Follow the Stars Home

ALSO BY LUANNE RICE

Cloud Nine
Home Fires
Blue Moon
Secrets of Paris
Stone Heart
Crazy in Love
Angels All Over Town

Follow

the Stars

Home

* * *

Luanne Rice

DOUBLEDAY DIRECT LARGE PRINT EDITION

Bantam Books

New York   Toronto   London   Sydney   Auckland

This Large Print Edition, prepared especially for Doubleday Direct, Inc., contains the complete, unabridged text of the original Publisher's Edition.

FOLLOW THE STARS HOME
A Bantam Book / February 2000

ISBN 0-7394-0793-7

Bantam Books are published by Bantam Books, a division of Random House, Inc. Its trademark, consisting of the words "Bantam Books" and the portrayal of a rooster, is Registered in U.S. Patent and Trademark Office and in other countries. Marca Registrada. Bantam Books, 1540 Broadway, New York, New York 10036.

PRINTED IN THE UNITED STATES OF AMERICA

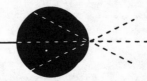

**This Large Print Book carries the
Seal of Approval of N.A.V.H.**

For
Andrea Cirillo,
my beloved friend and amazing agent,
with love and gratitude

Acknowledgments

I would like to thank Sam Whitney, a girl I've known since the Thanksgiving Day she was born. Sam is an intrepid writer, mountaineer, explorer, and nurse. She trekked the Nepal Himalaya, worked with Mother Teresa in Calcutta, and now she's a full-time O.B. RN taking a full load of graduate courses. Her help was invaluable in my research on Rett Syndrome. Sam is spiritual, compassionate, and hilarious, and I am proud to have babysat for her. She is a seeker of great spirit.

The people at Bantam are wonderful and supportive. I am shepherded through the publications of my books with their kindness, belief, and insight. I ask that Irwyn Applebaum, Nita Taublib, Christine Brooks, Barb Burg, Susan Corcoran, Gina Wachtel, Betsy Hulsebosch, Carolyn Willis, each person on the incredible sales force and in every office, please accept my thanks, affection, and a bouquet of herbs from Point O'Woods.

Lucinda was inspired by my mother and the librarian of my youth: Mrs. Virginia Smith of the

New Britain Public Library. With deep appreciation to librarians everywhere.

Thank you to Juanita Albert. She inspires me with stories of family, devotion, and faith. She has been a true friend through grief and joy.

Point O'Woods is a place in Connecticut of sea, sand, tall pines, and golden salt marshes. It is in my heart and soul forever. My parents met there, and their spirits—along with Mim's—inhabit our house and herb garden. My mother helped me learn to love to write at our old oak table, and I write there still. May my family and neighbors know how much I love them.

Introduction

FOLLOW THE STARS HOME was inspired by something I experienced last December, on a cold snowy afternoon as it darkened into the longest night of the year. A group of neighbors had gathered together for a holiday celebration. We stood in an old stone church, listening to ancient music being played on organ and bells.

Beside me were a mother and daughter. I had seen them around my neighborhood often, had been struck by the woman's posture, her attitude of strength. Her daughter, about ten years old, was in a wheelchair. Her limbs were thin and frail, her backbone curved, her head resting on her shoulder. Her hands moved through the air, dancing in front of her face as if in ballet, as if she was listening to private music none of the rest of us could hear.

At a certain point in the ceremony, we in the congregation were asked to join hands. I glanced down at the little girl, hesitating. She looked so fragile, so *apart.* At that moment, I caught her mother's eye. Her expression was nearly fierce with suspense, with the desire that I take her daughter's hand, that I not leave the little girl out.

I took the child's hand.

It was cold. I squeezed it gently, wishing she

would squeeze back. She didn't, but she turned her head, gazing up at me with enormous dark eyes. Again, I noticed her mother's expression: pure gratitude and joy. She was thanking me, a stranger, for treating her disabled child like the beautiful, ordinary, luminous, common human being that she was.

That experience humbled me. For years, throughout many books, I have written about love. I write about families—mothers and daughters, fathers and sons, sisters, grandparents—and the extraordinary trials of everyday life. But I had never before written about anyone like that mother and daughter. I thought about courage. I started to think about loving someone others consider damaged.

I began thinking about loving a person others might think unlovable, and I realized a great truth—something I've always known but never named; we are all, every one of us every day of our lives, being perfectly loved by imperfect people.

That's the secret. We spend so much time searching, wishing, fixing, planning, bargaining: *if only they were better, happier, nicer, healthier, closer.* When the fact is, we already have exactly what we need. When we fill our hearts and minds with compassion for the ones around us, we realize that love is already there.

I believe that writers are made of experiences, that everybody we see, feel, do, and receive adds up to our lives and our material—which are actually one and the same thing. Some novels coalesce like a cloud; bits of material swirling together, events from the near past and the distant past, emotions that have built up over time. Others start with a bang, a flash of divine inspiration. FOLLOW THE STARS HOME is a little bit of both.

My characters—Dianne, Julia, and Alan—were just waiting for that amazing mother and child to breathe them into life. But my own life, like most, has had its share of challenge, chances to care for the people who need me most. Once again, I see family and home—my own, my characters', everyone's—to be the most intense, romantic, passionate, dangerous, thrilling inspirations there are.

The title, FOLLOW THE STARS HOME, comes from the practice of celestial navigation. I come from a family of sailors, and many of them have gone to sea for days and weeks at a time. Most boats carry extensive electronics, but the sailors I know learned how to navigate using the stars and a sextant. They use the stars in the sky to find their way home.

If we know where to look, we don't need a sextant: we don't even need a boat. We just need the stars and the knowledge of where we belong. And, especially, we all need the love in our hearts that was there the whole time.

Luanne Rice
February 2000

One

$\ast \ast \ast$

Snow was falling in New York. The flakes were fine and steady, obscuring the upper stories of Midtown's black and silver buildings. Snow covered the avenues faster than city plows could clear it away. It capped stone monuments and the Plaza's dormant fountain. As night closed in, and lights were turned on in every window, the woman stood with the young girl, breathing in the cold air.

"The snow looks so magical in the city!" Amy, twelve, said in amazement.

"It's so beautiful," Dianne agreed.

"But where do the kids go sledding?"

"In Central Park, I think. Right over there," Dianne said, pointing at the trees coated in white, the yellow lights glowing through the snow.

Amy just stared. Everything about New York was new and wonderful, and Dianne loved seeing the city through her eyes. Fresh from the quiet marshlands of eastern Connecticut, they had checked into the Plaza hotel, visited Santa at Macy's, and gone ice skating at Rockefeller Center. That night they had tickets to see the New York City Ballet dance *The Nutcracker*.

Standing under the hotel awning, they took in Christmas lights, livery-clad door-men, and guests dressed for a gala evening. Three cabs stood at the curb, snow thick in their headlights. At least twenty people were lined up, scanning the street for addi-tional cabs. Hesitating for just a moment, Dianne took Amy's hand and walked down the steps.

Overwhelmed with excitement, her own and for the child, she didn't want to risk missing the curtain by waiting in a long taxi line. Standing by the curb, she checked the map and weighed the idea of walking to Lincoln Center.

"Dianne, are we going to be late?" Amy asked.

"No, we're not," Dianne said, making up her mind. "I'll get us a cab."

Amy laughed, thrilled by the sight of her friend standing in the street, arm out-stretched like a real New Yorker. Dianne wore a black velvet dress, a black cashmere cape, a string of pearls, and her grand-mother-in-law's diamond and sapphire ear-rings: things she never wore at home at Gull Point. Her evening bag was ancient. Black satin, stiff with years spent on a closet shelf, it had come from a boutique in Essex, Connecticut.

"Oh, let me hail the cab," Amy said, danc-ing with delight, her arm flying up just like Dianne's. Her movement was sudden, and slipping on the snow, she grasped at Dianne's bag. The strap was very long; even with Dianne's arm raised, the bag swung just below her hip. Nearly losing her balance on the icy street, Dianne caught Amy and steadied them both.

They smiled, caught in a momentary embrace. Although Thanksgiving had just passed, Christmas lights glittered every-where. Beneath its snowy veil, the city was enchanted. A Salvation Army band played "Silent Night." Bells jingled on passing horse-drawn carriages.

"I've never been anywhere like this," Amy

said. Her enormous green eyes gazed into Dianne's with the rapture of being twelve, on such a wonderful adventure.

"I'm so glad you came with me," Dianne said.

"I wish Julia were here," Amy said.

Bowled over with affection for the girl, and missing her own daughter, Dianne didn't see the cab at first.

Spinning on the ice, the taxi clipped the bumper of a black Mercedes limousine. A snowplow and a sand truck drove by in the opposite direction, and the Yellow Cab caromed off the plow's blade, crushing its front end, shattering the windshield. Dianne lunged for Amy.

The violent ballet happened in slow motion. Pirouetting once, twice, the cab spun on the icy street. Dianne grabbed the child. Her low black boot fought for traction. Glass tinkled on the pavement. Onlookers screamed. Arms around Amy, Dianne tried to run. In the seconds it took to register what was happening, that she wasn't going to get out of the way fast enough, she wrapped her body around the child and tried to shield her from the impact.

The taxi struck the crowd. People flew up in the air together, tumbled apart, and landed with separate thuds. Skidding across the pavement, skin scraping and bones breaking, they slumped in shapeless heaps. For one long moment the city was silent. Traffic stopped. No one moved. The snow was bright with red blood. Down the block, horns began to blare. A far-off siren sounded. People closed in to help.

"They're dead!" someone cried.

"So much blood . . ."

"Don't move anyone, you might injure them worse."

"That little girl, did she move? Is she alive?"

Five people lay crumpled like broken toys, surrounded by people not knowing what to do. Two off-duty New York cops out for the evening with their wives saw the commotion from their car and stopped to help. One of them ran to the wrecked taxi. Leaning through the shattered window, he yanked at the door handle before stopping himself.

The driver was killed, his neck sliced through by a sheet of door metal. Even in death, the man reeked of whiskey. Shaking his head, the cop went to the injured pedestrians.

"Driver's dead," he said, crouching beside his friend, working on the girl.

"What about her?" he asked, pulling open Amy's coat to check her heartbeat.

With the child their first priority, the two policemen had their backs to Dianne. She lay facedown in the snow. Blood spread from her blond hair, her arm twisted beneath her at an impossible angle. Moving quickly, a stranger bent down beside her. He leaned over her head, touching the side of her neck as if in search of a pulse. No one saw him palm the single diamond earring he could reach, or pull the pearls from her throat.

By the time he grabbed her bag, a woman in the crowd noticed. The thief had the strap in his hand, easing it out from under the fallen woman's arm.

"Hey," the observer yelled. "What the hell are you doing?"

The thief yanked harder. He held the bag, tearing at the clasp. It opened, contents spilling into the snow. A comb, ballet tickets, a crystal perfume flacon, some papers, and a small green wallet. Snatching the wallet, the man dashed across the street, disappearing into the dark park.

One victim, an old man, was dead. A wife lay motionless while her husband tried to crawl closer to her. Bending over the child, one policeman barely looked up. The other moved to the woman—had to be the girl's mother—noticing the blood pumping from her head. Taking off his jacket, he pressed it to the open wound. Police cars arrived along with an ambulance, and the technicians turned the blond woman over. She was lovely, her face as pale as ice. The policeman saw a lot of death, and the chill that shivered down his back told him the mother was in bad shape.

The crowd stood back, everyone talking at once. "The taxi . . . out of control . . . skidded on the ice . . . five people hit . . . mother tried to save the little girl . . . scumbag stole her wallet."

"Crackhead got her ID?" the ambulance driver asked. "No. Shit, no. You mean no one knows their names? We got no one to call?"

"That's right," one of the cops said. He knew the ambulance driver wasn't neces-

sarily being altruistic, imagining someone waiting for these two somewhere
with no way to get in touch with him.
Unidentified victims were a paperwork
nightmare.

"Goddamn," his friend said, watching the
EMTs load them into the ambulance. The
lady was so pretty, delicate and petite.
Bystanders were saying she had curled her
body around the child to protect her from
the runaway cab. Ten to one she was from
out of town, staying at the Plaza for a special holiday treat, nailed by some celebrat-
ing cabbie on his way back to the garage
with a bellyful of cheer.

Throwing the useless handbag into the
ambulance, they watched the vehicle
scream down West Fifty-ninth Street, heading for St. Bernadette's Hospital.

Speeding crosstown, the ambulance driver
ran every light carefully, easing through
intersections. Storms brought out the worst
in New Yorkers. They panicked at the first
sign of snow. The driver stayed steady,
focused on avoiding the slow traffic and
numerous fender benders. Aware of his crit-

ical passengers, he called ahead to alert the emergency staff.

Oxygen masks covered the victims' faces. The attending EMT pulled away the woman's cape, searching for a heartbeat. Checking her blood pressure, he felt shocked when her eyes opened. She lay still, her lips blue. The intensity in each small movement was frightening to behold as she opened her mouth to speak one word: "Amy," she said.

"The little girl?" the technician asked.

"Amy . . ." the woman repeated, panic apparent in her eyes and in the effort it took her to whisper.

"Your daughter?" the EMT asked. "She's right here beside you, she's just fine. You're both going to be just fine. Lie back now, there you go. Just—" he said, watching her unimaginable distress behind the oxygen mask before she slid back into unconsciousness.

The kid's arm's a mess, he thought, silently chastising himself for the blatant lie.

The trauma unit was ready. Intercepting the ambulance beneath the wide portico, they slid the woman and girl onto gurneys. IV lines were hooked up. Blood and plasma were ready, just waiting for blood samples to be typed. Nurses and doctors in green surrounded the victims, assessing the worst of their injuries. Woman and child were wheeled into separate cubicles.

While the doctors worked, an EMT brought the black satin handbag to the desk. The head nurse checked it for ID, but the police report was right: The wallet was missing. She found two tickets for the ballet, two Amtrak ticket stubs originating in Old Saybrook, and two business cards, one for a lumberyard in Niantic, the other for a fishing boat called *Aphrodite*.

"Find anything?" a young nurse asked, coming from the injured woman's cubicle. "It would be awfully good to call someone."

"What's her condition?" the head nurse asked, glancing up.

"Critical," the younger woman said, discarding her gloves. She was thirty-eight, about the same age as the woman she'd just been working on. She had children herself, including a ten-year-old daughter, just a little younger than the girl, and nothing made her count her blessings and fear the universe like a badly injured woman and child. "Both of them. Extensive blood loss, bruising, concussion and contusions for the woman, fractured humerus and severed artery for the girl. They're prepping her for surgery."

"There's nothing much here," the head nurse replied. "Cards for a lumberyard and a fishing boat . . ."

The head nurse squinted, taking a closer look. She saw a fine zipper she had missed the first time, along the seam of the bag's lining. Tugging it open, she reached inside and fished out a small card filled out in elegant handwriting:

In case of emergency, please call Timothy McIntosh (203) 555-8941.

"Connecticut number," the young nurse said, reading the card. "Think it's her husband?"

Dialing the number, the head nurse didn't reply. She got a recording: The area code had been changed. Using the new numbers, she learned that the phone was out of service. She tried the lumberyard: no answer at this hour. Frustrated, she looked at the last card and wondered what good could come from calling a fishing boat at the end of November. Since she had no options, she called the marine operator and requested to be put through to the *Aphrodite*.

Waves pounded the hull and light snow sifted from the dark night sky. Tim McIntosh gripped the wheel, steering a long course due south. He had been lobstering in Maine, saving enough money to last the winter in Florida. He wore thick gloves, but even so his hands were chapped and rough. His leather boots were soaked through, his feet blocks of ice.

He glanced at the chart, illuminated by light from the binnacle. Point Pleasant, New Jersey, was his destination. He'd put in at Red's Lobster Dock for one night, then leave on the dawn tide for his trip south. Tim had had enough winter to last him for the rest of his life. Malachy Condon had once tried to talk him out of leaving for good, but that was before their final breach. Tim was heading for Miami.

A foghorn moaned over the sound of waves crashing against the steel hull. Checking his loran, Tim swung right into the

Manasquan Inlet. The water grew calmer, but he could still feel the Atlantic waves pounding in his joints. He had traveled a long way. Great rock and concrete break-waters flanked either side of the channel. Houses looked warmly lit; Christmas trees twinkled in picture windows, and Tim imag-ined other sailors' homecomings.

The radio crackled. Tim's ears were ring-ing from the constant roaring of the wind and throbbing of the Detroit diesel, but nev-ertheless he heard the high seas operator calling him.

"*Aphrodite*," the voice said. "Calling ves-sel *Aphrodite* . . ."

Tim stared at the set. His first thought was that Malachy had relented. Tim felt a quick spread of relief; he had known Malachy couldn't stay mad forever, that he wasn't cold enough to just banish Tim from his life. Malachy Condon was an old oceanographer, scientific as they came, but he had a family man's romantic vision of the holidays. Malachy believed in setting things right. He would want to fix things between them, press Tim to change his ways toward his daughter, her mother, Tim's brother.

"McIntosh, aboard the *Aphrodite*," Tim said, grabbing the mike, ready to greet the old meddler with "Happy Thanksgiving, what took you so long?" A click sounded, the operator connecting him to the caller.

"This is Jennifer Hanson from the emergency room at St. Bernadette's Hospital in New York City. I'm afraid I have some bad news. . . ."

Tim straightened up, the human response to hearing "bad news" and "emergency room" in the same sentence. He hated New York, and so did every other fisherman he knew. Even worse, he despised hospitals and sickness with every bone in his body.

"A woman and child were brought in several hours ago. They have no ID save a card with your boat's name on it."

"The *Aphrodite*?" he asked, bewildered.

"The woman is slender, with blond hair and fair skin."

He held on, saying nothing.

"Blue eyes . . ." the nurse said.

Tim bowed his head, his pulse accelerating. His mind conjured up a pair of familiar periwinkle eyes, searching and ready to laugh. Marsh-gold hair falling to her shoulders, freckles on pale skin. But with a child in New York? It wasn't possible.

"Thirty-four or thirty-five," the nurse continued. "Type O blood. The child is about twelve, has type AB."

"I don't know them," Tim said, his mouth dry. Didn't his daughter have type A? His head felt strange, as if he had the flu. The rough seas getting to him. Payback time for running out on his daughter time and again. He felt guilty enough already, obsessed with the way he lived his life. Malachy had never written him off before, and the old man's final rage had shaken Tim to the core.

Throttling back, Tim turned toward Red's. The docks and pilings were white with snow. Ice clung to the rigging of the big draggers. Woman with a twelve-year-old kid. In New York City? He had thought she was too sick to travel, but she *had* been on Nova Scotia last summer.

"The woman was wearing one earring. A small diamond and sapphire, kind of dangling . . ."

That did it. Glancing up, Tim saw himself reflected in the wheelhouse glass. Flooded with shame and regret, he remembered the little house by the Hawthorne docks, and he could see those trees his wife had loved so much, the ones with the white flowers that smelled so sweet. She wouldn't be calling him though. Not after what had happened last summer.

"The bag is satin," the nurse continued. "It has a tag inside, with the name of a place—"

"It came from the Schooner Shop," Tim said, clearing his throat. "I gave it to her one Christmas. The earrings belonged to my grandmother. . . ."

"Then, you do know her?" the nurse asked tensely.

"Her name is Dianne Robbins," Tim said. "She was my wife."

The Briggs taxi was an old blue Impala. Tim sat in back, staring out the window as the driver sped up Route 35. From the bridge, he saw suburban houses under snow, decorated with wreaths and lights. A few had snowmen in the yard. As they approached the Garden State Parkway, kids bombarded the taxi with snowballs.

"Heh," the driver said. "I should be offended, but in my day I'd've been doing the same thing, snow like this."

"Yeah," Tim said, thinking of himself and his brothers.

"Heading up to the city for a good time?"

"To the hospital," Tim said, his throat so dry he could hardly speak.

"Hey, man," the driver said. "Sorry." He fell silent, and Tim was glad. He didn't want to talk. The heater was pumping and the radio was on. Tim didn't want to tell some stranger his whole life story, how he had been running away for eleven straight years and had been just about to run even farther when he'd gotten this call.

Christmastime. Maybe Malachy had been right about this time of year: Families reunited, women forgave, children got better. Tim had wrecked his chances with everyone. He had stolen Dianne from his brother, married her, then walked away from her and their daughter.

Tim had just barely been able to live with himself all these eleven years, way out at sea. But he had burned his bridges with the old Irishman, the man who had made listening to dolphins off Nova Scotia his lifework, and that had woken him up. Malachy Condon had always urged him to make things right with Dianne. Maybe this was Tim's last chance.

Amy woke up slowly. Her first thought was *Mama!* Her second was *Dianne*. Amy was in a hospital bed. The walls were green and the sheets were white. She had a cast on her arm, which was held up over her head by a metal triangle that looked like a trapeze.

"Is Dianne okay?" she asked the nurse standing by her bed.

"Is that your mother, honey?" the nurse asked.

Amy shook her head. She felt tears hot in her eyes. Her mother was back in Hawthorne. Amy wanted to call her, wanted her to come. "Tell me, please," she said, choking on a sob. "Is Dianne—" she tried to ask.

The cabdriver took the Holland Tunnel. Tim hadn't been in a tunnel in more years than he could remember. His life was the sea: crustaceans, the price of lobster at the Portland Fish Exchange, cold feet in wet boots, the smell of diesel fuel, and regret.

Tim's life could have been different. Passing the nice houses decorated for Christmas, he wondered why he had given it all away. Once he had had it all: beautiful wife, nice house, prosperous lobstering business. Sometimes he felt guilty for taking Dianne from his brother, but the choice had been hers. She could have stayed with Alan—the great doctor—if she had wanted, but she had chosen Tim.

"I'm gonna take Hudson Street uptown," the driver said. "West Side Highway's stopped deader'n hell."

"Just get me there," Tim said. Dianne was in some New York hospital, just minutes away now. The closer he got to her, the harder his heart pounded. He had made mistakes, no doubt about it. But maybe he could undo some of them: He could go to the hospital now, see if he could help. Tim was a good guy at heart; his intentions had never been bad. He wanted Dianne to know that.

Maybe she understood already. Hadn't she gotten the nurse to call him?

Tim would like to show Malachy. He hated picturing their last time together: spit flying from Malachy's angry mouth, shouting at Tim as they stood on the Lunenburg dock. Acting more like Alan than Malachy: sanctimonious, looking down on Tim for his shortcomings. But this might be Tim's chance to help Dianne, to prove both Alan and Malachy wrong.

Besides, didn't the stars point to something? Why had Tim been steaming into Point Pleasant instead of somewhere else? He might have bailed into Nantucket, avoided yesterday's storm. Or he could have veered into the Gulf Stream, headed farther south than New Jersey for his first port, had the radio off, not heard the call.

"Dianne," he said out loud.

New York was filled with people and cars. Couples stood at every street corner. The Empire State Building was lit up green and red. Christmas trees down from Nova Scotia, where Tim had been the previous summer, filled the city air with the lovely fragrance of deep pine forests. Dianne loved the holidays. She was a good person, full of love, and she saw the holidays as one more chance to make her family happy—to bring joy to their daughter, he was sure.

As he thought of the little girl he had never met, Tim's eyes stung. Dianne had told him her name was Julia. It didn't help that Alan was her pediatrician, that he used to send letters to Tim through Malachy. Tim had torn them all up. The child had been born damaged.

No renegade lobsterman wanted to be reminded of lousy things he'd done. Dianne had given birth to a sick baby, and Tim hadn't been able to handle it. That's what fishing the Atlantic was for: tides and currents and a big lobster boat named after the goddess of love to take him the hell away.

Tim handed the driver a pile of money and jumped out at St. Bernadette's Hospital—a complex of redbrick buildings too huge to figure out. He ran into the ER, pushing past a guard who told him he had to sign in. The nurses were nice. They took one look at him and knew he needed help fast. Tim had been aboard *Aphrodite* for days, and he needed to wash and shave.

"The woman and girl," he said to the head

nurse. "Who were brought in earlier, the accident, you called me . . ."

"You're the fisherman," she said kindly, handing him his grandmother's earring.

Tim shuddered and groaned. He dried his face with the oil-stained sleeve of his brown Carhartt jacket. His knuckles were cracked and bloody from winter in northern waters. He clutched the ancient earring Dorothea McIntosh had given Dianne on their wedding day, and he remembered it sparkling in the Hawthorne sun as they'd said their vows.

Tim had been roaming for so long, searching for something that would help him forget he had run out on his wife and daughter. Julia had been born sick and crippled. Tim had been too afraid to see her.

"Where's Dianne?" he asked, wiping his eyes.

The nurse led him through the hospital. Tim followed, their footsteps echoing down long corridors. The hospital seemed old, several brick buildings connected by a warren of hallways. Accustomed to starlight, Tim blinked under the fluorescent lighting. Entering a more modern wing, they rode an elevator to the twentieth floor.

"I'm taking you to see the child," the nurse said. "Her mother is still in surgery."

"No—" Tim began.

"The girl is scared," the nurse said. "She's hurt, and she's all alone."

"My daughter," Tim whispered. Was it really possible? After eleven years, was he about to meet his little girl? His stomach clenched. He had never seen her, but in his imagination she was stunted and palsied, like other damaged children he had seen. By then, sure he was on the brink of meeting her, Tim steeled himself for what he would see.

"In here," the nurse said, opening a door.

"Which one?" Tim asked.

It was a double room. Both beds were filled. The occupants of each were quiet, their faces in shadow. The nurse indicated the girl with a broken arm. She lay in traction, her arm suspended overhead with lines and crossbars, like the elaborate rigging of a brigantine. Stepping closer, Tim was stunned.

Lying there was a beautiful young girl. Her arm was in a cast, her forehead was bruised, but she was perfect. Dark lashes lay upon delicate skin. Her face was oval, her nose straight, her lips full. As Tim stared, he began to shake.

"My daughter," he said, his voice croaking.

"She's waking up," the nurse said.

The child began to stir. She licked her lips, tried to move her arm. Her cry was awful to hear, and Tim wanted to put his arms around her.

"Oh," she wept. "My arm hurts."

"There, honey," the nurse said soothingly, bending over the girl. She spoke quietly, helping the child to orient herself, blocking Tim from her sight. Tim pulled himself together the best he could. He didn't want to meet his daughter for the first time in shock and looking like Captain Ahab—or worse.

"I want to go home," the girl cried. "I want to go back to Hawthorne."

"It's okay," the nurse said kindly. "You're going to be fine, honey. And you're not alone. There's someone here to see you."

The young girl blinked. Stepping out from behind the white-clad nurse, Tim watched the child bring him into focus. Blood pounded in his ears like waves smashing over a ship's bow. He tried to smile, not wanting to frighten her. But he needn't have worried. Her fearful expression changed instantly the moment she saw him into one of sheer delight and love.

"Dr. McIntosh!" she exclaimed, bursting into tears.

Tim was too choked up to speak. Hearing only his last name, he thought for one minute that his daughter knew him already. Dianne had showed her his picture. Maybe they kept it on the mantel. They had talked about him all this time.

"Oh, Dr. McIntosh," she said again, and now Tim heard the rest, the "Doctor." Shit. She was calling for his brother. Alan. In her groggy, posttraumatic state, she had caught sight of one McIntosh and mistaken him for the other. Tim's heart fell. He closed his eyes and knew that the little girl had made a mistake.

And so, he thought, probably he had too. But he was going to set it straight. He had to see Dianne.

Two

Conscious only of bright light and searing pain in her arm and head, Dianne moaned. Her eyes tried to focus. Shapes swam before her, green beings saying her name over and over.

"Dianne?" she heard. "Dianne, can you hear me?"

"Mrs. McIntosh, how many fingers am I holding up?"

"Amy . . ."

"Hold steady, that's right." She felt the pressure of a hand on her forehead. The Plaza, Christmas lights. Headlights came at her, and she cried out. But they weren't headlights. A man in green was standing there, shining a light in her face.

"Dianne, do you know where you are?" came a woman's voice.

"She's lost so much blood," a male voice said.

"Her pressure's dropping," came another voice.

"Please, help," she murmured. Was this a nightmare? She could not move, and her thoughts swarmed in her mind. "Julia," she mouthed, but she had been with Amy, hadn't she? Julia was at home with her mother. Alan should be here . . . if he came, he would know what to do. He would save her. Memory fragments began to materialize, shifting around like parts of a terrible puzzle.

"Mrs. McIntosh," the nurse said gently. "Amy is being taken care of. Everything we can do is being done. You need to be strong. Stay with us."

Dianne's mind was fuzzy with pain and injury and blood loss and whatever drugs they had given her. She felt herself losing consciousness. She wished she could open the door and walk through the snow to the marsh. Trying to see, her eyes would hardly focus. She was in New York. That's right, they had come to New York to see *The Nutcracker*.

Shivering, thinking of Amy's imagined terror, Dianne cried out in anguish.

"Stay with us, Dianne," one voice said. "Mrs. McIntosh!" called another. She thought of her home by the Connecticut marshes, her mother and daughter, and Alan. The nurse had called her "Mrs. McIntosh" as if she were still married to Tim. A long time ago Dianne had dated both McIntosh brothers. They had both loved her, and at different times she had loved each of them. Alan was day, Tim was night. Dianne, for whom life had always been gentle, fair, and kind, had chosen the brother with a dark side. She had married Tim, and she had paid a price.

But over the last three magical seasons, she and Alan had started to come back together. For the first time in eleven years, Dianne had just started to love again, and now she lay in this strange bed in a New York hospital, so far from home, feeling as if she were starting to die. She spun back: winter, fall, summer, all the way to last spring. . . .

It was April, and the scent of flowering pear trees filled the air of Hawthorne. The trees had been planted one hundred years earlier, along the brick sidewalks around the water-front, and their blossoms were white, frag-ile, and delicate. Looking up as she passed underneath, Dianne Robbins wondered how they survived the fresh sea wind that blew in from the east.

"Flowers, Julia," she said.

Her daughter slept in the wheelchair, unaware. Reaching up, Dianne stood on her toes to grab hold of the lowest branch and break off a twig. Three perfect blossoms curved from thread-fine stems. The petals were pure white, soft pink in the center. Dianne thought they were beautiful, the more so because they lasted so short a time. The flowering pears of Hawthorne stayed in bloom less than a week.

Julia had once seen a flower and said "la," her first word. So Dianne placed the twig on her sleeping child's lap and continued on. She passed White Chapel Square, named for the three churches that surrounded it. The sea captains' houses came next, gleaming white Federals with wide columns and green-black shutters, overlooking the harbor and lighthouse. Dianne had always dreamed of living in one of these houses, ever since she was a child.

She slowed in front of the one she loved most. It had an ornate wrought- iron fence surrounding the big yard and sea-flower meadow. At age nine Dianne had stood there gripping the black fence rails and imagining her life as a grown-up. She would be an architect and have a wonderful husband, beautiful children, two golden dogs, and they would all live blissfully in this house on the harbor.

Glancing at her daughter, Dianne pushed the wheelchair faster. The breeze had picked up, and it was cold for April. Low clouds scudded across the sky, making her wonder about rain. They had been early, with time for a walk after parking the car. But now it was almost three o'clock, time for Julia's appointment with her uncle, Dr. Alan McIntosh.

Alan McIntosh sat as his desk while Mrs. Beaudoin went through Billy's latest pictures in search of the perfect one for the Wall. She was a very young mother—Billy was her first baby—and Alan had long since learned that every patient's mother's goal was to see her child properly enshrined in the collage of photos hanging behind his desk.

"In this one he's drooling," she said, smiling and proudly handing it over nevertheless. "And in this one he's squinting. He looks just like an old man!"

"He is one," Alan said, cradling Billy in one arm while he wrote out a prescription for ear drops with his other. "Six months on Tuesday."

Martha Blake, his nurse, appeared at the door. She raised her eyebrows, as if to ask whether Alan needed help in hurrying Mrs. Beaudoin along. He'd had an emergency at the hospital that morning, so now he was backed up with a packed waiting room. He'd been so busy, he hadn't had time for lunch, and at that moment his stomach let out such a loud grumble that Billy's brown eyes flew open with surprise.

"I like this one where he's squinting," Alan said, glancing over for permission to hang the picture on the Wall. "He looks like he's thinking deep thoughts."

Walking Mrs. Beaudoin to the door, he gave her the prescription and told her to keep Billy's ears dry when she bathed him. His office was in an old brush factory dating back to the early 1800s, and some of the doorways were very low, built for humans two hundred years shorter of bone. Alan, six four since eighth grade, had to duck to walk through.

When he straightened, he saw the waiting room packed with patients: mothers and children everywhere. Children sniffling, huddled at their mothers' sides, trying to read picture books, their big eyes looking in his direction as if the big, bad wolf had just stepped off the page. Only two children looked happy to see him, and they filled his heart with the kind of gratitude he had become a doctor to feel. They were both young girls, just a year apart in age, and only one of them had an appointment.

Amy was sitting in the big playhouse in the corner. She was twelve, slight, with silky, uncombed brown hair and big green eyes, and she was theoretically too old to be playing there. Hidden in shadows, she ducked down so she couldn't be seen by any of the mothers, but she gave Alan a wide grin. He gave her a secret smile, letting her know he was playing the game and would find time to talk to her later.

Julia was in her wheelchair. She had huge,

eloquent eyes. When she smiled, every tooth in her mouth showed. Seeing Alan, she let out a bellow of joy, causing her mother to lean over from behind and wrap her in a hug. Dianne Robbins laughed out loud, pressing her lips against Julia's pale cheek. When Dianne looked up, the expression in her blue eyes made her look as happy and carefree as a young girl sailing. Alan started to say he was running late, but something about the moment left him temporarily unable to speak, so he just walked back into his office.

Amy Brooks was invisible. She was as clear as her name: a clean brook that ran over rocks and stones and pebbles, under fallen trees and arched bridges, through dark woods and sunny meadows. Amy was water. People might look in her direction, but they'd see right through her to things on the other side.

Amy felt safe there in Dr. McIntosh's playhouse, and she wasn't sure which part was best. Knowing that Dr. McIntosh was in the next room or sitting in the little house itself. Some lady in Hawthorne had made it to look just like one of those white mansions down by the water. Outside, it had glistening white clapboards and dark green shutters that closed. The heavy blue door swung on brass hinges, with a bronze sea horse door knocker.

A little kid knocked on the door, wanting to come in.

"Grrrr," Amy growled, like the new puppy in the cage at home. The little kid couldn't see her because she was invisible, but he could hear her. That was enough.

"Mine again," Amy whispered to the house.

Glancing at her father's watch, a huge Timex weighing down her wrist, she wondered what time Dr. McIntosh would see her. She had had a good day at school—she was a sixth-grader at Hawthorne Middle, three blocks from his office—and she had purposely missed the bus to tell him about it. Just then she heard a strange noise.

It was a kid: From across the room, some child with its back to Amy started making funny sounds, like water trying to flow through a broken pipe. Its mother was pretty, like the golden-haired mother in storybooks, with silver-blue eyes and a smile meant only for the child. The two mothers on either side bent double like jackknives trying to get a peek at what was wrong. The kid's ratchety noise turned pretty, like a dolphin singing, and suddenly the kid's mother joined in.

The nurse called them, and they disappeared down the corridor. The mother caught Amy's eyes as she passed the playhouse. She smiled but just kept going. When the office door shut behind them, Amy missed their odd song.

"Pretty music," Alan said.

"Julia was singing," Dianne said, holding her daughter's hand as the young girl rolled her eyes. "I just joined in."

"Hi, Julia," Alan said. He crouched beside Julia's wheelchair, smoothing the white-blond hair back from her face. She leaned into his hand for an instant, eyes closed with what appeared to be deep trust. Dianne stood back, watching.

Alan spoke to Julia. His tone was rich and low, the voice of a very big man. But he spoke gently to Julia, tender and unthreatening, and the girl bowed her head and sighed contentedly. He was her uncle; he had been her doctor for the eleven years she had been alive. In spite of their history, the awkwardness between them, Dianne would never take Julia to anyone else.

Alan encircled Julia with his arms, easily lifting her onto the exam table. She weighed very little: twenty-nine pounds at the last visit. She was a fairy child, with a perfect face and misshapen body. Her head bobbed against her chest, her thin arms flailing slowly about as if she were swimming in the bay. She was wearing jeans, and a navy blue Gap sweatshirt over her T-shirt, and Dr. McIntosh must have just tickled her because she suddenly gasped. At the sound, Dianne turned away.

She let herself have this fantasy: Julia was healthy, "normal." She was just like all the other kids in the outer office. She could read books and draw pictures, and when you took her hand, it wasn't ice cold. She would jump and dance and demand her favorite cereal. Dianne would know that her favorite color was blue because Julia said so, not from hours of watching for slight changes of expression as Dianne pointed at colors on a page: red, yellow, green, blue.

Blue! Is that the one you like most, Julia? Blue, sweetheart?

To be a mother and know your own child's heart: Dianne couldn't imagine anything more incredible. Could Julia even distinguish colors, or was Dianne just kidding herself? Julia could not answer Dianne's questions. She made sounds, which experts had told Dianne were not words at all. When she said "la," it did not mean "flower"; it was only a sound.

"How are you, Dianne?" Alan asked.

"Fine, Alan."

"Julia and I were just having a talk."

"You were?"

"Yep. She says you're working too hard. Every kid in Hawthorne wants a playhouse, and you're backed up till Christmas."

Dianne swallowed. Nervous today, she couldn't manage the small talk. She was at her worst during Julia's exams. Her nerves were raw, and just then Alan reminded Dianne of his brother, of being left, and the worst of everything that could happen to her child; waiting for him to examine Julia made her want to scream.

Julia had been born with defects. A blond angel, she had spina bifida and Rett syndrome, a condition similar to autism. No talking, no for-sure affection. There was the maybe affection, where she'd kiss Dianne's face and Dianne wasn't really sure whether it was a real kiss or just a lip spasm. Dianne tended toward optimism, and she gave each smooch the benefit of the doubt every time.

Since birth Julia had had thirteen surgeries. Many trips to the hospitals—here, in Providence, and in Boston—had produced wear and tear on the spirit, sitting in those oddly similar waiting rooms, wondering whether Julia would survive the procedure. Hydrocephalus had developed after one operation, and for a time Dianne had had to get used to a shunt in her baby's brain to drain off the excess fluid.

Dianne, so desperate to lash out at Tim, would often talk to herself.

"Hello! Darling! Kindly bring me a sponge—I seem to have spilled this little bowl full of our daughter's brain water. Oh, you've left for good? Never mind, I'll get it myself."

Dianne's heart never knew which way to

twist. She teetered between hope and rage, love and terror. She hated Tim for leaving, Alan for reminding her of his brother, all doctors for being able to keep Julia alive but not being able to cure her. But Dianne loved Julia with a simple heart. Her daughter was innocent and pure.

Julia could not walk, hold things, or eat solid food. She would not grow much bigger. Her limbs looked jumbled and broken; the bones in her body were askew. Her body was her prison, and it failed her at every turn.

Her organs were hooked up wrong. Most of those early surgeries had been to correctly connect her stomach, bladder, bowels, and to protect the bulging sac on her smooth little baby back containing her meninges and spinal cord. Julia was the baby every pregnant mother feared having, and Dianne loved her so much, she thought her own heart would crack.

"You okay?" Alan asked.

"Just do the exam," Dianne said, sweating. "Please, Alan."

She took off all but Julia's T-shirt and diaper. They had been in this very room, on this exact table, so many times. Alan was frowning now, his feelings hurt. Dianne wanted to apologize, but her throat was too tight. Her stomach was in a knot: She was extra upset this visit, her fear and intuition in high, high gear, and it wasn't going to get better till after Alan did the exam.

Unsnapping Julia's T-shirt, Alan began to pass the silver disc across Julia's concave chest. His wavy brown hair was going gray, and his steel-rimmed glasses were sliding down his nose. He often had a quizzical, distant expression in his hazel eyes, as if his mind were occupied with higher math, but right then he was totally focused on Julia's heart.

"Can you hear anything?" she asked.

He didn't reply.

Dianne bit her lip so hard it hurt. This was the part of the exam Dianne feared the most. But she watched him, restraining herself and letting him work.

Julia's body was tiny, her small lungs and kidneys just able to do the job of keeping her alive. If she stopped growing soon, as the endocrinologist predicted she would, her organs would be sufficient. But if she sprouted even another inch, her lungs would be overtaxed and her other systems would give out.

"Her heart sounds good today," Alan said. "Her lungs too."

"Really?" Dianne asked, although she had never known him to tell them anything but the truth.

"Yes," he said. "Really."

"Good or just okay?"

"Dianne—"

Alan had never promised to fix Julia. Her prognosis since birth had been season by season. They had spent Julia's whole life waiting for that moment when she would turn the corner. There were times Dianne couldn't stand the suspense. She wanted to flip through the book, get to the last page, know how it was going to end.

"Really good?" she asked. "Or not?"

"Really good for Julia," he said. "You know that's all I can tell you. You know better than anyone, any specialist, what that means."

"She's Julia," Dianne said. The news was as good as she was going to get this visit. She couldn't speak right away. Her relief was sudden and great, and she had a swift impulse to run full tilt down to the dock, jump in his dinghy, and row into the wind until she exhausted herself.

"For so long," Dianne said, her eyes brimming, "all I wanted was for her to grow."

"I know . . . How's her eating?"

"Good. Great. Milk shakes, chicken soup, she eats all the time. Right, sweetheart?"

Julia looked up from the table. Her enormous eyes roved from Dianne to Alan and back again. She looked upon her mother with waves of seeming joy and adoration. Her right hand rose, making its way to Dianne's cheek. As always, Dianne was never sure whether Julia meant to touch her or whether the movement was just a reflex, but she bowed her forehead and let her daughter's small fingers trail down the side of her face.

"Gaaa," Julia said. "Gaaa."

"I know," Dianne said. "I know, sweetheart."

Dianne believed her daughter had a sensitive soul, that in spite of her limitations, Julia was capable of deep emotion. Out in the waiting room, with those mothers staring at her, Dianne had started singing along with her, to help Julia feel less alone and embarrassed.

Eleven years earlier she had given her deformed baby the most elegant, dignified

name she could think of: Julia. Not Megan,
Ellie, Darcy, or even Lucinda, after Dianne's
mother, but Julia. A name with weight for a
person of importance. Dianne still remembered a little boy looking through the nurs-
ery window, who started to cry because he
thought Julia was a monster.

Julia sighed, long and low.

Dianne touched her hand. When she had
dreamed of motherhood, she had imagined
reading and drawing and playing with her
child. They would create family myths as
rich as any story in the library. Dianne's child
would inspire her playhouses. Together
they would change and grow. Her baby's
progress, her creative and intellectual
development, would bring Dianne unimaginable joy.

"That's my girl," Alan said, bending down
to kiss Julia. As he did, his blue shirt
strained across his broad back. And now
that the exam was over, other feelings
kicked in, the other part of why it was hard
to be around Alan. Dianne folded her arms
across her chest.

She could see his muscles, his lean waist.
The back of his neck was exposed. Staring
at it, she had a trapdoor feeling in her stom-

ach. She thought back to when they'd first met. To her amazement, he had asked her out. Dianne had been a shy girl, flattered and intimidated by the young doctor. But then she had gone for his brother instead—dating a lobsterman made much more sense, didn't it? Life had thrown Dianne and Alan together for the long haul though, and she couldn't help staring at his body. *Oh, my God*, she thought, feeling such an overwhelming need to be held.

"I can't believe Lucinda's retiring," Alan said. "Lucky for you and Julia—you'll have a lot more time with her."

"I know." Her mother was the town librarian, and even though she wasn't leaving until July, people were already beginning to miss her.

When he looked over his shoulder, Dianne bit her lip. This was the crazy thing: She had just been staring at Alan's body, wishing he would hold her, and now she had the barbed wire up, on guard against his familiar tone, against his even thinking he was part of the family. She couldn't handle this; the balance was too hard.

"The library won't be the same without her."

Dianne glanced at Alan's wall of pictures, catching her breath. He and her mother shared the same clientele: Alan's patients learned their library skills from Mrs. Robbins. Julia couldn't use the library, had never even held a book, but many nights she had been lulled to sleep by her grandmother, the beloved and venerated storyteller of the Hawthorne Public Library.

"We're lucky," Dianne said to Alan, half turning away from Julia.

Alan didn't know what she meant; he hesitated before responding.

"In what way?" Alan asked.

"To have that time you mentioned."

Wringing her hands, Julia bowed her head. She moaned, but the sound changed to something near glee.

"My mother, me, and Julia," Dianne continued. "To be together after she retires. Time to do something important before Julia . . ."

Alan didn't answer. Was he thinking that she had left him off the list? Dianne started to speak, to correct herself, but instead she stopped. Holding herself tight, she stared at Julia. *My girl*, she thought. The terrible reality seemed sharper in Alan's office than it did anywhere else: The day would come when she would leave them.

"Dianne, talk to me," he said.

He had taken off his glasses, and he rubbed his eyes. He looked so much like Tim just then, Dianne focused down at her shoes. Coming closer, he touched her shoulder.

"I can't," she said carefully, stepping away. "Talking about it won't change things."

"This is nuts," he said. "I'm your friend."

"Don't, Alan. Please. You're Julia's doctor."

He stared at her, lines of anger and stress in his face.

"I'm a lot more than that," Alan said, and Dianne's eyes filled with tears. Without his glasses he looked just like his brother, and at that moment he sounded as dark as Tim had ever been.

Stupid young woman, Dianne thought, feeling the tears roll down her cheeks. She had been full of love. She had chosen the McIntosh she had thought would need her most, take every bit of care she had to offer, heal from the sorrows of his own past. Tim had been brash and mysterious, afraid to open his heart to anyone. Dianne had thought she could change him. She had wanted to save him. Instead, he had left her alone with their baby.

"A lot more than that," Alan said again.

Still, Dianne wouldn't look at him. She bent down to kiss Julia, nuzzling her wet face against her daughter's neck.

"Maaa," Julia said.

Dianne gulped, trying to pull herself together. Kissing Julia, Dianne got her dressed as quickly as possible.

"It's cool out," Alan said, making peace.

"I know," Dianne said, her voice thick.

"Better put her sweatshirt on," Alan said, rummaging in the diaper bag.

"Thanks," Dianne said, barely able to look him in the face. Her heart was pounding hard, and her palms were damp with sweat. He kissed Julia and held her hand for a long time. She gurgled happily. The adults were silent because they didn't know what else to say. Dianne stared at their hands, Alan's still holding Julia's. Then she picked up Julia, placed her in the wheelchair, and they left.

By the time Alan finished seeing all his patients, it was nearly six-thirty. Martha said good-bye, rushing off to pick up her son at baseball practice. Alan nodded without looking up. His back ached, and he rolled his shoulders, the place he stored the pent-up tension of seeing Dianne. He knew he needed a run.

He had Julia's chart out on his desk, studying her progress since the last visit. Maybe he should have done an EKG today. But he had run one two weeks before and found the results to be within normal limits.

Hawthorne Cottage Hospital was a great place to have healthy babies, to schedule routine procedures. Few pediatricians did electrocardiograms; most didn't even own the equipment. Alan had bought his as soon as it became obvious that Julia was going to need frequent monitoring. She had specialists in New Haven, but Alan didn't see any reason for Dianne to drive all that way when he could do the test himself.

Alan had a picture in his mind. Dianne was standing in the doorway, waiting for him to come home. She wore her blond hair in one long braid, and she was smiling as if she knew all his secrets. Her blue eyes did not look worried, the way they did in real life. She had finally decided to let Alan love her and help her; she had finally figured out that the two things were really the same.

"Ah-hem!"

Looking up, he saw Amy Brooks standing in his doorway. Her brown hair was its usual tangle, she was wearing one of her mother's pink sweaters over lint-balled red leggings. Her wide belt and turquoise beads completed the ensemble.

"Oh, it's the young lady who lives in the playhouse," he said. With his mind on Dianne and Julia, he felt lousy for forgetting about Amy.

"You saw me?" she asked, breaking into smiles.

"With those beautiful green eyes looking out the window—how could I miss?"

"I was hiding," she said. "Sick brats were pounding at my door, but I put spells on them and sent them back to their mamas. What do they all have?"

"Never mind that," Alan said. "What brings you to my office today?"

"I like that little house," she said, turning her back to stare at the black-cat clock, its tail ticking back and forth each second. "I like it a lot."

"I'll have to tell the lady who made it," he said.

Amy nodded. She moved from the clock to the Wall. Scanning the gallery, she found her pictures in the pack. Last year's school photo, one from the year before, Amy at Jetty Beach, Amy sitting on her front steps. She had given him all of them.

"Are there any other kids with four pictures here?"

"Only you."

"No one else has more?"

"No," Alan said.

Wheeling around, she bent down to read the papers on his desk. Alan heard her breathing hard, and she smelled dusty, as if she hadn't taken a shower or washed her hair in a while. Her forearms and hands were already summer-tan, and she had crescent moons of black dirt under her fingernails.

"Julia Robbins . . ." Amy read upside down. Gently Alan slid the pages of Julia's chart under a pile of medical journals. He knew that Amy was jealous of his other patients. She was one of his neediest cases. Alan had the compulsion to help children who were hurting, but he knew some things couldn't be cured.

Amy came from a lost home. Her mother was sinking in depression, just as Alan's mother had drowned in drink thirty years earlier. She didn't hit Amy or give him any clear cause to contact Marla Arden, Amy's caseworker. But the state had gotten calls from neighbors. There were reports of Amy missing school, the mother fighting with her boyfriend, doors slamming, and people shouting. They had an open file on Amy. But Alan knew the terrible tightrope a child walked, loving a mother in trouble. They were always one step from falling.

Amy had latched on to Alan. From her first time in his office, she had loved him all out. She would clutch him like a tree monkey. His nurse would have to pry her off. She would cry leaving his office instead of coming in. Her mother slept all day to kill the pain of losing her husband, just as Alan's mother had drunk to survive the death of his older brother, Neil.

"Come on," he said to Amy. "I'll drive you home."

She shrugged.

Alan knew the cycles of grief. They spun all around him, taking people far away from the ones they were meant to love. His mother, Amy's mother, Dianne, and Julia, even his brother Tim. Alan wanted to save them all. He wanted to heal everyone, fix entire families. He wished for Julia to live through her teens. He wanted Dianne to meet Amy because he believed they could help each other. People needed connection just to survive.

"I'll drive you," he said again.

"You don't have to," Amy said, starting to smile.

"I know," he said. "But I want to." Doctors were like parents; they weren't supposed to have favorites, but they did. It was just the way life was.

Amy worried that someday Dr. McIntosh would stop her from coming to his office. She didn't need to be there: She was as healthy as a horse, her fourth favorite animal following dolphins, cats, and green turtles.

"I only got two spelling words wrong today," she said.

"Only two?" he asked. "Which ones?"

Amy frowned. She had wanted him to congratulate her: She had never gotten so many right before. "*Judge* and *delightful,*" she said.

"How'd you spell *judge*?"

"J-u-j-e," she said. "Like it sounds."

"Did you read those books I gave you?"

Amy fiddled with a loose thread. Dr. McIntosh had bought her two mystery books he thought she'd like. Amy had never read much. She kept feeling as if she were missing the key all other readers received at birth. Plus, it was hard to concentrate at home, where there were real mysteries to be solved.

"Do you have a maid?" she asked, changing the subject.

"A maid?"

Did he think she was dumb for asking? Amy slid down in her seat, feeling like an idiot. They were in his station wagon, driving past the fishing docks. This part of town smelled like clams, flounder, and powdered oyster shells. Amy breathed deeply, loving it. Her father had been a long-liner, and fishing was in her blood.

"You know, someone to clean your house," she said.

"Not exactly," he laughed, as if she had said something outlandish.

Amy tried not to feel hurt. He was rich, a doctor—he could afford it! He didn't wear a wedding ring, and once she had asked him whether he was married and he'd said no. So he was alone, he needed someone to take care of him. Why shouldn't it be Amy?

"I love to clean," she said.

"You do?"

"It's not exactly a hobby, but I'm very good at it. Mr. Clean smells like perfume to me—why do you think I like your office so much? Can you think of many other people who like the smell of doctors' offices?"

"It's a rare quality," he said. "And I appreciate it."

Turning inland, he drove onto the so-called expressway. In Hawthorne they had three kinds of roads: the beautiful ones down by the harbor, this one-mile highway leading away from downtown, and the ugly streets near the marshlands, where Amy lived.

"I could do it part-time," she said.

"What about schoolwork?"

"I'd fit it in."

Dr. McIntosh was pulling onto her street.

The houses here were small and crooked. Hardly anyone had nice yards. Broken refrigerators leaned against ramshackle garages. Stray cats—half of which Amy had tried to save—roamed in packs. It was a neighborhood where kids didn't do their homework and parents didn't make them. The air was sour and stale.

"You know I want to help you," he said, looking at her house. "Is it really bad, Amy? Do you want me to call Ms. Arden?"

"No," Amy said with force.

"I know you worry about your mother. Maybe it would be good for you to stay somewhere for a little while, see if we can get her some help."

"I'm not leaving," Amy said. The whole idea filled her with panic. Her mother might die if she weren't there. She would fall asleep and never wake up. Or her mother's boyfriend, Buddy, might hurt her. Or—and this was the worst fear—her mother might just run away with Buddy and never come back.

"Do you have friends? Girls you hang out with?"

Amy shrugged. He didn't get it. Her best friend was Amber DeGray, but Amber smoked and wrote on her legs with razor blades. Amy was scared of her. Other kids didn't like Amy. She believed she wore her life on her person, that good kids would look at her and see her mother depressed in bed, Buddy's angry fingers plucking out "Midnight Rambler" on his expensive electric guitar, Buddy's new dog cowering in the back of its cage.

"I'm asking," Dr. McIntosh said, "because I know someone you might like. She's a young mother with a daughter. Do you ever baby-sit?"

"No," Amy said. Who would ask her? Besides, Amy wanted only Dr. McIntosh for her friend. He already knew her and didn't think she was gross. He was kind and funny, and she trusted him.

"It's my sister-in-law and niece," Dr. McIntosh said.

Amy gasped. She hadn't known he had a family! Suddenly she felt curious, excited, and horribly jealous all at once.

"Julia's disabled. She needs a lot of attention, and sometimes Dianne gets pretty worn out. They live nearby—I know they'd like you."

"You do?" Amy said, feeling so happy he

thought she was worth liking, her eyes filled with tears.

"Sure I do," he said.

Amy swallowed her feelings. *Disabled*, he had said. Was Julia one of those children with braces and crutches, hearing aids and glasses? Amy sometimes saw kids like that and felt just like them: different, set apart, very badly hurt.

"I used to be special . . ." Amy began, wanting to say something about her father and mother when they were young, when Amy had been their beloved newborn babe in a dark blue pram, when they had lived in the fishermen's park, where the air was always fresh and the smells were of saltwater, spring blossoms, and fish.

"You're wonderful just the way you are," Dr. McIntosh said.

My mother's depressed . . . she cries and sleeps all day . . . no one wants to come to my house . . . I'm so lonely!

Those were the thoughts running through Amy Brooks's mind, but since she couldn't begin to put them into words, she just jumped out of the doctor's car and ran straight up the cement sidewalk into her house without a look back.

Dianne built playhouses for other people's children. Tim had run a lobster boat, and Dianne had set up shop in the oyster shack, where they lived, on the wharf. During their thirteen months together, her playhouses had smelled a lot like shellfish. By then she had orders pouring in from everywhere. She advertised in magazines appealing to parents, romantics, and lovers of New England. Word of mouth did the rest. Her houses were big enough to play in. They had gingerbread, dovecotes, eaves, peaked rooftops, and cross-and-Bible doors; her company was called Home Sweet Home.

Dianne's HMO paid for several hours each week of physical therapy and nurse's aides. If Julia were left alone, she would spend all day in the fetal position. She would curl up, drawing herself inward like the slow-motion nature films of a flower at dusk. Therapy helped, but Dianne didn't like strangers in her home. She preferred to work with Julia herself. No one loved Julia like Dianne did.

Many people had suggested Dianne institutionalize Julia. She could go to St. Gertrude's Children's Hospital or to Fresh Pond Manor. They had told Dianne that Julia would be too much for anyone, even a saint. Sometimes Dianne felt guilty, imagining those people thought she wanted credit for her sacrifice and devotion. She asked herself: Wouldn't Julia get expert care in a place like that? Wouldn't she be exercised and changed and fed and monitored? Wouldn't Dianne be set free to live a less burdened life, be lighter of heart during the time she spent with Julia?

But Julia needed massage. Her muscles would knot up. Her stomach would tighten, and she'd get constipated. And only Dianne knew exactly how she liked to be rubbed. With baby oil on her rough hands, Dianne would soothe her baby's woes. Julia liked circular motions on her angel wings. She liked light pressure around her rib cage, in the area of her kidneys, and she hated being touched on her scars.

Who at the institution would know that? Even if one nurse's aide got used to Julia's preferences, what if that person got transferred or moved away? Julia would have to go through the whole thing again, getting used to someone new. Also, there was the matter of her constipation. Most newcomers didn't realize it was part of the territory for Rett syndrome kids. Medical people were always so quick with laxatives, when all Dianne needed to do was gently rub her belly—using a flat palm, no fingers—to help things along.

Julia would sigh. She would gurgle like a baby, and Dianne would talk back in words: "There, honey. Is that better? Let me tell you about the owl and the pussycat. . . . Ever hear about how monarch butterflies migrate to Belize? . . . About the otters that live in the marsh and the hawks that hunt along the banks . . ."

Dianne was no saint. Her anger and frustrations knew no bounds. She banged nails with a vengeance. She'd yell while she sawed, swearing at God, the universe, and the McIntosh boys. Money was tight. She charged huge sums for her playhouses, targeting the richest people possible. But production was limited; she lived rent free with her mother and paid nearly everything she made to insurance and deductibles. When the aides were there, she'd take off on breakneck runs along the beach, rows through the marsh in her father's old dinghy. Crying and exercise were free.

Her studio was now in the small cottage

behind her mother's house, where she and Julia had come to live after Tim left. The windows overlooked the estuary, the green reeds golden in this twilight hour. Sawdust was everywhere. Like pollen carried on the spring air, it filmed the cottage floor, work-benches, table saw, miter box, and the inside of the windowpanes. Stella, her shy tiger cat, hid in her basket on a high shelf. Julia sat in her chair.

They listened to music. Dianne loved out-of-date love songs that expressed mad longing and forever love; she sang them to Julia while she worked. "The Look of Love," "Scarborough Fair," "Going Out of My Head."

Dianne had been without a man for Julia's entire life. Sometimes she saw women with husbands and imagined what it would be like. Did they have all the love they needed, was it worth the fighting and disagreements to be part of a secure family? In the dark, Dianne sometimes felt lonely. She'd hug her pillow and imagine someone whispering to her that everything would be okay. She tried not to picture a face or hear any certain voice, but the night before she had imag-ined how Alan's back might look under his shirt, how his muscles would strain if he held her really tight.

Measuring carefully, she used a pencil to mark lightly the places she wanted to cut. The table saw let out a high-pitched whine as she guided the wood through. Her father had been a carpenter. He had taught her his craft, and Dianne never cut anything without hearing his gentle voice telling her to mind her priceless hands.

"Home from the wars," Lucinda Robbins said, walking in.

"Hi, Mom," Dianne said. "Tough day?"

"No, darling," said her mother. "It's just that I can *feel* my retirement coming in July, and my body is counting the days."

"How many?" Dianne asked, smiling.

"Eighty-seven," Lucinda said, going over to kiss Julia. "Hello, sweetheart. Granny's home."

Lucinda crouched by Julia's side. Julia's great liquid eyes took everything in, roaming from the raw wood to the finished play-houses to the open window before settling on her grandmother's face.

Dianne stood back, watching. Lucinda was small and thin, with short gray hair and bright clothes: a sharp blue tunic over brick-red pants. Her long necklace of polished agate came from a street market in Mexico, bought on the only cruise she'd ever taken with Dianne's father, eleven years earlier— the year Julia had been born and he had died.

"Maaa," Julia said. "Gaaa."

"She's saying our names," Lucinda said. "Ma and Granny."

"She is?" Dianne asked, dumbstruck by her own need to believe.

"Yes," Lucinda said soothingly. "Of course she is."

Julia had hypersensitive skin, and Dianne smoothed her blond hair as gently as she could. Her hair felt silky and fine. It waved just behind the girl's ears, a white-gold river of softness.

"At Julia's age, you had the same cornsilk hair," Lucinda said. "Just as soft and pretty. Now, tell me. What did Alan say?"

"Oh, Mom." Dianne swallowed hard.

Lucinda touched her heart. "Honey?"

Dianne shook her head. "No, no bad news," she said. "No news at all, really. Nothing definite one way or the other."

"Has she grown?"

"An eighth of an inch."

"Isn't that a lot?" Lucinda asked, frowning. "In so short a time?"

"No!" Dianne said more sharply than she intended. "It isn't a lot. It's completely normal, Mom."

"Good, honey," Lucinda said, striking what Dianne had come to consider her Buddha pose: straight back, serene eyes, hands folded in prayer position under her chin. She might have the same turmoil inside as Dianne, but she hid it better. "Were you nice to him?" she asked.

"Nice?" Dianne asked.

"To Alan," her mother said. "When you saw him today . . ."

"Well . . ." Dianne said, remembering the look on his face as they'd left his office.

"Dianne?"

"Why does he have to remind me so much of Tim?" she asked.

"Oh, honey," Lucinda said.

"They move in identical ways," Dianne said. "Their voices sound the same. Alan's hair is darker, but it gets light in the summer. He wears glasses, but when he takes them off . . ."

"Superficial similarities," Lucinda said.

"I tell myself that," Dianne said. "I feel so

bad, holding this miserable grudge against him. But my stomach hurts every time I think of what Tim did. I lie awake hating him for hurting Julia, but I also hate him for leaving me too. It's horrible, like I swallowed a rock."

"Ouch," Lucinda said kindly.

"I know. And every time I look at Alan, I think of Tim. He makes me think of all the hurt and betrayal, of how much I hate his brother—"

"No," Lucinda said sharply. "That I don't believe."

"I do, Mom. I hate Tim."

"But I don't believe Alan *makes* you feel that way. He can't. He wouldn't—he's too good. He cares for you and Julia, he's always been there. Those feelings are yours alone. Wherever they come from, you're taking them on yourself."

Dianne thought of Alan's eyes, how kind and gentle they were when he looked at Julia. She pictured his hands examining Julia's body, holding her crooked hands as if they were the most precious things on earth.

"I know he's good," Dianne said quietly.

"Listen to me, honey," Lucinda said. "When you talk about swallowing that rock, I can see what it's doing to you. I can. You're tough as can be, you carry the weight of the world on your shoulders, but those hard feelings are tearing you up."

The reality of her mother's words brought tears to Dianne's eyes. Her stomach clenched, the rock bigger than ever. Once the sorrow over Tim's departure had gone and the only things left were bitterness and anger and the rock in her stomach, Dianne had realized in a flash that she had made a mistake from the very beginning: She had chosen the wrong brother.

"I'm fine," Dianne said.

"You say that, but I can see how worried you are. And then when Alan calls, you snap at him—as if it's him you're mad at instead of Tim. When he's just trying to help."

"Sometimes he gets me at a bad time," Dianne said.

"With him it's always a bad time," Lucinda said.

"I'm tired, Mom," Dianne said, uncomfortable with the conversation and the way her mother was smiling at her.

"When I retire," Lucinda said, putting her arm around Dianne, "I'm going to spend some time taking care of you."

Dianne's throat ached. It felt so good to be loved. She closed her eyes and let her mother's strength flow into her. She may have chosen the wrong brother, screwed up her life, but she had the best mother in the world.

"Julia and I have big plans for your retirement," Dianne said.

"Oh, honey," Lucinda said. "Not a party, okay? I know you want to do something for me, and I appreciate it, but I'm not the surprise-party type."

"No party," Dianne said.

"Besides, there's the library dance," Lucinda said. "I think they're going to give me a plaque or something this year. I'll have to pretend to be surprised. How's this?" She made a Betty Boop face: round eyes and mouth, fingertips just brushing her jaw.

"Very convincing," Dianne said, laughing.

"Not that I'm not appreciative," Lucinda said. "I am—I love them all and I'll miss them like crazy. But I'm ready, honey. My feet have been swollen for forty years, and I just want to kick these dumb oxfords right into the marsh and never see them again."

"Julia and I will come up with something that involves bare feet," Dianne said.

"Ahhh," Lucinda said, closing her eyes in bliss, ticking off the time until July fifteenth.

"Gleee," Julia said.

"Just imagine, Julia. I'll have all this free time, I'll be able to read all the books I've missed. Will you help me catch up?" Lucinda asked before opening her eyes.

Dianne exhaled slowly. Julia's life was full of love, but it was so horribly, disgustingly unfair: to have her grandmother be the town librarian and be unable to read, to have her mother make real-life playhouses and be unable to play.

"Do you think she's happy?" Dianne heard herself ask.

"Well, I know she is," her mother said. "Just look at her."

Dianne opened her eyes, and it was true. Julia was rolling her head in slow rhythms, as if she were keeping time with music in her head. She stared at Dianne. Lucinda touched Dianne's shoulder, and Dianne leaned against her.

"My happy girl," Dianne said, wanting to believe.

"Maaa," Julia said. "Maaaaaa."

Could a person die from loving too much? Could the weight of Julia crush her, squeeze the breath right out of her? Summer seemed like a sweet dream. Her mother would be retired; she, Dianne, and Julia could lie on the beach, feeling the hot sand under their backs, letting the breeze take away all their troubles.

"Go for a row, sweetheart," her mother said. "I'll stay with Julia."

Dianne hesitated. She thought of that perfect white house down on the harbor: Lately all her own dreams went into the play-houses she built. Her own home was broken. Dianne felt hard and frozen inside. Her muscles ached, and she knew it would feel good to pull on the oars, slip through the marsh into open water.

"Thanks, Mom," Dianne said.

Lucinda held her gaze. She was small and strong. Even without touching Dianne, her support and force were flowing into her.

Outside, a light breeze blew through the golden-green rushes. Sea otters slid off the banks, playing in the silty brown water.

"Go," her mother urged.

Nodding, Dianne ran down to the dock.

Three

As kids, the McIntosh boys had lived by the sea. Neil, Alan, and Tim had grown up on Cape Cod, ten miles east of the Woods Hole Oceanographic Institution. Alan had spent several summers working in the hydrophone lab there. His mentor, Malachy Condon, told him he had the best ear for dolphin talk of any student he'd ever met. But Alan was destined to be a pediatrician.

Now, eighteen years later, on his Wednesday afternoons off Alan went to the library to read the latest issues of *Delphinus Watch* and *Whale Quarterly*—to keep up with his old interest and to see an old friend—Lucinda Robbins. The Hawthorne Public Library was two blocks from his house. But Alan went running first, so it took him forty-five minutes to get there.

"Did you do six miles?" Mrs. Robbins asked, standing behind the counter.

"Seven today," he said.

She handed him a folded towel she had picked up from a cart of books to be reshelved.

Several months after Tim had walked out on Dianne, Alan had stopped by the library after his run. He had been missing Mrs. Robbins. She had always been good to him, accepting him into her family from the very start. He had more in common with her than Tim did—he had practically lived in libraries at Woods Hole and Cambridge, and during Tim and Dianne's marriage, Alan and Lucinda were always talking books and ideas.

But that day, eleven years ago, he had stood there, noticing the trail of sweat dripping on the brown linoleum floor, feeling the librarian's wrath. What had he expected? He was a McIntosh, Tim's brother, and that fact alone was bound to set her off.

The next week he had gone home to shower first. He didn't want to alienate Mrs.

Robbins. He had realized how important she had become to him, and now she wanted nothing to do with him. Taking care of Julia, he felt the family connection more than ever, and he had come to apologize. To his surprise, Mrs. Robbins had greeted him with a striped towel.

"I'm sorry about last week," she had said. "My evil eye is an occupational hazard."

"You had every right," he had said.

"No," Mrs. Robbins had insisted, vigorously shaking her head. "You come in here sweaty anytime you want. What Tim did isn't your fault. You do so much for Julia and Dianne. . . ."

Alan had started to protest, but he'd stopped himself, accepted her offer. His relationship with Dianne was tenuous, and he'd do whatever he could to guard it. He had considered the towel a one-time peace gesture, but Mrs. Robbins continued to bring it in every Wednesday afternoon.

Today he said thanks, took the towel, and found his favorite armchair. The oldest library in the state, its rooms were bright and lofty. The reading room had a stone fireplace large enough to roast an ox, and Alan settled beside it with a stack of journals to read. Clear April light flooded through the arched windows; he lost himself in the latest literature on marine mammals. And then he thought of his own family.

Their oldest brother, Neil, had loved whales. When they were only teenagers, he, Tim, and Alan had run their own whale-watching business, taking people out in their runabout to the feeding grounds off Chatham Shoals. Leaving from the steamship dock in Hyannis, they had charged ten dollars per person. It had been Neil's idea to give full refunds, no questions asked, if they failed to spot whales or dolphins. That was Neil through and through— generous, good-hearted, and confident enough of their whale-finding abilities to know those refunds would be few and far between.

Neil died of leukemia. The summer they were sixteen and fourteen, Alan and Tim had watched their older brother slip away. Locked in the house, the curtains drawn and no one allowed to make any noise or enter Neil's room, Neil had suffered horribly. Not just from the pain of his disease, but from isolation. He had missed the sea, the whales, the boat. He had missed his brothers. At eighteen Neil had died of leukemia, but also of a broken heart. Tim had spent the last two nights of Neil's life sitting on the grass under his window. Alan had snuck inside to be with him.

Alan's parents had been afraid the cancer was catching. It didn't matter that Neil's doctor had told them it wasn't. They had a primal fear of the blood disease, and they had lived in terror of losing all their sons. They were simple people, a fisherman and his wife. Alan's dad would go to sea, barely coming home at all. His mother had turned to drink.

Alan and Tim had spent the next few years caring more about fish and whales than about people. Tim had dropped out of school to lobster. Like his father, he would lose himself at sea. Alan had latched on to Malachy Condon at WHOI. The old guy was as crusty as a fisherman, but he had a Ph.D. from Columbia. Tim would steam in from a night off Nantucket, meet Alan on the docks at Woods Hole, and listen to Malachy's colorful stories about research trips to the North Sea and the Indian

Ocean. Both brothers were numb with losing Neil and the attention of their parents, and Malachy had been a steadying force.

In Alan's senior year at Harvard, he had found himself dreaming every night of Neil. One cold November morning he ripped up his application to Woods Hole and applied to Harvard Medical School instead. Malachy had been disappointed, and Tim had thought he was crazy. Tim had had the idea they could share a boat, him catching fish and Alan studying them. He had confronted Alan on the steps of the Widener Library, wanting to talk some sense into him.

"Stick with fish," Tim had said. "If they die, who cares?"

"Exactly," Alan had said. "I'm studying plankton past midnight every night, and I can't get that worked up about it. I'm going to be a doctor."

"And do what?"

"Help people," Alan had said, thinking of their brother, their parents.

"You want to spend your life with sick people?" Tim had shouted. "You think you can make any difference at all?"

"Yeah, I do," Alan had said.

"Like Dr. Jerkoff did with Neil?"

"He should have talked to us," Alan had said. "Told Mom and Dad what could happen. Helped them to understand, to prepare us better. He should have helped us help Neil die, Tim. I hate thinking of us all going through that alone."

"What's the difference, how it happened?" Tim had asked wildly. "He's gone. Nothing can change it."

"But he suffered," Alan had said. "It didn't have to be so bad—"

"I know he fucking suffered," Tim had shouted, shoving Alan. "I was there. You think you have to tell me?"

"Quit acting like an asshole," Alan had said. "Neil would hate it."

"He's dead," Tim had shot back, hitting Alan's chest with the heel of his hand.

With Neil gone, Alan was the oldest brother. Tim was tougher, but Alan was big and had never lost one of their fights. He'd stepped away, shaking with rage.

"You sat outside his window," Alan had said. "You were afraid to go in. I want to help people not be afraid."

"Fuck you, *afraid*," Tim had said. "I'll shove it down your throat. . . ."

He hooked a right, and Alan took it in the gut. Their eyes met, wide and surprised. Alan grunted and swung back, driving a left into Tim's side. Tim moved in, and Alan tried to push him off, but Tim raked his fingers down Alan's neck, and the brothers were rolling on the sidewalk in the middle of Harvard Yard.

Alan slammed him with a right to the head. Tim had him by the hair, and Alan jerked his arms hard to break the grip. A gash over Tim's eye was bleeding, and Alan felt the nail marks down his throat. Springing up, he reached down to yank Tim to his feet. Tim wasn't done fighting. He swung blindly through the blood in his eyes. Alan came to his senses.

"Hey, knock it off," he'd said, shaking Tim by the shoulders.

Another left hook.

Alan caught it in the air. The brothers circled, unsteady on their feet. Both were wary, but Alan's burning anger was gone. As Tim swung again, Alan hit him in the solar plexus and sent him to his knees. He stepped away, but Tim kept coming back for more. It's insane, Alan thought. All he wanted was to help children, cure them when he could and comfort them when he couldn't, and here he was, fighting to the death with his brother.

After the fight, Alan and Tim drifted even further apart: Alan buried himself in his studies, Tim chose to escape back to the sea.

For the next few years Tim had stayed at sea. Lobstering took most of his time. It weathered his face and toughened his hands; even more, it hardened something deep inside him. He forgot how to be with people. He'd drink and fight, or he'd flash a smile that let some girl know how lonely he was. That he needed her to hang on to.

One of those girls was Dianne. Knowing that Dianne was interested in Alan made Tim go after her full blast. He had pulled out all the stops. Tim wanted someone to save him, and he chose a woman with a special talent for giving. Some of his behavior was an act, he thought, as he played the part of a lonesome, drunken lobsterman just to get her attention. But it worked, because it was real. So he thought he was playing a role, but he really wasn't. And Alan had watched it happen, Dianne falling in love with his brother.

Alan gave up without a big fight for only one reason: If he couldn't have Dianne, maybe she could at least straighten his brother out. At least that was what he told himself. Dianne was strong and solid, and Tim had been heading downhill since the day Neil had died. Maybe marriage and children would fill the void, make him stop hurting. But they hadn't.

"I hear you saw my girls yesterday," Mrs. Robbins said, startling Alan as she wheeled in a cartload of periodicals to be shelved.

"I did," Alan said.

"How is Julia?"

"She's a champ," Alan said.

Mrs. Robbins had been the Hawthorne librarian for forty years. Alan had heard kids in his office claim she had read every book on the shelves, and he could almost believe it was true. Her blue eyes were clear with intelligence and compassion. Curiosity kept women like Mrs. Robbins young.

"But how *is* she?" Mrs. Robbins asked evenly.

"You know," Alan said. "She's holding her own."

Mrs. Robbins bit her lip. She shuffled

through a pile of *National Geographic*s as if to make sure the issues were in order. But Alan knew she was just pulling herself together.

"Well, Alan," Mrs. Robbins said. "We count on you."

"Thanks," he said.

"I'm worried for Dianne," she said.

"Why?" he asked, alert.

"She wears herself out," Mrs. Robbins said, starting to whisper. The words came out fast, and her brow was creased with worry. Alan leaned forward to hear her. "Julia's light as a feather. She's no weight at all. But the effort . . . even when she's just sleeping, resting in the corner of Dianne's workshop. It takes every bit of energy Dianne has just to let her be. Not knowing the future."

"That's the challenge . . ." Alan said, pulling something out of his generic repertoire. Doctors were supposed to be wise. Inside, he was a mess, hearing about Dianne's pain.

Thinking of Neil, Alan understood what Mrs. Robbins meant. Seeing a person you love suffer is the hardest thing there is. Taking action—bandaging the wound, setting a fracture, cleansing a burn—was always easier than sitting back, accepting there was nothing you could do.

"Dianne's brave," Alan said.

"Most of the time."

"She could ask me for more help than she does."

"Oh, Alan," Mrs. Robbins said. "Don't you know how hard it is for her to be around you—as kind as you are—you will always be a reminder of Tim."

"Yeah," Alan said, hurt to know the truth from Lucinda.

"Heard from him lately?"

Alan shook his head. Two months earlier, Tim had called from Camden, needing to borrow a thousand dollars. Before that Alan would get collect calls or postcards from ports from Lubec to Halifax. Tim had become a seafaring drifter. Sometimes he visited Malachy. He had no home, no address. That was the price he'd paid for what he'd done: leaving his wife and child.

"The poor wretch," Lucinda said. "It's almost impossible to loathe him when he's so tormented. But not quite."

"I know what you mean," Alan said, feeling Lucinda's gaze. He wondered whether she had figured it out. She was too loyal to Dianne, too discreet to ask, but he believed she knew.

Alan was in love with Dianne.

The feeling had never gone away. Even when she'd chosen Tim, with Alan tricking himself into thinking Dianne was stopping Tim's decline, saving his life, he loved her anyway. He'd do anything to help her, then or now.

He told himself he was a doctor, his compassion was natural. Dianne's eyes showed everything. Her hair was the color of Cape Cod marshes in autumn, golden in the October sun. She smelled like paint, lumber, and the sea. Frustration often creased her brow, but when she looked at Julia, the lines would disappear into such deep love that Alan sometimes felt pressure in his throat.

Psychiatrists—and Malachy Condon— would say he loved his sister-in-law because she was totally inaccessible. *Fear of commitment? No problem—pick someone your brother has left, a woman who hates your family with a passion.* Alan was screwed up in the area of relationships—he knew it well. He dated good women. They were all better than he deserved. He had a lousy habit of forgetting to call after the third or fourth time. He had never been married, and as much as he loved children, he had none of his own. And it would probably stay that way.

"Dianne's hoping for a good summer," Mrs. Robbins said.

"I know," Alan said.

"I'll be home to help her out more."

"Do you think Dianne would consider a baby-sitter?" he asked. "I'm thinking of someone, kind of like a mother's helper."

"She might," Mrs. Robbins said. "You could try."

"Coming from me, I'm not sure."

"You're very good to her, Alan," she said. "She might not show it, but I know she appreciates it."

"It doesn't matter," he said.

The librarian's eyes connected with his. "It matters a lot," Mrs. Robbins said. She took his damp towel and hung it on the metal handle of her cart. Alan knew she would wash it and bring it back for him next week. He understood that Lucinda wished that he had been the one to win.

That Dianne had stayed with Alan, never married Tim at all.

Things that Alan wished himself.

Amy came home from school early. Her mother was in bed, and her mother's boyfriend, Buddy, was rehearsing with his band. They were in someone's garage down the street, and Amy could hear the ugly metal sound. *Who wanted to make music that sounded like train wrecks?* But the good news was, he was busy and she would hear if he stopped playing.

The shades were pulled down, but spring sunshine outlined the window frames like square halos. Emptied beer bottles gave off their usual fragrance. Amy walked through the dark room with a can of pine-scented air freshener, spraying full blast. She thought of brooks and forests, hoot owls and whippoorwills. Peeking into her mother's room, she saw her mother lying under the blankets.

"Mama?" Amy whispered.

Her mother didn't move. Thick curtains were pulled over venetian blinds, so the air was dark and heavy as brown corduroy. It was stiflingly hot, and Amy resisted the impulse to throw open the window. She knew her mother needed her rest. Wanting company, she went back to the living room.

"Hi, puppy," she said, falling on her knees before the dog cage.

The young dog bared his teeth, growling and cowering in the back of the cage. Buddy, training him to be a guard dog, had named him Slash, but there was no way on earth Amy would ever call him that.

"I'm your friend," she said.

"Grrrr."

"You don't believe me?" Amy ran to the kitchen and came back with two slices of American cheese—even Buddy wouldn't miss two little slices. Breaking them up into small pieces, she placed one near the front of the cage.

"Grrr," the dog growled. Amy thought back to an early time in Dr. McIntosh's office. Amy had been scared—she had had a sore throat, burning like fire, and a fever of one hundred and four. She had been so afraid to open her mouth. Dr. McIntosh hadn't rushed her at all, just won her over slowly with a lollipop, a story about dolphins, and his gentle voice.

"I'm your friend, puppy," Amy said, trying to imitate Dr. McIntosh's voice. And it was working, because soon the small black dog began creeping forward. Both eyes on Amy, he inched ahead.

It took ten whole minutes, but the little dog finally took the cheese. Then another piece, and another. Very carefully Amy unlatched the metal door. The hinges squeaked, and the dog scurried back. But Amy just kept putting out cheese, and the little guy came up to eat it all. Soon he was eating out of her hand. His coat was bristly and warm, and he had that baby-animal smell that made Amy wish she were a dog.

"The music!" Amy said, realizing one second too late that it had stopped.

"What's going on here?" Buddy asked, standing in the door.

Amy tried to shield the dog from his sight. The room was so dark, even with the window halos, he might not be able to see. The little dog could crawl back into his lair, and everyone would be safe. Amy lay full-length in front of the cage, praying for the dog to retreat.

"Nothing," Amy said. "How was band practice?"

"Lousy. I broke a string, and our bassist had to get to work. What—"

"You sounded great," Amy said, her heart pounding. Reaching behind her, she tried to shove the puppy back.

"You heard us?"

"Yes. Even with a broken string, you play the best. Who's that famous guy, the one Mom listens to—not James Taylor, the other one . . ."

"Eric Clapton?"

"Yes! You play better than him."

"Huh," Buddy said. No one could get more out of the word "huh" than Buddy. Coming from his string-thin lips, he could make the word sound like a ton of cement falling from the Empire State Building. But just then he made it sound like an expression of wonderment. When Ponce de León had emerged from the hot jungle to find the Fountain of Youth his "huh" had sounded just like Buddy's.

"Much better," Amy said warmly, her chest cracking with anxiety. The puppy had discovered her cheese-flavored fingers again and was licking them madly.

"You think? I think I'm more Hendrix myself. When my string snapped, I damn near . . . what's that?"

"That noise?" Amy asked, thinking fast. The puppy was slurping away.

"Did that dog get out?" Buddy asked.

"No," Amy said immediately, pushing the puppy inside his cage, blocking the door with her outstretched arms. "I let him out, it's my fault, I just wanted—"

With one motion Buddy lifted Amy away from the cage and tossed her onto the sofa. Reaching in, he grabbed the dog by the scruff of his neck. Amy's eyes were open wide. She watched the terrified puppy dangle from Buddy's hand like a ham on a hook.

"What did I tell you?" Buddy asked, and Amy didn't know whether he was talking to her or to the dog.

"It's my fault," Amy said again. Her voice sounded funny, like the sandpaper she sometimes used in art class.

"I don't care about fault," Buddy said softly. "What I care about is obedience."

"Don't hurt him," Amy said.

"What good is a guard dog that won't obey? You teach them young, or you have to shoot them later."

"Don't hurt him though," Amy said.

Without another word Buddy kicked the dog with his pointy cowboy boot. The dog yelped in pain, and Buddy kicked him again. "For your own good," Buddy said, holding him down. "For your own stupid good."

Amy started to sob. The little dog couldn't get away. He struggled and squirmed, yelping loudly. Buddy kicked him over and over, and when he was done, he hurled the dog into his cage. Picking up a rolled-up newspaper, he smacked the palm of his open hand.

"Got it now?" he asked. He never hit Amy, but she had the definite feeling he was threatening her then. "Are we clear who's master around here?"

In the bedroom, blankets rustled. Amy's stomach ached. She didn't know what she wanted more, for her mother to rescue the dog or for her to stay out of the way.

"C'mere," Buddy said.

Amy refused to look, afraid he was talking to her.

"Come here," Buddy said, and the cage door rattled. He was reaching in, pulling the dog out again. He was petting the dog, whispering to him, scratching him behind the ears. The dog whimpered, trying to get away.

"I'll break you, boy," Buddy said. "If that's what it'll take, that's what I'll do."

"Don't break him," Amy whispered.

"What?" he asked.

Amy shut her mouth. She didn't want Buddy to hear her. She knew from experience it made him mad when people intervened—like Amy would do with her mother.

The puppy pulled to get away, crying almost like a human child. Amy's body ached, straining to get over there and help him, but she was glad the dog had fight left in him. It would be worse if he licked Buddy's hand the way he wanted the puppy to. Amy knew she had to be very quiet so Buddy would leave the room. If she made herself invisible, this would stop sooner.

"I said, what?" he asked softly.

But Amy slipped away in her mind, turned herself into a babbling brook. She was tumbling over mossy ledges, through shady glens and sylvan glades. Herons were nesting on her banks, and spiders spun glassy webs across her clear water. She was flowing downhill, toward the sea, where her father had fished. She was on her way when the phone rang.

"Hello?" Buddy said.

Amy watched him. He was ramrod-straight, the king of his castle, when he picked up the receiver. Beating the puppy must have given him confidence, because he sounded very sure of himself. But as he listened to the voice at the other end, Amy watched him wilt before her very eyes. His spine gave out, and he drooped like a tulip stem.

"Yes, she's right here," he said. "I'll get her."

"For Mom?" Amy asked.

"For you," he said, covering the receiver. He seemed about to admonish her, to tell her he was expecting a call, or remind her to keep family matters private. His thin lips opened and closed a couple times, but he just handed her the phone.

"Hello?" Amy asked.

"Is this Amy Brooks?" came the deep

voice, and she recognized it right away. Relief spread through her like a heat wave, tears cresting in her eyes.

"Hi, Dr. McIntosh," she said.

"What are you doing next Saturday?" he asked.

Four

On Saturday morning Dianne was wallpapering the parlor wall of a small Victorian. The blue and white paper was English, a pattern of tiny white peonies. Dianne worked from the interior out. She would do the inside work first, making sure every detail was perfect, then nail the house together.

"Your grandmother would like this paper," she said to Julia. "Peonies are her favorite flower."

Julia sat close by, propped up in her chair. Every window was open, and a warm wind blew off the marsh. Stella crouched on the sill, inside the screen, watching life in the yard. Julia was very quiet today, enjoying the breeze in her hair. Everyone got spring fever in their own way. Dianne felt April moving toward May.

A car door closed, and the cat instantly slid out of sight. Born in the wild, Stella was intensely shy. Dianne craned her neck, but she couldn't see the driveway from the window. Washing wallpaper paste off her hands, she went to the door.

"Oh, my God," she said, feeling her stomach lurch as she saw Alan getting out of the car. Dianne thought of Julia's test results, wondered whether he had come by to break some bad news in person. But then she saw the young girl, and she relaxed a little. He wouldn't have brought someone with him if that were the case. Dianne's hands were trembling as she dried them with an old rag, and she watched them come toward the studio.

Alan shielded his eyes, looking around. The marsh was bathed in sunlight, a hundred shades of green. Cattails rustled, and red-winged blackbirds darted in and out. Long Island Sound sparkled beyond. The Robbinses had the last house on Gull Point, ten blocks and a world away from Amy's.

"You know these people?" Amy asked, standing beside him with wide eyes.

"I do."

"They're witches," she said. "All the kids say so."

"What kids?"

"In my neighborhood."

"What do they say?"

"That the ladies cast spells and turn kids into monsters and trolls. Then they keep them prisoner." Amy was staring at the house. It was a tidy Cape, its white cedar shingles weathered to silver. The blue shutters had cut-out sea horses; the white window trim gleamed. Window boxes were filled with purple and yellow pansies.

"Well . . ." Alan said.

"Is it true?" Amy asked, standing so close, her shoulder bumped his jacket.

"You're going to have to decide for yourself," he said, feeling a shiver under his skin as he saw Dianne standing in the doorway.

Amy had never doubted Dr. McIntosh before, but she couldn't imagine why he was bringing her to the witch-ladies' house. She had been so happy about spending the day with him, she had prepared by taking a bath in Rain Magic bath salts, then putting on fresh jeans and the cleanest shirt she could find. But now, standing in the clamshell driveway on Gull Point, she felt afraid.

Tall privet hedges lined the yard, blocking any view from the street. Although Amy lived just a few blocks away, she had never seen the house before and was surprised that it looked so cute. Would witches live in a Cape with sea horse shutters? Instead of walking up the front path, Dr. McIntosh headed around the side yard. It was a meadow of sea grass, bristly and greenish-brown, but there were gardens of daffodils, pink azaleas, and tiny blue scillas.

Set back at the edge of the marsh was a small white cottage. *Most unwitch-like!* Amy thought. And standing in the doorway was the golden-haired lady Amy had seen once before, at Dr. McIntosh's office.

"Oh!" Amy said.

"I should have called," the doctor said to the lady.

"What's wrong?" she asked, sounding scared.

"Nothing. Nothing at all," he said quickly. "I happened to be in the neighborhood, picking up my friend Amy Brooks, and I wanted to introduce her to you."

The lady bowed her head, looking relieved. She wore a white shirt tucked into blue jeans. The sleeves were rolled up; she wore old sneakers. Her hair was pulled back in a loose braid, and she'd tied the end with a thin piece of marsh grass. Her eye color reminded Amy of periwinkles, just as they had the other time she had seen her.

"I know who you are," the lady said, smiling slowly.

Amy stood slightly behind the doctor.

"You were in the playhouse," the lady said.

"Dr. McIntosh lets me," Amy blurted out, thinking maybe the lady was going to give her a hard time about it.

"It makes me happy you like it," the lady said.

Amy frowned, unsure of why the lady should care one way or the other. Confused, she looked at the doctor, and he placed his hand on Amy's shoulder.

"Miss Robbins made that playhouse," he said. "I bought it from her to put in my waiting room. And my brother delivered it in his truck. That's how we all met."

"That's a very old story," the lady said. "I'd like Amy to call me Dianne. Come on in."

Once Dianne got past that first lurch, seeing Alan's car and thinking *bad news*, she felt herself relax. Their eyes met and held for a moment. She took in his open expression, the smile lines every mother in Hawthorne loved, and she was so aware of the distance she wanted to keep between them, she forgot to open the screen door.

"How are you?" he asked, entering her studio.

"Fine, thanks. Is everything okay?" she asked.

"Yes," he said, looking around as if her studio were new to him. He made frequent emergency visits, but they were mainly up at the house.

"You've been in here, haven't you?" she asked.

"You usually have it pretty well barricaded," he said.

She glanced up, saw him smiling wryly.

"You're related," Amy said. "He told me."

"Distantly," Dianne said.

"I'm her daughter's uncle," Alan explained

with kindness in his voice that even Dianne couldn't miss. He was nice to all kids—no one could mistake the fact that he had a gift for talking to them.

How could someone so different from Tim remind Dianne so much of him? Alan was brainy, Tim was cocky. Alan wore the most faded blue shirts Dianne had ever seen, old blue jeans, and hiking boots. His glasses were slipping down his nose, and Dianne had to fight the urge to push them back up. Tim was the family bad boy, and Alan was the scientist. But they were both tall, lean, with an easy, graceful style of movement. Seeing Alan, Dianne always pulled back, as if from Tim himself.

"Deeee," Julia said, coming to life. "Deeeee!"

"Oh!" Amy said, shocked, stepping back at the sight of Julia.

Dianne's stomach flipped. Whenever someone saw Julia for the first time, all Dianne's mother-lion instincts kicked into gear. If the people seemed upset, un-friendly, or disgusted, Dianne found a way to get them out fast. She might have expected Alan to warn the girl, but it seemed obvious that he hadn't.

"Is that—" Amy began.

"My daughter," Dianne said steadily.

"Her name is Julia," Alan said. "You were asking about her the other day."

"I saw her chart!" Amy said. Her eyes wide, she took a step toward Julia.

Dianne's shoulders tightened. She clutched herself with folded arms. The young girl had sounded so scared, and now she had a look of morbid fascination on her face. Anger welled up in Dianne, and she started forward to get between Amy and Julia.

"You showed her Julia's chart?" Dianne asked, furious.

Alan just shook his head as if it didn't merit an explanation.

"This is Dianne's workshop," Alan said.

"Where you make the playhouses?" Amy asked.

"Yes."

"Hmm," Amy said. She cast a low glance at Julia, then looked quickly away. She was curious about the little girl. She wanted to stare, but she was polite enough not to. While Alan visited with Julia, Dianne pointed at the half-finished house, directing Amy's attention away.

"I'm wallpapering this section," Dianne said, feeling like a protective bird, leading the girl away from her nest. On the other hand, the child seemed so vulnerable. She had fly-away brown hair, bitten-down fingernails, a deep worry line between her eyebrows.

"Ooh, pretty," Amy said, touching the white flowers.

"I do one wall at a time," Dianne said. "Then put them together."

"Oh," Amy said, looking back at Julia.

"Once the house is assembled, I add the trim. These wooden curlicues are called gingerbread. I'll attach that to the eaves, then add this little dovecote, these shutters. Then I'll paint it. . . ."

"Does she have one in her room?"

"What?" Dianne asked.

"Julia," Amy said carefully. Leaning to see around Dianne, she looked across the room. "Does she have her own playhouse?"

"Well, no," Dianne said slowly. Couldn't Amy see?

Amy must have picked up on her surprise, because she blushed. "I just thought, her being your daughter and all . . ."

"That Dianne would build her a house," Alan said, stepping in to help.

"Julia is . . ." Dianne searched for the words to explain.

But Amy couldn't contain herself anymore. She walked straight over to Julia, bent down to look her in the eyes. Her face was full of warmth and friendliness.

"Gaaa," Julia said.

"Hi, little girl," Amy said, crouching beside Julia's chair.

Dianne stepped forward, wanting to get Amy away from her.

"Let them . . ." Alan whispered, grabbing Dianne's wrist.

"Pretty little girl. Oh, you pretty little girl," Amy said.

"Gaaa," Julia said again. She had seemed happy to see Alan, but she was utterly entranced with Amy. Julia's hands drifted in their strange ballet, gently tracing the air in front of Amy's face.

"How old are you?" Amy asked.

Dianne wanted to reply for Julia, but she found that her voice wouldn't work.

"She's eleven," Alan said.

"Almost my age," Amy said, holding Julia's left hand. She spoke not to the adults but to Julia herself. "I'm twelve."

"Deeee," Julia said. "Deee . . . Gaaaa . . ."

"She's not surprised," Dianne said quietly to Alan. "Most people see Julia and think she's so much younger."

"Amy's young for her age," Alan said. "I got it into my head she could baby-sit for Julia. Maybe not by herself, but when you or your mother are around. It would give you a little free time, and I think it would be good for Amy. I mentioned it to your mother. . . ."

"You don't have to look after us, Alan—"

"I know that," he said.

"This is my father's watch," Amy said, holding out her wrist for Julia to touch. "It weighs a ton, but I don't care. I've had it eleven years now, and it's still running strong. It was being fixed at the jeweler's the day he died. He was a hero, he went down with his ship. . . ."

Dianne had to turn away. She walked to the window and stared out at the garden. The tall, purple irises swayed in the wind. A wild cat hunted along the edge of the rushes. Dianne felt like howling. Emotion flooded her chest, and she had to hug herself hard to keep it in. Alan came up behind her; Dianne felt his presence before he said a word.

"Do you hear the way she talks to Julia?"

Dianne asked, tears rolling down her cheeks.

"I do," Alan said.

With her back to Alan, Dianne covered her face and wept silently. Her body shook, and she felt his fingers brush her shoulder. His hands were big, and they felt strong and steady. She felt the heat of his fingers through her thin shirt. Across the room, Amy was telling Julia about the puppy at her house, imitating its bark so well, she sounded like a young dog.

"Julia's never had a friend before," Dianne whispered.

"I don't think Amy has either," Alan whispered back.

Five

Amy began stopping by occasionally after school. By the second week she was coming every other afternoon. Julia liked Amy and seemed soothed by her. So often Julia seemed to be fighting demons in her head. She would wring her hands over and over. When Amy was there, she didn't struggle as much. She seemed more placid and serene, and she smiled.

By two-thirty each day, Dianne had started glancing out the screen door of her studio, listening for Amy's footsteps. Amy would run so fast across the marshy land, she sounded like a young filly in the homestretch, bursting through the screen door with a wild grin. She was a little hellion, awkward and messy. Dianne had taken to making lemonade, and she would set out the pitcher on a tray bearing glasses, oatmeal cookies, and square linen napkins.

Their second Tuesday together, they had their snack at the small table beside Julia's chair. Sunlight streamed through the windows, and the marsh smelled warm and salty. They ate a cookie in silence, then, as was becoming their custom, talked for a few minutes before Dianne returned to work.

"I love these glasses," Amy said, admiring one. Old juice glasses, they were enameled with tiny baskets overflowing with wildflowers. Each petal was a distinct, nearly microscopic brushstroke of scarlet, cobalt, cadmium yellow, or sap green.

"They were my grandmother's," Dianne said.

"All your things are . . . so careful."

"How?" Dianne asked, tickled by the word.

"Everything is just *so*. You make things seem like they matter. Beautiful glasses, real cloth napkins, the way you tie your hair with a piece of marsh grass . . ."

"That's just because I couldn't find an elastic," Dianne said.

"Hmm," Amy said, glowing as she took a small bite of cookie. Dianne didn't think of herself as careful: Sentimental was more like it. She liked things to remind her of other people. She had loved her grand-mother, and she had loved Tim's. Dorothea McIntosh had lived in a meadow, and she had tied *her* hair with long grass and flower stems. She had married a sea captain who brought jewels and rosewood back from a trip to India, and Dianne had her diamond and sapphire earrings tucked safely away.

Dianne held the cup close to Julia's chin, guided the straw to her lips. The first day, Amy had tried to feed Julia a bite of cookie, and Dianne had had to explain that Julia could choke. She loved the way Amy accepted Julia's reality without question, without trying to change it, make it better, conform to hers. Amy leaned forward with a napkin to dab away the lemonade that spilled down Julia's chin.

"Thank you," Dianne said.

"Rats, don't thank me," Amy said, blush-ing.

"Your mother doesn't mind you coming over here?"

Amy shook her head.

"Does she work?" Dianne asked, trying to get a feel for what made Amy want to spend the afternoons away from home. Maybe her mother didn't get home till five or six; probably Amy didn't like staying in an empty house.

"No," Amy said, looking down. "She's home."

They didn't say anything for a while after that. There was a rhythm developing to their time together. They didn't have to do anything to rush it along; it was growing at its own pace. Dianne tried not to ask herself why this meant so much to her, that a twelve-year-old girl from the neighborhood would want to hang around with her and Julia.

Amy was helping her see something. This was how life would be if Julia were normal: a mother and daughter going through their days together. Dianne was a mother with so much to give. Alan had put them together; Dianne was grateful, but sometimes she felt she was already beholden to him for too many things. And he was always there, even when she least expected him.

Last Wednesday she had driven over to the library to drop off her mother's lunch.

From behind the glass partition in the librarians' office, Dianne spotted Alan jogging up the library's wide front steps.

"It's Wednesday," Lucinda said, following her gaze. "He visits on his day off."

"I forgot," Dianne said, holding Julia.

"Just a minute," Lucinda said. "Be right back."

Her mother took the towel she had folded on her desk and walked out to the front desk to meet Alan. Rocking Julia, Dianne watched them greet each other. Alan's T-shirt was soaked, and wet hair hung in his eyes. She half rose, thinking she'd walk out and say hi. This was her chance to thank him for sending Amy over.

Lucinda gestured, beckoning him around the desk. She directed Alan behind a corkboard partition. From behind the glass Dianne watched him glance around to make sure no one was looking. Then he pulled his wet shirt over his head. His body was strong and glistening with sweat. He dried himself off with the towel, and she watched him rubbing the mat of curly dark hair on his chest.

Dianne was frozen in place. She couldn't move or look away. She felt like a spy, the library voyeur. The blood was pumping to her brain, leaving her mouth open and dry. Alan's skin was ridiculously smooth, glossy and taut across his muscles. The two young librarians had walked in to have their lunch. They giggled, and Dianne realized they were checking Alan out too. She mumbled a few words.

The pediatrician's body. She stared at it: his flat stomach, the narrow line of dark hair trailing into his waistband. His thighs looked massive, the rest of his legs long and lean. When he had finished drying himself, he pulled his wet shirt back on. As his head popped through the opening, his eyes met Dianne's.

She blinked and looked down. The door opened and Lucinda walked in. The younger librarians were teasing her about keeping Alan to herself. Lucinda bantered back. Julia waved her arms, trying to call her grandmother. When Dianne glanced up, remembering that she still hadn't thanked Alan for sending Amy to them, he had disappeared.

Having finished the little Victorian yesterday, Dianne was beginning a Greek Revival for the seventh birthday of a little girl in Old

Lyme. This required building a portico and positioning ionic columns. While Julia dozed, Amy sat on a high stool watching Dianne work. Stella, still unsure about the newcomer, perched in a wicker basket on a shelf, spying from on high.

"Why doesn't Stella like me?" Amy asked. "Cats usually do."

"Stella is a squirrel," Dianne said.

"No, really. Why doesn't she like me?"

"She does. She's just very shy," Dianne said, measuring the distance between columns. "Her mother was killed by foxes the day she was born, and she was raised by a mother squirrel in the stone wall out back."

"Poor little thing!" Amy said, staring at the cat, gray-striped with a brown undercoat. "She looks a little like a squirrel. . . . How do you know?"

"I found her mother's body. I'd see the tiny kitten going in and out of the wall. After a couple of weeks, when she got too big, the mother squirrel stopped nursing her and kicked her out. She probably thought her babies were in danger—"

"Cats hunt squirrels," Amy said. "They were her prey."

"Eventually, but she was still too young. I had to feed her warm milk with a doll bottle. She was tiny, the size of a teacup. I'd hold her in one hand."

"She must have been so cute," Amy said in a small voice.

"And wild. At night she'd tear through the house. Once a bat got in, and she chased it till dawn. When people dropped by, she'd hide so completely, I sometimes couldn't find her all day."

"Hide where?"

"In my sweater drawer, under my quilt—she'd flatten herself out so much, you couldn't even see a bump in the bed. Up the chimney, on the smoke shelf."

"And now she's up there, hiding in the basket," Amy said, tilting her head back to see. Stella was there watching them, her eyes an unusual shade of turquoise.

"See, it's not you," Dianne said.

"I thought she'd know me by now," Amy said. "I've been coming almost a month."

"She doesn't even meow—she chatters like a squirrel. In the morning she peeps. Sometimes I call her Peeper. She's just a very unusual cat." Dianne hated the idea of anyone thinking they were rejected, left out, unloved. Including Amy. She came over every day now, sat with Julia, talked to Dianne for hours on end. Gazing up at Stella, Amy seemed thin and unkempt, a lost ragamuffin.

"You raised a wild cat with a bottle . . ." Amy said, turning to Dianne. Her eyes were full of pain. "People don't usually do that."

"You would," Dianne said.

"How do you know?" Amy asked.

"I can tell how much you care by the way you are with Julia."

Clearing her throat, Dianne began to make Stella's sound, the chirping of a squirrel. "Eh-eh. Eh-eh."

The cat perked up her ears. Julia awoke, her eyes rolling up to Stella's hiding place. Dianne kept on making the noise. Amy sat very still, and Julia's hands began to drift, conducting her imaginary orchestra. Tentatively, Stella slid out of her basket. With great stealth, she came down from the shelf.

This was a game Dianne often played with her cat. Stella could play; Julia could not. Amy watched openmouthed.

Afternoon sun bathed the room, and Dianne tilted her watch crystal to catch the light. Directing it against the white wall, she sent the bright disk of reflected light careening along the baseboard. Stella began to chase it, making the "eh-eh" noises as she stalked her prey.

"She thinks it's alive," Amy exclaimed. "She wants to catch it!"

"You try it," Dianne said. "With your father's Timex."

"Okay," Amy said, and Julia sighed.

Dianne watched Amy get the hang of it, sending the tiny moon along the floor, Stella chattering in hot pursuit.

"Watch, Julia," Amy laughed. "You have one crazy cat!"

Julia strained to focus. Her hands moved rapidly. Her eyes seemed to follow the action, and when Amy sent the tiny moon onto Julia's tray and Stella jumped into Julia's lap, Amy squealed with surprise and delight.

"Stella means 'star,'" Dianne said. "I named her because when I first brought her home, I found her sitting in the window one night, staring at the sky. She always looks toward the same constellation."

"Which one?" Amy asked.

"Orion."

"I love the story of Stella," Amy said.

Dianne nodded. As she watched Julia and Amy pet the cat, she tried not to let Amy's comment make her feel too sad. She thought of loving the strange, the unlovable. She knew the value of play, of imagination and symbolism. It was every mother's dream to see her child grow and develop, and to help the child along that path. Dianne had been able to do that more for a cat than for her own daughter.

Leaving the girls alone, she went silently over to her workbench, back to the columns. She loved the ionic capitals; their scrollwork reminded her of moon shells. The girls' voices drifted over. They were soft and harmonious; at their feet, the cat chirped and peeped.

Listening, Dianne thought: This wasn't the life she would have chosen. Dianne loved to talk, tell stories, exchange tales about the mysteries of life. Her child, her darling, her beacon of light, was incapable of reflection. Gazing into her eyes, she saw blankness, as if Julia's eyes saw only inward, deep into her own soul—or nothing at all. Dianne pretended that Julia spoke in words and gestures, and sometimes she was more able than others to admit her own maternal lies.

Somewhere along the line Dianne had turned into an eccentric who talked to cats. Then, since she couldn't communicate with her daughter, she captivated another woman's child. To escape the hurt of her life, she imagined that her daughter was aware. That Julia was more, somehow, than a broken human body.

Much more, Julia. Much more, my love.

Dianne glanced over: The girls were talking. Amy was imitating the cat, and Julia was expressing her pleasure with the elaborate hulalike motion of her arms. Dianne bent over her work, positioning columns.

"Does your mother want you home?" she called to Amy.

"Nope," Amy called back.

Amy rarely spoke of her family, but Alan had given Dianne to understand that all was not well in the Brooks household. Dianne had respect for all mothers, no matter how troubled or imperfect, and she took a long breath to make herself mindful of that fact.

"What do you think we should do for my mother when she retires?" Dianne asked, changing the subject, knowing that she had touched a raw nerve. Amy was clearly not ready to open up to Dianne about the goings-on at home.

"A surprise party," Amy said.

"She says she'll kill us if we do that."

"My friend Amber's mom took her parents on a cruise for their golden anniversary."

"A cruise . . ." Dianne said, mulling it over.

"Dianne," Amy said. "Julia's wet."

"Okay, be right there," Dianne said.

The game was over, and Stella crept back to her basket. Dianne went to the bathroom and returned with a clean diaper. During Amy's first visits, Dianne had taken Julia behind the rice-paper screen to change her. They were beyond that now. Julia was eleven. If she went to camp, to gym class, to sleep over at a friend's house, other girls would see her naked. Amy was Julia's friend, her good friend.

"Here's powder," Amy said, handing Dianne the bottle.

"Thank you," Dianne said, sprinkling it on.

"I love baby powder," Amy said to Julia. "It's better than perfume. I wear it to school."

"Laaa," Julia said.

"I always think she means flower," Dianne said. "when she says *la*."

"She does," Amy said solemnly. As if she knew more about Julia's language, could hear more, translate better, than even Dianne herself. Dianne was silent, wishing Julia would say something else. But she didn't.

"La, Julia," Amy said. "Marigold, lily, daisy, and rose."

Julia blinked her eyes, rolling her head.

Dianne listened, watching Julia play with her friend, glad she had told Amy the story of Stella. Maybe someday she'd tell Amy the other story, the story of Julia.

The story started with the McIntosh brothers.

Dianne had dreamed of love her whole life. Her parents were wonderful people, devoted to each other and to her. She had always wanted that for herself, to find that kind of true love. Dianne's mother had been an orphan, and she claimed Emmett had saved her. Dianne was shy, and she lived at home long after other kids her age had left. It was as if she knew that the real world was harsh, that she had to be ready before she stepped out into it.

Taking after her father, she went into carpentry. He had built her a playhouse when she was a little girl, and Dianne made one for the third birthday of a daughter of a childhood friend. She had modeled it after that white house on the harbor, the place where she fantasized someday living with a family of her own, and every mother who saw it wanted one for her own child.

Alan was then a new pediatrician in town and he commissioned Dianne's father to build shelves in his office. Alan was young, just getting his practice off the ground, and Emmett had liked him a lot. He had suggested he buy one of Dianne's playhouses for his waiting room. Dianne had gone to the medical arts building to get a feel for the space, and Alan had come out to meet her.

"Your father did such a good job," he said. "I wanted to see what you could do."

"I learned everything from him," Dianne said, feeling shy and a little intimidated. "From the best."

"I'll be the only doctor in town with a Robbins playhouse. All the kids'll want to come to me. I'll have the edge," he joked in

a way that let her know he was partly serious, a little insecure. He was tall and thin,
not much older than Dianne. He had light
brown hair that kept falling into his eyes.

"Are you from around here?" she asked.

"Cape Cod."

"And you decided to be a doctor in
Hawthorne?"

He nodded. "I did my residency in New
Haven, and I took over this practice when
Dr. Morrison decided to retire."

"Do you miss Cape Cod?"

"It's not that far away," he said, "but, yes,
I do."

"Do you have family there?" Dianne
asked, knowing how much she'd miss her
parents if she ever moved.

He shook his head. "Not anymore. My
brother's a lobsterman, working off Block
Island this year. Half the time he ties up right
here in Hawthorne."

"That's good," Dianne said, nodding.

"I like the hospital here," Alan said. "The
town's growing, and the area's beautiful.
But fitting in . . ."

"My dad says Hawthorners take forever to
accept newcomers," Dianne said. Even
though she was just a carpenter and he was

a doctor, something about Alan made her feel she could say these things to him. "Even my business started off slow, and I was born here."

"People will find me," Alan said.

"I'm sure they will," Dianne said, sizing him up. If she had a child, she could imagine wanting this man to take care of her. He seemed gentle, and when he'd said 'people will find me,' he'd sounded quietly confident, as if he knew he was a good doctor and he knew parents would bring their kids to him.

"Don't worry," she said, nodding her head. "I'll make you a beautiful playhouse." She didn't know why, but the promise was incredibly important to her. Back at home, she riffled through architecture books and all sorts of magazines in search of quirky details. Little kids loved things like sea horse door knockers, shutters that really closed, a mailbox to hold letters.

One night a few weeks later her mother called her to the phone and told her it was Alan McIntosh. Thinking he wanted to discuss her progress, she picked up the extension. But instead, he wanted to ask her out to dinner. Dianne was silent, holding the receiver. Working for a doctor was one thing, going out with him was another. What would they have to talk about? What would he think when he found out she'd dropped out of Connecticut College?

"Yes," she heard herself say. "Yes, okay."

Saturday night he said. He thought she might like to try the Rosecroft Inn.

Dianne loved the place and the evening. They sat in the grill room. Drinking champagne, she had felt the bubbles on her upper lip. It was such a romantic night. There was a pink rose on the table, a fire in the fireplace, candles flickering around the darkened room.

Alan was handsome and attentive. He seemed interested in her background, the fact that she had spent her whole life in Hawthorne. He hadn't acted surprised when she told him about not liking college, about knowing she wanted to work with her father. He talked about his brother Neil, the reason he had become a doctor. He told her about his brother Tim, the wild man who fished the eastern seaboard, coming home only when he had to.

Curious about how two brothers could be so different, Dianne wanted to hear more.

She and Alan were talking so much, the waiter had to stop by four times before they were ready to order. When the time came, she realized she had barely even looked at the menu. She ordered sweetbreads, something she had never tried before.

Alan asked her to tell him her happiest memory. She asked him about his favorite dream. He wanted to know about all her pets, and after she told him, he wanted to know how they got their names. She asked him if he believed in heaven.

She had never had a date like this before. Most of the guys she dated were locals like her. Many of them had gone to grade school together, had known each other their whole lives. But just two hours of talking to Alan gave Dianne the idea she'd been missing something. She had never imagined getting so much pleasure from telling a man about the Scottish terrier she'd gotten for her fourth birthday.

He had shoulders like a football player's, broad and solid, yet he moved with a sexy kind of grace. He ordered oysters and fed Dianne one, tilting the shell against her lips. His brown hair was a little shaggy, in need of a haircut. Listening to him talk about medicine, she could hear the passion. He wasn't in it for the money or prestige: He had a true calling to help people.

That night when he drove her home he held her hand across the seat. When he stopped the car, he kissed her. The blood rushed into her face and her knees went weak when he tangled his long fingers in her hair, kissed her hard and steady as she leaned into his chest. He felt strong and sturdy as any workman, even though his hands didn't have calluses. He was a doctor, what did she expect?

A week went by while she worked on his playhouse. She hoped he would like it enough to take her out again. But he was busy with his practice, and she was busy creating the playhouse. He called once, and she was out; she returned his call, and he was at the hospital.

Then came delivery day.

The playhouse was ready. She had it in her studio, and she and her father had planned to carry it over in his truck. But then Alan said his brother Tim was back in town. Since his boat was tied up at the lobster dock, Tim would swing by to pick up the finished house.

She had been wrapping the playhouse in batting to protect it on the drive when Tim McIntosh walked into her studio. He was as tall as Alan but blonder. He spent his life in the sun, and it showed in the lines on his face. He wore a plaid shirt with the sleeves rolled up, exposing muscular forearms, and his front tooth was slightly chipped. His eyes looked as intelligent as Alan's, but haunted, as if he were pondering the end of the world.

"Hey" was all he said as he walked over to grab the roll of batting from Dianne's hand. "Let me do that."

"No, I—" she began.

But he didn't listen. He just took the roll of thick padding and began to wrap the house as if he'd been doing that sort of work his whole life. Without speaking, or even really smiling, he stared at her across the small house's gabled roof. Dianne felt a long shiver down her spine and along the backs of her legs. She wondered how he had chipped his tooth, gotten that scar over his right eyebrow.

"What're you thinking?" Tim asked.

"Me?" she replied, embarrassed to have gotten caught staring. "Nothing."

"That's not true," he said.

"Then tell me what I'm thinking about."

"You want a boat ride," he said.

"No," she said. "If I'm thinking anything, it's that you did a nice job. Wrapping that playhouse."

"You always do your work in that outfit?"

Hoping that she and Alan might have dinner after the delivery, Dianne had put on a dress. It was blue and white striped, with a white collar that suddenly seemed too big. Standing in front of Tim, she felt so awkward, felt sweat rolling down her back. She couldn't stop staring at Tim's wide grin. She looked like a schoolgirl in her striped dress, she thought, and she wondered what he would think if he knew she still lived with her parents.

"Strong woman," he said. "To build this house all by yourself. Tell the truth—did your father help you? Because you honestly don't look like the hammer-swinging type."

"I am," she said.

"I'm a laborer myself. That's why I don't expect someone as pretty as you . . ." He smiled again, showing his broken tooth.

"I love my work," she said.

"Me too," he said. "A woman after my own heart."

With his light hair and ruddy skin, the fine white lines radiating around deep blue eyes, there was no missing the fact that he was a fisherman. He was ruggedly gorgeous, and he had a way of glowering that made Dianne think he was harboring a bad secret. He was full of life, and she could imagine him standing on deck, navigating by the stars. When he took her hand and shook it, she felt the thrill all through her body.

"Tim McIntosh," he said. "Pleased to meet you."

"Dianne Robbins," she said, staring at his strong and callused hand. It took a long time for him to let go.

"How about that boat ride?" he asked.

"Your brother's waiting for us."

"He can come with us," Tim said.

"Stop." She laughed. "We have to take the playhouse over to his office."

"An island," Tim said. "That's where I'll take you on our boat ride. Somewhere in the Bahamas. We'll go bone fishing and sleep on the beach. You like the sound of palm trees rustling in the wind?"

"I've never heard them."

"You will," Tim McIntosh had said, his blue eyes blazing.

"No, I—" Dianne began, unable to take her eyes off Tim. He held her hand lightly, as if he had known her for years, as if he planned to walk her straight off into the sunset. She pulled away, convinced him that Alan was waiting, that they should deliver the playhouse to his waiting room as they had promised.

"Whatever you want," he said, wrapping his arm around her waist. "You don't love him, do you?"

"We've gone out only once," Dianne said, her voice cracking.

"Good," Tim said.

"Why do you say that?" she asked, feeling his hand on the small of her back. Their faces were close, and she knew it was all over. He was a cowboy with a boat, a broken tooth, and a dark secret. Her heart was pounding, and she felt liquid inside. Just looking at him made her smile, made her nervous, made her feel like laughing out loud.

"Because we're going for a boat ride, and if things work out, I'm going to ask you to marry me," he said. "What would you say to that?"

"I'd say you're crazy," Dianne said as he touched the side of her face with his rough fingertips. But she knew that her time with Alan was over forever.

The truly crazy thing was, Tim McIntosh proposed to her for real less than a month later. He asked her to marry him on the deck of his boat, with all the new spring constellations overhead.

"I need you," he told her.

"We hardly know each other," she said.

"It doesn't feel that way to me," he said, clutching her. "It feels as if I've known you my whole life. Marry me, Dianne," he said.

"Marry you . . ."

"You'll never be bored."

"Tim!" she laughed, thinking that was a funny thing to say.

"I'm not like Alan," he continued. "With him you'd have it easy. Stable as hell." He made it sound dull. "You'd never have to ask him twice to mow the lawn. Perfect all the time. With me . . ." He bent her over backward. "You wouldn't have a lawn."

"No?" she asked, staring into his eyes.

"Just this," he said, sweeping his arm out

to take in the sea, the silver-topped waves spreading to the horizon. "That's all I can give you."

"Only the sea." She laughed again.

"Marry me," he said again.

Dianne had a sudden strange feeling that Tim was in competition with his brother and she was the prize. The thing was, she was shy and humble, and she didn't trust her instinct. Alan was a successful doctor, Tim was a handsome fisherman: They could have any woman they wanted. Why would they fight over her?

Shy girls are sometimes insecure. They don't know how they shine. One date with Alan, and Tim seemed to take it more seriously than she did. If Alan liked her so much, why hadn't he asked her out again? That night at the Rosecroft Inn, she had had such a wonderful time. Alan seemed solid and true, as if he knew exactly where he was going.

Tim was something else entirely. He trembled when he held her. He said "I need you" at least as often as "I love you." He told her he kept time by the tides, and she found that incredibly romantic. The first time he was late, he blamed it on an east-setting current. Then he wrapped her in his arms and told her when he'd been out of sight of land, he'd been afraid he might drown without ever seeing her again.

He told Dianne she was all he had.

He called her ship-to-shore twice a day. Anchoring on the Landsdowne Shoal, he shot off white flares spelling "Dianne" in Morse code. He saved the best lobsters he caught and cooked them for her dinner. They drank wine every night.

They made love. Holding her so tenderly, his arms quivered, and Tim whispered her name over and over. They'd lie in the bunk of his boat, wrapped in wool blankets and feeling the rhythm of the sea. At those times his eyes would look serious and afraid. He'd gaze at her face as if trying to memorize every feature.

"Don't ever leave me," he'd whisper.

"Never," she'd whisper back.

"I can't lose you," he said. "This has to be forever."

"How can you think it wouldn't be?" she asked, feeling scared. She was taking the same risk: To give herself this totally to another human being, she had to believe that he was going to stay always, be true to his word, love her until the end of time.

"Things change," he said. "For some people."

"Not for us," she promised.

"My parents," he said. That night he told her his version of what had happened to his family. They had been so close: His parents had been childhood sweethearts. They'd gotten married at twenty, had three little boys. Life had been a dream. They had fished, and crabbed, and swum. Their mother had made them picnics. And then Neil had gotten sick.

The family fell apart. His mother lost her mind: The sheer agony of seeing her son die drove her to drink. Unable to help her, his father stayed at sea. Alan turned to books, Tim went fishing. And Neil died anyway. Alan had told Dianne before, but that didn't make the story any easier to hear.

"I'm so sorry," Dianne whispered.

"No one's ever going to leave me again," Tim said. "Ever."

"You can't control fate," she said. "As much as you want to."

Pulling back, Tim's eyes were dark and

troubled. He peered into her face, wiping tears from his cheeks.

"I have to," he said. " 'Cause I'm not going through that again."

"Losing someone you love must be awful," Dianne said. "But look at Alan—he used your brother's death for something positive. Deciding he wanted to be a doctor."

Tim moaned.

"Tim!"

"I'm sorry," he said, and she could feel him shaking. "It's just that there's nothing positive about Neil dying. And I don't like you talking about Alan like he's so wonderful, the great and powerful doctor. He had his chance with you and . . ." He trailed off, his face bright red.

"I love you," Dianne said, brushing his hair out of his eyes, scared at the expression on his face. "Not Alan."

"No woman's ever come between us before," he said.

"I don't want to come between you."

"Then take my side," he said.

"I will. I do," she said, confused.

"I've never loved a girl before," Tim said.

"Never?" Dianne asked, shaken to her

core. She had her bad boy all right: He was too handsome, too wild, too charming not to have had girlfriends. He was telling her a blatant lie, and she knew it.

"I've been with girls, but I've never loved anyone," he said, kissing her forehead, smoothing her hair. "Never until you."

"People have to love each other through the worst," Dianne said, her voice trembling. She had lived a blessed life: There was so much love in her family, and thankfully no one had ever been sick. But for some reason, she thought of Alan asking her about her happiest memory, her family pets, telling her about his life, and she swallowed hard.

"You think we can?" Tim asked, holding her face in his hands.

"Oh, I know we can," she said.

"We're sticking together," Tim said. "Starting now."

And Dianne believed him. He needed her. Life had hurt him badly, left him damaged, and Dianne was ready to nurture him in their marriage. For the first time in her life, she could believe that her own motto, "Home Sweet Home," applied to *her*. Happiness was possible. Love was true. She and Tim would have many sweet babies, and she would build playhouses for all of them. Life would be so beautiful.

They would love each other through the worst.

She would always support Tim's point of view, and she would try to ease his rivalry with Alan, so the McIntosh brothers could stay close.

She and Tim would never be apart.

They had promised.

Alan hadn't felt like ripping Tim apart since that day on the Widener Library steps. But the day Tim told him he was going to marry Dianne, the old feelings came tearing back. Tim was going on about how they wanted Alan to be in the wedding, would he be Tim's best man? Cold fury filled Alan's chest.

"What d'you say?" Tim asked. "You plan on keeping me in suspense?"

"You asked her to marry you and she said yes?"

"No," Tim said, his eyes sharp and bright. "We're walking down the aisle for a joke. What's wrong with you?"

"Nothing," Alan said, his blood racing.

"Bullshit. I know you." Tim exhaled as if he had the north wind inside him. He began to pace around Alan's office.

"It's pretty quick, isn't it?" Alan asked. "I mean, you hardly know her."

"I know her fine. Listen, this isn't because you used to go out with her, is it? Because I've been under the impression there was nothing much between you. Correct me if I'm wrong, but I thought you had only one date."

"Yeah," Alan said. "One date."

"So what's the problem?"

The problem was, Alan hadn't been fast enough. The world could change in the course of one date, and when he'd been out with Dianne, he had known he had met someone amazing. He had felt a deep connection looking into her eyes and kissing her in the car, and he could have sworn she had felt it too. But then he had worked some late nights at the hospital, called Dianne at the wrong time, and lost his chance to see whether the connection was real or just a dream.

"So what's the problem?" Tim asked again.

"You're going to marry her and settle down?"

"Yep."

"Really settle down?" Alan asked, making himself a disapproving jerk so Tim wouldn't detect the fact he was being eaten alive by jealousy.

"As much as I can," Tim said. "She knows about the boat, the lobster license, the fact I work offshore. I don't think it bothers her."

"She hasn't watched you come and go," Alan said. "For the last ten years."

"Hey, you had your chance. You could have been an oceanographer. You're the one who nailed yourself to a medical practice."

"I know."

"Dianne has no problem with my work," Tim said. He grinned, showing his broken front tooth. Trying to pull pots in a high sea six winters before, he'd gotten smacked in the face with the winch handle. It pissed Alan off that Tim wouldn't go to the dentist and get it capped. It was almost as if he had decided to live a role, play a part.

"She likes the maverick lobsterman," Alan said. "That it?"

"Yeah, she likes it."

"The renegade home from the sea."

"Hey . . ." Tim said, picking up on the sarcastic tone.

"Hope she likes it as much when you're *not* home from the sea," Alan said. "When you decide to head into Newport instead of back to Hawthorne."

"Those days are over," Tim said. He grinned again, and there was something of a brother-to-brother wink in his eye. Alan felt the jealousy surge again, and he wanted to knock his brother flat on his back. Tim was right: Alan had dated Dianne only once. But whether he liked it or not, Alan still felt the connection. Alan knew his brother, and he didn't want him hurting her. Taking a step forward, he stood toe to toe with Tim.

"They'd better be," Alan said.

Tim stared him down, his eyes lit up and ready to fight. Neither brother had forgotten their last fight up in Cambridge, and Alan could almost feel the heat pouring off Tim's skin. They were each waiting for the other to throw the first punch.

"She's different than we are," Alan said. "She comes from a family where they look out for each other. You hear what I'm saying?"

"You warning me?" Tim asked, jabbing Alan's chest with his index finger. "About my own wife-to-be?"

"I'm warning you to be good to her," Alan said.

"Don't worry."

"Her parents stick around," Alan said. "For each other and for her. Not like Mom and Dad. Not like what happened after Neil died."

"I was there for Neil," Tim said, head up, chin out.

Alan stared, harsh challenge in his eyes, unable to contradict something his brother held as gospel truth. But thinking back all those years, Alan remembered Tim sitting outside Neil's window.

It was summer, and the sky was blue and birds were singing, and Tim had sat in the grass throwing his baseball into his mitt over and over again. Alan had snuck past his parents to be with Neil. They could hear the thunk-thunk of Tim's baseball going into the mitt. That dark bedroom had smelled of sickness and death, and Neil's eyes had been wide as an owl's, staring at Alan with the sheer terror of not knowing what was going to happen to him.

"Don't hurt Dianne," Alan said now, with a bad feeling in the pit of his stomach.

"Go to hell," Tim said. Stepping back, he turned and started to walk away. "You my best man or not?" he asked.

"Yeah," Alan said, because Tim was his only living brother. For his sake, and for Dianne's, he'd finish this right then. Dianne would never know about this fight or about the misery he was feeling inside. "I am."

"I don't know why," Tim said, "but I'm glad."

Weary and fed up with the fight, Alan had stood by his desk, watching him go. His brother was tall, his posture straight and proud. Why shouldn't it be? He had won the girl. Alan had the diplomas and degrees, Tim had his boat and Dianne. When he got to the doorway of Alan's office, he turned around.

Tim's blue eyes were fierce. Alan's stomach tensed, knowing that his brother was claiming victory in their latest battle of life. But staring across the office, he saw something else too. Deep in those eyes Alan saw fear. He saw the glimmer of a man who was already lost.

For a moment Alan tried to think of something to say, something to call Tim back and keep him from walking away, make up for the latest breach between them. After all, the brothers were each other's only living relative. But once Tim McIntosh had decided to walk, nothing anyone could say was going to stop him.

Six

* ✳ *

The last Wednesday in May, Alan felt tense, as if he wanted to run twenty miles. Instead, he only ran three, heading over to the library early. Mrs. Robbins wasn't at the counter, a fact that disappointed him straight off. But there was his yellow and white striped towel, folded like a book, on top of the reshelving cart. Nodding to the young library assistant, Alan reached across the counter to get it.

He picked out his journals, settled down in the reading room, and opened to an article called "Krill: Life Force and Food Source for Blue Whales." His heart was still pounding from his run. His left knee had started aching lately—for the first time in years—from an ancient injury, the time he'd crashed straight into Tim, sliding home at a baseball game behind Barnstable High School. His throat had been hurting all day, and now he sneezed.

He had taken Rachel Palmer, a nurse he knew from the hospital, to the movies Sunday night. Afterward, she'd wanted to get a drink and have dinner. Instead, Alan had convinced her to walk out on the curving sand spit to the lighthouse. It was dark. There was no moon, and they could hardly see their way.

Her shoes were wrong, the too-high heels sinking into the cold sand. She didn't complain though. She kept up with Alan, talking about the movie. Alan had strode along, hands jammed into his jacket pockets. Across the bay was Gull Point. The channel was black ink, the tide rushing out. The lights of Dianne's house blazed beyond the dark marsh.

Alan stood under the lighthouse. The beacon swung across the water, lighting a path to Dianne. Rachel held his hand. She was tall and sexy in her tight beige sweater. Alan eased her onto the damp sand, taking off her clothes so roughly, she'd exclaimed. She pulled her own lacy black bra off herself. Lust, thrills, they'd had it all. Alan had held her tight, trying to catch his breath. Wanting to make up for his thoughts, for the fact he couldn't stop staring at Dianne's house across the channel, he'd let her wear his sweater and jacket.

"Call me," she said when he dropped her off.

"I will," Alan said, kissing her. She gave him back his clothes. Shivering in his T-shirt, he left them on the seat. She was divorced. She worked in the ER, and she had a six-year-old son. Alan felt like a creep who deserved the cold he'd caught. He knew he'd never call her again. Truth, when it came to romance, had never come easy for Alan. He thought back to how he had pretended to forgive Tim for stealing Dianne, when instead he had wanted to kill his brother.

He sneezed.

"Gesundheit," the reference librarian whispered loudly.

"God bless you," Mrs. Robbins said simultaneously, coming around the corner with a stack of new magazines.

"Thank you," Alan said to both of them.

"Are you coming down with something?" Mrs. Robbins asked.

"I always catch the kids' colds," he said.

"Then you shouldn't be running."

"I need the exercise," he said.

"Exercise, my foot. Get yourself home and spend your day off in bed," she said sternly, but then her face softened into a wonderful smile. "If the doctor won't mind my saying so."

Alan sneezed again. His throat hurt, and his chest felt heavy. Mrs. Robbins put her hand on his forehead. It reminded him of his grandmother.

"You have a fever, my boy," she said.

"Hey, how're Julia and Dianne?" he asked, trying to sound offhand. "Things seem to be working out okay with Amy?"

"Never mind Julia and Dianne," Mrs. Robbins said. "Never mind Amy. You go lie down and try taking care of yourself for a change. Okay?"

"Okay," he said. Chills came over him suddenly, and he shivered. He was really sick. Being cared for felt strange. Again he thought of his grandmother. Dorothea had done her best after Alan's parents had absconded into their misery. But she had lived on Nantucket, a sea voyage away, and Alan had hardly ever seen her.

"And call me in the morning!" Mrs. Robbins said.

His grandmother might have joked the same way.

The minute Lucinda Robbins got home, she took two cans of chicken broth out of the cupboard. When Emmett used to get sick, she would boil a chicken and make the stock from scratch. But for now, she made do with canned, throwing in some shallots, carrot, celery, peppercorns, bay leaf, and thyme from the garden. She set the pot to simmering.

The girls were in Dianne's studio. They were listening to Carly Simon today: The love songs floated on the air, straight into Lucinda's open window. Dianne loved Carly. She always had. She'd listen to that voice— full of passion, singing about lost love and a broken heart and the joys of her children and hope about tomorrow—as if only Carly could express the things Dianne felt so deeply inside.

Dianne was a wizard with wood. She had her father's carpenter hands, his common sense, and his patience. Patience, above all, was the key to good carpentry. The ability to take a careful measurement, down to the last fraction of an inch, to fit pieces of wood together in a tight squeeze with no gaps or buckles. And faith: that she was making the right cuts, that she wasn't going to ruin a piece of expensive wood with carelessness.

Dianne had all that patience and faith when it came to wood.

But Dianne had no faith at all about love. Why should she? Sometimes Lucinda looked at Dianne's life and wondered how she had survived the despair. To be madly in love, the way Dianne had been with Tim, to marry him in the wedding of her dreams, to have his baby, and to lose him when the baby didn't turn out to be the right kind.

Dianne had nearly died. Literally. Lucinda had spent those early days after Tim's departure caring for Julia while Dianne was too sad to get out of bed. For so many days, once she realized the extent of Julia's problems, she was flattened by postpartum depression, and the only thing Dianne could do was cry. Julia had pulled her through though. Eleven years ago, that tenacious little baby with her terrible troubles and fierce needs had saved her mother from dying of love.

But Alan McIntosh helped too. He had stopped by every day. There weren't many doctors who made house calls, but he had never considered not making them. He was a forgiving man to look past Dianne's leaving him for his brother. He'd come over straight from the office, minister to Julia's peculiarities. Her third week alive, she'd had surgery to repair a twisted intestine, and they had attached a temporary colostomy bag to catch her little baby bowel movements.

Dianne, wild with grief, had fumbled with the bag. She had pulled the adhesive away from Julia's stoma, the open place in her tiny belly, and Julia was screaming in pain.

Lucinda still remembered the pandemonium. Julia wailing, Dianne sobbing. Alan had walked into the kitchen, put his black case on the table, and taken Julia from Dianne. He held the infant against his chest, calming her down. A little trail of yellow baby poop stained his blue shirt, but he didn't seem to mind.

"I hurt her," Dianne said, trembling as she wept.

"No, she's fine," Alan said.

"When I went to change the bag, I pulled too hard, and the connection ripped right off! Her skin's so raw already, she's been through so much . . ."

"You didn't hurt her," Alan said more firmly. "It was like taking off a Band-Aid, that's all. It'll sting only for a minute. We'll get a new one, get her all set up."

Gently handing Dianne her daughter, he rummaged through his case. He tore open the packages. Within two minutes he had cleaned Julia's stoma, attached a new bag, wrapped her in her baby blanket.

Lucinda had stood back, paralyzed. She had raised a healthy daughter, hadn't had a clue about how to fix a colostomy bag, how to help Dianne from losing her mind. In awe of her own daughter, she had felt afraid to move.

Alan had brought the courage to carry them all. Although he never pretended Julia was normal, he never acted as if she were different. Dianne had given birth three weeks earlier, the same week Tim left. She was pale and nearly insane, a quivering wreck with her dirty hair and blue robe. Afraid to hold her own baby, she had stood in the corner, tearing at her hair.

Lucinda would never forget what happened next. It was summer, and the marsh was alive with crickets. Starlight burned the black sky. A wild cat howled, and it had reminded Lucinda of her own daughter. Alan had walked across the kitchen, tried to put Julia in Dianne's arms. But she wouldn't take her.

"She's your baby," Alan said.

"I don't want her," Dianne wept.

You don't mean that, Lucinda wanted to say. But maybe she did. Dianne lost her husband and so much more: her sense that love could overcome everything, that the world was a safe place, that good people had healthy children.

"She needs you," Alan said.

"I want Tim," Dianne begged. "Make him come back to me!"

"He's gone, Dianne!" Alan nearly shouted, shaking her arm to wake her up. "The baby needs you!"

"I'm not a good enough mother for her," Dianne said. "She needs someone much stronger. I can't, I'm not . . ."

"You're the only one she has," Alan said steadily.

"Take her," Dianne begged.

"Your daughter is hungry," Alan said. He led Dianne almost roughly to the rocking chair by the window and pushed her down. Then, in the tenderest gesture Lucinda had ever seen, he opened the front of Dianne's robe. She had been fighting, but now she stopped. She just sat there, unable to move.

Alan placed Julia at Dianne's breast. Tears rolling down Dianne's cheeks, she sat there in the dim light, refusing to look at her child. Outside, galaxies blazed in the night. She stared up, as if she wanted to leave this torment and become the blue star in Orion's belt. Stubborn, she wouldn't embrace her daughter. Kneeling before her, Alan supported Julia while she nursed at Dianne's breast.

A long time passed. Minutes seemed like an hour. After a while, Dianne held her child. Her arms moved up from her sides, seemingly of their own accord. Taking hold of Julia, she touched arms with Alan. Lucinda watched their foreheads nearly brushing, looking down at the baby. Their faces were together, their arms were entwined. Julia sucked hungrily.

Lucinda stood at the stove, remembering.

Glancing at the table, she could almost see them now: Dianne, Alan, and Julia.

Lucinda decanted the soup into a big container, leaving the lid off to let it cool a little. She packed some fresh bread and butter into a bag, poured some lemonade into a jar. Then, heading across the side yard, she went to tell her daughter that the doctor was sick and it was her turn to make a house call. There were times, she swore, that Dianne was blind to her own life.

At first Dianne felt impatient. Building a widow's walk to sit atop her newest playhouse, modeled after one she admired in Stonington, was taking all her concentration. But her mother was insistent, telling her she'd made some chicken soup for Alan, and that Dianne had to drive it over to him.

"Do you know how long it's been since I've been to his house?" she asked.

"Well," her mother said dryly. "You have his address in your book. Look his street up in the gazetteer if you've forgotten where he lives."

"Only a librarian would have a gazetteer," Dianne said.

"Librarians aren't so different from carpenters," she said. "The right tool for each job."

"I know where he lives," Dianne said reluctantly.

"Julia is so lucky," Amy said.

They both turned to look at her. She had brought over a game of checkers, and she was playing a brand-new version with Julia.

"To have Dr. McIntosh for an uncle," Amy explained.

"It has its ups and downs," Dianne said.

"That's terrible, Dianne," Lucinda said. "He's very good to you both."

"Mom, I have to finish this order by Sunday," Dianne said, trying again. "Can't you take it over?"

"I have the girls coming over for reading group tonight, and I have to get things ready."

"And you found time to make him soup?"

"Like Amy said. He's Julia's uncle," Lucinda Robbins said.

Dianne had the truck windows open, letting spring air blow through the cab. The birds were in high gear, making the twilight hour zing with feeling. Swallows caught bugs in the fields. Flocks of starlings swooped and swirled in one black cloud. A lone kingfisher sat on the telephone wire above Silver Creek. Dianne smelled rose gardens, fresh earth, and the salt flats. Her mother's package was in back, nestled among weighty bags of hinges and two-penny nails.

Pearl Street was smack in the middle of Hawthorne. One of the oldest streets in town, many prosperous whaling captains and merchants had built their houses there in the 1800s. Two blocks back from the harbor, it was a little quieter than Front and Water streets.

Driving slowly down Pearl Street, Dianne breathed the salt air. The sun was setting, and the white facades glowed with peachy iridescence. She hadn't visited Alan at home in many years. His street brought back old memories of being happy with Tim, and she drove a little faster.

Alan's house was a Victorian. White clapboards, gray trim, three steps leading up to a wide porch. Gingerbread, dovecote, a grape arbor. But the place was in disrepair.

Paint peeling, one shutter on a side window missing, the weather vane cockeyed. The grass needed cutting, and the day-sailor on its rusty trailer had not seen saltwater in a long time. She remembered long sails with her husband and brother-in-law.

Their relationship had been smooth back then. She had sensed that Alan wanted the best for her and Tim. He would invite them sailing, and they would invite him to dinner. Everyone was on his, and her, best behavior. Those sailing days were bright and sparkling, the three of them on Alan's small sloop. He'd be at the tiller, Tim stretched out with a cap over his eyes, Dianne manning the jib as they sailed the Sound.

One brilliant sunny day, the waves splashing over the rail, Dianne had felt incredible joy. They were sailing to windward, Tim trawling for bluefish off the stern, Dianne crouched in the bow. She had turned, mouth open in sheer delight, to say something about the sun or the wind or the three of them being together, and she caught Alan looking at her. His eyes were narrowed, the expression full of regret and longing. In that one glance she knew that his mood had to do with what had once briefly been between them, and for that instant she felt it too. She turned quickly away.

Dianne and Alan kept things polite and superficial. They were each other's in-laws. She would make fish stew every Friday night, and Alan would come over for dinner between office hours and hospital rounds. He would ask her opinion on what color carpeting he should get for his office. Tim would grin, holding Dianne's hand, glad to include Alan in their happy family life. But the pretense between Dianne and Alan collapsed the day Tim took to the sea for good.

Crossing the unkempt lawn, she spied something in the grass: an old birdhouse. Dianne had made it for Alan many years earlier, before she had had Julia. As a promise to Alan's future kids, that she would build them the greatest playhouse in Hawthorne, Dianne had made him the birdhouse. She remembered Tim holding the ladder while Alan climbed up to hang the house in the tall maple. Now it had fallen down. Propping it against the stone foundation, Dianne walked up the front steps.

Dianne rang the doorbell again and again, but no one came to the door.

"Hello," she called. "Hello!"

It felt strange to be standing there. She remembered the night she and Tim had come to tell Alan their amazing news: that she was three months pregnant. She had stood in the foyer with Tim's arms around her as Tim invited Alan to touch her belly. She had felt embarrassed for Alan; she could see the discomfort when he met her eyes, but he'd done what Tim asked to please his brother. His touch had been sure and steady. Closing her eyes, Dianne felt Alan connecting with the baby inside her, and she'd shivered.

"Alan," she called now. "Are you home?"

She tried the doorknob. It turned. Creaking open, the heavy door led into a small entry hall and living room. The decor could be considered minimal: one mahogany table, one rolltop desk with chair, and one bleached-cotton covered love seat. His decorating skills hadn't improved.

"Alan!" Dianne called. She gave a whistle.

The walls were lined with shelves overflowing with books: Dickens, Shakespeare, Norman MacLean, Yeats, William Carlos Williams, Hemingway, Freud, Dos Passos, Trevanian, Robert B. Parker, Ken Follett, Linnaeus, Jung, Lewis Thomas, Louis

Agassiz, Audubon, Darwin, Winnicott, and many more. Tim had never been able to sit still long enough to read books like those.

Turning away, she noticed an upper shelf full of framed photos.

Alan was very tall, so the pictures would be at his eye level. Dianne, standing on tip-toe, could barely see. A portrait of his parents—he looked just like his father, tall and lean. A silver-framed photo of Dorothea, his grandmother. A picture of three young boys in baseball uniforms. The same three boys on a sailboat, at the beach, holding surf-casting rods. Alan, Tim, and their big brother, Neil.

"Tim," she said, almost shocked by the sight of him.

Dianne and Tim's wedding picture. She took it down, her hand shaking. People often talked to her about "letting go." Of the past, anger, her ex-husband. Eleven years had passed. So why was Dianne filled with rage at the sight of him?

They had loved each other once; she could see it in the way her body leaned toward him, the way he couldn't take his eyes off her. His touch made her melt, his voice had made her want to promise him the stars. His shoulders looked ready to burst out of his tuxedo. His tie was crooked. Dianne had tried to make it her life's mission to give Tim the happiness he'd lost when Neil died.

Remembering how hard she had tried, Dianne dug her nails into her palms. Eleven years hadn't diluted her feelings. He hadn't just left her; he had left their daughter.

She remembered one night, several months into the pregnancy, lying on the deck of his lobster boat. The starry sky curved overhead, and Dianne had whispered: "We can name the baby Cornelia if she's a girl, Neil if he's a boy. Either way, we'll call our baby Neil."

Tim had kissed her; he had seemed overjoyed. They had been relatively young, just twenty-seven years old. Her doctor had suggested the prenatal testing, not because of her age but because he'd found high levels of protein in her blood. He had ordered amniocentesis.

Two words: genetic abnormalities. Dianne remembered the shiver down her neck, the way her insides had turned to ice. Hugging herself, praying for time to go back and for the results to be a mistake, she had cried for days. How could such a thing happen? She and Tim were healthy. They loved each other, they were good people, they worked hard. Their baby was a girl, and it was abnormal.

Was it her diet? The fact they lived too close to a power plant? Had Dianne drunk too much wine before she'd known she was pregnant? Had Tim smoked too much pot down on the docks? Was it air pollution? Something in the water? Were there chemicals in the milk they drank? The meat they ate? Was she using the wrong detergent, shampoo, skin lotion, fabric softener? Did she lack folic acid? Had she neglected to eat the proper green, leafy vegetables?

Dianne had sat in a rocking chair in her workshop, going back and forth on the creaky floor, for days. She hadn't washed her hair, eaten a meal, spoken to her mother. Tim would go out lobstering, come back, go out, come back. She had wanted him to hold her, tell her everything would be all right, but that wasn't happening. So she had held herself.

Inside her, the baby was still. Maybe it's dead, she had thought. She'd been in love with the little child, called it Neil, but now she'd begun thinking of it as It. As in "It's not moving." "It's genetically abnormal." "It's sick."

"We can't have it," Tim had said one night. Keeping his distance, he spoke from across the room. "No one would think we're wrong."

"What do you mean?" she asked.

"An abortion," he said.

"Oh," she said, feeling nauseated.

He came close. His face wet with tears, he pressed his lips against her neck. "When we said we'd have the amnio," he said, "we knew we might have to face this. That's the reason for the test—to give us a chance to decide. We have to decide, Dianne."

"I'm glad you're saying 'we,'" Dianne whispered. She had been feeling so alone. Tim had been fishing all this time, not wanting to talk to her about their baby and the nightmare they found themselves in. She understood—sickness drove him crazy. He was so afraid, but she wanted them to go through it together.

"We can call the doctor," he said. "Schedule the abortion. We can get started on a new pregnancy right away. . . ."

"I'll think about it," Dianne had said.

And she did think about it. She rocked herself through the days, trying to imagine how relieved she would feel when this problem was lifted. She would go to the hospital, the doctor would give her a sedative, and the baby would be gone. It was a sick baby anyway. It would have horrible problems. It might be retarded; other children would make fun of it.

Remembering those days in the rocking chair, Dianne reached up to take Julia's picture down from Alan's shelf. There she was, six months old. It was her official baby picture, a little late because she had spent so much of her early life having surgery. She was wrapped in a pink blanket, her tiny face peeking out. Dianne had been holding her. Alan had taken the picture.

Dianne stared at her daughter's face. It was so pretty and fine. Looking at those blue eyes, one would never guess at the mess inside her body, under the pink blanket. Julia's tiny pink tongue glistened. Dianne felt the same surge of love every time.

"Julia," she said as if her daughter were right there. "Oh, Julia."

Dianne thought back to those days in the rocking chair. She didn't hate herself for considering the options; most of the time, she didn't hate Tim. For her, the decision to have Julia had been gradual. Rocking slowly, she had felt the baby move. A slight shift, her bones clinking against Dianne's rib cage. The baby had tiptoed up her spine. Dianne had felt her heart flutter.

Alan stopped by. He walked into the room, stood in the doorway. Dianne hadn't told anyone the test results, not even her mother. Tim's reticence on physical matters was renowned; Dianne would never have expected him to confide in his brother. *Especially* not his brother.

"Tim told me," Alan had said.

Dianne was shocked. Hugging herself, she knew that nothing either of the McIntosh brothers could say would make her change her mind. She was rocking her baby, just the two of them, and everything would be fine.

"He showed me the test results."

"They don't matter," Dianne said.

"I'm supposed to talk to you," Alan said. "Talk some sense into you. I guess he thinks because I'm a doctor—"

"Doctors and lobstermen," Dianne countered. "You're both very practical."

"He's scared," Alan said. "He's seen some very bad suffering. He knows what can happen between parents when they have a sick child."

Dianne lowered her head. She was scared too. Her eyes welled up and tears spilled down her cheeks. She had known about Tim's parents fighting, his mother's drinking, their turning against each other, and she had smelled beer on Tim's breath ever since getting the test results.

"Don't," she said, "say anything against my baby. Don't tell me not to—"

"I won't," Alan said.

"Don't tell me not to have her."

"No," Alan said. Walking across the room, he knelt beside Dianne. Taking her hand, he waited for her to look up. Tears were running down her face, and she felt too tired to wipe them.

"I'll take care of her," he said. "I'll be her doctor."

His words hung in the air. She saw the circles under his eyes, imagined he had lost some sleep coming to this decision.

"You will?"

"Yes."

"Did Tim show you the piece of paper?" she asked then, grabbing his hand tighter. "Could you understand the results? Will it be very bad?"

"I don't know," Alan said.

"Will she be in pain?"

"I don't know that either."

Dianne wept, feeling Alan's arms around her shoulders. She had already made up her mind: She was having this baby no matter what, but the questions were still hard. The child's problems could be great or small, but she was going to be born, and Dianne was going to be her mother.

"I want Tim to love her," Dianne had said. "I want him with us. Tell him he has to accept this."

"Don't ask me that," Alan said. "He's my brother, and I can't tell him what to do. Okay?"

Tim was gone before the next full moon. So much for loving each other through the worst. Dianne wept for weeks, remembering the broken promise.

Alan had kept his though. He had been there from the beginning. Tim had walked out on his family, saddling them on Alan, a doctor and an uncle, but not a father. A fine man who made Dianne crazy because he was Tim's brother. Dianne took down the picture of the three young McIntosh brothers fishing. They had been inseparable. When Neil had died, so had parts of the other two. The parts that knew how to love, Dianne thought now.

She had no business being at Alan's house. Deciding to leave the soup on his kitchen counter, she walked around the corner into the sunroom. And there he was, sacked out on a sofa.

"Alan," Dianne said, not wanting to scare him.

Well, her mother had been right. He really *was* sick. Anyone could see it by the way he lay on his back, fast asleep, breathing through his open mouth, one arm flung over his eyes, the other flopping down to the floor. He hadn't shaved that morning, and his beard was dark. With his glasses off and a five o'clock shadow, he looked almost like a different man. A little dangerous, too mysterious to be Alan.

He wore khakis and a T-shirt. Dianne stared at his bare arms. They were strong and lean, the forearms covered with hair.

Those were real muscles, and his patients' mothers would never guess they were there. His stomach was flat and lean.

Feeling weird, Dianne just stood and stared. Her insides flipped, and she felt she was doing something forbidden. He really did look awfully cute lying there. His tousled hair, the way his mouth looked, those arms: She was used to thinking of Tim as the McIntosh with muscles. The plaid blanket had slipped, and Dianne reached down to pull it a little higher.

She walked out. But on her way down the front steps she stopped. Her heart was pounding. She told herself it was the bizarre intrusion of standing beside a person while he unknowingly slept, and maybe it was. The birdhouse was leaning right where she'd left it. Picking it up, she put it in the back of her truck.

And then she drove home.

Seven

Alan woke up to the smell of chicken soup. His head was thick and stuffy, and his mind swirled with a thousand dreams.

He was in Italy or Greece, somewhere hilly and green with shimmering light silhouetting everything from dark cypresses to goddesses. Water flowed, and Alan lay helpless on a blanket of moss. The goddess stood over him. She had small hands and clear eyes and messy, straw-colored hair. Wanting to reach for her, he was paralyzed by love. The goddess was Dianne. She had come back to him after all this time.

When he woke up, he went to the kitchen for a glass of water. On the butcher-block island he saw an unfamiliar paper bag. It smelled like his dream. Starving, he pulled out the container. The soup was still hot, and there was a hunk of fresh bread included as well.

Sitting at the island, he ate the soup straight from the jar. Had Dianne actually been here? Dazed from his cold, he couldn't figure anything out. What would she be doing, delivering chicken soup to him? She wasn't the chicken-soup-making type. And usually she didn't want anything to do with Alan that didn't involve Julia.

Chicken soup seemed more like Rachel, other people he could think of. He had a few regular mothers who knitted him sweaters, baked him cakes, dropped off casseroles. His friend Malachy Condon called them the SMB—Single Mom Brigade. They were nice women, grateful for the way he took care of their kids. They were kind and generous, and their gifts usually came thoughtfully packaged in wicker baskets strewn with fresh flowers, pinecones, seashells, and chocolates. Heartfelt notes always accompanied the offerings.

The soup had come in a paper bag: decidedly original. He rifled through, looking for clues. No note, no flowers. No sign it was from Rachel or anyone else.

Alan knew he was willfully stupid about the gifts. Some of the women who gave them were divorced, a couple were widowed. He knew how hard it could be, raising kids alone. These were conscientious people: They read all the good-parent literature, and they tried hard. Being alone hurt. Always being the parent to answer the nighttime crying, to soothe the sore throat, to hold the bowl that caught the throw-up. The single pediatrician could start to look pretty good. So they'd knit him a sweater, bake him a pie.

Alan would ask some of them out. They had good times. The women were nice, fun, smart, pretty. Alan would always wish he felt more than he did. Marriage and a family sounded so fine. He had started to wonder what he was missing in himself: Why couldn't he love these women who seemed so ready to love him?

One answer came to mind: They weren't Dianne.

When Alan made house calls to Gull Point, Dianne would answer the door looking like the wrath of God. Her face would show however she felt, and at those times it generally wasn't good. Wild hair, madwoman eyes, clothes stained with Julia's spit and urine, bearing almost no resemblance to the girl he'd taken to the Rosecroft Inn. She'd talk to Alan but all the while be staring at Julia. No dislike, no affection for him at all. At those times Alan was incidental. He wasn't her brother-in-law nor a man she'd once dated—someone who had once been a friend, a guy she'd grown to resent—he was just the person she had called to stop her daughter's suffering.

She had mentioned time. She had wanted to know that they—she, her mother, and Julia—would have time together. He glanced at the calendar hanging by the phone, sent to everyone in Hawthorne by the Layton Pharmacy. It showed the lighthouse where he'd gone with Rachel, where he'd caught his cold. There was the exact spot where they had—Alan looked for the word: *coupled*. It couldn't be called making love. He ripped the picture off and threw it in the trash.

Then he stared at the days. All those white squares stretching through June, July, August, September, October, November, December. Seven pages, seven months. Alan's head was thick and heavy, and his eyesight blurred. He didn't think Julia was going to live more than seven months, seven calendar pages.

On the other hand, Julia had confounded him again and again. He hadn't expected her to survive her first birthday. He would never have believed she would see her fifth. Children with such severe health problems rarely lived long, so every year was a gift. But this year Julia had decided to grow.

Alan dragged his hand over his eyes. He had only one niece. Staring at the calendar, he saw how fast summer was coming. Julia loved the sea. When the water was warm, she and her mother would lie on the tide line at the protected lighthouse beach, letting small waves wash over them. Alan had seen it, two summers earlier at Jetty Beach, Dianne holding Julia in her arms as the sea swirled all around. The clean green wash, the cream-white foam, the two blond heads.

They seemed so free: Dianne unencumbered by worry, Julia afloat in her mother's arms. Alan heard Dianne singing, saw her smiling. The summer sun was pouring down, and the tide was going out. When they finished their swim, Dianne built a castle from the wet sand. Julia lay peacefully beside her, warm and content.

The sand castle was vast, elaborate. Dianne built turrets and a moat. She used jingle shells, sea glass, and driftwood for decorations. This was her beach version of a playhouse, and it was for Julia alone. Taking her daughter's hand, Dianne helped Julia to pat the sand. Julia did her part, unaware. But the look on Dianne's face was pure joy. She was playing with her daughter, and no one could say she wasn't.

Seven months, Alan thought. Seven pages. He didn't know how many more times he had left to see her, to see Dianne— once Julia was gone, Dianne would disappear from his life. Alan would have no reason left to see her. Their worlds would go dark with missing Julia.

White squares on the calendar. Alan wanted to go after Dianne. She had asked whether they would have time "together." Alan wanted to be part of that. He wanted to marry Dianne. He wanted to help her raise Julia for the little time she had left, be with her through it all. The little girl deserved a father. Alan wanted to be that for her.

Holding the chicken soup someone had left in his kitchen, Alan stared at the days and wondered which one would be Julia's last. He thought of his brother Tim, far away on a lobster boat. Out of sight of land, alone with himself and the stars, the focus of so much unfinished business. Alan wanted to haul Tim back to shore, force him to settle things with Dianne. With Alan. Give everyone a chance to move on.

Before it was too late.

Lucinda Robbins had been hoping to talk to her daughter all evening. But Dianne was late getting back from her mission and Lucinda's reading group had gotten wrapped up with layers and irony and symbolism and love in Shakespeare, staying a full forty-five minutes later than usual. Then Dianne rocked Julia to sleep and Lucinda went for a walk in the fog. Finally they were alone in the kitchen.

"Well?" Lucinda asked.

Dianne stood at the stove, stirring squares of bitter chocolate into the pan of steaming milk. She wore a white summer nightgown, and from the back she looked thinner than ever, as if she were shrinking right down to Julia's size.

"It's almost ready," Dianne said.

"Not the hot chocolate," Lucinda said. "That's not what I mean at all."

"How was your reading group?"

"Marvelous. Ducky beyond belief. We're all wondering how we got through college without reading *Love's Labor's Lost*. All of us English majors, and not one—"

"I'd like never to do that again," Dianne said.

"What, honey?"

"Deliver soup to Alan McIntosh."

"Why? Did he—"

Dianne shook her head. She tasted the chocolate, added more milk, continued stirring.

"He was asleep. I know, because he didn't answer the door and I walked in. I should have just left the soup on the porch, but I wanted him to find it—I feel like a jerk."

"But why? It was a caring thing to do."

"It was *your* caring thing to do, Mom."

"He's all alone, dear. You think of him as the great doctor, but let me tell you: He comes into the library on his days off just because he's lonely through and through. He's not Tim, you know."

Dianne gave her a look. It was completely smileless, a serious signal for Lucinda to back off.

"Let's not get into this," Dianne said.

"Dear . . ."

"Mom, please. I'm not mad. I swear I'm not. But I like things the way they are. Alan takes care of Julia. I need him for that, you know? I don't want to mess it up with chicken soup and dropping by and thinking maybe, someday . . ."

Lucinda watched her pour the hot chocolate into blue mugs. Dianne's hands were shaking a little; the spoon clattered against the rim. Stella jumped up on the counter to lick a spot of milk, and Dianne leaned down to let the cat rub her cheek.

"Someday what?" Lucinda asked.

"Someday we could be friends like we used to be."

Lucinda didn't answer. She remembered way back, to the early days of Dianne's involvement with the McIntosh boys.

One day, just before Dianne's twenty-seventh birthday, she bloomed. She turned gorgeous and radiant: their carpenter swan.

Dianne had wreaked havoc between two brothers without even realizing it. She had had no sense, at least at first, she'd really wounded Alan: She had not understood his attraction to her in the first place. She must have seen the hurt in Alan, though. After a while it was unmistakable.

So Dianne came home with a boyfriend and his brother—Tim and Alan—and the three of them had become nearly inseparable.

"Emmett loved those boys," Lucinda said. Although she had wished things had worked out between Dianne and Alan, Emmett had felt more comfortable with Tim. Never mind that Emmett was the smartest man Lucinda knew, he had that old blue-collar inferiority complex about being around men with degrees. "Both of them."

"I know."

"He liked seeing you so happy." Lucinda thought back on the years they'd all had together. Emmett had gone out lobstering with Tim many afternoons. He had built cupboards for Alan's exam room. He'd been overjoyed by the news of Dianne's pregnancy, but he'd died of a heart attack a month later. And then Tim left. Eleven long years ago.

"Dad never even knew Julia," Dianne said, staring into her cocoa.

"No, but he was thrilled the day you told him you were pregnant," Lucinda said, taking her daughter's hand.

"So was Tim."

"Tim couldn't help himself," Lucinda said. "Poor weak thing."

"He never even saw her," Dianne said. "He just ran."

"A cowardly man," Lucinda said. "Does not deserve you."

"He always told me I made his life so perfect."

Lucinda hesitated, but she reached across the pine table to take her daughter's hand. "That was the problem," she said quietly. "He thought perfect could be only one way."

Lucinda watched Dianne. Dianne traced the knots and grain in the old table with her free hand. Her father had made it decades earlier, the first year of his marriage to Lucinda.

"I miss Dad," Dianne said.

"He rejoiced, Dianne. That's the only word

for it. He went out into the backyard, shouted to the stars. He *bellowed* that he was going to be a grandfather."

"But he died before that happened," Dianne said.

Lucinda cleared her throat, gathering herself together. Talking about Emmett, almost twelve years after his passing, brought him as close as ever.

"Oh, I don't see it that way," Lucinda said. "I don't believe he did either."

"But, Mom," Dianne said. "He died in my fourth month. . . ."

"Yes, but don't say he wasn't a *grandfather*," Lucinda said. "That would upset him just terribly! He was very attached to your baby, honey. Just because they never officially *met* doesn't mean much at all."

"She'd have upset him," Dianne said.

"He would have loved her," Lucinda said steadily.

"Her own father left her!"

Well, there was nothing Lucinda could say to that. It was true, men were more squeamish about sickness and such things. Emmett had never been able to sit up through Dianne's croup, chicken pox, strep throats. He hadn't changed many of her diapers, and he had gagged the one time Lucinda had asked him to clean her ears.

"She has us, darling," Lucinda said.

"I know."

Lucinda saw her staring at the table, tracing the grain with her fingernail. These late-night kitchen talks were worth the moon to Lucinda, and it broke her heart that Dianne would never be able to have them with Julia. Love came in such odd shapes, with such indecipherable rules, it was a wonder families got by at all.

"Emmett would have loved her. He was that baby's grandfather," Lucinda repeated, gazing up toward Julia's room.

Dianne nodded. She looked so frail and lovely, but she had a constitution of steel. Her hands were delicately boned, the skin as rough as Emmett's had been. Strangers stopped her on the street and congratulated her for not putting her baby into an institution. Lucinda knew Dianne wanted to find Tim's ship and sink it.

As Lucinda often did in times of stress, she pictured her husband. There he was, sitting at the head of the table. His leonine head, full of white hair, was nodding, his deep blue eyes steady as ever. He was chewing on one of the yellow pencils he had always carried to mark measurements on wood.

He had been difficult in many ways. Moody and intense, he had kept to himself. If Lucinda had had her way, they would have gone out more often. They would have given dinner parties. Lucinda had imagined literary evenings, with people reading their favorite poems, acting scenes from plays, drinking wine. Emmett would have laughed her out of town before letting that happen.

Early on, he had left the raising of Dianne to her. He was a little nervous around his baby girl, afraid he might harm such a fragile creature just by touching her. Emmett had yet to realize the strength and resilience of babies. So Lucinda, a full-time librarian, had stuck Dianne's playpen behind the front counter. But as Dianne grew, her father had started taking her in his truck. She would ride through town, standing on the seat, her arm slung around his neck. Love can take time to grow—even between a father and a daughter.

She thought of Alan, of the way he was with Julia. Wishing she could find something to say that would make Dianne see him in a different light, Lucinda smiled. "Well, I hope my chicken soup does some good. Alan is Julia's uncle, after all."

"He did look pretty sick," Dianne said.

"He was positively green around the gills when he came into the library."

Dianne laughed. Staring off into space, she seemed to be seeing something that amused her.

"You find it funny," Lucinda began, "to see Alan McIntosh laid up with the flu?"

"No," Dianne said. "I was just thinking of his arms. He's got that myopic-professor look down pat, but under his frayed blue shirt, he's actually pretty muscular."

"Surprised you never noticed before," Lucinda said. *She* certainly had, and so had the other librarians.

"Amy has a crush on him," Dianne said.

"Do you like having Amy around?"

"Yes," Dianne said. Her eyes scrunched up as if she didn't like the thoughts in her head. "She reminds me so much of how Julia would be if she could talk. And she seems to like Julia so much—she treats her like a real person."

"Oh, honey," Lucinda said.

"I wonder about her mother . . ."

"Maybe she can't talk to her. Maybe she needs to talk to you."

"That's how it feels," Dianne said.

Lucinda didn't think this was the time to point out that Alan had sent Amy to them. Her matchmaking instincts were buzzing, and she knew she'd better slow down. She didn't know what Dianne, in her present mood, was liable to read into any comment Lucinda might make about their helpful pediatrician. So she just smiled across the table and waited for her daughter to smile back.

Eight

* * *

One afternoon in the beginning of June,
waiting for a second coat of paint to dry,
Dianne discovered something else they all
had in common. She and Julia had always
loved driving: Something about the rhythm
of the road, the warm breeze in their hair,
the sense of moving ahead, of being together in a small space, brought them comfort. And now it was revealed that Amy
loved riding too.

Dianne's Ford pickup was dark green and
shiny. She had stickers from Mystic Seaport, the Mystic Marinelife Aquarium, and
the Connecticut River Museum on her back
window. Julia's wheelchair lay in the flatbed,
folded under a blue plastic tarp in case of
rain. With Julia buckled into her special car

seat, set in the middle, Dianne drove with her elbow out the open window.

"We're up so high!" Amy said.

"Ever been in a truck before?" Dianne asked.

"When I was a baby—my father used to have one. My mom told me. He needed it for his fishing gear. I wish we still had it. I'd get my mom to park it somewhere till I was sixteen, then I could drive and drive. . . ."

"My dad had one too," Dianne said. "Trucks are great for hauling things. Wood, fishing gear, wheelchairs . . . right, Julia?"

Julia gazed straight ahead. In the truck she didn't have to move her head from side to side. The world was spinning fast enough, whizzing by her window at forty miles an hour. She clasped and unclasped her hands.

"Can I ask you something?" Amy asked.

"Sure," Dianne said.

"Do you hate it when people call girls chicks?"

"By people, you mean guys?"

"Yeah, at school. They call us chicks. One guy called me something bad because I wouldn't let him copy from my test."

"Good for you for not letting him copy."

Dianne glanced across Julia, saw Amy frowning at her knees. "What'd he call you?"

"Two things. *Bitch* and the C-word."

"Poor fellow," Dianne said, shaking her head as if she were filled with true compassion and sorrow for the nameless sixth-grader. Admitting only to herself how murderous she'd feel if anyone ever said that to Julia.

"Why do you call him that?" Amy asked, looking confused.

" 'Cause he's so limited. Imagine revealing your ignorance that way, in the middle of school for everyone to hear. Pathetic, really. I feel sorry for him."

"Yeah . . ." Amy said.

"So, the boys call you chicks?"

"Mmm. Is that okay?"

"What do you think?"

"I kind of like chicks. My friend Amber and I talked about it. We like the word, and we like chicks themselves. Cute, peepy little things. All busy and happy and feathery."

Julia sighed and hummed.

"I love feeling feathery," Dianne said, turning on the radio. "But I'm picky about what

I want boys calling me. Like, you and Julia can call me a chick, but I don't want men doing it."

"Because it means something different when they do, right?" Amy said, her face screwed up as she worked on getting this ancient and vexing truth.

"I think so," Dianne said.

"But when it's just us together—you, me, and Julia—we can be chicks?"

"Sure."

"Huh."

"To men we're women."

"Women?" Amy asked doubtfully. "I'm only a sixth-grader."

"Still," Dianne said. "It's in the attitude."

Julia tilted her head, blinking at the sun.

"Women," Dianne said, "are strong."

"My mother says *lady.*"

"That's okay," Dianne said. "Everyone has their own path. They get strong in their own ways. For me, it means I want people to call me a woman."

"Even us? Me and Julia? We have to call each other women?"

"Nah," Dianne said. "As long as we know who we are, we can relax when it's just us. If we want, we can be chicks."

"In one week I'm out of school. Then next year I'm in seventh grade."

"Wow," Dianne said, meaning it.

"Seventh-grade woman," Amy said, trying it out.

"Smart and excellent," Dianne said.

"With my chick friends," Amy said, and she grinned.

"That's us, right, Julia?"

"Babes," Amy said.

"Girls."

"Gurlz," Amy laughed, spelling it.

"Gaaaa," Julia said.

"That's us too!" Amy said.

"Three gaaaas, off for a ride by the sea," Dianne said, smiling so hard her cheeks hurt.

Amy was free!

School was out, finally and forever. At least till September. Her first week off from school was hot and muggy. A heat wave had fallen on Hawthorne and all they wanted to do was keep cool.

Dianne gave Amy a straw sun hat. It had a wide brim, a blue ribbon, and it looked almost exactly like Dianne's. Amy loved her new hat so much, she wouldn't take it off.

The three "gurlz" went rowing in the marsh. Bluefish, the first good-sized ones of the season, turned the water silver-blue. A gray heron skulked in the shadows. Amy dipped her fingers in, trickled cool water onto Julia's bare legs. Dianne had made a little bed for Julia in the V of the rowboat, between the seats, shading her with a blue umbrella.

"What's your favorite animal?" Amy asked.

"A particular animal or a species?" Dianne asked.

Amy exhaled. Dianne had such a complicated way of thinking, it sometimes made Amy feel stupid. At home, people didn't talk like this. Their answers were so much easier: "dog" or "shut up, I'm watching TV." But the weird thing was, Amy wasn't embarrassed about feeling stupid around Dianne. She knew if she stayed with it, Dianne would help explain her way of thinking, and Amy would get it sooner or later. Amy was starting to feel smarter all the time.

"What do you mean?" Amy asked.

"Well, Stella's my favorite animal in particular, but cats aren't my favorite species. Sea otters are."

"Oh, yeah!" Amy still didn't know the exact definition of *species*, but she was ready to go with the flow. Drifting through the marsh, she looked for sea otters on the banks.

"What's yours?" Dianne asked.

"Gaaa," Julia said.

"I guess the puppy at home, or maybe Stella, is my favorite in particular. The best spee-sees"—Amy spoke carefully, getting it right—"in my opinion, are whales and dolphins."

"You're like your friend Dr. McIntosh," Dianne said.

"Yeah," Amy said. With Dianne in her life, she had stopped going to his office so much lately. Besides, his office was downtown, near her school. But the mention of his name still filled her with a warm glow.

"How's he doing anyway?" Dianne asked, gently splashing the oars.

"Dleeee," Julia said.

"Oh, he's fine. I called him yesterday."

"Hmm," Dianne said.

You and he should get married, Amy

nearly blurted out, but she stopped herself. She'd been thinking it for a while.
They seemed so comfortable together.
They had known each other forever. And
they both loved Julia. But life at home had
made Amy very sensitive to people's feelings, and she had the idea Dianne
wouldn't want her to say that about her
and the doctor.

Dianne was in a tie for third, in the most-
important-alive people in Amy's life. Her
mother was first, Dr. McIntosh second, and
Dianne and Julia tied for third. Amy's father
reigned over them all, but he was dead in
heaven. This was an earthly competition.

"Do you have brothers or sisters?" Amy
asked.

"No," Dianne said.

"Oh, another only child," Amy said.

"I always wished for sisters," Dianne said.

How often had Amy wished for sisters?
Girls to share the secrets of home life with,
concern for their mother, hatred of Buddy.
Older sisters would know what to do. They
would care gently for Amy, leading her out
of the maze. "Who's your best friend?" Amy
asked.

"I don't know. My mother, I guess."

Amy was silent. She wished so much that she could say the same thing, but she knew it was impossible. Her mother and Lucinda were about as far apart as two people could be.

"How about you?" Dianne asked. "Are you close to your mother?"

Amy coughed, pretending not to hear the question.

"How are the plans coming?" she asked. "For the retirement surprise?"

"I don't know," Dianne said. "I'm stymied."

"You'll think of something."

"It's funny," Dianne said. "Last night I had a dream of Julia graduating from school. In it I wanted to take her someplace, and when I woke up, I was thinking we should all take a trip."

"To Disney World!" Amy blurted out.

Dianne laughed. As if Julia could understand, she began to croon. Amy felt so excited. Did Dianne mean Amy too? She had said "We should *all* take a trip. . . ." Did that include Amy?

"Or somewhere," Dianne said. "The Grand Canyon, or the Rocky Mountains . . . the Mississippi River, Prince Edward Island. My mother loves *Tom Sawyer* and *Anne of*

Green Gables. We could go visit the story settings. That's what I thought when I woke up from my dream."

"How would you get there?" Amy asked, praying Dianne would correct her and say *we* again. But she didn't.

"I don't know," Dianne said. "My dream didn't get that far."

Julia's hands moved as if parting the air in front of her face.

"There's always tonight," Amy said, feeling solemn inside. "Maybe you'll dream again tonight."

Dianne rowed them through the marsh. Julia dozed at their feet. Whenever she slept, she curled up into a ball, just like the puppy at home. Amy saw Dianne watching her. Dianne reached down to brush Julia's damp hair off her brow, leaving her hand there for a minute. The expression on Dianne's face was serene. It wasn't always that way. A warm breeze blew through the reeds, and the sun beat down. Amy was glad they had their hats on and Julia's umbrella up, and she wished they could just keep rowing forever.

Nine

* * *

The sky was white and the air was hot. Waves of heat rose from the road. Dianne and the girls had stopped for ice cream, and they were eating in the shade of a picnic area.

Dianne hadn't slept well the night before. Julia had tossed and turned. She'd torn off her diaper twice. The second time, she had been out of breath, and Dianne had held her until her pulse returned to normal, until the rise and fall of her chest matched the gentle rhythm of distant waves breaking over the Landsdowne Shoal. When she fell asleep, she curled back into the fetal position.

"Mmmm," Amy said, licking her ice cream cone. "I love orange pineapple."

"I love black raspberry," Dianne said. She

and Julia were sharing a dish, and she spooned a cold bite into Julia's mouth.

"Why did you name her Julia?" Amy asked, letting the orange ice cream melt down the backs of her hands.

"Because it sounds dignified."

"Dignified?" Amy asked, frowning the way she did when she wasn't positive exactly what something meant.

By the way she talked, Dianne knew she hadn't been read to as a child, and that filled her with great sadness. "Yes," Dianne said. "I wanted everyone to know she's important."

"But she is important," Amy said as if that was the most obvious fact in the world.

"I know," Dianne said, thinking of Tim sailing away.

"What's her biggest wish?"

"I don't know," Dianne said.

They were sitting in a grove of trees, and the wind blew overhead, making the leaves slap like cards in bicycle spokes. Dianne took a spoonful of ice cream.

"Where's the farthest place Julia's ever been?" Amy asked.

"Just here," Dianne said. "Places around Hawthorne."

"I wish we could take her somewhere," Amy said. "On a trip." A huge motor home had rumbled into the picnic area. An old man was driving. Parking in the shade, he and his wife got out to stretch their legs. They had a collie on a leash, and the woman walked it in the grass.

"In one of those," Dianne said. She laughed, and so did Amy, staring at the Winnebago.

"Julia," Amy said, taking her hands. "Pretty girl!"

Julia wrung her hands, gazing at the sky.

"How about you?" Dianne asked, turning to Amy. "What's your greatest wish? Where's the most incredible place you've ever been?"

"Oh," Amy said. "I don't know." She sounded offhand, almost as if she didn't matter. "I don't know nothing but Hawthorne."

Dianne hesitated but only for a moment. She was the librarian's daughter, after all. "*Anything* but Hawthorne," she said gently. "Not *nothing.* You're too smart to use bad grammar."

"Thank you," Amy said. And Dianne suddenly felt sorry she'd said anything.

"Tell us something about yourself," Dianne said. "We spend so much time together, and you never talk about yourself."

"I have a dog at home. He sleeps on my bed and guards my room," Amy said, looking down. "He loves me."

"I'll bet he does," Dianne said. "What's his name?"

Amy didn't reply. She bit at her fingernail, then looked at her wrist.

"He doesn't—" she said. "He sleeps in a cage."

"Amy . . ." Dianne began, confused by the lie.

"My father left me his watch."

"I know," Dianne said.

"That big motor home—" Amy said, trying to laugh. "Would you really take a trip in one?"

"I was just kidding," Dianne said.

"It's like that story, where a whole family lived in one big shoe. I feel like you and Julia are going to climb in and walk away."

"Shoes that walk away can come back," Dianne said.

Amy shrugged. She clicked the toe of her shoe against the wheel of Julia's wheelchair. Julia had been wringing her hands, but she stopped. Her hands began their ballet, tracing the air between her and Amy's faces.

"They can, Amy," Dianne said.

Amy nodded, but she didn't speak.

Dianne's heart was bursting. She wanted so many things. To help Amy, to be a good mother, to be a good daughter, to give Julia the life of a real girl—take her different places, let her feel new air, let her know she mattered. Take her to New York to see *The Nutcracker* at Christmas, something every mother and daughter should do together at least once. Her mother was the person retiring, but Dianne felt like the one growing old.

"I know how it feels to be left," Dianne said out loud.

Amy turned to look at her.

"It hurts so much. I can't even pretend it doesn't."

Amy was crying, but she didn't want Dianne to see. She just kept playing with Julia. Dianne had the lonely feeling of being the only parent around, the only adult. She wished her mother were there. Even more, surprising herself, she wished Alan were.

But why should that be surprising? He cared about them all: Amy, Julia, and even Dianne. Dianne felt the tension building up in her chest, and was about to cry. At times like this, she felt such an overwhelming need for him. He was the only one who knew, really knew, what she went through. She wanted to be held by someone gentle, by Alan, but she couldn't. She had married Tim instead. Dianne knew her tragic flaw, had recognized it after all this time: She didn't know how to choose a man who would really love her.

She sat very still and watched her daughter and her friend write silent poetry in the warm air, in the sacred little grove of birch and pine trees, old picnic tables, and melted ice cream, and she imagined how it would feel to share times like these with a friend of her own. With Alan.

The next night, Julia cried out; when Dianne went to her, she found her child panting as if she had run a race. Dianne did what she always did: checked for obstructions in her throat, the wetness of her diaper, things sticking into her skin. Julia seemed bigger; was it possible she'd grown an inch in the night? Dianne's own heart was beating out of her chest. Grabbing the phone, she called Alan's answering service, told them it was an emergency.

"Hi, Dianne," he said, calling back five minutes later. Although it was three in the morning, he sounded wide awake. "What's the matter?"

As it often happened, the minute Dianne called him, Julia seemed better. Her breath was returning to normal, her heart slowing down. Perhaps she had had a nightmare. Sweaty and distressed, she was crying softly.

"Julia was breathing too hard. She's better now. . . ."

"I'll come over."

"No, Alan," Dianne said, feeling Julia's pulse. "I'm sorry I called. Honestly, she's—"

"Look. I'll meet you at the emergency room or I'll make a house call. It's your choice."

Holding Julia, feeling her sobs starting to subside, Dianne hated the idea of taking her out into the night. They were in their night-gowns, sleeveless white cotton that let the cool air blow across their warm skin. Crickets were chirping, and a setting half moon flooded the marsh in thin butter-scotch light.

"A house call, I guess," Dianne said. She thought back to that flood of great need for him in the picnic area, and she realized her hands were shaking. She tried to keep her feelings out of this; Julia was in distress, and she needed her doctor. "Thank you, Alan."

She got dressed.

Parking his old Volvo outside the Robbinses' house, Alan grabbed his medical case and walked to the door. He had done this a hundred times, stopped by when Julia was having a problem. But tonight his heart was pounding. He was there to help his niece, and he was in love with her mother. They had been going through this for years. Lights were on in the kitchen, and he could see Dianne sitting at the table. Her head was down, her face in shadow.

Walking up the pathway, Alan thought about false alarms. His service woke him three or four times a week, and by the time he called the parents, the emergency would have subsided. The coughing had stopped, the fall out of bed hadn't been serious, the yell had been worse than the injury. From Dianne's voice, Alan had been able to determine Julia's crisis had passed.

Yet there he was. Nothing could have kept him away. She could be bitter and angry till the day they both died, and he'd keep showing up. Nightbirds called, and animals having sex or killing each other screeched in the marsh. Taking a deep breath, Alan tapped on the kitchen door.

"I feel really stupid," Dianne said.

"She's breathing fine?"

"Not only that," Dianne said. "She's fast asleep."

They stood in the doorway, toe to toe. Moths flew around the porch light, bumping against the glass. Dianne wore jeans and a big white shirt. Alan wondered whether she slept in the shirt. He saw her beautiful body, her soft curves, and he wanted to hold her against his own beating heart.

"Let me take a look at her anyway," he said after a while.

Nodding, Dianne let him in. She led him upstairs, down the short hallway. Alan could have found his way blindfolded. Over the past eleven years he had walked the route so many times, the rhythm of his footfalls had become silent meditation; a prayer of protection for Dianne's daughter.

They entered Julia's room. Dianne always

kept a night-light burning in there. It cast a dim orange glow, like the half moon outside, on the sleeping child. Her hair fanned out on the pillow. The only time he ever saw Julia peaceful was in slumber. Dianne stood so close, he could feel the heat coming off her body.

"See?" Dianne whispered. "She's okay."

Taking out his stethoscope, Alan gently rolled Julia flat on her back. Her normal sleep breathing had a slight whistle, like air slowly leaking from an inner tube. Dianne slid down the straps of Julia's nightgown, and Alan listened to her heart and lungs.

"See?" Dianne said.

Closing his eyes to hear better, Alan listened harder.

"She's fine," Dianne said again.

Every seven beats, Julia's heart made a little click. Alan had been listening to it for a long time. The click had first materialized when she was three. Back then, it had come once every ten beats of her heart. The summer before it began coming once every eight. And now it was every seven; Alan had noticed the change last Christmas.

"See?" Dianne whispered, although her eyes looked worried.

Moving the stethoscope down, he listened to the fluid gurgling through her bowels. Palpating her belly, he felt for swelling. Gently unhooking her diaper, he glanced inside.

"Well, she's fine," Alan said suddenly, putting his stethoscope away.

They went downstairs.

"I'm sorry for panicking," Dianne said.

"You were right to call me."

"I was?" she asked. The worry had disappeared from her forehead when he had put away his stethoscope, but it came straight back at his pronouncement, so Alan put his hand on her shoulder to reassure her.

"I just meant it's better to be extra careful. We've been watching her. . . ."

Dianne waited for him to finish his sentence, hanging on every word. But Alan couldn't finish it. He didn't know what to say next. Dianne understood Julia's situation better than anyone. Standing in the kitchen, they stared at each other.

"What's happening?" she asked.

"With Julia?"

"Tell me," she said, her eyes wild.

Alan wanted to take her hands. He wanted to hold her, tell her he had loved her all these years. He was so filled with love for her: Couldn't she see? Life was short, and people threw the time they had away. Doctors were supposed to know that better than anyone.

"What?" Dianne asked.

"When you change her diaper," he began. "Do you look?"

"What do you mean? Of course I look!"

"She's in puberty," he said.

Sitting at the kitchen table, Dianne seemed to be in shock. She wrinkled her nose, shaking her head.

"Um, is that coffee?" he asked, gesturing at the pot on the stove.

"Yes, I just made it," she said. "Please, sit down."

Alan took a seat at the old pine table. He had been there plenty of times before. He had had his very own spot, back when Dianne and Tim were first married. Now, Dianne sat beside him, pretty and flushed. Her skin was lightly tanned, glistening in the warm night. Her lips were moist and full. He played with a spoon to keep from holding her hand.

"Puberty, really?" Dianne asked.

"What?"

"Julia . . ."

"She's young, I know," he said. "Some girls start maturing earlier than others."

"But how can you tell?" Dianne asked, sounding at once eager and embarrassed. Alan had been through this moment with plenty of mothers. Usually they were so attuned to their daughters' bodies; they remembered their own experiences, and they were on the lookout for signs. Had Dianne thought there wouldn't be any for Julia?

"She has three pubic hairs," Alan said as clinically as he could. "The areola of her right breast is somewhat enlarged."

"Oh, Lord," Dianne said. "My little Julia."

Alan sipped his coffee. He watched Dianne cover her mouth. Behind her hand was a smile, and it spread to her eyes. For one shimmering moment she let herself have this. Her bright eyes stared up, maybe imagining a vision of the teenage Julia. Her freckled face was radiant, and again Alan wanted to take her hand. He felt something powerful too: He'd been watching Julia grow up as long as Dianne herself.

Dianne looked at him across the table. Her smile deepened, and she stared at him so long, he felt himself smiling back. She reached out one finger, halfway across the pine table, and Alan touched it with one of his.

"I didn't think she would . . . develop that way," Dianne said.

"She's surprised us every step," Alan said.

"She has, she has," Dianne said.

"When she breathes hard, like she's doing tonight, I think it's due to hormonal surges. She's in flux, you know? That brings on emotional changes."

"Oh, I remember those," Dianne said.

Reaching into his medical case, Alan took out a paper bag. As he watched Dianne's face, he saw her eyes register something like embarrassment.

"Thanks for the soup," he said.

"You're welcome."

"I thought it was you. I was half awake, and I saw you. But then I told myself I had to be delirious. I had some fever."

"Jungle madness," Dianne said.

"Exactly. I figured it had to be someone else. But no one came forward."

Dianne removed the old plastic container

from the paper bag. She raised it, smiling. "To claim this lovely vessel? I wonder why. Thank you for bringing it to us though. We'll turn the alarms back on."

"The soup was good."

"I'll tell my mother."

So, Dianne hadn't made it herself. It had been Lucinda's idea, a fact that shouldn't have surprised Alan at all. Alan drank his coffee and stood to leave.

"Are you feeling better?" Dianne asked after such a long pause that it took Alan a minute to realize she was referring to his cold.

"Yes," Alan said. "Much. It's long gone."

"Good," she said. "I'm glad."

"Got to keep myself in shape," he said. "To keep up with Julia."

"Yes," Dianne said. "We count on that."

Alan laughed.

"Oh, Alan," Dianne said, suddenly rising up on her toes to hold him hard. He felt her breath on his skin, her arms tightening around his neck. He slipped one arm around her waist, and he felt the shiver down his spine, the backs of his legs. Her body felt so sweet and hot, and he was close to joy. They were standing in her kitchen, holding each other, laughing like fools.

"You're happy," he said.

"I am," Dianne laughed. "I really am."

It was so nice to hear her laugh, to see her take pleasure in her unusual and amazing daughter. Dianne and Alan were raising this little girl together, if only Dianne would realize it. He wanted her so badly. He wanted to take care of them both.

Alan felt he could have stayed in Dianne's kitchen until the sun rose over the marsh. But instead, he pulled on his tweed jacket and said good-bye. When he stepped into the cool outdoors, he felt terribly lonely. The half moon had set. The sun hadn't started rising. The lights were still on in the house. And Alan was leaving.

Ten

One rainy day, a bunch of kids were playing in the shed behind Amy's house. Amber had stolen cigarettes from her mother, and everyone was smoking. Amy had heard the laughter, gone out to investigate. David Bagwell was practicing to be a loser, leaning against the wall with a cigarette dangling from his lower lip.

"You shouldn't be in here," Amy said, upset.

"Make us get out," Amber said.

"Buddy won't like it—"

"Buddy's cool," David interrupted. "He's in my dad's band. You're lucky he's your step-father."

"They're not married!" Amy said, making an anti-vampire cross with her two forefingers. She tried to see through the smoke. It was like a night of heavy fog, only it smelled disgusting. Outside, it had started to rain, drops pelted the tin roof. She felt sorry for these kids, that they were smoking. She knew they didn't have people like Dianne and Dr. McIntosh to show them that life could be better than puffing their lungs out in a toolshed.

"You'll kill yourselves," she said sharply, embarrassed to hear her own voice. "Smoking's bad."

"Oh, go play with the retard," Amber said, blowing smoke rings.

"She's not—" Amy began, shocked and hurt.

"Get out, you bitch," David said, wadding up an empty cigarette pack and throwing it at her.

"Only an ignorant person would call someone that," Amy said, welling up as she used the words Dianne had told her to say.

"*Bitch* means girl dog—that's you!" David called as Amy walked out.

Passing David, she tried to feel sorry for him, but that was too much for her. Amy's head was jammed up with hurting thoughts. Running through the rain, she felt upset at being called a bitch, mad about what Amber had called Julia, but mainly worried about her mother. Something bad had happened behind her mother's closed door the night before. Amy hadn't seen her yet that day, and it was now three o'clock.

Rain poured down in sheets. The yard was one big puddle. Amy knew the basement would be flooded, making Buddy's mood even worse than usual. Anticipating his ups and downs was a skill of Amy's. She had learned what made him happiest and maddest, and she used those guides to stay out of his way. But right then, however Buddy might be feeling, Amy was going to see her mother.

Amy stepped inside as drenched as a marsh raccoon. She slipped off her sneakers on the kitchen floor. Her heart was beating fast, as if she were entering the haunted house at the Harvest Fair. The house was dark and silent, just as it had been all day. The puppy made a high, thin sound: his fearful greeting.

The fight had been loud. The evening had started off fine, with Amy, her mother, and Buddy having dinner together in the kitchen. Buddy was in a great mood. He'd gotten paid, and some bar owner had complimented him on his music; Buddy liked nothing better than being a big shot. Leaning back in his chair, arms outstretched along the wall behind him, he was telling them how his band was going to be bigger than Pearl Jam, Guns N' Roses, or Nine Inch Nails.

Buddy was drinking beer, and Amy's mother was sipping white wine. Watching Buddy's glass empty and be filled again, Amy felt a knot in her stomach. She saw all the danger signs, recognized every single one for what it was. The more Buddy drank, the worse it always got.

First, her mother served fish sticks. Buddy's skinny lips thinned to nothing when he saw that. Fish, even frozen little bland cutouts, reminded Buddy of Amy's father, the fact that Amy's mother had been married before. But Buddy said nothing: He was still feeling too good, and a soon-to-be-Grammy-winning rock star was better than a lost-at-sea fisherman, he knew.

Second, her mother requested James Taylor. Midway through the Tool CD, which was loud and obnoxious as dinner music, Amy's mother had gently asked if anyone would mind a little James. Buddy hadn't objected, but it was clear that he *did* mind. His lips and eyes *both* disappeared: turned into straight lines. James Taylor had started it all. Because his music had touched Amy's mother's heart, and that had made her feel sad again, and then she'd started looking at old photo albums, and pretty soon she was sitting on the sofa, tears running down her face as she stared at pictures of Amy's father.

Now, the next day, Amy tiptoed to her mother's door and tapped lightly.

"Mom?" she whispered. "Mama?"

The dog whimpered a little more loudly. Knowing he wouldn't make a sound if Buddy was home, Amy felt emboldened to push open the door. Her mother's room was darkest on rainy days. The curtains and blinds were both pulled, double protection against the lack of sun. Rain drummed on the roof. Her mother was huddled in bed as if she hadn't moved all day.

Amy moved closer, feeling scared. The room smelled disgusting, not just old cigarettes and Buddy's beer, but bathroom smells like Julia's diaper pail. At Julia's it was kind of nice, but here it seemed evil.

Amy couldn't explain it, but it made her want to shake her mother as hard as she could, yelling in her loudest voice.

At the same time, it made Amy feel too shy to move. Standing at the end of her mother's bed, she stared and stared. "Mom?" she whispered. "Mom, will you wake up? I want to ask you something. . . ."

It felt awful to be afraid to wake up her own mother. When had she started feeling this way? When Buddy moved in with them. *Three years, four months, and two weeks ago. That's when.*

"Mom!" Amy said loudly.

Her mother groaned.

"It's three o'clock in the afternoon," Amy said. The previous night she had felt so sorry for her mother, hearing Buddy yell at her, hearing the slaps and her mother's screams. Amy had lain in her bed, covers over her head, thinking of things to do. She could call the police, get a neighbor, hold Buddy at bay with a kitchen knife. But she hadn't known what to do, what her mother would want, so she hadn't acted.

"Ohhh," her mother whimpered.

"Mom!" Amy shouted, feeling growing

rage. What was her smart, pretty, funny mother doing wrapped up like a cocooned caterpillar in the middle of the day? She should be painting a picture, writing a poem, fixing Amy a snack.

"Get up!" Amy said, grabbing her mother's shoulder, rolling her over.

At the sight of her mother's face, Amy felt relief and disgust. The skin was unmarked; no bruises or swelling like that horrible time she remembered a few months back. But if her mother was okay, why was she in bed?

"Amy, I couldn't sleep last night," her mother said. "Let me sleep."

"Mom, let's go."

"Go?" her mother asked.

"Let's leave. Let's get away from here." As Amy spoke, she felt many things. She would miss Dianne, Julia, and Dr. McIntosh—miss them like crazy. But she and her mother could escape. They could start fresh, go somewhere else. Her mother would go back to feeling happier, the way she'd been before Buddy came. They could get a motor home like the Winnebago at the picnic area and visit beautiful places, see canyons and mountains and northern bays full of whales.

But her mother just lay there, staring at the ceiling, while Amy's enthusiasm gathered steam. "We have our money," she said, referring to the settlement they'd gotten from her father's fishing fleet. "We could move somewhere new! Mom, it would be so good. We'd get away from Buddy. . . ."

"Last night wasn't Buddy's fault," her mother said. "I started it."

"No," Amy said. "All you did was request James Taylor."

"I got stupid and sloppy," her mother said. "I make myself sick when I cry like that—what can I expect other people to think?"

"I heard him hit you," Amy said.

Her mother shook her head. Was she denying the truth? It made Amy so mad, she yanked back the covers, looking for the bruise. There—on her mother's upper arm. A rotten black-and-blue oval. And others on her chest.

"There," Amy said, pointing.

"Amy, you don't know what you're talking about. Go watch TV."

"If you worked, you'd feel better," Amy said. Staring at her mother lying in bed, she thought of Dianne. With Julia always needing to be adjusted in her chair, or needing to have her diaper changed, or to be fed, Dianne still found time to work hard all day long. Sometimes Amy saw Dianne looking just as troubled as her own mother, but she just kept working anyway. Instead of feeling sorry for her mother at that moment, Amy nearly hated her. Seeing those bruises, watching her just lie in bed . . . *Why doesn't she get up?*

"You know we're doing fine, Amy," her mother said. "The settlement should last a long time."

"You shouldn't give any to Buddy," Amy said. "For his stupid beer."

"You don't understand," her mother said.

"He's using you," Amy said.

"Shhh. You don't understand."

"Why are we with someone so mean?" Amy asked, something inside her melting fast. "We're not bad, are we? Did I do something?"

"Amy, let me sleep."

"Mama," Amy began, her chest starting to crack with all the tears she kept inside. She didn't feel hate, only love. Only love, she wanted to say, sick with guilt for hating her own mother, her very own mother.

"Go watch TV," her mother said again, sounding sick and frantic.

Amy tried to catch her breath. Didn't her mother notice that today was unusual? That Amy had spent the day at home instead of going to Dianne and Julia's? Didn't she miss Amy when she wasn't there? Didn't she notice anything at all? But instead of asking those questions, Amy let out one sharp sob and quickly left the room.

Dianne's music collection was romantic and out-of-date. Some of it had belonged to her parents, some was the music she had listened to as a young girl, wasting long hours dreaming of boys. Songs of desire, something no man could fulfill, and when she put them on now, she would sing them to Julia: "This Guy's in Love with You," "Sweet Caroline," "If Not for You," "The Look of Love."

Dianne had the Supremes playing. She sang her lungs out. Work was impossible today. This was a mother-daughter moment if ever there was one. Julia, still so tiny and young-looking, was on the verge of womanhood. Dianne smiled, frowned, shook her head, stared out the window, sang, paced, came back to Julia. She took Julia's right hand.

"I have so much to tell you," she said.

Julia's head swayed, and her left hand began to drift.

Diana Ross hit a high note. Dianne smiled.

"You're one of us, honey," Dianne said to Julia.

"Dleee," Julia said.

What's next, Dianne thought—her period, a bra? Dianne remembered herself at Julia's age. She had spent hours staring at lingerie ads in her mother's magazines. One day she and her best friend, Margie, had stayed home from school and tried on Margie's older sister's underwear, dreaming of the time they, too, would wear bras.

Breasts were the main thing. Dianne had them now and barely even gave them a second thought. But back then . . . Dianne had spent hours obsessing over when she'd get them. Lucinda had sat her down one day. She had told her the facts of life. The talk was straightforward and funny. She had brought library books for diagrams and illustrations.

"Okay, honey," Lucinda said, pointing at a

red and blue drawing of the female repro-
ductive system. She explained menstruation, ovulation, cramps, and bleeding.
Dianne stared, aghast at the thought of anything so revolting. Fallopian tubes deep in
her very own body? No, thank you.

"It might look confusing on the page and
sound scary in your head," Lucinda said,
"but it's not. It's just paying attention to your
body. Taking care of yourself, you know?"

"Like getting a cold?" Dianne asked.

"No, you're not getting sick! I'm supposed to tell you it's wondrous and mirac-
ulous and amazing, but it's mainly just
annoying. That's all. You go to Layton's
and buy pads, you go through them fast
and furious the first few days, and then you
slack off. I swear, I think the government
should subsidize sanitary napkins. Why
should women get stuck with a whole huge
monthly expense that men know nothing
about?"

"Does it hurt?" Dianne asked.

Lucinda smiled. "I wish I could say it
doesn't, but sometimes it does. It's a funny
feeling, kind of like waiting for a storm.
Once the clouds open up, it's all over and
you feel better. You feel fine."

"This happens every *month?*" *Dianne asked gloomily.*

"Every twenty-eight days," Lucinda said, patting her hand.

"Gross, Mom."

"Honey, look at this picture," Lucinda said, pointing at the headless red and blue road-map body. The artist had given it an hour-glass figure, with voluptuous curves and a tiny waist. "That's the secret of the universe," Dianne's mother said. "It's you—right there. You're a woman, and you're amazing. Don't get mixed up thinking you're weak or dainty or moody or any of the other things people—men—tell you when you have your period. Don't be one of those girls who has to miss gym and go to the nurse."

Dianne listened.

"Don't let people tell you your feelings aren't real, just monthly blowups. Don't be someone who blames every little thing on your period, because you'll only trivialize yourself if you do. And you are not trivial, my darling."

"Oh, Mom."

"Some women call it the curse," Lucinda said. "Or my little friend. I don't see it those ways. It's just a period. Like the tide's the tide and the wind's the wind."

"The curse sounds about right," Dianne said, staring at the veiny diagram in the anatomy book, still feeling the newfound horror of having a uterus, cervix, and labia. "I really look like that inside?"

"Yep. So does Margie. So do I. But you know the greatest thing?"

"What?" Dianne had asked.

"You came out of there. And when you're ready to have your baby, so will she."

Dianne stared at that baby now: Julia. What would happen when Julia started getting cramps? What would she think was going on in there? Dianne wanted to show her a body diagram and help her make sense of it all. She kissed Julia's hand, then pressed her cheek to Julia's soft skin.

"Julia," she said. "What are you thinking?"

"Gaaa," Julia said.

Dianne had bills to send out, catalogue copy to compose, and a checkbook to balance. The rain slanted down, blowing straight off the marsh with gale force. She wished they could see open water, because she had an idea.

"This storm is from the south," Dianne said, carrying Julia to the car. "Feel how warm it is?"

The rain came down hard, like driving bathwater. Dianne imagined it blowing up from Florida, across Cape Hatteras, over palm trees and barrier islands. She buckled Julia into the truck. She scanned the radio dial, listening for female voices: No men would do today. When she heard Blondie singing "Dreaming," she left it there.

They drove straight into downtown Hawthorne. The tide was up, and the boatyards were flooded. Alan's office was in one of the old brick buildings, and Dianne glanced up. Then she looked out at the storm; taking a deep breath, she held her daughter's hand.

Does it hurt? Dianne had asked her mother. *A storm*, Lucinda had said . . .

At thirteen Dianne *had* felt her body was a storm. She had swallowed a hurricane, and it felt like it would rip her apart. Her period came, she eventually got breasts, she began secretly pining for boys. But her mother had given Dianne words to match to her feelings.

How was it for Julia? She looked like a tiny child. She didn't know any boys, and what would she think if she did? Her body was acting just like every other preteen girl's, whether her head knew it or not.

"My grown-up girl," Dianne said.

Julia made a crying sound.

"Look, Julia," Dianne said, pointing at the water. Beyond the yacht club, the harbor was thrashing around. Waves broke over the jetties, sending rockets of spray up into the air. Dianne reached across the front seat. She placed her right hand on her daughter's abdomen.

"It's the same thing," Dianne whispered. "There . . . and there."

Could Julia understand? Dianne wanted to tell her it was all okay. She wanted to explain the birds and the bees, the sorrows of menstruation, the complicated joys of womanhood.

"I love you, Julia," Dianne said. "Don't be scared, okay?"

Dianne didn't say any more. She knew she couldn't make Julia understand with words. Pointing at the crashing surf with one hand, she gently pressed Julia's belly with the other again. *It's all the same. It's all the same*

*thing. Don't be afraid of a little storm inside.
Don't be afraid, my love.*

Alan's office overlooked the harbor.
Dianne wondered whether he was up there
now, seeing her truck out his window. It
made her feel better—yet nervous, and
crazy, all at once—to think he was.

She didn't want to think about why, but
she couldn't stop remembering how easily
she had rested her head on his shoulder the
previous night. He had held her tight, and
she'd felt desire starting to grow. Thinking
about his muscles, feeling his strong arms
around her, knowing that they had once
wanted each other. They had kissed once, a
million years ago.

She stared up at his office. Was that
him, standing in the window? She saw a
figure silhouetted in the glass, staring
down. It had to be. She felt flushed, as if he
had caught her watching him. Sliding
down in her seat, she felt her heart beating
hard. All these years of angst, and she felt
it still.

"That's Uncle Alan up there," Dianne said.

"Daaaa," Julia said, waving her hands.

Dianne looked across the boatyards.
There was the oyster shack where she'd

lived with Tim. Where they had conceived Julia. What had Dianne been thinking? Life with Alan would have been too easy, too comfortable and predictable? She had had to choose his brother, the scoundrel with scars and a broken tooth, just to prove that she was superwoman? That she could love Tim McIntosh into staying home, into mental health?

There was Alan standing by his window. It looked as if he were on the phone, staring over the water. He was tall and strong; he filled the window. Standing there, not moving or walking away, she sensed his amazing focus. Dianne couldn't stop staring up at him.

"Dlaaaa," Julia said. She sounded distressed, as if she was hungry or wet. The fussing got worse, and she started to cry.

"Okay, honey," Dianne said calmly. "We're going home."

Dianne felt so overwhelmed with reality. Glancing up at Alan, she wanted him to see them and come down. She needed someone to hold her, tell her everything would be okay, she was doing a good job. Thinking again of Alan's arms around her, she nearly broke down. She felt deserted right then. In the shadow of Alan's office, within sight of the old oyster shack, Dianne closed her eyes and held Julia's hand.

Alan stood at his window, finishing up a phone call. *Was that Dianne's truck down by the wharf? What was she doing here in the pouring rain?* If he told Martha to stall his patients, hold his calls, he could grab a jacket and see what was going on. But just as he decided to head out, Dianne drove away.

Alan was having a busy day. A three-year-old patient had swallowed some Monopoly houses, and Alan had spent the morning trying to determine how many. One? Thirteen? The frantic mother had walked in just as her son was popping one into his mouth. He got down another before she'd stopped him. X rays revealed three, so Alan had put the family on stool watch and sent them home. Now he picked up the phone on his desk and dialed a number in Nova Scotia.

"Yeah?" came the voice. It was low and gravelly, the voice of a cartoon bad man.

"That's nice," Alan said. "This could be the

International Dolphin Council wanting to throw you research money, and you'd scare them right off."

"I got their money already. Why should I kiss their asses again? Trouble with you doctors is, you put too much emphasis on bedside manner. Waste of everyone's time, in my opinion. Not that you asked."

"Hi, Malachy."

"Hi, Alan. To what do I owe the honor?"

"Honor?"

"Sure. Busy young doctor like yourself calling me."

Alan pictured Malachy in his wheelhouse. Since retiring from the Woods Hole Oceanographic Institution, he had started his own operation in Lunenburg, Nova Scotia. He lived and worked on an old tugboat, recording marine mammals to study the ways they communicated. Strange work for a guy whose own communication skills were shaky at best.

"What's it like up there?" Alan asked.

"Clear and fine. You coming up?"

"Too much work to do."

"I've got a great idea. Make all the sick kids better fast. Give yourself till Christmas. Then you can quit doctoring, come up to

Canada, and listen to whales all day. I could use you."

"Sounds tempting," Alan said.

"So what's holding you back? Stick a sign on your office door, tell 'em all good riddance, and come on up."

"Good riddance," Alan said, trying out the phrase as he stared at his wall of pictures—infants and children, his patients, all smiling out at him.

"What's the SMB gonna do?" Malachy asked. "That's my only concern."

"The SMB . . ." Alan said.

"Yeah . . . All those chicken pot pies are gonna go to waste. Those chocolate layer cakes and pullover sweaters."

"You should be so lucky," Alan said.

"They steer clear of me," Malachy said. "The lovely ladies of Nova Scotia. One wife was enough for my lifetime."

"Could be the skull and crossbones you've got on your door," Alan said. "Or the way you answer your phone."

"Quit picking on old coots," Malachy said, "and get to the point. I was out six hours with the hydrophones last night, and I've got two reels left to listen to. What's going on? Kids got you down?"

"They eat their toys."

"Ehhh," Malachy chuckled. "Mine ate a starfish once. He survived. What else is bothering you?"

"My niece," Alan said, staring at Julia's folder.

"Tim's girl?"

"Yes."

"I'm listening."

"She's eleven years old now. More wrong with her than right, Mal, and it's been that way since the beginning."

"I know, you think I don't remember the soap opera? What's different?" Malachy asked, all the abrasion gone from his voice.

"Why do you ask that?" Alan said.

"You've been standing by for eleven years—something's got you churned up all of a sudden. What is it, she's taking a turn for the worse?"

Alan stared out the window. "Not yet."

"But she will?"

"Yeah. You hear from Tim?"

"I hesitate talking to him about you, just as I'm slow to talk to you about him. You know? Might cause trouble. What does her mother say?"

"She knows the facts, but she doesn't want to see them exactly. She's—"

"Don't say 'in denial,'" Malachy growled.

"I won't," Alan said. His mentor had taught him to avoid jargon, to never trivialize situations with catchphrases that sounded like they belonged in magazine articles. "But that's the idea."

"Look," Malachy said. "You're the best pediatrician spit out of Harvard in the last twenty years. Bar none. You're doing everything for that child . . . she's in good hands. That's all you can offer."

"Seems like there should be more," Alan said.

"I told you way back when, it's easier being an oceanographer," Malachy said, his voice almost soft.

"Yeah, and sometimes I wish I listened," Alan said.

"How's she doing?"

"Julia? I told you, she—"

"No, the mother. Dianne."

Alan felt very cold. His heart was beating fast, and he felt it in his throat. "Is that you asking, or someone else? Is he up there with you?"

"It's me asking."

"She's good," Alan said, realizing that Malachy hadn't answered his second question. "She's very good."

"Glad to hear it," Malachy said. "It was never her fault."

"No, it wasn't," Alan said, feeling an old anger grab hold. "It never was."

"Lousy thing, one brother stealing the girlfriend of the other."

"She wasn't my girlfriend," Alan said. "We had only that one date."

"That might be what you told yourself, but it wasn't how you felt. You should've spoken up when you had the chance. You tried to keep the peace, and now you're paying the price."

"Huh," Alan said, staring at the rough harbor.

"You all right, Alan?"

"I want to settle this," he said.

"Settle with Tim, you mean?"

"Yeah."

"It's about time," Malachy said. "No use poisoning yourself, holding everything inside."

"So much for keeping the peace," Alan said.

"What was so peaceful about it?" Malachy asked. "I'd like to know."

"I get your point, Mal," Alan said. "So, if you see Tim, if he just happens to pull up to your dock, will you give him a message? Tell him I want to talk to him. Right away."

"I'll keep my eyes open," Malachy Condon said.

Buddy walked in from the rain, drenched and swearing. Sitting on the floor by the puppy's cage, reading *Anne of Green Gables* and watching TV, Amy ignored him. She heard him slamming around in the kitchen, opening and closing cupboards much louder than necessary. If there was one thing Amy had learned from her afternoons with Julia and Dianne, it was that positive attitudes were far superior in all ways to negative ones.

Let him swear, let him rage, Amy thought as she struggled to concentrate on the book Dianne had given her. She tried adopting the same approach to Buddy that was working so well with David Bagwell: feeling sorry for him. Anyone that mean was pretty pathetic, a very sorry human being. But as Buddy moved toward her mother's door, the sympathetic approach flew out the window.

"Don't go in there," Amy said.

"Excuse me?" Buddy asked, one hand on the doorknob.

"I said"—Amy swallowed—"leave my mother alone."

"I'm not going to be told what I *can* and *can't* do in my own home," he said. "Not by you, not by your mother."

"We live here too," Amy said. Her heart was thumping again. For courage, she tried to bring Dianne's face to mind. But she was too lost in the monster maze for it to help.

"Shut up, Amy," he said. "You might try turning off the TV while you read. Your last report card was nothing to write home about."

Amy's report card was her second sorest subject after the fact that her mother spent most days in bed. Feeling herself shrivel up like a salt-sprinkled slug, Amy made herself stare at Buddy. "You hurt Mommy," she said.

"What'd you say?"

"You hurt her," Amy said. "I saw."

"Leave fights to the grown-ups," Buddy said. "You don't understand nothing about it."

"*Anything* about it," Amy said. "Not *nothing*."

"Wise mouth, just like your mother. She's a show-off bitch, so why should you be—"

Amy's eyes filled with tears. How could some rat like Buddy say that about her mother? How could her mother stay under the same roof as him—and keep Amy there with her? Before she knew it, she was on her feet, flying across the room.

"Don't say that about her."

"You heard her last night, singing 'You've Got a Friend' like she has a voice. Stupid, that's what she was. Karaoke night without a stage."

"That's her and my father's song!" Amy yelled, staring up at him.

By the stunned look on Buddy's face, Amy could see that he hadn't known. He grabbed Amy's arm and twisted it. His ugly face came to a point, his lips and eyebrows and cheeks meeting at the end of his nose.

"You wanna rub my face in it?" he asked. "Then let's see how you like it."

Buddy had never been rough with her before. He yanked her arm, pulling her across the room. Amy screamed, but all Buddy did was throw her down while he opened the puppy's cage. Cowering in back, the puppy's eyes were wide with terror. Buddy tore him out of the cage, flinging him across the room.

"Buddy, please," came Amy's mother's voice. It was weak and thin, full of fear and panic. "Leave her—"

"Rub your nose in it," Buddy said, jamming Amy's face down into the puppy's newspapers. "See how you like it, little smart-ass."

Amy's mother was screaming, tugging at Buddy's arm, and Amy was gagging and crying. The smell choked her, stinging her eyes and the back of her throat. The puppy, in his terror, must have squatted on the carpet, because the next thing Amy knew, Buddy had let go of her neck and was kicking the dog.

"Goddamn son of a bitch," he bellowed. "Stupid fucking animal. You no-good, mangy mutt—get me a sack. Get me a sack right now."

Amy's mother ran into the kitchen after him. Amy's face was wet with tears and barf and puppy pee. Her mother was begging him to calm down, Buddy was knocking things over in his rage to make a sack materialize from

deep in the utility closet. Amy had no doubt
that he intended to drown the dog, and that
made her head clear in a hurry.

The puppy had run under the bed.
Following him into her mother's room, Amy
didn't hesitate. Buddy, for all his vileness,
had given her an idea. She yanked a spit-
yellowed pillowcase off one of the pillows.
Crawling straight under the bed, she didn't
waste time with any sweet talk. She just
shoved the puppy inside.

Then, with Buddy knocking things left and
right in the kitchen closet, cursing out all
women, Amy's father, James Taylor, and the
weak-bladdered puppy, Amy ran out of the
house. The puppy tussled in the sack,
scared half to death.

"Going somewhere better," she promised
the puppy as he bumped against her back.
"Somewhere much, much better."

The puppy yelped and wiggled. His claws
were sharp, and he tried climbing Amy as if
he were a tree sloth and she were a tree. His
jaws snapped in the darkness, occasionally
getting her shoulder and the side of her
head. In her haste she hadn't grabbed a
jacket or hat. She was barefoot—and she
didn't have real beach feet yet.

She heard tires squealing. Buddy always peeled out when he was mad. Cutting through backyards, Amy ran two streets over. Her feet hurt, and her shoulder was bleeding from where the puppy kept biting her. She was crying but silently. She had had plenty of practice hiding her tears, and this wasn't the time to have some neighbor deciding to drive her home.

A car glided around the corner toward Amy. It wasn't Buddy, because the muffler didn't sound like a machine gun mowing down an entire village. Amy was crying so hard, she almost couldn't see. She looked over her shoulder, past the puppy flailing in the sack. The car was a truck. It was green. It had seaport and aquarium stickers in the window.

"Hey there, Amy," Dianne said, grinning as she rolled down the window. "How about a lift?"

"Help me, Dianne," Amy wept, almost dropping the dog as she opened her arms wide. "Help us, please!"

Dianne drove straight home. Amy sobbed the whole way. The way she looked over her shoulder made her seem like a fugitive on the run. Julia was silent. Her hands drifted questioningly in space. When they had parked the truck and unlocked the work-shop door, Amy ran inside. Crazy-eyed, she stood in the middle of the room, clutching a writhing bag. Blood dripped down her upper arm.

"Amy, what happened?" Dianne asked, approaching slowly.

"I had to take him," Amy said. Her feet were planted on the floor, her body was tense as a spring. She held the bag with a kind of mad purpose, like a zealot about to commit a terrorist act in the name of patri-otism.

"Take who?" Dianne asked. "Honey, you're bleeding. . . ."

"Can I let him out?" Amy asked, starting to cry again. "My arms are tired."

"Yes—" Dianne said.

Amy lowered the bag, which appeared to be a filthy pillowcase, and a black puppy scrambled out. He was all legs, like a young deer. The whites of his eyes flashed with terror. Squatting where he stood, he peed on the wood floor. Then he dashed under the daybed in the corner.

Dianne walked straight to Amy. She approached her gingerly, unsure of what she might provoke. The child was shaking, pale, close to shock. Her lips were bluish-pink, and they opened and closed like a little fish. She stared at Dianne with help-less longing, and when Dianne opened her arms, Amy ran straight into them.

"You're safe," Dianne whispered to the sobbing child, not knowing exactly what she needed to be safe from. "I prom-ise."

"It's the puppy I'm worried about," Amy cried. "His name is Slash, but I can't call him that. It's an awful name. We have to think of something else. . . ."

"Yes," Dianne said, looking down at the blood, at the darkening red marks on Amy's neck. "I agree. He's much too sweet for Slash."

Helping Amy take off her shirt, she saw that the bleeding had come from where the dog had scratched and bitten her. Amy said almost frantically that it hadn't been his fault, that he'd been scared and confused, that he hadn't meant to hurt her. Dianne agreed that he probably hadn't. The cuts were superficial, and she washed them gently with soap and water. But there was one mark the dog hadn't made.

All along Amy's shoulder, at the crook of her neck, was a purple handprint. Dianne could see the palm mark, the four fingers on Amy's collarbone, the thumb pressing down her back into her angel wing. There was no medicine Dianne could rub on the bruises. Staring at them made her sick to her stomach.

"Amy, who did this to you?"

"No one," she said.

"I don't mean the bites. You have a bruise here that—"

"I bumped my shoulder," Amy said. "Getting the puppy out of his cage."

Dianne tried to breathe. Whoever had hurt her couldn't have left more blatant evidence if he or she had tried.

"Did someone hit you, Amy?" Dianne asked, and she found her voice shaking.

"No!"

"You can tell me, honey. I promise it's okay—"

"I'm fine," Amy said. "It's just the puppy. I wanted to show you the puppy."

After letting Dianne rock her for a few minutes, Amy became anxious. She

checked under the bed for the puppy.
Raising her eyes, she looked for Stella:
nothing but gray ears showing in the basket. Then she looked out the window.
Finally, she went to sit with Julia. Pulling her
chair close to Julia's, she put her head
down on Julia's tray. Julia's hands formed
delicate patterns in the air, as if she were
trying to soothe her friend.

Dianne went to her desk. Turning her back
on the girls, she dialed Alan's office number.
It was late, nearly six-thirty, but Martha
answered.

"Hi, Dianne," he said a few moments later.

"Hi," she said. "Amy's over here."

"Good," he said. "How is she?"

Dianne kept her voice low. She found it
shaking, not in her control at all. "Someone
hurt her, Alan," Dianne said. "She says they
didn't, but they did—"

"I'll be right over," he said abruptly.

It's a terrible thing to hope for marks, but
that's what Alan was wishing for on his way
over to Dianne's house. He had a Polaroid
camera in his medical bag. As a pediatrician, he had seen many horrors, heard

many lies. The malnourished children deprived of food. The cigarette burns said to have come from the radiator. The belt marks supposedly caused by falling.

In those cases Alan took swift action. One call to the police, and Alan would oversee the caseworker driving the child to the foster home. No questions asked. Beating and burning your child is not allowed.

But other cases were more subtle. The word *abuse*, incredibly enough, had shades of meaning. There were the cold parents who provided food and presents but withheld love. Never hugging or kissing their kids, never reassuring them with that all-powerful loving touch. Several shades more cruel were the parents who punished verbally, who took their own frustrations and limitations out on their children—called them stupid, ugly, wicked, slutty nobodies. Words the parents no doubt felt applied to themselves, but Alan wasn't their psychiatrist and had no sympathy at all.

Alan had special love for the children of depression. Children whose parents had once meant well, whose love was real and true; caring people who perhaps felt more pain than the rest of us, who couldn't make that pain go away. Some, like Alan's mother, turned to drink. Others, like Amy's, pulled the covers over their head, filling their children with loneliness and despair.

Buddy Slain wasn't a parent, but he was part of Amy's world. If Amy had marks on her body, Alan bet Buddy had put them there. And Alan would take her away from Tess Brooks, no matter how much she said she loved her daughter, before the sun went down.

Amy's heart was pounding. Sitting with Julia, she began to calm down though. Julia was doing her hand dance, casting good spells over Amy's head. Sending all the bad thoughts away, far away. Julia's hands were so gentle. Every so often, passing by Amy's ear, they'd brush her skin, caress her hair. Julia's voice was extra soft today, whispering "gleee, gleee" in a message of sweet peace.

Amy had pretended to be resting while Dianne called Dr. McIntosh, but she'd heard every word. So she had to decide what to do.

In one fantasy Dianne adopted her. She

would become Amy's mother. Julia would be her little sister, and they would all be so happy here on the marsh. Old Mrs. Robbins would be Amy's grandmother. Amy would get first pick of all the library books, and she would have the most perfect grammar in seventh grade.

This fantasy had merit. She continued on, making it more perfect. Why shouldn't she and Julia have a father? Dr. McIntosh. He and Dianne could fall in love. They would be good parents, and everyone would be happy.

Julia sighed as if she were having the same fantasy.

Amy had always loved dreaming. Dreams took her out of herself, away from her fears and worries. She had pretended to be dogs, cats, dolphins, ants, bats. She had imagined Buddy dying and her father coming back to life. She had lulled herself to sleep picturing her and her mother swimming underwater on a coral reef, being pulled through crystal waters by beautiful dolphins, becoming those dolphins themselves, swimming their way back to her father. So many happy dreams . . .

A tear rolled down the side of Amy's

nose. Right then she had to face reality.
Dr. McIntosh was coming over. He was
going to ask her about the bruise Dianne
had seen, and Amy was going to have to
lie. It was that simple. She knew the procedure. CWS—Child Welfare Services—
had a file on her already. It wouldn't take
much for them to take her away from her
home.

And sometimes Amy wanted to go.

That was the part that caused her grief.
The desire, deep in her heart, to get away
from her dark house. To leave the screaming and drinking, the fights and yelling, the
drawn shades and Buddy's beer bottles
behind. There were families in the world like
Dianne and Julia, places where life wasn't
perfect but the people loved one another
anyway. Amy would only have to say the
word, and Dr. McIntosh would put her in a
family like that.

But it would mean leaving her mother.

At that thought Amy swallowed a sob.
Amy loved her mother more than anything,
more than the perfect girls loved their perfect mothers. The feeling shook her whole
body from head to toe. She kept silent so
Dianne wouldn't hear and come over. But

Julia heard. Or she sensed. Whichever, her hands stopped dancing. They settled onto Amy's head.

Amy just lay there, quietly crying. Julia's hands rested steady, gently patting Amy's hair. She breathed in her Julia way, the air rasping in and out, with no words but whole libraries of meaning. Amy knew the language of no talk. She spoke it herself in a thousand different ways—even then, to the cat on the shelf and the dog under the bed. She lay still, silently communicating with her friend and the animals.

"Amy?" Dianne asked. "Can you talk to us?"

"No," Amy said calmly for the third time. "No one hit me. I just bumped my shoulder going into the cage."

"Amy," Alan said, looking her straight in the eye.

Children were born honest. They came into life knowing nothing but the truth: The bath was wet, the towel was dry, the milk stopped their hunger, their mother smelled like Mother. Some kids learned to lie as they got older, and it always got under Alan's skin. He could almost always tell. Amy had been doing it for a while.

"It's true," Amy said with the telltale side-long glance.

"Amy, you were so upset when I found you on the road," Dianne said quietly. She was standing back, arms folded across her chest, seeming a little unsure of whether she belonged in this discussion or not. Alan moved over so she would step forward, stand by his side.

"Yeah, Dianne says you were barefoot and you weren't wearing a jacket."

"So's she," Amy said, pointing.

Alan glanced down. It was true. There were Dianne's bare feet sticking out of the bottoms of her jeans. Over the years he had seen her shoeless in her home more often than not.

"I was wearing shoes in the car," Dianne said. "And outside."

"Yes, but—" Amy began.

"No getting off the track," Alan said. "Shoes aren't the point. That bruise on your shoulder is, Amy. I think by now you know I'm pretty worried about you. Why were you and the dog running away?"

"The dog doesn't like Buddy," Amy said.

"Buddy," Alan said. "Did Buddy hit you?"

"Buddy didn't hit me," she said finally.

Alan noticed the sidelong glance again. He could read her mind. She knew if she reported Buddy, she'd be taken out of her home. She'd be separated from her mother.

Alan could see the bed, covers pulled high over the sleeping woman's head. Alan could see it as if it were yesterday. He knew about mothers, pain, and hiding.

"Amy . . ." Dianne said. "We want to help you. No matter what." She knelt before Amy, taking her hand. Dianne loved her own daughter all out, with vibrant and piercing devotion, and she thought that was how it should work with all mothers. She was new to this kind of conflict, she would think it was as simple for Amy as telling the truth.

"Buddy hit the dog," Amy whispered, staring at the same spot. "That's all. He just hit the dog."

"Baaaaaaaa," Julia wailed. Julia had been calm when Alan had first arrived. She cried now, and Dianne went to her. Alan could sense Dianne's frustration. He sat there with Amy, watching her shut down. She would always do this after an incident at home: turn silent and secretive, retreat into her own private world. Even now, sliding off the window seat, she crawled into one of Dianne's half-finished playhouses.

Alan checked the camera for film; he still wanted to get his picture.

Dianne gazed at him across the room. Her eyes were curious and challenging. She wanted to see how he was going to handle this, help an abused child who was afraid to be helped. Alan thought of lies, how people told them because they were so afraid of truth.

It was no coincidence that he had called Malachy, starting to track down Tim. Alan had to set things right with his brother, and he had to begin to tell the truth—all of it—to Dianne. The stress of lying for eleven years had taken its toll. He felt overwhelming love for her; but not wanting to push himself on her, he'd done his best to protect her from the fact. He had been lying, and he was going to stop.

Lucinda Robbins had bought Cornish game hens as a treat for her and Dianne, but when she found out about Alan and Amy staying for dinner, she just hacked the birds in half and made extra rice. The party was starting off slow—what could you expect, considering the child welfare people had just spent a solid hour interviewing all concerned?

"Amy, do you like to cook?" Lucinda asked.

"Cook?" Amy asked as if she had never heard the word.

"The reason I ask," Lucinda said, "is that I have some new cookbooks for teenagers at the library. I haven't even put them on the shelves yet, I was so intrigued reading about Marshmallow Fizz and Chocolate-Raspberry Shebang."

"Amy's a good cook," Alan said, sitting between Amy and Julia. They were both staring at him as if he were their father.

"Gaaa," Julia said.

"You'd like her cooking," Alan said, holding Julia's straw close to her mouth. "She makes excellent milk shakes."

"You remember?" Amy asked, looking as if she were about to drown in heartbreak. She had dark crescents under her eyes, and her lids were puffy from crying.

"How could I forget?" Alan said. "You came over before the fireworks last Fourth of July and made me the best picnic I ever had."

"You two have been friends a long time?" Dianne asked.

Amy nodded. "Since I was little."

"You know that wall in my office?" Alan asked. "The one with all the cute kids on it? Four pictures of this one here—" He pointed at Amy.

"Wow," Dianne said, cutting a piece of hen.

Lucinda gazed at Amy Brooks hard. There weren't many kids in town she didn't know from the library, but Amy was one. Lucinda knew that when a child didn't use the library, it wasn't his or her fault: It was the parents'.

Lucinda had watched two and a half generations of readers, and the odd thing was, she would have expected Tess Brooks to have done better for Amy. Tess had read a lot when she was younger. A child without library books was like a plant without water: withered, stunted, and rootless. If only Julia were able to read. She looked from Dianne to Julia, feeling her chest tighten.

"What *is* this bird?" Amy asked, prodding her hen with a fork.

"A Cornish game hen," Dianne said.

"It's so little," Amy said, looking doubtful.

"You don't have to eat it," Dianne said.

"I will," Amy said, working away with her fork. "I just can't cut it right."

Dianne reached across the table to help her. Lucinda watched Dianne set Amy's knife and fork correctly. Such a little thing, teaching a child how to cut her food properly. She gazed at Julia, in her high chair and bib, eyes drifting around the table, and Lucinda gave her a long smile.

Julia and Amy, Lucinda thought. It was almost impossible to believe they were nearly the same age. Two darling girls in terrible need: There wasn't a thing Lucinda, Dianne, and Alan wouldn't give them if they could. Lucinda could see that Amy was like a sponge, soaking up the healthy love around the table. More startling to Lucinda was the way Dianne seemed to be absorbing love too. Helping that child, Dianne was glowing, something Lucinda didn't see every day.

Twelve years ago Dianne had sat at this table holding hands with Tim, telling Lucinda their incredible news. They were going to have a baby! Dianne had been radiant, happier than Lucinda had ever seen her. Almost shyly, as if Dianne couldn't believe she had life inside of her, she had kept her right hand on her flat belly the whole time. She had wanted children her whole life.

"What's this?" Amy asked, finding a currant in her rice. There were also shallots, walnuts, and snippets of chive.

"A currant," Dianne said. "Kind of like a raisin."

"In the rice?" Amy asked, doubtfully but with an open mind.

"When rice has stuff in it, it's pilaf," Alan said.

"I like to jazz things up when I cook," Lucinda said.

"You jazz good, Lucinda," Alan said. He had eaten every bite on his plate, and Lucinda couldn't help beaming.

"Thank you," she said. "You'll have to break bread with us more often."

"Bread?" Amy asked, frowning as she looked around the table for an explanation.

"Just an expression," Dianne said. "She means he should eat over more."

"Expressions . . ." Amy said glumly, as if she would never learn them all.

"It's raining cats and dogs," Dianne said. "There's an expression. In for a penny, in for a pound. Take the money and run. . . ."

"I'm kind of hung up on Lucinda saying I should break bread here more often," Alan said.

"Anytime," Lucinda said.

"It's nice," Amy said, her voice small and thin. "The way you just invite people. You didn't even know we were coming, and you have all this pilaf. . . ."

"Pilaf's a cinch," Lucinda said.

"We'll teach you," Dianne said so fast she gave herself away. Lucinda almost couldn't bear to see the joy in her eyes. Dianne had energy for giving, but Julia had such limited capacity for taking. There would be no cooking classes for Julia, no schooling in the expressions of life. In some ways Lucinda saw Amy as a godsend, but in others she felt scared to death: that Dianne would grow more attached to her and she would leave.

"Daaaa," Julia said.

"Hi, sweetheart," Dianne said.

"She wants more milk," Amy said.

Alan offered Julia the straw, and she took it in her mouth, sipping noisily.

"Where's her father?" Amy asked suddenly, watching intently.

"What?" Alan asked.

"Your brother. Julia's father," Amy asked. She seemed rattled and upset, and the question seemed to have deep meaning for her.

"Gone," Dianne said.

"He's at sea," Alan said, unable to keep the roughness out of his voice.

"Like my father," Amy said, her voice cracking. "Only still alive. He should be giving Julia her milk, not you. Oh, I wish Julia could have him. . . ."

"He's not like your father," Dianne said.

"Just because things aren't perfect," Amy said, "doesn't mean the family don't love each other."

"Or should," Alan said.

"You love your brother?" Amy asked.

"That's a tough one," Alan said, clenching his jaw. "But yes. He's my brother. I do love him." Dianne looked away. Lucinda's throat closed up; she felt like crying for all her sad, troubled children.

"You should rent a Winnebago," Amy said. "And go find him. Drive to every fishing harbor and put up signs. Get him home for Julia before it's too late."

"Too late?" Dianne asked as if Amy were an oracle and knew something she didn't.

"His boat could sink, like my father's. He could drown. He'd never get to know Julia at all. Never, never. There would never be another chance," Amy said, tears streaming down her face. "I feel so sorry for them. . . ."

"For who?" Dianne whispered, holding Amy's hand.

"All of them," Amy sobbed. "All the parents who lose their kids, and all the kids who lose parents. I love my mommy! I don't want to lose her."

"Oh, Amy," Dianne cried.

Alan was staring at Dianne with such wild intensity, Lucinda lost her breath. His emotions were right there in his eyes, in the tension in his neck and shoulders, as if he were oppressed beyond bearing with love for Dianne. He was swallowed up with it. Watching Dianne sob as she held Amy, Alan could barely hold himself back. Lucinda could see the strain in his whole being.

"She needs me," Amy cried. "Don't let anyone take me away from her."

"We all need each other," Lucinda whispered, watching Alan stare at Dianne.

Eleven

Amy was to stay with the Robbinses for a few days. Dianne made up the twin bed in Julia's room. Amy didn't sleep at all the first night. She climbed in and out of bed, wandering around the room, kneeling by the window and looking out, as if she hoped her mother would come to get her. Dianne couldn't sleep either. She wanted to call Alan and ask him to come over and be with them. When she saw Amy crying, she went in.

"You'll go home," Dianne said.

"She can't get on without me," Amy said.

"I'm sure she misses you," Dianne said.

"She forgets to take her vitamins," Amy sobbed. "Without me there, Buddy'll hurt her. He holds himself back when I'm around."

Children aren't supposed to protect their

parents, Dianne wanted to say. It's supposed to be the other way around. Julia slept fitfully, her breath rumbling like distant thunder. Kneeling by the window, Amy stared in the direction of her own house. Whippoorwills called in the marsh. The night was so dark, every constellation showed: Draco, Cepheus, Cassiopeia. The Milky Way was a wide river of stars.

"She'd want you to sleep," Dianne said, her hand on Amy's shoulder.

"I'm worried something bad will happen—"

"I know."

"I don't want it to," Amy said, her voice tight.

"I know that too," Dianne said. Alan knew the situation better than she did. If only he would come now, he could hold Amy and comfort her, say the right things. The way he always tried to do with Dianne . . .

Across the yard, she could see her studio. Stella sat in the window, staring as she always did at the stars. Her head was tilted up, and even from her room Dianne could see her eyes full of yearning.

"Look," Dianne said, leaning down so her face was next to Amy's. The child's cheeks were wet, and Dianne could hear the soft shudders of continued sobbing. "Your friend."

"My friend?"

"Stella," Dianne said. "Doing what she always does: searching for Orion."

"Every night?"

"Every night. Even when it's cloudy, she looks for that constellation. No matter what. She knows it's there, whether she can see it or not."

"She believes," Amy said brokenly.

"Yes. She has faith. I always imagine her living in that stone wall when she was tiny, looking up at the sky. I'll bet she thought Orion was her father. He's the hunter, but he kept her safe."

"Like my father . . ." Amy said, turning her eyes to the sky. Dianne looked down at Amy, then across the dark yard at Stella. There they both were, the young girl and the strange little cat, staring at Orion in the sky, thinking of their fathers. Tilting her head back, Dianne thought of Emmett. And she thought of another man, someone who had never been a father but knew just how to be a good one, Alan.

After four days the puppy still hid under the daybed in Dianne's studio and wouldn't come out. Dianne had architecture books and photo albums and interesting scraps of lumber she was saving under there, and he had wedged himself behind it all. Nothing of him was visible, not even his eyes.

Dianne had left bowls of food and water by her desk, but he wouldn't even emerge for sustenance. By the second night, when it was obvious he wasn't going to venture forth, Dianne pushed the bowls under the bed. She had never seen a creature so terrorized, and it disturbed her horribly.

Even worse was imagining what Amy had seen and endured. Dianne watched the child alternately stand by the window, then stare at the telephone. She missed her mother with burning intensity. Every seventy-two hours had brought new developments: first, an order of protection, with Amy not allowed to go home. Second, a hearing, at which Alan had been appointed temporary guardian. And finally, the decision that Amy would stay with Dianne in foster care for a period to be determined by the court.

Amy's bruise had turned black; it showed through the cotton of her summer shirt.

Gazing from Amy to Julia, Dianne felt her chest fill with rage.

Amy was every mother's dream: healthy, beautiful, active, smart, kind. To have a child and not love her with all your heart, how was such a thing even possible? How could a mother waste her life away, sleeping the free hours she could be spending with her daughter? How could Tess Brooks let her boyfriend hurt them both, especially Amy, so badly?

But it was the way that Amy loved her mother that broke Dianne's heart. Away from her, Amy had lost some of her spirit. She hardly talked. She wouldn't eat. When Dianne asked for her opinion on what color the newest playhouse's door should be, Amy just shrugged. Even Julia couldn't capture her attention. Amy just stared into space.

Until Stella came down from her basket.

The cat circled the bed. She didn't seem particularly afraid or curious; she just walked around, looking for the best spot. There was a dog under the bed. A strange dog. Nothing escaped Stella's attention, but by the way she was moving, Dianne knew that she realized the dog was there, that she had something in mind.

"Amy," Dianne said. "Look."

Amy watched, glanced questioningly at Dianne.

"What's she doing?" Amy asked.

Stella crouched. She wriggled slightly, settling on her haunches as if she planned to be there for a while. By her position, Dianne guessed that she was just about even with the spot the puppy had hidden himself. The cat's turquoise eyes were trained on the one-inch gap between the bedspread and the floor.

"She's waiting."

"Why isn't she afraid?" Amy asked, a little inquisitive brightness returning to her eyes. "He's so much bigger than she is."

"Well," Dianne began, but Amy figured it out.

"She wants to be his friend?"

"I think so. She's letting him know it's safe."

"But Stella never thinks it's safe," Amy said, looking up at the shelf. "She stays in her basket all day long! She never even comes down like this for us!"

"Maybe telling him it's safe will help her know it herself."

"Will she show him Orion tonight?" Amy asked. "When the stars come out?"

"I wouldn't be surprised," Dianne said.

"That's his name," Amy said suddenly. "Orion."

"The puppy. Orion!" Dianne said.

"Stella and Orion . . ."

Amy walked over to Julia. Julia had been drowsy all day, but she seemed to perk up at Amy's approach. She lifted her head, looked up with wide eyes. Amy crouched beside Julia's seat just as the cat was doing with the dog.

"We have pets," Amy whispered. "I've never named a dog before. His name is Orion. Men can see him from their boats, Julia. Your father and mine. When they follow the stars to come home, Orion will show them the way."

Julia swayed slightly. She seemed lulled by Amy's voice. Faithfulness and devotion were in her face. Her thin body leaned closer to her friend. Amy's eyes glittered with tears and the madness of loving people who weren't there. Dianne knew well about longing for absent people, and her throat ached hard. Julia had a father, and he wasn't Alan. The knowledge was as true as the stars, and it broke Dianne's heart.

• • •

At the week's end Alan stopped by Amy's house to pick up more things she needed. When Dianne heard his car, she ran outside. His eyes looked glazed, his face drawn.

"You look like you've seen a ghost," Dianne said.

"Tess Brooks. She's like Lady Macbeth," Alan said. "A blank stare on her face, haunted by what she's living with. Swore left and right that Buddy didn't mean to do it. The dog lunged to bite Amy, and he was just pushing her out of the way. Does the dog bite?"

"The dog is so far under the bed, we haven't even seen him since he got here. But Amy says no, and I believe her."

"So do I."

"Her mother lied?"

"To protect Buddy. Tess Brooks is depressed, and he's got her convinced she can't take care of herself. He's an abusive bastard, telling her she should be grateful to have him."

"I want to feel sorry for her," Dianne said. "But what about Amy? The woman would lie instead of defending her daughter?"

"She's lying because she's desperate and afraid," Alan said.

It seemed to Dianne like he could have been talking about his own mother. Tim had told her a few of the stories, how after Neil's death his mother would buy vodka. She'd drink it openly, tell the boys it was water. Later, when that didn't work, she'd hide the bottles and say she had quit for good. When she crashed the car, she said she had swerved to avoid a dog. When she'd smashed into the side of a van and sent it skidding through an intersection, she'd told the investigating officers that she had suffered from migraines since the death of her son, that she hadn't even seen the van passing by.

"What else did she say?" Dianne asked. The thought of Tess Brooks made her sick. She felt furious, her blood pressure skyrocketing.

"She wants Amy back."

"She said that?"

"Of course. She promises to get counseling, kick Buddy out, do whatever it takes. She's a nervous wreck."

"Letting Amy get hurt like that . . ." Dianne said. She stood there, shaking, her arms folded across her chest. She pictured Amy's bruises.

"She's filled with remorse."

"A little late," Dianne said.

"Everyone deserves a second chance," Alan said.

Dianne stared up at him in shock. How could he say that so easily? After everything his own mother had put Tim and himself through? Overcome with fury, Dianne shook her head.

"It's hard for me to reconcile," Dianne said, "what that woman has let Amy go through, when I think of how I feel about Julia. . . ."

"You're different," Alan said.

"I know, I don't sleep all day!"

"She's not a bad person," Alan said. "She's a sick person."

"I don't see how you can say that," Dianne said, staring down at her bare feet so he wouldn't see the angry tears in her eyes. "Coming from where you do."

"You think Tim would be here?" Alan asked. "If our mother hadn't drunk?"

Dianne's head snapped up.

"I'm past wanting that," she said, the tears streaming down her face. "But something hurt him early, made him into the man he was. I think about that, yes. I think about how the whole thing started. If she hadn't turned from her kids to the bottle . . . Yes, I think Tim's life would have been different. He'd have been able to stay with me and Julia. . . ."

"Come on, Dianne," Alan said, his face full of the agony she'd seen before. "You wish he'd stayed?"

"He's Julia's father," Dianne said.

"In name only," Alan said.

Dianne wanted to push him away. The reality of her life came crashing in. What did the words "in name only" mean when the subject was parents? Blood was the ultimate bond. Julia was Tim's daughter, and none of them were ever going to forget it. She could hear Alan's breath, feel it on her cheek. She felt utterly crushed, and she wanted to run away.

"I can't talk about Tim," she said.

"I want to drag him back here to face what he left."

"He can't face his own life," Dianne said, feeling the color drain from her cheeks. "He's not capable."

"I face mine," Alan said. "Every day, every minute. Sometimes it's not easy. . . ."

"You're different," Dianne said.

"We both are," he said. "You and I are alike."

"In some ways," she whispered, feeling the breeze blow across her arms, making the tiny hairs stand on end. She felt dizzy from how close he was standing.

"You're the most loving woman I know," he said.

"With Julia," she said.

"And with Amy. You took her in from the first day."

"I want Amy to stay with us, Alan. For as long as she needs to."

"As long as you realize her mother wants her home. And Amy wants to go."

"Oh, I know Amy wants to go," Dianne said, glancing at her studio. The girls were sitting by Julia's chair, keeping watch over the animals.

"I couldn't stand to see you hurt again," Alan said. "By someone you love leaving."

Dianne bowed her head. She had numbed herself to a dull ache, but the tenderness in his voice brought tears to her eyes. He stepped closer. She could hear him breathing, and she could see his shadow on the grass at her feet.

"Dianne," he said. "Look at me."

She shook her head. His arms had been full of boxes of Amy's clothes, but he lowered them to the ground. He placed the palm of his hand against her cheek, and she raised her head. Tears were running down her cheeks, and she couldn't stop them. Alan reached into his pocket for a handkerchief but couldn't find one, so he dried her tears with his bare hand. But they just kept coming.

Alan left his hand there, as if he couldn't stop touching her face. Dianne stared up at him. She swallowed, wanting to tell him she was okay, but she couldn't speak. Her heart was beating too hard. She felt the breeze blowing through her hair, and she felt something give out in her knees, as if someone had reached down and yanked a little pin. When Alan pulled her close to hug her, she held him as if they were both about to die there.

Alan mumbled something into her hair.

"What?" she asked.

She could swear she had heard him speak, she was positive she'd heard him say "This is it."

But he just shook his head. She felt his

lips on her part, on the back of her ear. He eased out of the hug, both of his hands on her upper arms, steadying her as if he thought she might fall.

"Did you say something?" she asked again.

She waited for him to answer, but instead he just raised his palms to the sky. The gesture was simple. It seemed to be a question and a prayer all at once. The summer sky was bright blue, with only a few clouds passing by. An osprey flew overhead, a large silver fish struggling in its talons. A pair of swans swam in the marsh.

Dianne watched Alan looking at the sky, and she turned toward the two young girls inside her studio. She thought of love, daughters, mothers, and fathers. She thought of people meant to be together. Her face felt wet, and her knees were still weak. People prayed in different ways, but Dianne believed the prayers might be pretty much the same thing.

Lucinda's retirement day arrived. Friday, July fifteenth, her alarm rang at six A.M., as it had for forty years. Padding downstairs, she half expected to see Dianne sitting at the kitchen table, ready to commemorate the moment. But the room was empty. Julia had been sick to her stomach the previous night, and Dianne had been up late.

Taking her coffee out to the porch, Lucinda read her devotions looking east over the marsh. The old blue heron stood in the reeds. Staring at the big bird, Lucinda had a strange lump in her throat. She could hardly focus on the psalms. She felt as if she were standing on a dock, about to wave good-bye to a great steamship loaded with people she loved. She wanted them to go, she hoped they'd have a thrilling voyage, but she'd miss them terribly.

Getting dressed, the feeling didn't go away. She put on her best blue suit, pinned her mother's cameo to the throat of her white blouse, and put on lipstick. Most days she dressed a bit more casually, but she thought maybe her coworkers would throw her a luncheon for her last day. She practiced her surprise face in the mirror.

Dianne was still asleep, and Lucinda slipped out quietly. With Amy there, Dianne was doing even more than usual. So

Lucinda pushed down her feelings, not wanting to admit she felt a little disappointed not to be seen off on her last day of work.

The library was cool, as it always was in the early mornings. Lucinda loved this time of day. She would walk through the shelves, straightening books, putting back the volumes on the cart. Yellow sunlight came through the tall windows, silver dust sparkling in the air. Lucinda knew she would miss every book, every window, every particle of dust.

"Good luck, Mrs. Robbins!"

"We'll miss you, Lucinda!"

"The library won't be the same without you. . . ."

All through the day her coworkers and library users said the same thing. Lucinda thanked them all. She must have made her thoughts about surprise parties very clear, because there was no special lunch. Two of the younger women ran out to their usual lunchtime aerobics class, and the reference librarian met her husband at the boatyard café.

Lucinda went about her tasks with an ache in her throat. She knew that she could never have had a better career. She had majored in English at Wheaton College, gotten her MLS from the University of Connecticut, started working at the library forty years before. She had overseen many changes, grieved when they took out the old oak card catalogues and brought in computers.

She had issued her own daughter her first library card. Standing right there, at the front desk, she had watched Dianne, five years old, sign her name on the card. Lucinda had watched her try to get all the letters on the line; she remembered how the N in Robbins had dangled off, but Lucinda had never felt prouder.

Emmett had built the oak shelves in the new addition. He had constructed the window seats in the children's library, installed a bay window in the reading room. Lucinda would grab the new Robert Ludlum novels the minute they'd come in, sign them out for her husband. And she would smile when he beeped his truck horn driving past, even though Lucinda repeatedly told him it was a quiet zone.

"Have you really read every book in the library?"

When she looked up, Alan was standing there. He held a bouquet of red roses and a wrapped package.

"You've heard that, have you?" she asked.

"It's legend here in Hawthorne."

"Just like the ghost in the lighthouse," she joked. "And pirate gold buried somewhere on Jetty Beach. I'm an institution!"

"That you are," he said.

Lucinda nodded. To her surprise, tears came to her eyes. She had been looking forward to this day for months. She had movies to see, languages to learn, places to visit. She had served the readers of Hawthorne for four decades, worked very hard. She told herself it shouldn't matter that the town hadn't hired a brass band to send her off, but she had a lump in her throat anyway.

"I'll have a ball," she said, forcing herself to sound jolly. "I have a list a mile long of things I want to do."

"Good," he said.

"I'll miss our Wednesdays though. Not many librarians have a handsome young doctor jogging by to sweat up their periodicals room."

Alan nodded, handing her the roses and

package. Lucinda had been trying her best to be upbeat, stay laughing, but Alan's eyes were serious behind his steel-rimmed glasses. He looked as if he knew how she really felt—how very sad she was to be leaving the library she loved so much. Alan carried his own suffering with noble silence, and Lucinda knew she could learn from him.

"Good luck," he said.

"Well, it's not like I won't be seeing you at our house. Now that we have two of your patients living under our roof . . ."

"It won't be the same," Alan said. Lucinda had been thinking his motives for coming had to do with the way he'd looked at Dianne at dinner the night before, but she could hear the honest compassion in his voice.

"Thank you," Lucinda said. Her throat caught as he kissed her cheek and backed away. The boy was trying to hide it, but he had tears in his eyes.

The rest of her day went by fast. She did her usual jobs. Everyone was so kind. The rooms grew hot as the sun took its westward journey, and the fans whirred. Air-conditioning was on the budget for the following year. When five o'clock came, the bells on White Chapel Square rang.

It was time for her to go.

The three younger librarians lined up to kiss her good-bye. They all told her how much she had influenced them, how much they would miss her. Lucinda had known them all for years. She had listened to their stories, counseled them on their love lives, held their newborn babies. Cheryl, Ramona, and Gwen.

As Lucinda walked down the wide steps, she heard the soles of her oxfords clicking on the stone. Bowing her head so no one could see her tears, she smelled the roses Alan had given her. The scent was heady and sweet. In her car, with her hands trembling, she opened the package. He had given her a brand new towel. She held it to her face, sobbing.

Driving home, Lucinda had her jacket off. The breeze blew her short hair, cooling her skin. She turned on the radio. Someone on NPR was talking about a trip to Tuscany, renting a farmhouse in an olive grove. Maybe Lucinda would learn Italian. By the time she reached Gull Point, her tears were gone.

The girls were in the yard. They were so busy playing, huddled over something, they didn't even look up. Parking her car, Lucinda tooted her horn. So what if Dianne had forgotten it was retirement day? With everything that girl had on her mind, she could be forgiven a momentary lapse. Lucinda gathered herself together, taking a breath.

But as she got out of the car she began to grin.

It was a parade. Amy marched first. Her smile had returned, and she carried a sign saying CONGRATULATIONS EXCELLENT LIBRARIAN! Dianne pushed Julia's wheelchair, decorated with red, white, and blue crepe paper and a sign reading MARVELS OF THE UNIVERSE LIE AHEAD.

Laughing, holding her roses and towel, Lucinda couldn't speak.

Dianne and Amy switched places. While Amy continued pushing Julia's wheelchair, Dianne ducked behind the hedge. She returned with her lumber cart, lined with blue silk and pillows, covered with two simple wire arches decorated with day lilies, Queen Anne's lace, and beach roses.

"Your float, madame," Dianne said.

"My what?"

"You're the star of the parade, Mom," Dianne said, kissing her cheek.

"Did you do this?" Lucinda asked, touching the flower-laden arches.

"I did," Dianne said, smiling as she helped Lucinda into the pillow-lined cart.

Settling down, still holding her roses, Lucinda allowed herself to be pushed through the yard. Amy was singing, and Julia was making her dolphin sounds. Lucinda held on tight as her daughter pushed the cart down the bumpy path to the marsh.

Swifts and swallows flew low, catching bugs. Two sea otters slid off the banks, gliding through the water. Tall golden grasses whispered in the wind, and a kingfisher dove for minnows. Still singing, Amy stopped pushing Julia. She stared straight at Dianne.

"Now?" Amy asked, grinning.

"Now," Dianne said, kneeling by Lucinda's feet.

"You're not planning to dunk me," Lucinda said.

"No," Dianne said, gently easing one of Lucinda's shoes off her foot. Amy untied and slightly more roughly pulled off the other. The two girls held Lucinda's shoes, her sturdy old oxfords that had hurt her feet all these years. They were heavy and stiff, and she had had them resoled more times than she could remember.

"Are we doing what I think we are?" Lucinda asked.

"You've said you wanted to do this many, many times," Dianne said.

"The minute I retired . . ."

"It's the ceremonial sinking of the shoes," Dianne said solemnly. "No retirement parade would be complete without it."

"Gleeee," Julia said, swaying in her wheelchair.

"Freedom!" Lucinda cried, wiggling her toes. The fresh breeze blew through her panty hose, cooling her sore feet. Dianne and Amy each held one oxford.

"Bombs away!" Amy said, throwing one shoe with such force, it scattered swans, otters, minnows, and blue crabs.

"Mom?" Dianne asked, grinning as she stepped forward, bearing Lucinda's other shoe as if it were a tiara on a satin cushion.

"But of course," Lucinda said, letting Amy pull her out of the wheelbarrow. Taking her

shoe, holding Dianne's hand, Lucinda tiptoed toward the water. The earth was soft
and damp, and her stocking feet sank into
the warm mud. Stretching closer to the
edge, holding on to her daughter, Lucinda
eased her shoe onto the water.

The oxford floated for an instant, and
Lucinda thought it was going to sail away.
Reflecting the late-day sun, the cordovan
shoe was burnished and glowing. It wob-
bled on the surface of the water. Amy knelt
by Julia, laughing so hard, she couldn't
stop. Dianne squeezed her mother's hand,
and Lucinda squeezed back.

As the four of them watched that old shoe
sink into the marsh, Lucinda really and truly
knew she was retired.

Twelve

Small, pine-spiked islands filled the sapphire bay. The dark trees were tall, and they grew right down to the rocky shore. In this part of Maine there was no gradual dropoff, no shallow sandy beach. Just deep water, steep rocks, and more lobsters than Tim McIntosh could catch. The *Aphrodite* glided so close to shore, Tim could hear moose munching on laurel leaves.

He pulled a pot, chucked twelve big lobsters into the basket, re-baited the pot, and threw it back in. On to the next pot, and the next. His buoys were red and white. Keeping the colors straight took concentration. Tim was working his way north, signing on to work with different lobster companies along the way, each with their own colors.

He caught lobsters, he got paid, he moved on.

The life of a nomadic lobsterman suited Tim fine. Moving kept him just off balance enough to keep from dwelling on his past. Introspection was a curse. Tim chose to look outward, not in: at the granite cliffs, the blue sky, the sparkling sea, a pod of pilot whales, a lone eagle flying in slow circles. Tim had practical matters to consider: his fuel level, a snagged line, a broken winch, low pressure moving up the coast.

For then, Tim was staying on Elk Island. Nice place, quiet people. The pay was average; Dirk Crawford was cheap, which made him exactly like any other fleet owner Tim had ever worked for. Dirk supplied the pots, which he figured gave him seventy-five percent ownership of any lobster Tim brought in.

So what? It wasn't as if Tim had a family to feed. He slept on his boat, ate by himself. The *Aphrodite* was his home. It was also his family, his wife, his only friend. Tim McIntosh had thrown the real things away, so he had to accept what he had. It was a good boat. It kept him warm at night. He'd lie in his bunk, listening to its creaks and rumbles, the way the water slapped the hull, and he'd let the *Aphrodite* lull him straight to sleep.

His boat took care of him.

That's what he got, naming his boat for the goddess of love. He had purchased it when he and Dianne were first married. She had encouraged him to get a new boat, Alan had given him the down payment; Emmett and Lucinda had lent him the rest of the money. Tim had been on top of the world. He wasn't the sharpest knife in the drawer, but he wasn't stupid—if this boat hadn't been a gift of love, then what was it? Clumsy at gestures, wanting to give thanks, Tim had named her *Aphrodite*.

Tim pulled his last pot of the day. A flock of screeching gulls followed him around the point. He stared at the old saltwater goose farm. Dirty geese waddled through the rock-studded field, and an old man and young boy headed up the path toward the barn. The white house was small and pretty, the kind of place Dianne would love. She'd be taking pictures right now, planning to turn it into a playhouse.

Shaking his head, Tim stared at the water ahead. Thinking of Dianne did him no good.

Hearing her voice in his boat at night was bad enough without scoping out houses for her to copy. Next thing he knew, he'd be imagining his daughter playing in a Home Sweet Home playhouse. He'd be hearing her call him Daddy, picturing himself holding her in his arms.

Nomad lobstermen weren't known for obeying rules, but Tim had a few he considered unbreakable. Men who didn't know their own children weren't allowed to dream about them. Same thing for guys who left their wives. They couldn't call, send birthday cards, ask to be taken back. They couldn't wallow in self-pity, ask themselves what might have been.

All they could do was keep moving. The sea made a good partner. It pulled him along, made him pay attention. Tides and currents, rough water, bad weather, uncertain skies, kept him alert. Other men lived other ways. The married ones Tim didn't know much about. He had tried that life but found himself insufficient. No one had told him that love was hard: His father had fished himself to death and his mother had died drunk before passing down the instruction manual.

His brother Alan was a nomad too, even if he didn't know it. He had his patients and the hospital. He owned a house in Hawthorne. To Tim, those things were no different from lobstering and the *Aphrodite: work to keep him busy and a place to keep him dry while he kept himself out of reach. For all his fancy degrees, Alan was just as big a loser as anyone.*

Tim missed his brother Neil. Sometimes he felt Neil—grown-up, no longer the eighteen-year-old he'd been when he died—standing with him in the wheelhouse. It was as if Neil had seen Tim through every fuckup along the way, as if he loved him so much, he could forgive him for it all. The stuff Alan could never forgive and forget.

Tim held the wheel and thought about his brother and Dianne. They'd known each other before Tim had come along. They'd gone out only once, but it had meant more to Alan than one casual date. Tim wasn't going to lie to himself about that. Alan had decided to play it down for the sake of harmony with his brother, but he might very well have already fallen in love with her.

All that stuff about treating her right and being a good husband: There'd been more to Alan's lecture than his being Tim's older brother. Tim had never seen Alan act that way over a woman before. Then Tim just took Dianne away, just like that. Without regard for his brother's feelings—or maybe *because* of them. Sibling rivalry, brotherly competition . . . Tim tried to come up with nice words for what had happened, but it left him with a knot in his stomach.

The bell buoy clanged. The town lay dead ahead, just past the breakwater. Tim saw the flag waving over the post office. Red, white, and blue, Old Glory. Seeing it, he felt choked up. The flag made him feel part of something bigger than himself. He had given up his family and home, so what he had was his country.

Soon he'd be leaving for a while. Once he left Elk Island, Tim was heading up to Canada. He needed a real friend, not just Neil's ghost or his good boat's voice. The feeling had come on strong, sometime during the spring; the need to touch base with an actual human being who knew him well. So Tim was going to see Malachy on Nova Scotia.

Just then, though, he had lobsters to sell, pay to collect. He was still paying off his boat loan. Every month, no matter where he was, he stuck a money order for two hundred dollars in the mail to Lucinda. So far he had paid her twenty-six thousand four hundred dollars; by the end of the year he'd be square.

He wondered what she thought, getting his envelopes postmarked all over the northeast. Out of courtesy to Dianne, he mailed the payments to her mother at the library so Dianne wouldn't have to open the mailbox and see his handwriting. He figured she had enough on her mind, handling the damaged child he'd saddled her with. What she didn't need was any reminder that Tim McIntosh was still out sailing the seven seas.

Amy was in the studio, alone with Julia. Dianne had trusted her with this great responsibility while she ran up to the house for a few minutes. Amy was trying to teach Julia to draw. She held a blue crayon in Julia's hand, guiding it across the paper. They were drawing Stella, who was crouched by the bed again, still waiting for Orion to make his first appearance.

"Cats aren't blue," Amy said to Julia. "I know you know that, and you're probably wondering why we're using a blue crayon. It's only because it's prettier than gray and brown, and I think—"

Suddenly Stella's ears stood up. She sprang up to her shelf, disappearing into her basket. Amy looked at the door and saw Amber standing there.

"Knock, knock," Amber said.

Amy froze.

"Aren't you going to ask me in?"

"Uh . . ." Amy began. She felt paralyzed. She didn't want Amber coming in. What if Amber asked Amy where she had been? Amy didn't want to explain about living here for a while instead of at home. But Amber didn't wait. She just opened the door. She was wearing low-slung pants and a tank top. Her bra straps were showing so much, Amy's face turned beet red. As Amber approached, Amy stood in front of Julia.

"Who's that?" Amber asked.

"You're not supposed to be in here," Amy said, blocking Amber's view.

"Where the hell've you been? I've called you thirty times at least. Your mother never answers, and I never would have found you if Buddy hadn't told David's dad you ran away."

"Huh," Amy said, surprised that David and Amber would even bother discussing her whereabouts. She wasn't completely upset that they thought she'd run away, even though it wasn't the exact truth. It sounded like something a person much cooler than Amy would do, and she liked it better than the fact of being removed from her home by the CWS.

"Why the hell'd you run here?" Amber asked, lowering her voice. "Witches and retards aren't my idea of fun."

"Shut up, Amber," Amy said.

"Let me see it," Amber said, trying to get around Amy.

"Stop."

"Come on," Amber said, grabbing Amy's shoulders and jostling her. She grinned, laughing as if she thought it was a big joke. Amy pushed back, hands on Amber's skinny upper arms as she tried to keep her away from Julia. It wasn't as if Amber was beautiful: Her eyes were close together, she had dandruff, and she had two growths on her neck that reminded Amy of potato eyes.

Amy felt deadly serious, cold and panicked by Amber's insistence. Craning her neck, Amber looked side to side, trying to see around Amy's head. Then she pretended to trip. When Amy tried to steady her, Amber pushed her out of the way.

"Jesus Christ," Amber said. Staring at Julia, her mouth fell open. "That's a *kid*? Moving her head like that?"

"Leave her alone," Amy said.

"That is a *girl*?" Amber asked. "She looks fake. Like she's a robot or something, the way she moves her head and arms. Like a wind-up girl. Jesus, Amy."

"Gleee!" Julia cried. Holding her arms out, she looked straight at Amy as if she wanted to be saved. Amy's throat caught. She knelt down, put her arms around her friend.

"You touch her?" Amber asked. "Amy, what's wrong with you? She has goobers all over her face."

"Do you ever think she might hear you?" Amy asked, holding Julia with loose arms the way Julia liked to be held. Amy had seen Dianne do it. You couldn't just grab her tight. Her insides were hurt or something, and she needed to be touched lightly. Amy's heart was pounding, and she could feel Julia's puffy little breaths on her cheeks.

"Shit," Amber said, bending down. "She understands? I didn't know—"

"You wouldn't even think," Amy said.

"Sorry," Amber said.

"Glaaaa," Julia said into the crook of Amy's neck.

"How old is she?"

"Eleven," Amy said.

"You're shitting me."

Amy was silent. She felt like butting her head into Amber's hollow stomach and shoving her out the door, but she didn't want to upset Julia any more than she was already. Julia's breathing had seemed so nervous, as if she were trying to blow a feather off the end of her nose, but now she was calming down.

"What's her name?" Amber asked.

Amy hesitated. "Julia," she said finally.

"Huh," Amber said. "Hi, Julia."

At the sound of her own name, Amy felt Julia relax. She totally did: Her muscles let go as if she knew the person making that sound must be a friend. Amy figured Julia didn't have many enemies. She would think anyone saying her name would be a good person.

"Gaaaa," Julia said.

"Let me say hello," Amber said, trying to pry Amy away. "Come on. I came over to see you, it's the least you can do."

"Just go, Amber," Amy said.

"Hey, I'm your friend. You ran away, I came to check it out. It's nice over here. I don't blame you for running away from Buddy's boozetown. Same as Dave's house, they never know when to stop. We stole a six-pack from his father Friday. He was so drunk he thought he drank it himself."

"You're drinking?" Amy asked. Her heart fell, and she didn't even know why. Why should she care what Amber did? They were so different. But it bothered her that anyone her age or any age could even touch a drop of the stuff after seeing what it could do.

"A few beers," Amber said, "is not drinking. Not like they do it anyway. Come out with us—we're partying at the beach tonight."

"Gleee," Julia said, her hands beginning to move.

"See? Julia likes me. Just listen to her. Let me see her."

Very slowly Amy pulled back. She

smoothed Julia's blond hair away from her face. Julia's big eyes rolled from side to side, and she grinned so wide, all her teeth showed.

"Nice smile," Amber said seriously.

"It is," Amy agreed.

"Will she talk to me?" Amber asked.

Amy glanced at Julia. Julia was entranced with Amber. She was staring at her, focused on Amber's dangly silver earrings. The thing was, Julia was much prettier than Amber. Julia was delicate and angelic, her eyes full of soul. As Amy watched Amber lean forward, she thought for a minute Amber had a heart. Face-to-face with Julia, Amber smiled.

"Polly want a cracker?" Amber asked, giggling.

"Gaaa," Julia said.

"Good bird, good humanoid," Amber said. "Now say, 'Take me to your leader. . . .'" She broke into laughter.

Leaping up, Amy shoved her. She slapped Amber's face so hard, it sounded like thunder cracking. "Get out," Amy said. "Get out and never come back."

"You stupid bitch," Amber yelled, rubbing her face. "You're trash, you know that?

Worthless shit. You think we don't know about the big scene at the trailer park?"

"I don't live in a trailer park!" Amy screamed.

"You might as well. It's just as much of a dump. Your mother never gets out of bed, she's so lazy. She's like an old lady in a nursing home, lying in her stinky sheets. Ever wonder why I stopped visiting you?"

"No," Amy screeched, shaking. "I was too busy being glad!"

"Yeah, well, it's because your house smells like shit. Everyone says so. Everyone! Like your mother took a big crap in bed and she's just rolling around in it. No wonder you like it over here. It smells the same way."

"Get out," Amy said, crying and breathless.

"The smell and your fathers. Two things you and retard-girl have in common . . ." Amber said.

"What about my father?" Amy asked. Just the thought of him gave her strength, helped her to swallow a sob.

"Her father walked out," Amber said, flicking her thumb at Julia. "My parents treat me like an adult, and they tell me shit you're too big a baby to hear. Her father screwed her mother and went for a nice, long boat ride before he even saw the kid's retarded face. Smart man. *Your* father, on the other hand—"

"He drowned," Amy said.

"I know," Amber said.

Amber smirked, and Amy felt her heart starting to pound again. "You know *why* he drowned?"

"Don't, Amber," Amy said.

"He was drunk, just like Buddy. He had a nice big bottle of booze in his boat, and he drank it all down. With you for a daughter, who could blame him? Doesn't that make sense? Lazy mother, drunk father, and you're just piss-poor trash."

Amy rushed at Amber so fast she knocked her down. She was sobbing too hard to see. Her chest was a lump of burning rage, hard and hot, scorching her blood. Julia was crying. Amy could hear the fear and pain in her friend's voice. She pictured her wonderful father going down with his ship, and she wanted to pound the smugness out of Amber's evil voice.

Suddenly she felt Dianne's arms embrace her from behind.

"Amy, stop," Dianne was saying. "Stop, honey."

Amy let herself be pulled up. She threw herself into Dianne's arms, sobbing with despair. Dianne held her tight for a few moments, but Amy couldn't stop thinking about Julia, the things Amber had said. Trying to stop crying, she eased herself out of Dianne's arms. Breathing hard, she bent down to Julia. They both had tears on their faces.

"Are you okay?" Dianne was asking Amber, offering a hand to help her up.

"No!" Amber shrieked. "She knocked me down! She just charged at me like a maniac, and she—"

"Well," Dianne said, brushing Amber off. "Maybe someday you'll be smart enough to realize that spreading lies about people's fathers isn't very good for your health."

"You're not . . ." Amber stammered, backing toward the door. "You're not supposed to defend her. You're the adult! Didn't you see what she did? See this?" Her arm snapped up, and she showed Dianne how she'd skinned her elbow hitting the floor.

"Yes, I see it," Dianne said evenly with the

iciest voice Amy had ever heard her use. "And I feel very sorry for you."

The marsh was dark gold. Fire-rimmed clouds raced across the setting sun. Ospreys began their twilight hunt, flying westward over the reeds. Martha told Alan that Dianne had called, something about a fight between Amy and one of the neighborhood kids, and he drove over as soon as he saw his last patient. Walking into the studio, he saw Dianne and the girls sitting together at the window.

"She was so mean," Amy said.

"She was," Dianne said.

"What happened?" Alan asked, standing still while they told him. He felt hot with anger, hearing the details, but he tried to remain professionally detached. Amber DeGray had been his patient since birth; he had once saved her brother from choking on a cotton ball.

"She said all that?" he asked.

"And she was *smiling*," Amy said. "And *laughing* as if she thought it was one big joke."

"Amy wiped the smile right off her face," Dianne said deadpan, her eyes meeting

Alan's. Their gazes held for a minute, and he felt the heat of her presence.

"My father wasn't drunk . . ." Amy whispered, starting to cry again. "He was *nothing* like Buddy."

They were sitting on the window seat, drinking lemonade. Dianne had her arm around Amy on one side and around Julia on the other. Both were shuddering with the aftermath of sobs, and Alan could see Dianne tighten her grip on Amy.

"I know he wasn't," Dianne said.

"He just wouldn't do that."

"Your dad was a good fisherman," Alan said, sitting on a pile of lumber. "I know that from Tim. And I never heard anything about his boat sinking being his fault. There was a big storm. Several boats up and down the East Coast were lost that day."

"I didn't know him well," Dianne said. "Tim knew a lot of fishermen, but I didn't go out with them much. But from what I heard, your father was a good man."

Hearing Dianne say his brother's name made Alan's chest ache. He breathed hard and low.

"Russell Brooks," Amy said, drawing in a knifelike breath.

"A good man," Dianne repeated.

Amy let out another shuddering exhalation. "Amber lied," Amy said. "She just lied."

"Some people do," Dianne said.

"Sad to say," Alan said.

"And she said," Amy said, lowering her voice, leaning around Dianne to make sure Julia wouldn't hear, "such mean things about Julia."

"Some people do that too," Dianne said.

"About how she moves," Amy said. "And how her body looks."

Dianne closed her eyes, and Alan watched her trail her fingers across the top of Julia's head. Her hair was so silky and fine. Her bones were so fragile; she was such a tiny girl. Dianne drew Julia against her body, knowing no mother had ever loved a baby more.

"Why?" Amy asked.

"You mean why did Amber say those things?" Dianne asked.

Amy shook her head. When she spoke, her voice was trembling. "No. I mean why is Julia like she is?"

"She had birth defects," Alan said. "She was born this way."

"But why?" Amy asked. "It makes it so

easy for people to be mean to her. To say bad things, to leave her alone. I don't want Julia to be hurt ever, by anyone."

"I know," Alan said, taking Amy's hand.

"You know," Dianne said, "I don't think she can. I don't think she *can* be hurt that way." Her voice sounded soft and low. She had taken her right arm from around Amy's shoulders and she was holding Julia in a tender embrace.

Julia closed her eyes. Her mother drew her closer. Her face was pale, and her lips began to move in a sucking manner.

"I used to think she could," Dianne went on, gently stroking her daughter's hair. "By the things people say, or the way they'd look at her. But I was wrong. I wasn't thinking straight."

"How are you thinking now?" Alan asked.

"Clearer," Dianne said, her eyes flying open. They were bright blue, and her smile was suddenly radiant. "Amy helps me so much. Amy is Julia's good friend. She likes Julia for who she is. . . ."

"I love Julia," Amy corrected Dianne softly.

"My mother reads the Bible every morning," Dianne said. "She's told me a million times: 'Man sees the appearance, but the Lord looks into the heart.' From Samuel. And Amy's helping me get it," Dianne said, still rocking Julia.

"I am?" Amy asked, her voice stretched and thin.

"Oh, yes," Dianne said, swallowing. "You are."

Falling asleep, Julia drew into the fetal position. Alan knew it was a symptom of Rett syndrome, but he imagined her wanting to climb back into her mother's womb, and he felt his throat tighten. He felt overwhelmed with love for them all. Amy leaned against Dianne from the other side. The sun had set, and the smells of Lucinda's cooking had begun to drift across the yard.

The four of them sat quietly, and after a while Dianne's cat climbed out of her basket. The ways of cats held no magic for the pediatrician, but Alan had never seen this animal do that before: She was shy and reclusive. Slinking off the shelf, she cast a long, cautious look in Alan's direction.

"She's making sure you're a safe person," Amy whispered.

"A friend," Dianne said.

"I'm a friend," Alan said, staring into Dianne's eyes.

They watched the cat circle the bed. She settled down finally, making herself as compact as possible, the size of a toaster, on the floor near the head of the bed. Staring at the gap between the bedspread and the floor, she seemed to be waiting, watching for something. Alan's heart beat faster. He didn't know why, but suddenly he knew that he was waiting for the same thing.

Thirteen

In many ways, it was the summer Dianne had dreamed of. The days were long and sweet, full of peace and closeness. One morning she rowed her mother, Amy, and Julia across the marsh. They hauled the dinghy onto the sand, then set the small anchor deep in the coarse beach grass and hiked across the dune to the lighthouse beach.

The surf was higher than on the marsh side, in the lee of the sand hill. A line of breakers rolled in, crested, folded into itself, and rolled in again. Dianne set up the umbrella while Lucinda spread the blanket and opened the beach chairs. Amy worried that she looked heavy in her navy blue tank suit, and Lucinda told her she was svelte and alluring. Amy asked for definitions.

Dianne carried Julia down to the water. The sand was wet and cool, with more pebbles than the fine sand up higher. Smoothing on sunscreen, Dianne felt her daughter's soft skin. Dianne dug out a little seat for her in the wet sand. She propped her up and started building a sand castle.

"Can I help?" Amy asked.

"Sure," Dianne said.

They worked at opposite ends of the castle, making it fantastic and elaborate. Dianne used her hands to shape the walls and turrets while Amy used a blue plastic pail to build parapets and ramparts. They scooped up handfuls of dripping sand, drizzled lacy zigzags along the ledges. Dianne made flags from bits of dry brown and green seaweed. They pressed crushed mussel shells, dark-blue sides down, into the sand so the castle glistened with iridescence. Seaglass framed the windows.

"It's beautiful," Amy said, sitting on her heels.

"Julia's castle," Dianne said, helping Julia to add the finishing touch: a piece of sea-silvered driftwood for the drawbridge.

"Is this how you feel when you build a playhouse?" Amy asked.

"Well," Dianne said, smiling. "Sort of." She loved carpentry, the fact her houses would be enjoyed by youngsters, and the arrival of a check. Sand castles were like summer days: sweet, fleeting, washed away by the sea. The only payment was the joy in building them, and that was greater than any check.

"You like working?"

"I love working," Dianne said.

"Hmm," Amy said, and she instantly fell silent.

Dianne knew she was thinking of her mother. Amy's stay with the Robbinses had been extended. Dianne had offered through Alan, and after initial protests, Tess Brooks had agreed.

Amber's mother had called to complain about Amy pushing her. A policeman had come to the house. Marla Arden said children learned violence from somewhere, and the CWS was not inclined to send her back to a dangerous environment without a thorough investigation. Amy's file was growing thicker, and Amy seemed to feel at times that her life was hopeless.

Sometimes Dianne felt Amy comparing her with her mother. Dianne worked, her mother slept. Dianne was busy, her mother was lazy. Amy was frowning, torn by the conflict.

"Most of all," Dianne said, smiling, "I love playing. Let's swim."

"I don't feel like it."

"No?"

Amy shrugged. She seemed morose, as if a dark cloud passing along the beach had settled over her alone. "The waves are too big here. We usually go to Jetty Beach, where it's calm."

"The waves won't hurt you, Amy. I could show you how to ride them."

"No, it's okay."

"You can think about it," Dianne said, disappointed.

The waves were definitely too rough for Julia, so Dianne carried her up to Lucinda.

"How's the water?" Lucinda asked.

"Warm," Dianne said.

"Going in?"

"I am. Amy's afraid."

"Don't rush her, honey. You weren't too thrilled with the big waves at first. Remember that time you got tumbled head-first into the sand? You scraped your nose and forehead."

"I remember," Dianne said. "But I was much younger—four or five."

"The first time is the first time," Lucinda said.

"Thanks, Mom."

Content, Lucinda nodded and helped get Julia settled beside her. She was adjusting to retirement fine: She had the beach, her book, her family, and her daughter's assurance the water was warm. The library dance was coming soon, and Lucinda was the guest of honor.

By the time Dianne walked down to the water, Amy had changed her mind. She didn't say anything, just rose from where she'd been working on the sand castle and walked into the water beside her.

"You're a good swimmer," Dianne said when they were out where the sea rose and fell without breaking.

"My mother taught me," Amy said. "When I was little."

"She did a good job," Dianne said. "My mother taught me too."

She glanced at Lucinda now, sitting under the green and white striped umbrella with

Julia. In her straw hat and dark glasses, reading a book in her faded striped beach chair, she looked timeless, the same as ever, Dianne's young mother.

"My mother's scared of waves," Amy said, sounding nervous. "There aren't any over at Jetty Beach."

"The secret," Dianne said, taking Amy's hand, "lies in not fighting them. Pretend you're a seal, and you live in the water. You're more comfortable here than any-where."

"Like a dolphin?"

"More like a seal," Dianne said. "You have to bob."

The sea felt fresh and cool. It tasted salty, and it took the pressure out of Dianne's chest. When Amy seemed ready, they started drifting in toward the beach. Dianne showed Amy how to look over her shoulder, anticipate the next crest. Stretched out like fearless women, arms extended over their heads, they flew into shore, borne by the foaming wave.

"Wow!" Amy yelled, brushing the hair from her eyes.

"Great job!"

"Lucinda!" Amy called. "Did you see?"

"I saw!" Lucinda replied.

Dianne felt so happy for Amy. Riding the waves was a big first. Now that she had done it, she didn't want to stop. She spent the rest of the day bodysurfing. Other kids were playing down the beach, but Amy stayed away from them. She seemed happier swimming with Dianne and Lucinda, playing with Julia.

The tide had been coming in all day, and Dianne watched it getting closer to their sand castle. She felt a lump in her throat. The first wave washed the smooth sand, its front edge barely approaching the moat. Dianne didn't want to see the castle wash away.

"Oh, the sea, the sea," her mother said, coming out of the water, drying her hair with a towel.

"Julia loves the sea too," Amy said.

"Her middle name," Lucinda said, "is Lea. It means 'a meadow by the edge of the sea.' L-e-a."

"Julia Lea Robbins," Amy said. "Oh, that's so pretty. It's a perfect name for her. Julia Meadow-by-the-edge-of-the-sea Robbins."

Dianne stared at the sand castle. The waves were getting closer. She leaned over Julia. The child was awake, silent, gazing into her mother's eyes. Dianne held her tiny hands. They were soft and sun-warmed, and touching them gave Dianne relief.

"I'm going to take Julia swimming," she said. "Across the hill."

Amy and Lucinda gathered up the beach things. Dianne carried Julia over the dune. From the top, she could see the half-circle of beach on one side, the sweeping marsh on the other. The white lighthouse stood on the point. The sea had washed away their beautiful sand castle, so Dianne turned the other way.

Julia moved in her arms. Dianne held her close. Their skin was warm together, their bare arms touching. Julia loved summer; she always had, and her favorite part—the swim—was coming. Dianne carried her down the lee side of the small dune. The open sea lay to their left, the marsh to their right.

The water was calm and warm. Holding Julia, Dianne walked straight in. The sand bottom felt soft and muddy. Dianne didn't like thinking about crabs and sharp shells, so she turned around, lifting Julia nearly chin height, and slipped backward into the water. The salt silkiness enclosed them with warmth.

"Maaa," Julia said.

"That's right, love," Dianne said. "I'm your mama."

Floating together on their backs, they moved away from shore. Dianne held Julia against her breast, kicking gently. Weightless, they felt the sun on their faces. Sandpipers skittered along the narrow beach, then took off in a brown blur. Dianne imagined flying, thought of Julia unburdened by her broken body.

"We're swimming, sweetheart," Dianne said.

Julia nuzzled her collarbone. Incapable of putting her arms around Dianne's neck, she let her mother do the holding. Dianne was swimming for both of them. The saltwater did the work. It held them up, swept them along without effort.

"Summertime," Dianne said, and the salt spray on her face tasted like tears. "You love summer, Julia."

"Maaa," Julia said.

"So much. You've always loved it so much, ever since you were born."

Julia moved, wringing her hands in Dianne's embrace.

"You're a summer baby," Dianne said.

"You love this season so much, don't you, Julia? This warm, wonderful time . . ."

Across the marsh Dianne could see their house. The weathered shingles looked silver in the light, the shutters as blue as the sea. Lucinda's garden blazed with color. Gold-green marsh reeds swayed in the breeze, and the flag waved. Her studio looked tiny, almost like one of her playhouses. The driveway was empty, but Dianne wondered whether Alan would be passing by later to check on Amy and Julia. She thought of how they had hugged the last time he was over, and she held Julia tighter.

"Helloooo!" Amy called, waving from the top of the dune.

"Hear that?" Dianne asked. "That's your friend Amy calling you."

"Gaaa," Julia said.

"Hi," Dianne called back. "Julia says hi."

Julia was weightless and free. Amy and Lucinda stood on the sand hill. Their faces were shadowed, but Dianne believed they were smiling. This day was blessed. The kingfisher perched on an old piling, watching them pass. The sun was hot, the breeze fresh. It was summer, and the girls were together.

• • •

Nine hundred miles north-northeast, Malachy Condon sat on his old red tugboat, listening to dolphins sing love songs to each other. He had the headphones on. Last night he had anchored off Big Tancook Island, dangling the hydrophone over the side. Dolphins had streaked by, trailing green fire. Their language was complex and mysterious, irresistible as poetry to an Irishman like Malachy.

Now he was back at his dock in Lunenburg, translating last night's recordings. He was seventy-two years old, white-haired and sturdy. Born and raised in the west of Ireland, his love for the sea dated back to childhood. His father had caught salmon in purse nets, and one summer he and his sisters had made holes to let the salmon out. An idealist from the start, his love of nature knew no bounds. Like right now: He'd listen to dolphins crooning over James Galway's flute playing or Pavarotti's singing anytime.

Out the wheelhouse window, the harbor was still as dark green glass. The bright red and blue buildings were as simple as children's building blocks. White gulls circled overhead. A fishing boat left the dock, and Malachy sighed. Beautiful music in his ears, the drama of a northern harbor to watch, what more could he want?

The question was a bitter one, and he bit down on his pipe. Malachy missed his wife. Brigid had died five years before. They had had a grand life together—in Ireland, in the States, and on many oceans around the world. An Aran Island girl, Brigid had encouraged him to study the sea. She had cleaned houses and taken in wash to put him through school. There weren't many students at the Kerry Oceanographic College with young wives chapping their hands and toughening their knees so that they might study eelgrass and shark livers.

"My day will come," she'd say with her low voice lilting and heather-green eyes twinkling. "You'll be hard at work studyin' your fish, and I'll be a lady of leisure. Me and the babies will stay home all day playing patty-cake."

"That's a promise," Malachy had said. "I'll support you and eleven babies until you're so happy, you can't take it anymore."

"Can a person ever be so happy?" she

had asked him, laying her red head against his chest. "So happy she can't take it anymore?"

"Maybe after eleven babies," he had joked. "She'd be so happy, she'd be beggin' her husband to leave her alone."

"Oh, Mal," she had laughed.

But there weren't eleven babies. There was only one. Malachy and Brigid had had a son. They had named him Gabriel, because he was their archangel. Brigid never had another child, but Malachy was glad. Gabriel was enough. He was their full moon, their rising sun. Small, funny, with his mother's curly red hair, he had been a poet.

No, he hadn't been published. But he would have been, Malachy knew. The boy had a gift. His language came straight from his forebears: Yeats, Synge, and Joyce. At fourteen he had the soul of a wise man. His words had the rhythm of songs, and when he wrote about moonlight shining on the bay, you could see the ripples. When he wrote about loving a girl, something he had not yet experienced, his poem had the power to pierce your heart and leave it bleeding.

Gabriel's agility and brilliance had its epicenter in his heart. The happiest baby ever born, he grabbed the life given him with passion and fervor. Everyone knew he was great. His teachers, friends, neighbors. His poems won contests. His English teachers were nurturing him, telling the Condons their son would be famous someday. Malachy didn't care about fame. If only he could hear his son's words for the rest of his life, that would be enough for him.

But Gabriel had been killed. He was only fourteen, killed in a car accident on Route 132 in Hyannis, just before the Airport Rotary. The shock had nearly destroyed his parents. If not for their faith . . .

Brigid had gone to mass at St. Francis Xavier Church every morning, kneeling a few pews back from Rose Kennedy. Sometimes their eyes would meet, the older woman well understanding Brigid's dark sorrow.

Malachy had buried himself in the lab. Woods Hole Oceanographic Institution was used to night owls, but even so, Malachy's office lights burned later than anyone's. Dolphins became his passion. He would listen to them talk for hours. He had far-fetched theories that no one wanted to hear about—

that dolphins were romantic, had elaborate rituals of courtship, that their voice tones changed when they were in love.

Hunched over, his earphones on, Malachy was lost in grief. All he could do was listen. How could a human being interpret dolphins' love songs without allowing the music to touch him? He nearly lost his grant that year. Unable to hear the love songs, he had been incapable of writing papers about them. Research without a theory didn't get funded.

Malachy's young assistant helped him out. Months after Gabriel's death, Alan McIntosh handed him a tape.

"It's from the Caribbean," he said. "Dolphins recorded in the Anegada Passage."

"More gibberish," Malachy said.

"Not the way I hear it," Alan said. "Not the way you taught me to listen. It sounds like poetry to me. We're reading Yeats in school, and it sounds like that."

"Yeats," Malachy said. Gabriel had been his Yeats. Gabriel had written words to break the heart and waken the soul. What did an American science student like Alan McIntosh know about Yeats?

Malachy hated the sight of him for months: a young man who went to school every day, who was alive, the things Gabriel was not. On the other hand, Alan had lost a brother. It was tragic and lousy, and it destroyed his parents. So, wanting to oblige, Malachy slipped on the earphones, trying to listen for Yeats in the dolphins' language. Instead, he heard Gabriel.

Alan gave Malachy that gift. Mentioning Yeats, he'd handed Malachy the key to Gabriel. And Malachy heard his son still. The dolphin songs were like Gabriel's poetry: beautiful, ethereal, too sweet for this world. After all this time, Malachy had met very few people who could hear it, truly get the magic. Most folks heard clicks, trills, crooning, keening. Only the emotionally intense, the spiritually advanced, the madly in love, the truly insane, the terminally foolish, the grief-stricken, the guilty, the enlightened, the people with souls of poets and hearts of children, could hear the dolphins sing their songs of love.

Alan McIntosh was one such man. His brother Tim was not.

The McIntosh boys: the only sons Malachy Condon had left. They weren't his flesh and blood, but did that matter? Malachy had adopted them in his heart, as they had adopted him. Malachy believed that people didn't choose one another. They were given to each other by God, companions for the journey. The McIntosh boys had entered Malachy's life for a good reason, whether he could always see it or not.

"Call your old man," he said out loud with his pipe in his mouth.

He was alone on his tugboat. The dolphins talked his ear off, not a human voice among them, unless he counted the spirit of Gabriel. Malachy believed that voices carried, that even though Tim and Alan were nowhere in sight, they could hear him calling all this distance away.

"Call me," he said again. "You know you want to, by God. What the hell're you waiting for? You think this life goes on forever?"

Alan had telephoned last month. He was due again, and so was Tim. The brothers had unfinished business with each other, deep trouble, and they couldn't rightly get on with their separate lives till they fought it through. Malachy had words of wisdom they both needed to hear.

He had an unusual variety of second

sight—common in the Irish but rare in men. He pictured Dianne, her stunning beauty quiet and natural, like Brigid's had been; he could see the girl, Julia, gnarled as a tree root, soaking in her mother's light and love. Malachy could have picked up the phone, contacted the boys, but it wouldn't be the same. Fathers liked to be called. Good men knew to call their elders. Malachy had faith, so he listened to the dolphins with one hand ready to pick up the telephone and take Tim's call. It was time.

Fourteen

"Who are you taking?" Amy asked.

"Taking where?" Lucinda asked.

"To the library dance."

"Oh," Lucinda said, smiling. They were sitting on the porch, having a cup of tea. Dianne had taken Julia to Alan's for her checkup.

"Considering you're the—what do they call it?"

"Guest of honor," Lucinda said as humbly as she could.

"Well, considering you're the guest of honor, you should be able to take anyone you want."

"Like you?" Lucinda asked.

Amy's mouth dropped open. She had been baldly hinting for days, but now that she was caught in the act, she acted shocked. "Me? Not me. I didn't mean that—"

"How's your reading coming?" Lucinda asked.

"Well, I'm almost done with the book Dianne gave me. *Anne of Green Gables.*"

"She gave you that two months ago! A smart girl like you, I'd have expected you to have read five or six more books by now."

"I just love it so much," Amy said, beaming. "Anne's all right. Going around that island looking for kindred spirits . . . she cracks me up! Do you like it, Lucinda? Don't you think it's a good book?"

"A very good book," Lucinda said dryly. "A three-months'-worth book." She knew she was being conned. *Anne of Green Gables* was her favorite book and she was certain Amy knew it. Like Anne, Lucinda had been orphaned as a child. She had lived in a Providence orphanage for three years, then been adopted by angry people. Although she had called them her parents, she had lived with a secret hole in her heart, the place where her real parents dwelled. She had wished she'd been sent to a kind home like Anne's.

"Is there a real Prince Edward Island?" Amy asked.

"Yes," Lucinda said. "It's one of Canada's Maritime Provinces."

"Have you ever gone there?"

"No," Lucinda said, sipping her tea. "Emmett always said he'd take me, but he died before we could get there."

"Was Emmett your kindred spirit?" Amy asked, gazing over the edge of her teacup.

"Oh, yes," Lucinda said. "He was."

"My father was my mother's kindred spirit," Amy said. "They were best friends, not just another married couple."

Lucinda smiled. The child had wisdom beyond her years. "That's how it's supposed to be," she said. "But sometimes isn't."

"Their song was 'You've Got a Friend,'" Amy said. "By James Taylor. They promised they'd always be there for each other. My father's name was Russell and my mother's was Theresa, and there's a tree downtown near the library that has their initials, R and T, in a big heart. He carved it."

"Good thing the librarian didn't catch him," Lucinda said.

"You'd have liked him," Amy said. "He was a good man. Dianne said so."

"Well, he has at least two fine things going for him: Dianne saying so and you for a daughter."

"Were Dianne and Tim kindred spirits?" Amy asked.

"Well . . ." Lucinda began.

"Wild for each other, madly in love?"

"Yes, they were very much in love," Lucinda said. "But I wouldn't say they were kindred spirits. There's a big difference. 'In love' has to grow an awful lot to approach the realm of kindred spirits. Things help it along—hard times, joy, sickness, humor, money worries, having children. All the events of everyday life. But when one person decides he can't stick around, that's the end of that."

"I hope," Amy said very quietly, "that I wouldn't be the type to leave."

"I have a feeling you're not," Lucinda said.

"They think I'm bad," Amy said, bowing her head.

"Who thinks that?"

"The State of Connecticut," Amy whispered, tears running off her nose. "They think I'm violent because I knocked Amber down."

"That means you made one mistake,"

Lucinda said. "It doesn't mean you're a violent person."

"They say I learned it from Buddy. That when a kid learns that stuff in her own home, she can turn bad."

"She might learn it," Lucinda said evenly, recalling her adoptive father's brute face and scalding tongue, the crack of his belt, the hours spent locked in her room. "But she doesn't have to incorporate it into her life."

"She doesn't?" Amy asked, looking up.

"No. In fact, I'd say it was her duty—to herself, to her parents, and to God—to rise above it."

"Huh," Amy said, drying her eyes.

"You make your own life," Lucinda said. "Your actions are your own responsibility. Blaming others is always an excuse. You're a good girl, Amy."

"Thank you," Amy said.

"You've brought a lot of joy to Dianne and Julia."

"I wish Tim hadn't left them."

"So do I."

"You don't leave your kindred spirit," Amy said.

"No, you don't," Lucinda agreed.

• • •

Dianne stood beside Julia while Alan did the EKG. He squirted white conductor gel on her skin, attached the suction cups. Her rib cage was malformed, her chest sunken. The lines of her bathing suit straps showed, a slight tan on her neck and arms. Her shoulder bore a fading decal of a tiny rose.

"Her tattoo," Dianne said, noting his gaze.

"Amy?" he asked.

Dianne nodded. "Yes. We went to Layton's, and Amy decided she and Julia should have tattoos for the summer. See?" She pointed at Julia's left foot.

Alan smiled. Just above Julia's ankle bone was a blue and orange butterfly. Clasped around it was an ankle bracelet, colored beads strung together in flowerlike clusters.

"That's pretty, Julia," Alan said. "My niece is the coolest girl on the beach."

"Alan," Dianne said, her voice shaking in spite of herself. "Could you please do the test?"

Alan nodded. He flipped on the machine. The engine hummed, and the printout began almost instantly. The machine turned out a long white tape, similar to a grocery store receipt, covered with black markings. He saw Dianne trying to read it, her head tilted to the side.

"Just relax," he said.

She let out a long exhalation.

"Sorry," he said. He was as nervous as she was. His palms were sweating as he handled the long paper. As he scanned the graph, he looked for changes. Julia's previous EKGs were in her file, but he was familiar enough to compare without looking. She had a murmur, an unidentified click.

"What does it say?" Dianne asked.

"Hang on," he said.

Julia lay on the table, staring up at the adults. She wrung her hands. Hand wringing was a common behavior of girls with Rett syndrome—the disease was genetic, affecting almost only female babies—but when Alan saw Julia twisting her hands, he felt helpless, as if she were expressing despair.

"Can you tell anything?" Dianne asked as Alan turned off the machine.

Alan lowered his glasses, peered over the rims at the minute markings. He scrolled through the long paper. He knew it was low and base to be excited by her closeness at this particular moment. Here they were, examining Julia's EKG, and he was drinking in the smell of Dianne's hair and skin.

"If you don't say something," she said, "I'm going to scream like a crane. I can't even help it. The scream's coming, it's in my throat right now—"

"I can't see any significant change," he said, feeling her lean against his side. He tapped the paper, and she looked closer. "This area here might be something, but I'm not sure. I'll fax it up to Providence, let Barbara Holmes take a look at it."

"Something like what?" Dianne asked, now holding Julia's hand. She hadn't moved away from Alan's side though. She was sandwiched between him and the child, touching them both.

"An irregularity," Alan said. "A very slight change in the pattern."

"You just said there's no significant change," she said.

"That's what 'very slight' means," he said. She was wearing a sleeveless white and yellow checked blouse. Her bare arm was tan and lightly freckled. It felt warm against Alan's arm, through the thin fabric of his blue oxford shirt. He wanted to bend over and kiss her naked shoulder, but she moved away so fast, suddenly his whole left side felt cold.

"I'm not a doctor," she said dangerously, leaning over Julia as she started to remove the suction cups from her skin.

"I know," he said.

"I don't like it when you patronize me," she said, her voice trembling. "I know the difference between 'significant' and 'very slight.' But you're faxing the results to Dr. Holmes, and you wouldn't do that if it was normal."

Alan watched her gently wipe the sticky gel from Julia's skin. She used baby wipes from her own bag, dabbing carefully, not wanting to hurt Julia or leave any residue behind. She soaked a wad of cotton balls in warm water, sponged off the remaining lotion. Bypassing the stiff brown paper towels, she dried Julia's chest with gauze squares. Her shoulders were tight.

"Dianne," Alan said, wanting her to turn around.

She just shook her head, her back to him, still cleaning Julia.

"I never want to be patronizing to you," he said, feeling the pressure in his throat. "Never."

She shrugged. He saw her shoulders lift, but she was so tense, they stayed somewhere up around her ears. She had said she was no doctor, but she knew her way around his office better than Martha. She had done medical procedures on Julia that would scare most laypeople far away, maintaining, at various times, shunts, colostomies, a feeding tube, a splint.

Taking hold of her shoulders, Alan turned her around. She was so resistant; he felt her not wanting to look at him. Her head tilted downward, staring at his feet. Her hair was pure gold, shiny in the light. She smelled of flowers and the beach. Alan's heart was beating so hard, he almost didn't trust himself to speak.

"I worry about Julia," he said.

Her head snapped up. Her blue eyes were deep and beseeching. Alan wished he could take her pain and fear on himself.

"I always will, when it comes to Julia," he said. "So will you. It's part of the territory that comes with having her in our lives."

"But the test—" she started to say.

Alan's hands were on her shoulders. He wanted to draw her close and kiss her. It was at moments like this when he knew he was too involved to be Julia's doctor, that he should give her over to someone not so close. But he couldn't. He would never abandon her or Dianne. He cleared his throat.

"The test is inconclusive," he said. "We're in limbo. There's no black or white, no clear indications. We're living in the gray area, where we've always been with Julia. Let it be okay. Let's take what we're given and enjoy every bit of our time with her. Every minute—"

"I need her so much," Dianne said.

"I know," he said.

"I never even know how much until we come here," she said. "Until I face the thought of someday losing her."

"You think that here?" Alan asked. His stomach fell. He had always thought of himself as Julia's protector, Dianne's beacon of hope. He had always tried to help. During Julia's roughest periods, he had stayed available—canceled appointments, passed up conferences, broken dates—just on the chance they would need him.

"Yes," Dianne said, gulping. "This is where we get the news. Whatever it is, this is where we hear it first."

"Some of it's been good," Alan said, stroking her back and trying to stop his own panic, wanting her to see him differently. Was he the voice of doom? She'd look at him and see the worst of everything that could happen to Julia? "So much of it has. So much of Julia's life has been good. Because of you." Did he sound desperate, as if he were trying to convince her?

"People used to ask me why," Dianne said. "Why I decided to keep her. Once I knew about her condition, after the prenatal testing, I could have just swept her away. . . . I had to choose between her and my husband."

Alan's body tensed. Holding Dianne, he pictured his brother somewhere out in the ocean, not knowing about any of this.

"They'd ask me that," Dianne said. "Can you imagine?"

"People don't always think," Alan said.

"It wasn't that I was that good," Dianne said. "Or that noble. I wasn't brave, even though people always said I was. I was chicken! I was so afraid. . . ."

"What do you mean?" Alan asked.

"Having a daughter," Dianne said. "I'd wanted her my whole life. I was so afraid I'd never get another chance. When I was a little girl, I loved dolls. I'd play with them constantly, and I'd get my mother to buy me real baby diapers and baby clothes. My father made them cradles. I had a playhouse. . . ."

"The one Emmett built for you?" Alan asked. He had heard this before.

"Yes," Dianne said. "It was so beautiful, I had it in my room. It had window boxes and a real doorbell hooked up to a battery. I played in it all the time. He made it to look like one of the houses here in Hawthorne, my favorite one. And I'd imagine growing up, having a baby of my own. Having a happy life in a house like that."

"And you did have a baby," Alan said.

"Julia," Dianne said, stepping away from Alan. He reached out, wanting to pull her back, but she had turned toward her daughter. She was still talking, but he had to move closer to hear, her voice was so low. "You can't pick and choose your children. If I didn't have Julia, who's to say I could have had another? Julia's mine."

"Dianne—" Alan said.

But Dianne didn't seem to hear him. She gathered Julia into her arms, holding her tight. "She's mine, and I'm hers. But don't say limbo, Alan. Just don't say we're in limbo."

"Okay."

"Limbo is where children go who can't get to heaven. That's not for Julia."

"No, heaven was made for people like Julia," Alan said.

"I love you," Dianne said, rocking Julia. The child's enormous eyes roved her mother's face. Her hands drifted up, fingers brushing Dianne's lips and chin.

"So do I," Alan said, stepping forward, putting his hands on the shoulders of his niece. Julia turned her head, giving him a huge smile. Dianne just kept rocking. She thought Alan was speaking to Julia alone. She didn't know his words were meant for them both.

"I want to take her somewhere," Dianne said.

"Where?" Alan asked.

"On a trip. To see the world a little. Can we do it?"

"Well," Alan said, unsettled by the idea of Dianne going away. "If you stayed near cities with good hospitals. Just in case. Where are you thinking of?"

"Not Disney World," Dianne said, holding her daughter's hand. "Somewhere beautiful, that's all I know."

Out his tall windows, the town of Hawthorne sparkled in the sun. The harbor was busy, filled with sailboats, trawlers, and sportfishermen. The big white houses lined the waterfront, and Alan wondered which one had inspired Dianne's father. Martha buzzed him. Her voice came over the speaker, telling him Bettina Gorey had called to ask him to meet her at the theater later instead of at her house.

"Change of plans," he said, explaining to Dianne. He had a date that night, and he watched her carefully for any sign of interest or jealousy.

"Oh," she said, beginning to get Julia dressed. "Sorry we've taken up so much time. I know you have patients left to see—"

"That's not what I meant," he said.

But she left the office anyway.

Alan often spoke of the patterns of Julia's condition, but as Dianne drove home, she noticed one of her own. Several days before Julia's appointments, Dianne would start to feel nervous. She'd get a headache, lose sleep, lose her temper. The pressure would build. She'd lie awake, imagining the worst news possible. By the time she got to Alan's office, she'd be a wreck. If he took ten seconds for small talk, she'd feel like biting his head off. And he never deserved that.

Once the visit was over, she felt like singing. Right then, alone in the car with Julia, she had the windows open and the radio playing. She could reach across the seat and touch her daughter's hand. It was summer, they were together; she felt lighter, as if they had been granted a reprieve. That was Dianne's pattern: Her tension would break the minute she left Alan's office. She thought of the white flag, the surrender she had wished for. If only she could stop blaming Alan for her everyday life.

When she got home, she carried Julia into the studio. Amy sat at her desk, and she jumped when they walked in.

"Are you mad?" she asked. "I just wanted to write a letter."

"You can sit at my desk anytime," Dianne said. "I don't mind."

"I'm writing a letter," Amy said again.

Dianne smiled, knowing what she was supposed to ask. "Who are you writing to?" she asked.

"My father," Amy said proudly. "He's my kindred spirit."

"You've been reading *Anne of Green Gables*," Dianne said.

"And talking to Lucinda. She says she talks to Emmett even though he's dead. So I figured, why not write to my father?"

"Why not?" Dianne asked, putting Julia into her chair.

"There's nothing like communicating with your kindred spirit," Amy said, taking up her pen again. "The person who loves you most, knows you best. I'll bet my father knows everything there is about me, but I have things to tell him anyway. How's Julia?"

"She's fine," Dianne said, brushing her hair back from her face.

"I'm going to tell my dad all about her. How's Dr. McIntosh?"

"He's fine too."

"He's my kindred spirit here on earth," Amy said. "And so are you and so is Julia.

But my father knows me longest, and I have a lot to say. Who's yours?"

"My what?"

"Your kindred spirit," Amy asked.

"Oh," Dianne said. "My mother, I guess. You, Julia." She found herself thinking of Alan, and she felt a flush spread up her neck.

"Huh," Amy said. She smoothed out her paper and started to write. By the way her pen flew, Dianne could see that she did have a lot to say.

For some reason Dianne felt unsettled by watching Amy. Torrents of words were flowing, as if Amy's heart were full and she'd finally found the right person to talk to. Dianne hadn't talked like that in so long, she wouldn't even know where to start. She pictured Alan listening, and somehow she knew he would hold her hand the whole time. Tired from her day, she decided to lie down on the daybed. The springs creaked, startling Stella. She was maintaining her post, staring under the bed.

Dianne slept. She dreamed, fragments of her life slipping by. Alan holding her in the waves. Tim leering at her from his wheelhouse. Julia flying like an angel, golden hair streaming behind her. Amy's voice through it all, calling her name.

"Dianne!" Amy whispered. "Wake up. You have to see this!"

Dianne's eyes flew open. Immediately she looked at Julia, but Julia was fine, sitting upright, her hands drifting in the air. Amy seemed frozen at the desk, afraid to move. But she was smiling, pointing at the floor.

"It's Orion!" Amy whispered.

Rolling onto her side, Dianne looked.

The puppy was coming out. Dianne could see his black nose. Wet and quivering, it poked out from under the bedspread. Instead of moving back, Stella inched closer. As if she wanted to assure the puppy that life was safe, she was exhibiting incredible courage. Her whiskers twitched, and her pink nose touched his.

"He's coming!" Amy whispered, clasping her hands.

They knew he had come out at night to eat his food and use Stella's litter box, because they had found evidence. But so far, until then, Orion had been too timid to show himself while humans were around.

Dianne's throat caught to think of the terrors that had driven him so deeply under the bed.

Julia sighed. Orion whimpered and Stella peeped. Dianne smiled at Amy, but when she turned back to the puppy and cat, her heart began to hurt. At first she told herself it was because the dog had suffered cruelty, but she knew that wasn't all. The creatures were nose to nose. Stella, Dianne's shy cat, had lured the beaten dog into the light.

"She got him out!" Amy said with delight.

Dianne suddenly knew the source of her hurting heart. She was watching what love could do: make frightened beasts brave, give hopeless creatures faith. Orion edged his way out. Stella backed up, giving him room. He shook as if he had just walked out of the sea. Dianne had always dreamed of love like this: the kind that made kindred spirits of a damaged cat and puppy.

"Good boy," Amy called, holding out her hand. "Remember me? I'm the one who gave you the cheese."

"And rescued you," Dianne said. She was closer, so the dog approached her first. He gave her hand a tentative lick, then backed away.

"Here, Orion," Amy said, and Dianne wished hard that the puppy would go to her. "Here, boy."

Orion walked over to Julia. He sniffed her toes, her heels, her ankles. Stella followed right behind him, stopping dead in her tracks each time he turned around. Julia's hands moved over the dog, as if bestowing a blessing. A breeze blew through the screen door, and Orion walked over and raised his nose to smell the world.

"He doesn't want me!" Amy said. "He doesn't remember me!"

"Wait, Amy," Dianne said. She could feel the child's impatience, her fear of rejection. Dianne had felt that way so often, wishing Tim would turn his boat around and return home. The memory hurt her stomach, and she thought of how it had felt to lose the man who she had thought was her kindred spirit.

Very slowly Orion turned toward Amy. Four feet planted on the floor, he gave her a long, hard stare. Perhaps she reminded him of the beatings, of his fearsome life with

Buddy. Perhaps her scent brought back recollections of terror. Dianne watched Amy's lip quiver. The child reached out her hand.

Orion walked across the floor. He moved cautiously, his eyes alert. Amy's hand stayed steady. He smelled her fingers. Edging closer, he licked the back of her hand. Amy was crying without sound. She let the dog lick her hand, and when he was finished, he let her pet his head.

Love is a miracle, Dianne thought. She lay on the bed, watching love unfold all around her. The puppy lay his head on Amy's lap, and Amy buried her face in his neck. Dianne waved at Julia, and she could almost imagine Julia was waving back. Kindred spirits stayed. They helped each other through it all. They understood that love was nothing less than a miracle, through all the days of all the years.

Thinking of the McIntosh who had stayed, Dianne closed her eyes. She had been hard on Alan today, as she was so often. He was still there though. She reminded herself that he had a date that night. She wondered what it meant that she felt jealous of some-

one she had never met, a woman named
Bettina Gorey.

The dog let out a small bark, and with her
eyes still closed she heard Amy say, "This is
your home now, Orion. You don't have to be
afraid."

Fifteen

Since Lucinda was the guest of honor, she decided she could invite whomever she wanted to the library dance. She chose Dianne and Amy. A nurse's aide would come that night to stay with Julia. Orion would serve as watchdog while the family was gone.

The dance was to be held in the library itself, on the second Saturday of August. Dianne took Amy shopping, and they bought dresses at the Schooner Shop in Essex. This was *the* shop in the area, the place where all special-occasion clothes were bought. Dianne's mother had taken her there many times, and Dianne felt happy to be sharing it with Amy.

"Is it okay?" Amy asked, coming out of the

dressing room in a yellow dress that made her dark curls and green eyes look even more beautiful.

"You look gorgeous," Dianne said.

"I do?" Amy asked, turning as she looked in the mirror. Her face was a combination of shyness, pride, and excitement. Dianne had the feeling she'd never been to a nice dress shop before.

"You do," Dianne said, turning Julia's stroller so she could watch Amy.

"You make me feel like a princess," Amy said, flinging herself into Dianne's arms. "I've never been to a store like this. Thank you."

But on the way home Amy seemed quiet. Crossing the Baldwin Bridge, she stared down the Connecticut River to Long Island Sound, deep in thought.

"What's wrong?" Dianne asked, glancing across the truck seat.

"Nothing," Amy said, clutching the bag to her chest.

"You really look lovely in your dress."

"Hmm."

"I know who else would think so," Dianne said.

Amy looked up.

"Your mother," Dianne said. "Would you like to show her?"

"She doesn't have many pretty things," Amy said, staring at her knees. "I'm afraid she'd feel bad."

"Mothers usually hope their daughters can have the things they can't have themselves," Dianne said.

The court had mandated that Amy be removed from her home until school started in September, and they were midway through the summer. Her mother had visitation rights as long as Buddy was nowhere on the premises. It was decided that Tess Brooks should come see Amy at the Robbinses on Saturday mornings, but she had canceled twice so far, saying she was sick.

Dianne had watched Amy close down each time her mother had backed out. Amy would stop playing with Julia, stop talking, stop eating, and just watch TV. She could stare at the screen for hours on end, no matter what the programs were. When Dianne or Lucinda tried to ask her how she felt, Amy would just say she wasn't upset, her mother got sick a lot.

But it was clear to Dianne that she missed

her mother terribly. She would wake up at night, hear Amy crying into her pillow. It frustrated Dianne all the more because Tess was supposed to drop off Amy's birth certificate. If they stopped by now, they could pick it up.

"We could call," Dianne began.

"To make sure Buddy's not there?" Amy asked, sounding excited. "And then go see her?"

"Yes," Dianne said.

They stopped at a Dairy Mart, and Dianne used the pay phone. There was no answer. They decided to drive past Amy's house. There was no sign of Buddy's truck, but the curtains were drawn in every room.

"Should we go in?" Dianne asked. "Would you like me to go first to make sure he's not here?"

"That's okay," Amy said, staring at one window in particular. "We'd better not go inside. She gets pretty tired."

Dianne imagined Amy's mother lying in bed, and she could see Amy worrying about what state she would find her in. It would be embarrassing with Dianne there. But as Dianne pulled away from the curb, Amy looked back over her shoulder, boundless love and longing in her green eyes.

Dianne was determined that Amy should see her mother. Besides, she needed that birth certificate. When she got home, she would call Alan. She knew he'd come through.

Anyone paying twenty-five dollars could attend the library dance. They were encouraged to contribute more if they could. The Hawthorne Public Library needed more books, more computers, a new roof. The librarians were all underpaid. Every year Alan McIntosh wrote out a check for a thousand dollars, hauled out a blue blazer, and put on a tie.

This year he had a mission to perform on the way. Dianne had called, asking him for a favor. It was early when he stopped by to pick Amy up; Dianne was over in her studio with Julia. Lucinda was upstairs getting dressed, but Amy was ready and waiting. She stood just inside the screen door, looking out with anticipation and shy pride.

"Hi," she said, beaming.

"Amy Brooks, is that really you?"

"Yep," she said. Twirling around, she let him see her new dress. It was just right for her coloring, for an end-of-the-summer party. Alan felt as if he were picking up his own daughter, taking her to her first dance.

"Let's go, then," he said, holding the door open, taking her arm, and walking her to the car. "You look beautiful, Amy. I'm proud to be seen with you."

Amy beamed as he held the car door open. Alan looked up, saw Lucinda, a towel wrapped around her head, waving good-bye from upstairs. He glanced at the studio, saw Dianne in her work clothes, watching from the open door. Their eyes widened and locked, and they both smiled. He felt her watching them drive away.

"Mom knows we're coming?" Amy asked as he drove toward her house.

"Yes," he said. "She's all ready."

"Do I look okay? Will she think I'm too fancy?"

"You're wonderful," Alan said. "That's what she'll think you are."

Walking up her own front steps, Amy seemed anxious, twisting her hands like Julia. Alan rang the bell. Footsteps sounded inside. Amy let out a big breath. She posed herself as if standing before a mirror: straight back, folded hands, unfolded hands, pleasant smile, no smile. But as soon as the door opened, her nervousness evaporated.

"Mommy!" Amy yelled, throwing herself into her mother's arms.

"Amy," Tess Brooks cried. "Oh, sweetheart."

Alan stood aside, watching the reunion. The mother and daughter just stood there, holding each other, rocking back and forth. After a while, taking Amy's hand, Tess led them into the living room. It was clean and bright, the curtains wide open.

"Look at you," Tess said. "Just look at you!"

"Too fancy?" Amy asked, plucking her skirt.

"No, honey. You're beautiful. Oh, I miss you so much. . . ."

"Mom, I miss you," Amy said.

"You know, there's something I need to tell you. About being sorry those Saturday mornings," Tess said. "When I didn't go see you."

"I know there's something going around.

Some flu or some awful thing," Amy said quickly, as if she couldn't stand to hear this.

"It wasn't the flu," Tess said, her hands shaking. "I've been sick in another way. I've been depressed . . . I have depression. That's what it's called. I wanted you to know it's an actual condition. I'm not just making it up or anything."

"It's okay, Mom," Amy said quickly. "You don't have to apologize."

Alan remembered the feeling, wanting to let his mother off the hook. He admired Tess Brooks for what she did next. Taking Amy's hands in her own, she gazed into her daughter's eyes.

"Yes, Amy," Tess said. "I do."

"Shhh, Mom," Amy said. "You don't have to—"

"Since your father died," Tess continued on, "I haven't taken care of myself very well. It was so awful, such a nightmare, losing him. I just wanted to curl up in a ball and go to sleep, so I wouldn't have to think. And that's what I did."

Amy listened, wide-eyed.

"That was bad enough," Tess said. "But the worst part was, I didn't take care of you very well either. I've been neglecting you—"

"No," Amy said. "You don't—"

"I have, honey. It's okay. I have to start being honest, or we won't get anywhere. I've kicked Buddy out."

"Mom!" Amy's eyes brightened.

"And I'm seeing a therapist to help me with my depression. Like I said, it's real. It's as real as pneumonia."

"Then . . . I can come home?" Amy asked.

"Soon," Tess said.

"Why not now? I don't have to go to the dance. Dr. McIntosh can take me back to get my things, or we can get them later. I don't care. I just want to stay home with you."

"Amy, we have to wait and see," her mother said gently. "The state says you should stay with the Robbinses, and I think that's a good plan. Just to make sure."

"Make sure what?" Amy asked, aghast. It was as if someone had shown her paradise, then locked the door on it. Her face was twisted with disappointment and grief. "That you still love me enough?"

"Oh, Amy," Tess said, pulling her daughter close. "That could never be in doubt."

"Then what?" Amy cried.

"That she loves herself enough," Alan said. "To keep taking care of herself."

Tess looked up at him with gratitude. She nodded, unable to speak. Helping Tess and Amy, he felt he was being given a second chance with his own past. He was a physician now, a lot wiser than he'd been when his own mother had been so sick.

"You have to," Amy said to Tess, holding her mother's face in her hands, staring sternly through tears into her eyes. "You have to take care of yourself."

"I'm getting help," Tess said. "It doesn't happen as fast as I want it to."

"You have to get better or else!" Amy said, and her mother laughed.

"My little tyrant," she said. "Always trying to boss me around."

"I want to stay . . ." Amy said, clinging to her mother.

"Come on, Amy," Alan said, pulling her gently from behind. "What would Lucinda think if you weren't there in the audience to see her get her plaque?"

"She did invite me," Amy said solemnly to her mother.

"Then you'd better go," Tess said.

"What made you kick him out?" Amy asked.

"When I saw the picture," Tess said, swallowing. "Of your bruises. I was standing right here when he did it, but somehow I didn't see. I believed his story, that it was an accident. But when I saw that photo, saw his big handprint on your beautiful shoulder . . ." Bending over, Tess kissed Amy's neck and shoulder.

"Thank you," Amy whispered.

"Now, it's a beautiful night," Tess said, her eyes bright. "I want you to go to the library and dance one for me!"

"I will," Amy promised.

"I'll make sure," Alan said, giving Tess Brooks a long look. She handed him the white paper he had come for. He nodded his thanks.

"Have a wonderful time," Tess said, "and send me . . ."

"Send you what?" Amy asked.

Tess just shook her head. She seemed young and hopeful, but Alan could see the raw hurt in her eyes, watching Amy leave. She was taking care of herself, trying to be honest, loving her child the best she could, letting go for now. From the doctor's point of view, that was how the healing began.

The library was transformed. The band played at the far end of the main reading room. All the tables and chairs had been taken out to create a dance floor. People sipped punch and ate small sandwiches made by volunteers. The only decorations were the books themselves, shelves full of them, their spines garnet, topaz, and verdant in the lamplight.

Dianne had pinned up her hair, put on a little makeup. She wore a brand-new dress, a sleeveless silk sheath of periwinkle blue she had bought because Amy said it matched her eyes. She also wore Dorothea McIntosh's diamond and sapphire earrings. As she stood in the corner, listening to the music, she felt excited and happy. She hadn't had a night out in a long time.

Watching her mother, she felt so proud. Everyone wanted to talk to Lucinda. They surrounded her, telling stories of how she had helped them do research projects, find favorite authors, learn about poetry. Lucinda took it all in, beaming.

When the band stopped, Mrs. Theophilus Macomber stepped up to the microphone. One of Hawthorne's most imposing figures, she was chairman of the library board. Grand in black crepe and a four-strand pearl choker, she made a speech thanking everyone for their generous donations.

"Now, the moment all you readers have been waiting for," she said. "I'm going to ask Gwen Hunter, our newly appointed librarian, to come up here and introduce our beloved guest of honor."

"Well, thank you, Mrs. Macomber," Gwen said in her soft Tennessee accent. She held the microphone, giving it a funny look. "I am none too sure about talking into one of these things, but if there's one person I'd do anything for, it's our guest of honor. I know she needs no introduction at all, Mrs. Lucinda Robbins. . . ."

The entire room broke into applause. Lucinda bowed her head, smiling and blushing. Dianne clapped louder than anyone. As she gazed at her mother, she saw Alan and Amy come through the door, and her heart jumped.

"Mrs. Robbins has been so influential in my life, I don't even know where to begin.

When Paul and I moved up here ten years ago, I didn't know a soul. I needed a job, I didn't have a college degree, but I did love books. . . ."

She went on to tell how she had come to the library, at first as a reader and then as a part-time library assistant. Mrs. Robbins had taken her under her wing. Over the years she had encouraged Gwen to apply to schools, to study library science, to apply for library jobs as they became available. She had been a friend and a mentor, showing Gwen how to help readers, especially young people, discover books they would love to read.

"Around here," Gwen said, "we think Lucinda Robbins is as special as they come. We love her so much, and we miss her every day. We're happy for her though. She'd come to work, and all she'd talk about was her daughter and granddaughter, how she wished she had more time to spend with them."

Lucinda looked through the crowd, caught Dianne's eye. She nodded, sending her daughter a kiss. Dianne smiled through proud tears.

"She has that now," Gwen continued.

"Time with her family. We want her to know that her legacy here will continue. We love our young readers, and we try to steer them toward books best suited for their particular tastes. We do, however, often start by suggesting one book Mrs. Robbins was always particularly fond of. . . ."

"*Anne of Green Gables!*" *the crowd called, Amy's voice above them all.*

"She steered three generations of readers toward that wonderful classic," Gwen went on. "Set one hundred years ago on a verdant island off the coast of Canada."

"Prince Edward Island!" Amy said, her voice ringing out.

"Yes," Gwen said, smiling. "Very good, young lady. As an expression of our gratitude and affection, Lucinda, on behalf of every single holder of a Hawthorne Public Library card, I would like to bestow upon you this road map. . . ."

People parted so Lucinda could make her way to the stage. Standing beside Gwen, she gazed at the young librarian with tears in her eyes.

"We had planned to give you an airline ticket to Prince Edward Island," Gwen said. "So you could visit the setting of your very favorite book. But when I talked to your daughter, she told me she'd been planning to drive you there herself in a Winnebago. So here's a gift certificate to cover the rental costs of a big old motor home, for you and your family. Thank you for everything, Lucinda Robbins."

They embraced, the old librarian six inches shorter than the young one, holding on tight before the cheering crowd.

"Oh, my," Lucinda said, gazing at the certificate, tears streaming down her face. "You have no idea what this means to me. No idea at all . . . I thought maybe I'd get a plaque! But a trip to Canada . . . to see where Anne lived and grew . . . with my Dianne!"

Looking out into the audience, Lucinda found her daughter again. They smiled at each other over the heads of everyone. Dianne wished her father could be there. Wiping her eyes, she blew a kiss.

"My years as librarian have been so rich," Lucinda went on, barely able to speak. "You have all given me so much. As a little girl, books were my best, sometimes my only friends. I would lose myself in the pages, and there were many days I wished I never had to come out. Working here," she said, pausing to gather herself together, "has been like that. With all these wonderful books"—she turned, looking around the room—"and all of you, I've had a life beyond my wildest dreams."

"We love you, Lucinda," Gwen whispered, trying to cover the microphone.

"I'd like to thank my daughter, Dianne," Lucinda said, "whom many of you know made the playhouse in the children's library, for all her love and support. And my beautiful granddaughter, Julia, who makes every day a joy. And I'd like to thank my granddaughter's wonderful pediatrician, Alan McIntosh, for jogging by all those Wednesday afternoons off, reading up on dolphins instead of golfing with the other doctors. But most of all . . ."

The room was hushed, everyone watching Lucinda stare out the window as she swallowed back tears.

"Most of all, I'd like to thank my darling husband, Emmett. Emmett Robbins. He'd drive by the library twice a day on his way to and from the lumberyard, beeping every time. Oh, I'd scold him for making noise . . . he always said that's what he got for marrying a librarian. Someone whose favorite word was *shush.* He always said he'd take me to Prince Edward Island, but . . ." She gulped. "He didn't quite get the chance." Waving her road map, she looked out the window again. "We're on our way, sweetheart," she called. "Meet me in Canada!"

The whole crowd broke into mad applause. Lucinda was swarmed by friends, but she held out her arms for Amy to run onto the stage and into her embrace. The mike was still on, and Dianne heard Amy cry to Lucinda, "Will you send me a postcard?"

"No, darling," Lucinda said, wrapping her in her arms, gazing at Dianne with love and gratitude in her eyes. "You'll be coming with us. I'm sure that's what Dianne was thinking when she thought of a motor home. We'll be on the road, all of us."

"You'll get to see your kindred spirit soon, Lucinda," Amy cried. "Oh, he'll be waiting!"

Overcome with emotion, Dianne ducked out of the room. The crowd spilled into the main hall, and she pushed through them on her way down the hall. She wasn't sure where she was going, but she had to get away. Sobbing, she stumbled into the stacks of fiction. It was quiet here, she was all alone. Down the hall the band began to play. They must have asked Lucinda for a request, because the music was "Ev'ry Time We Say Good-bye," her and Emmett's song.

"Dianne . . ."

She jumped at the familiar voice.

"I saw you run out," Alan said, standing at the end of the stacks, silhouetted by the hall light. He had his glasses off, holding them in his hand. For one second she had thought it was Tim. The voice, the shape of his body, everything. It made her sick, the way this kept happening, the way she made herself a victim of her own bad memories.

"You scared me," Dianne said, hand on her heart.

"Why do you say that?" he asked.

"I thought you were Tim," she said. "For one second . . ."

Alan drew back. He stepped away, and Dianne watched his spine curve over. She could almost hear him groan, and she could see the hurt in his eyes as he leaned against the shelf of books.

"Just for one second . . ." she repeated, wishing she could take the whole thing back.

"I'm not Tim," he said sharply, still holding his glasses.

"But you look like him," she said. "When it's dark, and I see you . . . with your glasses off . . ."

He put them on, yanked them off again.

"For God's sake, it's not what I look like," he said, his voice rising with anger and frustration. "It's what's in my heart. I didn't leave you, Dianne!" His words rang through the stacks; the music played down below, and happy voices carried.

"I know you didn't!" Dianne said, lashing out. "Don't you think I know that?"

"Hey—"

"It's impossible for me *not* to feel this way," she cried.

"What do you mean, impossible—"

"I know you're not Tim, I know you're a good man, so good to me and Julia and Amy. Jesus, Alan! Do you think I want to feel this way?" They both stood in stunned silence for a moment. Then Dianne spoke again before she could think to stop herself.

"I made the wrong choice," she said, holding her head, the words spilling out. "All that time ago. If I had it to do over again, if I could go back in time, I would have—"

"Made the wrong choice?" Alan asked.

Dianne looked at him. Their eyes locked and held for a long while, and Dianne leaned against the closest bookshelf.

"Chose the wrong brother," she said. She felt switches being thrown, gears shifting as she heard herself tell the truth. She swallowed, because she felt afraid to touch him yet she wanted to. She made herself take a step forward. Very slowly she reached up and brushed the hair out of his eyes.

He raised his head. She was looking at him face-to-face. His glasses had slid down his nose, and she gently pushed them up. Her throat was aching very hard as she realized the depth of feeling she had for this man. He had been looking hurt and perplexed, but now his eyes were starting to clear and she thought she saw the beginning of a smile.

They had been through years of this. Pain, blame, misplaced resentment. Dianne was so tired of it. Alan's eyes looked bruised, as if she had hurt him worse than she knew.

"Please forgive me," she said.

"For what?"

"All of it," she said, her throat hoarse. "For thinking you were Tim tonight. And for—"

"What?" he asked.

"This library," Dianne said, seeming lost in thought, her fingers trailing along the books as she gathered herself together. "Mom would come to work here when I was little, and I used to think it was *hers*. That all these books belonged to her. I used to think she wrote them all."

"My patients think she's read them all."

"She has," Dianne said.

"Is that why you're crying?"

"No," she said. Tears were streaming down her face, and she couldn't stop them. "I'm just thinking about what she said."

"About the gift?"

"About my father," Dianne said, covering her face.

"I remember him," Alan said, standing so close, she could see his shoes when she looked down at her own.

"Tell me something you remember," Dianne said.

"He was such a good guy," Alan said. "You were married to Tim, but he treated me like part of the family too. He built the cabinets in my office, and we'd take our coffee breaks together and talk. He was funny, and he'd make me laugh. He liked kids, and he loved the fact I had your playhouse in my waiting room. He loved you, Dianne."

"I know," Dianne whispered.

"Not many fathers inspire their daughters to become carpenters."

"It was that or a librarian," Dianne said. "I had two good role models."

The music drifted through the books, and Dianne felt Alan's hand on her cheek. It felt so gentle. A strand of her hair had fallen, and he brushed it back, tucked it behind her ear. He moved one of her earrings with his fingertip: his grandmother's earrings. Dianne closed her eyes.

"When do you leave?" he asked.

"Tomorrow," she said.

"Here's Amy's birth certificate," Alan said, suddenly remembering. "Tess had it all ready when we stopped by. I just came after you to give it to you."

"Thanks for getting it," Dianne said, taking it. She had requested permission to take Amy on the family vacation, and Marla Arden had discussed it with Tess Brooks. Tess had said yes, it was a wonderful opportunity for Amy, she wouldn't stand in the way.

"I'll miss you," he said.

"Dance with me," she said.

The music played. There were horns and strings, and the melody filled Dianne with yearning so deep, her heart ached.

"Dance?" he asked as if he had never heard the word.

"You can dance," she said. "I've seen you. At the boat club, and down at fisherman's row—"

He didn't wait for her to finish. He just swept her into his arms and pulled her hard against his body. With one arm tight around her waist, he danced her through the books. The light was dim and mysterious, and she felt her breasts pressed hard against his chest.

"Kiss me," he said in a voice so low she almost couldn't hear, and didn't give her the chance to reply anyway.

Dianne melted into his arms. His kiss was wild and sweet. She felt hesitant and excited, as if she were doing something totally forbidden. All these years they had been so close and ferocious and their passion had taken the shape of anger, and this kiss had been waiting to happen all that time.

"Alan," she whispered. The intensity amazed her. The way her skin tingled, the shiver that ran from the top of her head down the backs of her legs. She couldn't quite catch her breath. They were kissing in the darkened library stacks, amid the dusty books, right in front of Hemingway. Her eyes were closed, and her knees were so weak, she was going to collapse.

The band was playing Gershwin, and as they stopped kissing, Alan didn't release her from his arms. Their feet began to move, and Dianne found they were dancing after all. She was gazing through his glasses into his eyes, wondering how this could be happening.

"Dancing in the library," she said.

"Don't tell the librarian," he said.

"She'd be happy," Dianne said.

"I know," Alan said.

"You do?"

"She knew," Alan said. "A long time before you did."

"Knew what?" Dianne asked.

"That you chose the wrong brother," Alan said, his mouth against Dianne's ear.

Dianne nodded, believing that her mother had known all along.

"It's getting hot in here," Alan said after another minute. "Feel like taking a walk?"

"Oh, yes. I could use some fresh air," Dianne said, wiping her brow as they walked out of the stacks of fiction.

Alan waited while Dianne checked on Lucinda and Amy. Standing on the library steps, he said hello to friends, neighbors, parents of patients. He tried to look normal, as if he weren't in the middle of his dreams coming true. Maybe she wouldn't come out. Probably she'd realize she'd made the biggest mistake of her life, kissing him in the library.

But she came walking through the crowd.

"They're fine," she said. "They're so excited, they want to go home and pack right now. My mother's teaching Amy the box step."

"I'm sure every guy in there wants to dance with your mother," Alan said. "She's the belle of the ball."

"I don't think my mother's danced with any man since my father died," Dianne said.

Heading down the wide stone steps, they walked along the harbor. The night had an end-of-summer feel, with a sharp breeze blowing off the water. Streetlights shone brightly, and some of the trees had scarlet vines twisting up their trunks. Alan wanted to take Dianne's hand, but he held himself back.

"That was wonderful," she said. "Back there."

"The party? The music? I know, all for Lucinda," Alan said.

"You and me," she said quietly.

"Yeah?" he asked, his blood pumping. "You think so?"

"I was swept away," Dianne said. "By my mother's sentimental speech. By leaving for Canada tomorrow. That's what you think, right? That that's the only reason it happened?"

"Is it?" Alan asked.

"Let's walk," she said.

Now he did take her hand.

Dianne didn't pull away. Instead, she linked fingers with him. With her other hand she took off her shoes and carried them so she could walk barefoot. They were strolling through the town, along the street where the whaling captains had built their houses.

"Which one?" he asked.

"Excuse me?"

"Which house inspired your father?" he

asked. It seemed odd that after all these years, he didn't know. "To build your play-house? The one that got you started?"

"Oh," Dianne said. "We're not there yet. It's around the corner."

The harbor glittered through the trees and houses. Boat lights played on the black water. The lighthouse beam shot across the sky, east to west, back again. Cars passed on the street. Dianne didn't seem con-cerned about being seen walking around Hawthorne holding his hand. He didn't understand the change, but he also didn't care.

"Bettina Gorey couldn't make it?" she asked quietly.

"Make it where?" he asked, confused.

"To the dance tonight."

"I didn't ask her," he said.

"I wondered," Dianne said. "Martha men-tioned her the other day . . . that day I was in your office. Something about meeting her at the theater. Is she your girlfriend?"

"No," Alan said as they rounded the corner, as the houses got bigger and the yards wider. The town lights weren't as bright here, and the streets were darker. "I don't have a girlfriend. It's always been you," he said, his heart slamming. She had told the truth in the library, and now it was his turn.

Dianne didn't reply. They were passing a meadow, the easternmost edge of one of the waterfront properties. The grass grew tall here, and it was filled with the wildflowers of late summer: asters, goldenrod, Indian paintbrush. Alan saw them glinting in the single streetlight. A wrought-iron fence surrounded the field, which gave way to a manicured lawn. The stately white house was dark.

"There," Dianne said, pointing. "That's the one."

"Your playhouse," Alan said.

Dianne gripped the iron fence posts with both hands, looking inside. The house was white, square, with a mansard roof and ionic columns. It had dark green shutters and window boxes filled with geraniums. The paint looked new, glossy in the light. The house looked well kept but dark and deserted. Alan's house, just two streets away, was the opposite: very lived in but in need of paint and repairs.

"I used to dream of this place," Dianne said.

"You did?"

"When I was a little girl . . . I thought that anyone who lived in a house like this would have the most wonderful life."

"And your father built you a playhouse that looked just like it."

"He did," Dianne said. "It was the closest he could get to giving me my dream. I understand that, wanting to wrap up happiness and give it to your child. . . ."

"Do you still believe," Alan asked, looking down at her, "that the people who live here have a wonderful life?" He wanted so much for her to say that she did.

Dianne didn't reply for a minute. Still holding on to the fence, she stared at the dark house as if trying to see through the walls, past the closed curtains, into the quiet rooms.

"I'm not sure," she said in a voice so low, it was almost a whisper.

Alan wanted to kiss her again. He wanted to wrap his arms around her, hold her close, make her believe.

"You could hope they do," he said quietly. "Even if you're not sure."

"Hope their life is wonderful?" she asked.

"Yes," Alan said.

"Do *you* believe it is?" Dianne asked, her voice barely a whisper.

Alan closed his hand around hers and held it. "I do," he said. "And you do too. You wouldn't be packing up your family for the trip of a lifetime if you didn't."

"The trip of a lifetime in a Winnebago," Dianne laughed. "Is that even possible?"

"I'd say so," Alan said, looking into her eyes. "Listen. You have to pass through Nova Scotia on your way to PEI. I'm going to give you Malachy Condon's phone number. Just in case—"

"Malachy," Dianne said. He had been Alan's mentor and Tim's father figure; he had been at her wedding. "He's Tim's friend."

"He's mine too," Alan said, writing on the back of a card. "He's a good man, and he knows his way around up there. I'll feel better knowing you have his number."

"We'll be fine . . ." Dianne said.

"Are you coming back?"

"We have to. Amy has to start school in September."

"I knew there was a reason I sent her to you," Alan said.

"Alan . . ." Dianne said.

"You don't have to say anything."

A wall had broken between them, but he didn't want her to move too fast. She didn't have to feel vulnerable, lay herself on the line. He put his arms around her, held her in silence for a long time.

"I want to," she said.

"I'll be here," he said.

Her eyes were shining, and she was smiling up at him. He felt her step closer to him, and as he put his hands on her back, he felt her slim body through her dress.

"Something's different tonight," she said.

Everything, he thought.

"I said it out loud," she whispered. "It took me a long time, but I did. I've wished . . ."

"What have you wished?"

"For this," she whispered. They were holding each other in the warm summer night. Alan felt the breeze in his hair, and he heard it in the trees. Overhead, the stars were as bright as they were going to get this close to town. The sky was wrapped in haze, a sheet of sheer silk, and the stars were orange globes.

"Dianne . . ." he whispered into her hair.

"For this," she said, standing barefoot on the toes of his shoes, reaching up to kiss his chin, the side of his face. He brought his mouth to hers and rocked her back and forth in the sultry night.

They kissed for a long time, and then Alan felt Dianne's arms slide from around his neck so that she was holding his face in her hands. Her cheeks shone in the starlight, and he knew they were wet with tears.

"For a chance," she said, smiling as she cried. "That's what I wished for. For a chance to be with you. To let go of the past."

"The past brought us together," he said, his throat tight.

"And it's been tearing us apart," she said.

"So you wished . . ."

"To be brought together," she said, swallowing. "If that's possible."

He held her again. Was it possible? If Alan had his way, it was. His pulse was throbbing and words raced through his mind, ways to convince her it would work, as long as they both wanted it. To be together . . . What more could he want? He'd take her as she was, as she'd always been, without changing a thing.

"I've dreamed of being with you," he said. "For a long, long time."

"All this on the night before I leave for Canada," she said.

His heart sank. She was leaving tomorrow. He held her tighter, as if it could stop her from going away.

"I wish you weren't going," he said.

"In a way, so do I," she said.

"How do wishes work?" he asked.

"What do you mean?" she asked, laughing, kissing the underside of his chin as they stood leaning against the wrought-iron fence. She thought he was kidding, but he wasn't. He was a doctor, a scientist, and he wanted to nail this down. He wanted to pin down a guarantee that they were going to be together.

"How?" he asked.

"You look up," she said. Taking his hand, she raised it overhead. "You point."

"Yeah?" he asked, scanning the heavens.

"And then you wish."

Alan nodded. He closed his eyes and wished. When he opened his eyes, she was still there.

"So far, so good," he said, kissing the knuckles of her right hand, her left hand, and then kissing her mouth.

Sixteen

They left before dawn the next day. Dianne drove. Everyone was so excited at first, but after about thirty miles, Amy and Lucinda fell asleep. Stella found a shelf in the galley, and Orion curled up on one of the bunks. Dianne kept reliving the night before, thinking of Alan. They had kissed and held hands and kissed again until her knees gave out, and Dianne knew it was good that she was going away for a little while. She needed time to sort this out. Wishes and reality needed time to merge.

"Just you and me, Julia," Dianne said.

"Gaaa," Julia said, twisting her hands.

"You can be my navigator, okay? Amy and Granny don't know what they're missing."

"Gleee," Julia said, and it sounded to Dianne as if she understood.

The motor home was enormous, capacious, and luxurious. Everyone had her own bunk, there was plenty of storage room, and there was a little dinette table that folded down for meals. Dianne had stocked the cabinets with soup, bread, peanut butter and jelly, raisins, and fruit bars.

When Dianne was young, her father had gotten Bill Putnam down at the lumberyard to let her practice on some of the big trucks. She had driven a forklift, dump truck, and once, an eighteen-wheeler. Driving the motor home, with its power steering and power brakes, its automatic transmission, was easier, the hardest part being getting used to the rearview mirrors.

They headed north on Route 395. The road was quiet. The last stars twinkled, the dark blue sky like velvet draped over the rolling Connecticut hills. She thought of her wish. It was a strange wish, one without shape or edges: Who would ask for such a thing, the readiness to surrender? And surrender from what? From being so hard, she guessed. So unforgiving, so resistant to love.

But life could be so tough. Caring for Julia took every ounce of her strength, and it left her short-tempered and quick to blame. Not much room for love in a life of constant tension: Some days Dianne's spine was a steel rod with no give whatsoever. Now, heading north, Dianne knew she wanted nothing more complicated than the chance to bend. To let another person in. The sun rose over Worcester, Massachusetts, turning the old brick factories orange-red in the early light. They ate breakfast as they drove.

At the Portsmouth, New Hampshire, traffic circle, Dianne pulled into the Howard Johnson's parking lot to walk Orion. From there they took the coastal route. They had ten hours until nine that night, when they'd catch a ferry from Portland, Maine, to Yarmouth, Nova Scotia. Amy wanted to send her mother postcards from every pretty town.

"They really have a lot of lobsters up here," Amy said, noticing how nearly every restaurant had lobster buoys, traps, or claws nailed to the roof.

"We'll eat so much lobster on this trip," Lucinda said, "we'll turn into crustaceans."

"Could you spell that?" Amy asked,

pulling out her notebook. She had started keeping a list of new words, wanting to improve her vocabulary. Lucinda had given her a reading list, and she had moved beyond Anne to Jo: She was in the middle of *Little Women*.

"Crustacean," Lucinda said. "Try sounding it out."

"C-r-u-s," Amy began, "t-a-s-h-u-n."

"Progress, not perfection," Lucinda said patiently.

They cruised up and down peninsulas, admiring the scenic lanes and pretty houses. Fishing villages sparkled in the sunlight, and white spires graced distant hills. They drove through the Yorks, passed the sandy strands of Ogunquit, meandered through the village of Kennebunkport.

"I feel like a total tourist," Dianne said, both hands on the wheel as she tried to squeeze the motor home down a narrow street lined with boutiques and candle shops.

"Well, you are one," her mother said.

"You have to admit," Dianne said, "we're doing it up right. Winnebago and all. I feel kind of bad that our windows aren't filled with stickers of all the places we've been, like some of the others." They were in a line of trailers and motor homes trying to make their way along the water to catch a glimpse of George Bush's house.

"We don't own ours, dear," Lucinda said.

"Someday, Mom," Dianne said. "We can dream, can't we?"

Lucinda laughed. They were wearing shorts and polo shirts, and the sea breeze blew through the open windows as they slugged diet Cokes from the can. Amy and Julia sat in back, playing their version of checkers and gazing out the windows. Stella seemed content, and Orion was happy as long as they walked him every couple of hours.

"Since we're in tourist mode," Dianne said, "and since our ferry doesn't leave till nine tonight, let's make a pit stop at L.L. Bean."

"What's that?" Amy asked.

"What's *that*?" Dianne and Lucinda asked at once.

"Amy, every New Englander worth her salt has to get at least two things from L.L. Bean," Dianne said. "Mud boots and moose pajamas."

When they got to Freeport, they found

special parking for oversized vehicles. Other motor homes filled the area, and they couldn't help noticing that none was larger or more elegant than theirs. They sent a postcard to Gwen and everyone at the library, thanking them for making the trip possible. Dianne sent one to Alan that she didn't show the others. Then they shopped. Entering L.L. Bean, Amy seemed confused by all the canoes, snowshoes, and skis. Lucinda explained how it used to be, a good old-fashioned outfitter that hit the big time. They found the pajamas with grinning moose imprinted all over heavy green flannel. Lucinda bought some for everyone, along with slipper-socks. Dianne treated everyone to long underwear for chilly Canadian nights, pocketknives, and packets of freeze-dried beef.

"Survival gear is very important," she said, "on a trip like ours."

"Did you bring the bird book?" Lucinda asked.

"Forgot it," Dianne said, and they let Amy choose a field guide to buy.

"You guys think of everything," Amy said, her eyes sparkling, pushing Julia through the store on their way to the checkout.

By six-thirty they were in line to board the *Scotia Prince*. The ferry had limited high space, so they wanted to leave plenty of time. They had to present their tickets and proof of U.S. citizenship before boarding. Only Lucinda had a passport. Dianne, Julia, and Amy had their birth certificates, and as Dianne got the documents together to hand to the official, she felt a pang: so busy with Julia, she had never even traveled abroad. She had never bothered to get a passport. She had kept herself from so many things.

"What's wrong, honey?" Lucinda asked, noticing the stricken look in Dianne's eyes.

"Nothing, Mom," Dianne said, taking her mother's hand. "I was just thinking how wonderful this is. All of us taking this trip."

"I'm so grateful," Lucinda said. "That you wanted to do it for me."

"I thought I did," Dianne said, gazing at the sunset over Portland harbor, the brick waterfront rosy and warm. "I thought it was for you and Julia, and maybe Amy. But I'm realizing it's for *me*. It's your retirement, and I've wanted Julia to see a little of the world. . . ."

"But you're seeing it too," Lucinda said, speaking because she could see that

Dianne was too moved. "You're seeing the world right along with her."

Dianne nodded, smiling at her mother. The girls played in back, trying to get Orion to notice a poodle in the trailer beside them.

"It's one of the best parts about having a daughter," Lucinda said, reaching for Dianne's hand. "They take you places you never would have gone on your own."

"Thanks, Mom," Dianne said, hugging Lucinda with all her might. She kept thinking of what Alan had said, that he would be there when she got back. For eleven years she had kept herself from loving any man, but as she traveled north, she felt that changing. Dianne's heart was opening.

They were taking a night voyage! It was mysterious and divine. Amy was actually on a ship, the *Scotia Prince*. It was a fifteen-hundred-passenger vessel, half ferry and half cruise ship. It had a casino and a floor show, movies and bingo. They had a private stateroom! The animals had their own kennel. If this wasn't living, Amy didn't know what was.

"Is this like the *Queen Elizabeth?*" she asked Dianne.

"Maybe a little smaller," Dianne replied.

They were standing at the rail, watching the town of Portland recede. The sea felt smooth, the air was cool. Amy waved at people standing on the dock. She wished she had a hanky, to make it look right. The only thing wrong was, her mother and Dr. McIntosh weren't there.

They had dinner in the restaurant, heard a lady sing songs from Broadway plays. Then it was time for bed. Down in the cabin, they had four bunks, two on top of the others. Dianne wanted to be down below with Julia, so Amy and Lucinda got the upper ones. They all wore their moose pajamas.

"Good night," they said to each other.

"Sweet dreams."

"Sleep well," Lucinda said, reaching across the narrow space to touch Amy's fingers. Down below, Dianne was singing a lullaby to Julia, and Julia was breathing as if she had never been so comfortable in her life. The ship felt like a big cradle, rocking them all to sleep as it took them to Canada.

Amy felt so close to her father. She had

never been at sea before, and she imagined that this was the life he had loved. The waves tapped the hull, ringing through the ship like church bells. She felt the boat rise and fall; it moved with her breath and every beat of her heart. Her father lived in the sea now, his bones and his boat, but his spirit lived forever in Amy herself.

"'Night, Dad," she whispered, holding herself tight.

Driving off the ferry, they entered Canada. The sky in Yarmouth, Nova Scotia, was bright blue, filled with fair-weather clouds. The dock bustled, and the town was waking up. They had come through the Bay of Fundy, where the tide differential was the greatest in the world, but the most amazing thing was, they had seen a whale and several dolphins.

"Did you see them?" Amy asked. "I mean, was that a dream come true, or *what?*"

"Such graceful creatures," Lucinda said.

"Your first whale, Julia," Dianne said, thrilled. Julia had actually turned her head when the whale surfaced, its glossy back appearing like a tabletop in the water, spraying like a fountain as it breathed and sounded.

"Gleee," Julia said.

"And dolphins, Julia," Amy said, hugging her with joy. "We'll have to write to Dr. McIntosh right away. Or even call him!"

"Alan would know what kind they were," Lucinda said.

"Which way to Prince Edward Island?" Dianne asked, coming to a fork in the road. A right turn would take her toward Lunenburg, where Alan's friend Malachy kept his boat. The thought occurred to her that they could stop by, visit the old man. He could certainly tell them plenty about marine mammals. On the other hand, her night with Alan felt pure and precious. Getting away from Hawthorne was good for many reasons, and she didn't want to make a connection, way up here, that would take her back to bad McIntosh territory and remind her of Tim.

"That way, darling," Lucinda said, pointing as she read the road map. "Go left."

"It is so beautiful here!" Amy cried. "We're in a foreign land."

"Left?" Dianne asked with a glance at the road for Lunenburg.

"Leftward ho," Lucinda said.

"Okay, then," Dianne said. And she swung the bulky vehicle onto Route One, the Evangeline Trail, which would lead them north toward the ferry from Pictou to Prince Edward Island, leaving Lunenburg and the McIntosh boys' mentor far behind.

Tim McIntosh didn't have a license to lobster in Canada, and he didn't care. He needed to hang up his work gloves for a while. Steaming east with the tide, he had pulled into Lunenburg nearly a week earlier. Malachy's tugboat was nowhere to be seen.

"I thought he lived here," Tim had said to an old man hanging around the dock.

"That's the thing about living aboard a boat, young fella," the old fisherman said. "Wherever your vessel is, that's where you live. And Malachy's vessel ain't here."

"Got it," Tim said.

On the morning of the seventh day, when Tim had planned to head back to Maine, he woke up to find Malachy's tugboat berthed across the harbor in its usual place.

"Tim, boy!" Malachy said, slapping him on the back as Tim climbed aboard.

"Where the hell have you been?" Tim asked.

"Gulf of St. Lawrence," Malachy said. "Wanted to see if the dolphins up there sing prettier'n they do down here."

"Christ, Malachy," Tim said. "They don't sing. They jabber. They get caught in tuna nets and make the tree huggers crazy. Everyone thinks dolphins are so god-damned romantic, and what they are is a big nuisance. Every fisherman with a rifle knows exactly where to aim. . . ."

"They do, as a matter of fact," Malachy said, lighting his pipe.

"They do *what*?"

"They do sing prettier up north than they do here."

"They must be doing something interesting," Tim grinned, "to keep you gone for so long. I was just fixing to pull out."

"Well, I'm glad that didn't happen."

"Yeah."

"Your brother would've been mighty aggrieved," Malachy said. "He's been tryin' to get word to you."

"Alan?" Tim asked, his heart thudding. "Alan's looking for me?"

"Well, as 'lookin' for' you as he can do

from all the way down in those Hawthorne tropics. He called here." Puffing on his pipe, Malachy gazed out across the glassy harbor. The day was going to be a beauty. The sun had just risen over the land across the water, spreading clear, golden light over everything. "Good to be home, it is. Come down below, and let me fix you a cup of tea."

"Jesus Christ," Tim said gruffly. "I'm American. I like black coffee."

"Black coffee then, son," Malachy said, smiling around his pipe stem. "Whatever you want. You know all you got to do is ask."

"What's he want?" Tim asked.

"You know I don't butt in," Malachy said sternly. "If you want to know, you're going to have to ask him yourself."

Tim nodded at the old Irishman, respectful and apologetic. Hearing about Alan's call had put him in a belligerent state of mind. Here he was, a thousand miles away, in another country, and it all came back: his family, his past, his guilt. Days like this were bad. By nighttime Tim would be looking for trouble. Maybe a woman, maybe a fight, maybe both. Malachy stared at him with affectionate silence as if he could read his mind, as if he knew he had all day to talk him out of it.

Prince Edward Island was everything Lucinda had dreamed it would be. A land of meadows and rivers, swept by the wind and coddled by the sea. There were beaches everywhere, some with red sand, others with sand so white and fine it looked like powdered pearls. It was like stepping into the pages of her favorite book, where nearly every scene had brought tears to her eyes.

Dianne drove the motor home slowly, so Lucinda could savor every inch of the island. There was the Acadian parish of Tignish; the capital city of Charlottetown and the Gothic spires of St. Dunstan's Basilica; the lazy land of Summerside, where they saw a pair of silver foxes; and finally, Blue Heron Drive, which took them along the red sandstone coastline into *Anne of Green Gables* territory.

"'Blue heron,'" Amy read from the bird book. "'A large water bird that migrates to the maritime provinces every spring to nest in the shallow bays and marshes.' Will we see any on this trip?"

"We see them in the marsh at home," Dianne said. "All the time. You know that big bird that stands in the shadows. . . ."

"With the knobby knees," Amy said.

"He's a great gray heron," Lucinda corrected her daughter.

"Same thing," Dianne said, steering up a long and scenic hill.

"Is it the same thing, Amy?" Lucinda asked. "Is the blue heron the same thing as the gray heron?"

"They're different!" Amy said, waving the field guide. "The same species, but different birds!"

"My mistake," Dianne laughed, thrilled by the way Amy was starting to love learning. She and her mother exchanged a small smile. Julia dozed in her seat, her knees tucked into her belly.

They visited Cavendish. Here Lucinda's enthusiasm waned slightly. *Anne of Green Gables* seemed to have become a local industry. There were water slides and go-carts, an amusement park and a national park. Lucinda couldn't wait to move on, make a connection with the young orphan Anne, who had brought her so much comfort in her youth, but Orion needed a walk.

While Lucinda and the puppy went for a stroll, Dianne and the girls wandered toward the rides. They wore shorts and sleeveless shirts, and the summer sun felt just as warm as it did in Hawthorne. There was a merry-go-round and Ferris wheel, bumper cars and a flume.

"Gleee," Julia said, tilting her head back to look up.

"What do you see?" Amy asked, crouching by her side.

"Maybe a blue heron," Dianne teased. "In flight."

"No," Amy said, following the line of Julia's sight. As Dianne tilted her head up to look, she saw the Ferris wheel. It rose high over the amusement park, shiny silver and colored metal gleaming in the sun. Moving slowly around, it looked like a giant pinwheel, the kind Dianne had held up for Julia, to let the wind blow around and around, when she was very young.

"She wants to go on it," Amy said.

"She can't," Dianne said.

"Why?" Amy asked, her eyes glistening as

she grabbed Dianne's hand. "Let me take her."

"No," Dianne said, feeling panic.

"Kids love rides," Amy said. "We do. You've brought her all this way, on her trip of a lifetime. . . . Can't she go on the Ferris wheel?"

Julia gazed up. Her eyes were full of joy and light. Carnival music jangled, and Dianne's throat ached the way it did whenever she had a glimpse of Julia as a normal girl. What would be the harm? Children younger than Julia had ridden. . . .

"Okay," Dianne said. "She can go."

"Yay!" Amy said, jumping up and down, pointing at the sky. "That'll be us, Julia. Way up there!"

Dianne paid for two tickets. Afraid the man would say something, look at Julia strangely, prevent her from going on the ride, she tensed up. But he just took her money, waved them away from the window, moved the line along. Dianne insisted on strapping the girls in herself. The attendant seemed not to mind.

"These seats are safe?" Dianne asked, her heart pounding.

"Yep," he said.

"Has there ever been a problem?"

"Never lost a kid yet," he joked.

"Dianne . . ." Amy said, embarrassed.

"Maaaa," Julia said, touching Dianne's nose, her hair.

"Okay, next!" the attendant called as the Ferris wheel turned slowly, sweeping Amy and Julia out of her reach so the couple standing behind them in line could climb on. With every turn, Julia was inching away from her. Dianne stood on the ground, her head thrown back, wanting to get her baby back.

"Honey, where are the girls?" Lucinda asked, coming over.

"I'm crazy, Mom," Dianne said. "I let them on the Ferris wheel."

Now Lucinda tilted her head back, shielding her eyes against the sun as she searched them out. Waving madly, she grinned. Julia and Amy were all the way at the top. They stayed there for a long while, as the last passengers were loaded on, and then the ride began to move.

"Look at them," Lucinda said, still waving.

"I can't," Dianne said.

"Wheeee!" Amy's voice screamed above the music, above other people's laughter. "We're flying!"

"Oh, Mom," Dianne said. Panic closed in, and she felt it clutching at her chest. She had sent her baby, her little helpless Julia, into oblivion. Dianne had left her with baby-sitters, left her overnight at the hospital, but she had never felt so out of control before. What if Julia got scared? What if she slid under the bar and fell out?

"Wheee!" Amy yelled again.

"Whee! Whee!"

"Oh, my God," Lucinda said, holding Dianne's free hand. "Do you hear that?"

"Yes," Dianne said, covering her face. "Amy's excited."

"It's Julia, honey," Lucinda said. "That's your daughter."

Dianne uncovered her face. The Ferris wheel turned merrily, music tinkling through the summer air. The carriages were full, twirling around the spokes of the great wheel. Dianne located her daughter, fixed her in her gaze, saw her mouth wide open, grinning, calling out in sheer, joyful abandon.

"Wheeeee!" Julia called. "Wheee!"

Dianne held her mother's hand, watching her little girl have fun in the sky. When the ride stopped and Dianne rushed over, she heard Amy: "Wow. Oh, my God. Can we do it again?"

"Maybe later," Lucinda said, helping her off.

Dianne half expected to find Julia in tears. Ready to wrap Julia in an embrace, she held herself back. Her daughter was smiling, head swaying from side to side in pure bliss.

"Wheee," Julia whispered, gazing into her mother's eyes. Dianne found herself wishing Alan were there to see and hear her.

Seventeen

Alan returned to his office from the hospital. One of his patients had been brought in with a cut head suffered at Jetty Beach, and the ER had called Alan. Chris Wright, a seven-year-old with two older sisters, had banged his head, playing with a boogie board. His sister Abigail had been in charge, as their parents were out sailing on their boat, and she had asked the ER to call Dr. McIntosh. He rushed right over.

Now, back at work, he stared at the message on his desk, at first unable to make sense of the words: "Your brother Tim called." It was followed by a wrong number.

Alan buzzed Martha. She was on hold on another line, waiting to speak with Chris's neurologist, but she answered right away.

"Yes, Dr. McIntosh?" she asked.

"This phone message from my brother," he said.

"Oh, yes. He called while you were at the hospital. He—"

"You made a mistake with the number," Alan said, interrupting her.

"No, I didn't," she said.

Martha was a great nurse, but secretarial skills were not her forte. He kept planning to hire a receptionist to take the burden off her. In the meantime, backed up with patients in his waiting room, he snapped at her.

"Look, Martha," he said. "You wrote down Malachy Condon's number. Now, wherever the hell my brother's fishing these days, it's not in Canada. So will you go to your desk, look for—"

"He is with Malachy," Martha said coolly. "He said so expressly."

"Oh," Alan said, stunned. "I'm sorry."

"Now, if you don't mind, I have Chris's neurologist on line two—"

"Hello, Jake?" Alan said, clicking onto line two, ready to hear Chris's test results from Jacob Trenton, the best neuro guy Hawthorne Cottage had on staff. Alan listened, pleased to hear there'd been no concussion, no need for worry, Chris would be fine. But Alan was distracted.

When he got off the phone, Alan stared at the phone message. His brother was with Malachy Condon, up in Lunenburg, Nova Scotia, exactly where Alan had told Dianne to go if she needed anything. Sending the woman he loved into his brother's arms wasn't going to make Alan's day go any better.

He dialed the familiar number of Malachy's tugboat.

Dianne was enjoying every mile. Why had they never done this before? After this trip, they'd have to motor-home their way through all the great sights of the United States: the mountains of Colorado, the caves of Kentucky, Memphis, the Grand Canyon, the Mississippi River. They visited Woodleigh Replicas, getting deliciously lost in the medieval maze. They saw Cape Traverse, where one hundred winters ago passengers in iceboats were pulled across the strait by men harnessed like horses. She sent Alan postcards along the way.

They built sand castles on every beach they saw. They found strands of white sand in the north, red sand along the south shore. At each one, they built wonderful castles, taking pictures of every one. Julia seemed to enjoy being with her family on the sand, patting seashells and dry seaweed into place for decoration.

"Maybe I'll change tacks," Dianne said. "From now on I'll make sand castles instead of playhouses. Julia can help me."

"You can't sell sand castles," Amy said sadly. "They don't last."

"I know," Dianne said, helping Julia drizzle wet red sand onto a turret. "But they're so beautiful while they're here."

"Maaaa," Julia said.

They visited the places known to Lucinda's beloved Anne. They saw the grounds of Lucy Maud Montgomery's Cavendish home, where the novel's author had lived with her grandparents after the death of her mother.

"She knew from her own experience," Lucinda said.

"How it felt to be orphaned?" Amy asked.

"Yes," Lucinda said. "You can't imagine, it's the loneliest feeling in the world."

"I can only guess," Amy said, taking her hand.

They were walking through the homestead fields and old apple-tree gardens. The foundation and white picket fence were all that remained of the actual house, and Dianne felt disappointed. She would have liked to take photographs so she could duplicate the house for some little Hawthorne girl. Listening to her mother and Amy talk, Dianne pushed Julia and felt so grateful that they had each other. That she had her mother, and that Lucinda was healthy.

"Coming here means so much to me," Lucinda said, linking arms with Dianne and Amy.

"I know you loved the book," Dianne said.

"My childhood was very lonely," Lucinda said. "My adoptive parents fought all the time, and it often turned violent."

"Huh," Amy said. "I know what that's like."

"I wish you had started reading sooner," Lucinda said, kissing the top of Amy's head. "I used to escape into books. I'd hear my father yelling, and I'd open my book and dive in. I don't know what I would have done without reading."

"I just wished they'd stop," Amy said. "I'd

lie in bed with my fingers crossed and wish my head off. I'd pray to every angel flying by that something would happen, that somehow Buddy would disappear and things would get better."

"One of those angels listened," Lucinda said.

"Yeah," Amy said, nodding. "I think so."

"Buddy's gone, and your mother's getting better."

"It used to be so awful," Amy whispered. "Hearing him hit her . . ."

"That sound," Lucinda said, closing her eyes as if she could still hear the fights of her own family. "The crack of a big, bare hand slapping skin . . . it was worse when he used his fists. . . ."

"And the way she'd scream," Amy said. "And knowing there was nothing I could do to help."

"Even though you wanted to," Lucinda said.

"More than anything," Amy said.

Pushing Julia, Dianne felt she had no part in this conversation. It was so rare, hearing her mother talk about her troubled childhood. That was the part of herself Lucinda kept private. Dianne had always felt compassion for the idea of her mother as a child, orphaned and alone, but her mother had seemed to feel it too painful to discuss.

And Amy usually said so little about her own difficult home life. Dianne knew that Alan believed she would benefit from therapy, that she had been traumatized by her home life. That violent existence was the equivalent, he said, of the experiences of people who went to war.

The four of them strolled through the fields. Apple trees laden with fruit glowed in the afternoon sunshine, and the cider smell was pungent. Dianne thought of Alan, knew that he would be happy to hear Amy letting some of her story into the light.

"We're so lucky," Dianne said.

"Honey?"

"Julia and I," she said. "We're having a good life."

"But, Dianne," Amy began, a quizzical look in her eyes. "How can you say that? Julia's been so sick. . . ."

"She has," Dianne said. "And I've been so angry about it. More than I like to admit. But we're blessed anyway. We've known only love."

"Her father left," Amy said quietly, reminding Dianne.

"But she's had so much from other people," Dianne said, "it almost doesn't matter now. She has me, her grandmother, her uncle . . ." As she said the words, she realized how much she missed Alan.

"Who wouldn't love Julia?" Lucinda asked, bending down to kiss her granddaughter.

"Buddy," Amy said solemnly.

"You have a point," Lucinda said. "My adoptive father. People that sick simply can't love. They don't have it in them."

"I love it here," Dianne said, feeling the warm breeze blow through the orchard. She closed her eyes, wanting to remember it forever. Not just the setting, but the conversation: these people she loved so much, trusting one another enough to be open with their hearts. She felt Alan's steady presence, and she knew that somehow everything would be right when she returned home.

"Me too," Lucinda said.

"Let's take something," Amy said. "For souvenirs."

"Oh, honey," Lucinda said. "It's not right to take things—"

"These," Amy said, running to gather four withered apples. "No one would mind if we took these, would they?"

Dianne looked at them quizzically. The apples were rotten, shriveled. Their stems stuck out at crooked angles, and they smelled like vinegar or wine. Why had Amy chosen something so ugly? She could have picked flowers, found pretty pebbles, searched for four-leaf clovers, gathered yellow leaves.

But Lucinda understood. She stood there nodding, touching each apple as gently as she could.

"They'll dry nicely," she said.

"They will?" Amy asked.

"Yes. We'll set them aside in the galley, and by the time we go home, they'll be fine. I love them," Lucinda said. "I just adore them."

"But why?" Dianne asked. "I don't get it. Why take rotten old apples?"

"They're us," Amy said.

"Don't you see?" Lucinda asked, her blue eyes gleaming. "You of all people should see, honey. Amy's right, they're us. They're hurt and ugly, ruined things. Unlovable things lying on the ground . . ."

"Till someone picked us up," Amy whispered. "Till you picked me up, Dianne."

"Oh!" Dianne said, covering her mouth with one hand.

"Things other people would find unlovable," Lucinda said, and now Dianne did understand: Her mother was thinking of herself as a child. Dianne looked at Julia, her great eyes roving heavenward, listening to the sea breeze rustle the leaves overhead. Thinking of all the people who would see Julia only as deformed, find her unlovable, Dianne's throat ached.

"We'll cherish them forever," Amy said solemnly in a tone Dianne believed only a twelve-year-old could use. Until Lucinda used it a moment later . . .

"Forever and ever," Lucinda said.

As Dianne held her old apple, she closed her eyes. She thought about dropping from a tree. She thought about being abandoned, picked up, cherished by the brother of a man who had seemed to consider her unlovable. Dianne was falling in love.

"They're us," Dianne, finally getting it, said out loud as she held the apple. To Julia, her mother, Amy, and someone many miles over the sea.

• • •

That night they parked the camper in a trailer park by the sea. Up there, the stars seemed brighter than at home. Stella sat in the window, staring at her constellation. The puppy lay on Amy's bunk, asleep at her feet. With a chill in the air, everyone wore the moose pajamas.

Dianne and Lucinda sat in folding chairs outside, wrapped in blankets and wearing their new slipper-socks as they listened to the waves. A candle burned on the table between them, driving away bugs. They sipped honey-orange tea, letting the steaming mugs warm their hands.

"Do you feel retired?" Dianne asked.

"I feel young," Lucinda said. "Happy, excited, energized . . ."

"Are you enjoying your trip?" Dianne asked.

"It's a dream come true," Lucinda said. "It's more than I ever expected, a thousand times better because you and Julia are here with me. And Amy adds so much. . . ."

"Only Dad is missing."

"For me," Lucinda said. "But who's missing for you?"

"I don't know," Dianne said.

"You were gone quite a while the night of the dance," Lucinda said.

"Mmm," Dianne said, gazing at the sky. This far north, the air was perfectly clear. Against a field of blue-black, the stars blazed. The Milky Way coursed its white path through the night, and a meteor streaked into the ocean. "Did you see that?" Dianne asked.

"Yes," Lucinda said. "A shooting star—how fitting."

"Another one!" Dianne said, jumping up. She looked down at her mother. "What do you mean, fitting?"

"To be talking about people we love and to see shooting stars. You were about to tell me about your walk."

"Mom—"

"Your walk with Alan."

"We just strolled along the harbor," Dianne said, her heart kicking over as she remembered, trying to decide how ready she was to talk about it. Shooting stars crisscrossed overhead, long trails of white fire searing the sky. "What *is* that? Does Prince Edward Island attract meteors or something?"

"It's a meteor shower," Lucinda said.

"Happens every August, down in Connecticut too. You and your father used to watch it every summer."

Dianne nodded, remembering now. Standing by the marsh with her dad, holding his hand, he promised her shooting stars. They had never stopped coming— one meteor after another. She hadn't realized it was a natural phenomenon; she had just thought her father was so wonderful he could command shooting stars.

"I haven't seen it in years," she said.

"You've been so preoccupied, darling," Lucinda said. "You've been too wrapped up in Julia to look at the sky."

"I know," Dianne said, watching the stars now.

"Or to notice that someone wonderful wants to love you."

"Mom . . ." Dianne said.

"He does, honey," Lucinda said.

"I'm figuring it out," Dianne said, holding herself.

Dianne stared upward. She hadn't seen a meteor for several seconds, and she found herself holding her breath. Then one shot by, and she relaxed a little. She thought of how she'd shown Alan how to wish on a star. It was so easy to get used to amazement. Just as quickly, to become accustomed to sorrow. So why not love? Life could change in a heartbeat, and you could forget it was ever any other way.

"Dianne?" her mother asked, wanting her to say more.

"I told him something the other night," Dianne said quietly.

"What?"

"I told him I'd chosen the wrong brother."

"Well," Lucinda said, and Dianne could hear the smile in her voice. "Well, well."

"I want everything to work out," Dianne said.

"I have every reason to think it will."

"Why?" Dianne asked. "What reasons?"

"You, Alan . . ." Lucinda said, still smiling.

"I've screwed things up for a long time," Dianne said. "Everything's not going to be perfect all at once."

"Or ever," her mother said.

"Or ever."

"What you need," Lucinda said, "is to move on."

Dianne didn't speak. Behind her, in the Winnebago window, Stella had spied the constellation Orion standing on the sea, and she began to peep with joy.

Lucinda continued. "In some ways, I've spent my whole life learning how to move on. First, I had to forgive my parents—my real ones for dying, and the others for adopting me."

"But how?" Dianne asked.

"There's only one way," Lucinda said, reaching across the space between their folding chairs to take her daughter's hand.

"Love," Lucinda said.

"How did you do it? When you felt so bad inside?"

"It started with Emmett," Lucinda said. "And it continued with you."

"I want to try," Dianne whispered.

"The biggest mistake any of us can make," Lucinda said, "is thinking that love is a feeling, an emotion. It's not that at all. It's an action, a way of life. It's what you do with Julia. It's what you want to do with Alan."

"I know I want that," Dianne whispered. "I've known it for a while."

"Then, let yourself, darling," Lucinda said. "Let yourself love him."

Dianne nodded, staring at the shooting stars.

The animals made their sounds, the children slept inside. The waves broke on the shore. The Atlantic Ocean stretched a thousand miles south, and Dianne imagined Alan hearing the same waves in Hawthorne. She knew Alan was waiting for her to get back, and she knew that she was on her way.

On the road to the ferry, Dianne decided to walk Orion and pulled onto a rutted lane, stopping at the back side of a scruffy dune. Everyone felt sad, hating to leave Prince Edward Island on such a brilliant, sunny day. Scrambling up the dune, Amy saw it first: a black sand beach nestled in the hidden cove.

"Come on, everyone!" she yelled. "We have to build a castle here. Black sand!"

"There's not enough time," Lucinda said, checking her watch. "We have to catch the boat."

"Dleeee," Julia said. She had been overheated last night. Dianne had rubbed her with a damp washcloth, opened the vents for a cool breeze. But now she seemed back to normal, and Dianne knew how much she loved playing in the sand.

"I think we have time for a quick one," Dianne said, "if we build fast."

"You're the architect," Lucinda said. "I leave all matters of building to you."

So they climbed over the dunes and ran down to the water's edge. The sand squeaked under their bare feet. It felt fine, the texture of talcum powder, and it stuck to them, sparkling like chips of black diamonds. Together they smoothed out a section above the lapping waves. They began to mound the sand, then to shape it with their bare hands.

"Maaa," Julia said as Dianne helped her scoop some hard sand.

"Sweetheart," Dianne whispered. "This is so rare. We've never seen black sand before." The sand held its shape, and they carved out ramparts and balconies. The shells were as unusual as the sand, pink and delicate. Dianne helped Julia ring each window with shells and pebbles, trying not to look at her watch.

"A black castle," Amy said.

"Our masterpiece," Lucinda said sadly. "On our last day."

"Why do we have to leave?" Amy asked, carefully forming ledges along the castle walls. "Why can't we just stay and stay?"

"I agree," Lucinda said. "I'm retired. I don't have anywhere I have to be."

"You could teach me," Amy said. "We could live in the Winnebago, and it could be our schoolhouse. Julia would like it too."

"Absolutely," Lucinda said. "Our never-ending pilgrimage. We came, we saw, and we stayed."

"Gaaaa," Julia sang into the crook of Dianne's neck. They were sitting together, across the black castle from Amy and Lucinda. Dianne was lying on her side, using a driftwood stick to cut a doorway through the wall, with Julia curled beside her. Mica stuck to their skin, twinkling like black stars. Dianne listened to the others play, planning ways they could stay on the island longer, and she dropped the stick.

She held her daughter closer. The voices were music, along with the gentle waves. If only this feeling could last forever: the warm sun, the soft breeze, the sense of together-ness. The summer was ending; next week, it would be September. As Dianne listened to her mother and Amy laugh, she held Julia tighter.

Would she stay if she could? If she could make a new wish, prolong this moment for-

ever, would she? Black sand felt warmer
than any other kind. It pulled in the heat,
held the sun in its dark grains. Dianne
thought of the shooting stars, of the excitement she had felt about seeing Alan again.
But didn't she have it all here, everything
she could ever want, on this rare and amazing beach?

Did she need any other kind of love?

She had her daughter, her mother, their
friend, this beautiful castle. . . . If only she
could stop the tide from coming in, washing
it away. Lucinda stood, brushing sand from
her hands. As usual, she got out her camera
and took a picture. Time was flying; they
would have to rush to the ferry. The puppy
ran in mad circles, knowing he had to get
back inside the camper.

"Come on, Orion," Amy laughed. "Want a
drink of water? Follow me."

"Forty minutes," Lucinda said. "That's
how much time we have to make our boat.
If we miss it, we're staying on this island for
good. You'll never get me off."

Dianne hesitated. What if she took her
time? She could drag her feet, make them
late. They could stay in this enchanted
place, she wouldn't have to return home

and face her feelings, reality would never come again.

"Gaaa," Julia said.

"Go, honey?" Dianne asked. "Is that what you're telling me?"

"Gleee," Julia said.

Julia's sounds. Julia's words had no translation, but to Dianne they were filled with meaning. Just like the splashing waves, the whispering sand, the crying gulls. Everything in nature meant something, alive with private poetry for any person willing to listen. Julia was braver than her mother. She was telling her to go, return to Hawthorne, see what the future held.

Lifting Julia, Dianne began to walk toward the dunes. The tide was out, and it wouldn't begin to flood for another few hours. They'd be on the ferry to Nova Scotia by then, on their way home. Holding her daughter, Dianne was grateful they wouldn't have to see their black sand castle wash into the sea.

And soon she would be with Alan.

Malachy kept the telephone turned off most of the time when he was working. He didn't want the music of the dolphins having to compete with bells ringing. But soon after he plugged in the cord, he picked up a call from Alan.

"You missed your brother," Malachy said. "He's out provisioning his boat for the trip back to Maine. He should be back within the hour."

"He's leaving?" Alan asked. "When?"

"When?" Malachy said, watching a pair of loons fish the harbor. Attuned to shades of meaning in dolphin talk, he picked up a strange mixture of disappointment and relief in Alan's voice. "Why don't you ask him when he calls you back? I'll give him the message."

"Tell me, Mal," Alan said, sounding urgent. "What's his plan?"

"Jaysus," Malachy said. "You want an affidavit? He's departing the dock on the dawn tide. What's the matter?"

"I'll tell you, Malachy," Alan said, sounding short. "Dianne's vacationing up there, and I gave her your number and told her to look you up. I don't want her walking into a big mess with Tim. She doesn't need that."

"She's a grown girl," Malachy said. "Maybe that's just what she needs. You let her fight her own battles. Or make her own peace. It's not for you to control."

"Malachy," Alan began.

"You listen to me," Malachy said. "If she's meant to be yours, you'll know it. Manipulating the situation with Tim won't do you any good. Let nature take its course, let God's will be done, however you want to put it. But don't ask me to get in the middle of your blasted love triangle. I care about all of you too much to do that."

"Okay," Alan said, staring out the window at Hawthorne harbor. He knew Malachy was right. But that did nothing for the knot in his stomach, the fear that Dianne and Tim might see each other after all this time and remember what they'd once had. Alan was far away, and there was nothing he could do.

Eighteen

Traveling across Nova Scotia to the ferry that would take them back to the mainland, Julia had a seizure. Her body went rigid, she bit her tongue until it bled, and she thrashed for two full minutes. Amy began to scream, and the animals hid under the bunk beds. Pulling off the road, Dianne nearly drove the Winnebago into a ditch.

"Julia," Dianne said, trying to hold her. Blood and foam gushed from the girl's mouth, and her eyes rolled back into her head.

"What's wrong, what's happening?" Amy cried.

"Dianne, here's a spoon," Lucinda said, trying to force a spoon into Julia's mouth. "We have to hold down her tongue, keep her from swallowing it."

"Away!" Dianne screamed. "Get Amy out of here and leave us. I know what I'm doing, Mom. That'll just hurt her. Give me room. Get out!"

Shaken, Lucinda helped Amy out of the camper. Dianne heard their voices, Amy's upset and Lucinda's soothing. Dianne had never been through this before, but Alan had warned her to watch for seizures. He had told her never to put a hard object into Julia's mouth while she was seizing, that it could break her teeth or damage the soft tissue. Dianne just had to hold her and wait. The seizure was stopping. Her muscles let go. Her body twitched once more. The child sighed.

Dianne wanted to weep. She wanted to apologize to her mother for yelling, make sure Amy was okay. She wanted to set everything straight that Julia had kicked over—a bottle of fruit juice, a pile of guidebooks. But she knew something bad was happening, and she had to get Julia help.

"Mom!" she called.

Lucinda and Amy came back, standing in the doorway.

"Drive, Mom," Dianne said, rocking Julia. "Get us to a hospital."

Nodding, Lucinda climbed behind the wheel. Nova Scotia was rural, breathtakingly beautiful. Fields of flowers spread in all directions. Distant blue hills stretched toward the sea. Tall pines cast long shadows on the road, but there were no towns in sight. Amy read the map, directing Lucinda as best she could.

"Honey," Lucinda said after ten miles. "Tell me what to do."

"Find a pay phone," Dianne said. Julia lay in her lap, trembling. Her breathing was shallow and her skin tone was pale. Her eyelids flickered as if she were having a deep dream, but she wasn't waking up. Dianne felt primal fear in the pit of her stomach, as if she and her baby were lost in the wilderness.

The next rest area had four phone booths. Lucinda held Julia with Amy hovering beside while Dianne ran out. Her heart was pounding, and she felt so panicked, she couldn't think straight. Did Canada have 911 emergency service? Where would she tell them to come if they did? Hands shaking, she remembered Malachy's number.

"Is that you again?" he snapped as soon

as he picked up the phone. "I thought I told you, it's between your brother—"

"Malachy!" Dianne cried. "It's Dianne Robbins. I'm on Nova Scotia, and—"

"Slow down, Dianne," he said, his voice changing. "I know you're here. I heard all about it. Now, what's wrong? What has you sounding so frightened?"

"My daughter's sick, Malachy," she said. "I need to get her to a hospital, and I don't know where to go—"

"Tell me where you are."

Dianne did her best. She told him about coming into Pictou, heading west toward Yarmouth, mentioned the last road sign she remembered.

"You want Halifax," he said. "It's the best, and you're as close to there as anywhere. Can she make it, dear? What's her condition?"

"She's unconscious. She had a seizure. Her pulse is fast, and her . . ." Dianne burst into tears. Malachy's voice was deep and kind, and he made her think of how her father might sound.

"I know she's had the devil of a time, poor little girl," he said. "You just get her to Halifax, and we'll meet you at the hospital. Are you okay to drive?"

"I think so," Dianne said. "For Julia I'll make myself be okay. Thanks, Malachy. I'm glad I called you."

It was only after she hung up that she stopped to wonder who Malachy would be meeting her with, and how Malachy knew she was in the province in the first place.

"Lunenburg's nice," Tim said, coming aboard the tugboat with an armload of groceries. "Pretty town. Maybe I should—" One look at Malachy's expression, and he knew something was wrong.

"It's your daughter, Tim," he said. "She's in a bad way."

"Julia . . ." Tim said, stunned.

"Dianne just called."

"Called *here?*" *Tim asked.*

It had to be serious. Malachy's ruddy face was mournful, his eyes deep and sad. Of course, he was Irish, and he could look tragic at anything, at thick fog or melting ice cream. Still, Tim swallowed hard and waited to hear. He had been running a long time, but that didn't mean he didn't think about her, that baby he'd left. His heart was pounding.

"She has suffered," Malachy said.

"I know."

"Suffered terribly," Malachy said. "Life should never be so hard for a little girl. It shouldn't be so hard for any mother, or any father. Put those groceries down and come on."

"What?" Tim asked.

"You're coming to Halifax with me. That's where they are."

"Halifax, Nova Scotia?" Tim asked, shocked. "Just up the road?"

"That's the place," Malachy said. "Your brother Alan's been busting a gut trying to contact you. Dianne's vacationing up here, and the child had a seizure. Now, grab your jacket, and—"

"I can't," Tim said in shock.

"The hell you can't," Malachy said, shoving his arm. "She's your daughter, Tim. Whatever Dianne's facing, she'll face it better with Julia's father by her side. Put your stupid pride aside and act like a man. For the girl's sake."

"I want to," Tim said. "But I can't." He was picturing Dianne the last time he'd seen her: nine months pregnant, tears flowing down her face, pulling on his hand as she'd begged him to stay. He had spent eleven years sailing away from that memory, and he could only imagine what she had done. For her sake, he didn't want to enter her life again.

"For God's sake, Tim," Malachy said. "You're a ghost as it is. Haunting your own life! What kind of life is it, pulling lobster pots for any company'll have you? You've got no family, not even Alan anymore. You've got no home port, you've got no love. This is your chance, Tim."

Tim stood frozen, eyes closed as if he could block the whole thing out.

"Are you blind, son? It's a miracle, that's what it is. Your daughter needs you right now, and you're right here. You think these things happen by chance?"

"I don't know," Tim said.

"Well, I do," Malachy said, glaring at him. "And they don't. This is your chance, maybe your last chance. If I could have one minute, one *second*, with Gabriel and Brigid, I'd give the rest of my life. Grab it, Tim!"

Tim's throat ached. What if Malachy was right? What if he could see Dianne, meet his daughter? Why had he come to Canada right now, this summer, this week? Why had they?

"Halifax?" he heard himself ask. "That's where they are?"

"It's where they're heading," Malachy said. "Come on."

Tim shook his head. He knew he wasn't going.

"Come on," Malachy said, tugging his arm.

Tim yanked himself free.

"Knock it off, Malachy," he said. "Leave me alone."

"*Leave you alone?*" Malachy roared. He drew himself up to full height and he bellowed without shame or restraint. "Your daughter's up here and needs you now and you're too spineless to show up for her?"

"I can't—" Tim said.

"You shit," Malachy said. "You spineless shit."

"Mal—"

"This is it," Malachy said. "This is the end. The day you wouldn't give your child blood I blamed it on you being young and far away and panicked. But this. She's right here. Right up the road—"

"Don't blame me, Mal," Tim said, feeling

like a little boy, like the days his mother would abandon him for the bottle. "Don't say—"

"Don't say the truth?" Malachy spit out the words. "I wash my hands of you. I loved you like a son, but no son of mine would ever be so weak. You're a fucking coward, Tim McIntosh, and I never want to hear from you again."

"Hey, Malachy," Tim yelled, running after the old man, tears flowing down his red cheeks.

"Leaving you alone," Malachy said, walking faster. "That's what I'm doing. You asked me to, and I'm obliging. Go to hell."

Tim stopped where he was, on the dock in Lunenburg harbor, and sobbing with rage watched the man he had considered a father these last twenty-some years leave him behind forever. As if he were just a piece of trash.

By the time they reached the hospital, Julia was stable. Whatever had caused the seizure was not recurring. She was awake and fairly alert. She kept opening her mouth as if to speak. She had resumed her hand wringing, but her movements were weak and listless. Dianne held her for as long as she could, but the doctors wanted to take her down to do an MRI.

"Can I go with her?" Dianne asked.

"It would be better for you to wait here," the technician said. "But she'll be fine. We'll bring her right back to you."

Watching them wheel Julia away, Dianne held her hand over her heart. She felt terrified, and she hated to think what Julia was feeling. Dianne wanted to be with her through everything, so when Julia was afraid, at least her mother would be there. Looking around, Dianne wished for her *own* mother, but Lucinda had taken Amy down to the cafeteria.

Dianne felt very nervous. The waiting room had a television playing, but she couldn't concentrate enough to watch. By the nurses' desk she saw a row of pay phones. Almost without thinking, she walked over and dialed Alan's number. Her hands were trembling.

"Dr. McIntosh's office," Martha said.

"Martha, it's Dianne Robbins. I have to talk to Alan."

"He's with a patient, Dianne. May I have him—"

"Martha," Dianne said, gripping the receiver with both hands. "I can't wait. I need him right now. Please, get him. Please—"

Within ten seconds Alan was on the line. He said hello, and Dianne's eyes flooded with tears. Her body shook with repressed sobs, and the relief of hearing his voice made everything flow out.

"Alan, it's me," she wept. "We're at the hospital. Julia had a seizure, and they took her down for an MRI. Our trip has been so wonderful, she was having such a good time. . . ."

"Is she conscious?" Alan asked gently. "Is she breathing?"

His questions had a calming effect on Dianne. They were specific and practical, and they made her think and focus.

"Yes," Dianne said, "to both. By the time we got here, she was starting to seem more like herself again."

"Trying to catch invisible butterflies?" Alan asked, describing Julia's arm waving so perfectly, Dianne could almost smile.

"Wringing her hands," Dianne said.

"That's our girl," he said.

They had been through bad episodes before, and they had survived them all. No one knew Julia's case like Alan. Dianne had watched these new doctors take one look at her deformities, shake their heads with pity. To Alan, Julia was his beautiful little niece. He was acting very calm, so Dianne could fall apart.

"Who's the attending there?" Alan asked, writing down his name and number.

"Should I let them admit her?" Dianne asked, feeling very far away.

"I'll talk to her doctor," Alan said. "But I'd like to get her back home as soon as possible. Is there an airport nearby?"

"I'm in Halifax," Dianne said as she remembered seeing the airport symbol on the map.

"If she gets the green light, I want you two on a flight home today. I'll meet you in Providence and we'll take her straight to Hawthorne Cottage."

"Oh, I hope they let her," Dianne said, her eyes filling again. The idea of home and Alan was so comforting, she could hardly stand it. The thought of Julia being admitted way up here, in a strange hospital with doctors who didn't know her baby's history, filled Dianne with fear. She began to cry. Her head down, she jumped when she felt the hand on her shoulder.

It was Malachy Condon. Larger than life, the old man stood there in his faded overalls and chamois shirt, white hair hanging in his eyes. His face was lined and tan, and his eyes were filled with compassion. Dianne didn't know him well, but when he put his arms around her, she leaned against his chest and wept.

"Who's that, Dianne?" Alan asked.

Dianne tried to respond, but she couldn't speak. Malachy smelled like tobacco and salt air. She knew he had lost a child, and his kindness had reduced her to blind tears. He was patting her back, offering to take the phone from her. Gulping, she handed it to him.

"Dianne?" Alan asked. "Are you there?"

Her sobbing filled the air. Alan had heard a male voice, and his heart was skidding. Was it Julia's doctor with bad news? Or was it Tim? Dianne had said she was in Halifax; that was just an hour from

Lunenburg, and for all he knew, Tim was with her.

"Who's that, now?" came the deep, Irish voice.

"Malachy?"

"It's me, Alan. I just arrived."

"What about Tim?" Alan asked. His mouth was dry, his heart banging out of his chest. Julia was in the hospital, and all he could think about was his brother getting his hands on Dianne. She was so vulnerable, so worried. All she needed was for her child's father to come waltzing in and save the day.

"Gone," Malachy replied, the word sharp and clipped.

"What d'you mean?"

"What I said. Gone."

"He was there this morning when I called," Alan said, wanting details. Had Dianne and Tim talked? Was he simply gone from the hospital or gone from the area? The questions raced through his brain, but then he realized Malachy was standing there with Dianne just inches away, that he was trying to protect her from the truth.

"Has he seen her?" Alan asked. "Did they talk?"

"No," Malachy said.

"Has she seen him? Does she know he's there?"

"Jaysus," Malachy said, exhaling.

Alan took a breath of his own. He lowered his head, leaned his forehead on his desk for a moment. He was acting crazy, out of control. He was a physician, and his niece was in the middle of a crisis. Instead of keeping his cool, he was acting like an idiot in love.

"Have you seen Julia?" Alan asked. "Do you know the status of her condition?"

"That's better," Malachy said calmly. "But no, I haven't. And I don't."

"Do me a favor, Mal," Alan said. "Stay with Dianne. I'm going to call up there, talk to the doctors, see if I can arrange a transfer to Hawthorne. Will you see to it Dianne has all the help she needs?"

"Aye."

"A ride to the airport, an ambulance for Julia if it seems warranted?"

"Aye."

"Her mother's with her," Alan said. "Is she right there?"

"Not that I can see," Malachy said. He must have turned to Dianne, because Alan could hear him soothing her. "There, dear.

There now. She's a little angel, your Julia. She's in the best of hands now. The doctors of Halifax are first rate. Maybe not what you're used to in your own backyard, but nearly. Nearly. Where's your mother, now?"

Alan strained to hear. The sound of Dianne's voice was soft and sweet, and he could hear the fear and tension. He wanted to jump through the telephone, hold her in his arms. He wanted to bring them home himself, and it took everything he had to pull himself back.

"Her ma's out with Amy," Malachy said. "Whoever Amy might be. Seems they've got a young dog that needs walking."

"Orion," Alan said.

"Aye," Malachy agreed. "That's just what she said."

Staring at the Wall, Alan found Julia's baby picture and stared at it. Dianne had been holding her on her lap: There were her two hands, laced across the baby's chest. Her head had been cut out of the picture, but her fingers were long and slender, the most graceful hands Alan had ever seen. His eyes filled with tears, and it took him a moment to find his voice.

"Take care of her, Mal," Alan said.

"Count on it, Alan," Malachy said.

"Can you put her on?" Alan asked.

Malachy paused. "She's not quite able to speak just now, son. You take care of those telephone calls, and I'll look after things on this end. All right, then?"

"All right," Alan said.

Blood was thicker than water.

Hanging up the receiver, Alan thought back ten years and felt the same black rage at Tim he had felt then. Julia was one, in the hospital for a third surgery on her twisted bowel, and she had needed a blood transfusion. Blood supplies were down, and there'd been a shortage of her type at Hawthorne Cottage Hospital.

Using the Coast Guard and fishermen friends, Alan had tracked Tim down. He was in port in Newport, Rhode Island, hardly an hour's drive away. Leaving Dianne and Julia at the hospital, Alan had jumped into his car and headed north on I-95.

Most of the time, Tim docked at Long Wharf. Alan knew his habits, and he'd driven slowly along the waterfront, staring at the fishing boats docked there. No sign of the *Aphrodite*. He had swung down Thames Street, checking all the wharves, found him rafted at Bowens to a dragger out of New Bedford. From then it had just been a matter of checking the bars.

Hunched over his beer at the Ark, Alan found Tim telling his sad story to a girl with blond hair and tight jeans. She was wearing a halter, and her breasts pressed against the fabric. Tim was shaking his head, and although Alan couldn't hear the words, he knew the story was about Dianne and Julia, but it was designed to garner pity for Tim.

"Hey," Alan had said, clapping his hand on Tim's shoulder.

"Hey, Alan," Tim had said, happy to see him. He pushed back the stool and grabbed Alan in a bear hug. From Tim's steadiness, the way he moved, Alan could tell he wasn't drunk yet. That was good.

"It's Julia," Alan said. He'd wasted an hour driving up, and he had the same drive back. He wanted to get this done fast. As he faced his brother, looked into his sunken eyes, he realized he was doing this as much for Tim as for anyone. Giving Tim the chance to be a good guy and redeem himself.

"Your daughter?" the blond asked with sympathy as if she had heard the whole story—Tim's version anyway.

"Yeah, my little girl," Tim had said.

That was too much for Alan.

"Listen, Tim," he said roughly. "Let's step outside. I have to talk to you."

Disgruntled, Tim followed him into the street. It was summer, and Newport was teeming. Thames Street was ten-people deep, and Tim and Alan stood in the middle of the sidewalk being jostled right and left.

"She needs blood," Alan explained. "She's having a series of operations, and they're running low on her type. You and she have the same, type A, and I want you to donate some."

"Give blood?" Tim asked, red-eyed from last night's drunk, but still close to sober tonight.

"Yes," Alan said.

"Do I have to go to the hospital?" Tim asked, looking afraid.

"If you'd rather," Alan said. He knew Tim had a fear of hospitals. It was deep and primal, and it had been there ever since Neil had gotten sick. "But we can do it anywhere. I brought the equipment with me."

"What, you have it in your bag?" Tim asked, looking down. For the first time he seemed to notice Alan's medical case. Alan had everything he would need in there to help Tim do the right thing: needles, the IV line, the blood bags. Tim could give a pint. He could lie on his back in Alan's backseat or they could go to Tim's boat.

"I want to make it easy for you," Alan said. "She needs blood, and you're her best bet."

"I just had a beer," Tim said, trying to get out of it. "That's not good, is it?"

"A beer's not that much," Alan said.

"I've never given blood before," Tim said, looking pale.

"Don't be scared," Alan said, trying to be kind. "It won't hurt."

"Hey, man," Tim said. "I don't know. I don't think it's a good idea." He gazed at Alan's eyes, but he had to look away. It wasn't quite dark yet. He stared down the alley between two buildings across Thames Street at a deep red sunset. Two passing girls in tight skirts caught their attention, and he watched them go by.

Alan shoved him up against the wall.

"Don't look at them while we're talking about Julia," Alan said roughly.

"Cut it out, man," Tim said, breaking Alan's grasp.

"She's your daughter," Alan said. "She could die, Tim."

"Don't," Tim said, welling up. "Don't lay that on me."

"You've got to help her. Don't you want to? You think you'll be able to live with yourself years from now if you don't help her now?"

"It would be a blessing if she died," Tim hissed, the tears spilling over.

"No," Alan said, standing tall. "I don't see it that way, and neither does her mother."

"Her mother. I left town and you got what you wanted," Tim said, spit flying from his mouth. "You got Dianne. You get to be her hero. So don't act so high and mighty to me. You're the doctor—you can't get type A blood?"

"I wanted to get it from you," Alan said.

Tim shook his head. The cords stood out on his neck, and he was breathing as if he'd run a race. Tears were running down his face.

"I'm not giving blood. Is that what you want to hear? So you can feel better than me? I'm against it. I don't go to the doctor

myself, I haven't been once since Neil died.
I don't give a damn what you think. If you
think I'm superstitious or a moron, I don't
care. Okay, Alan?"

"Yeah, Tim," Alan said, backing away.
"Okay."

"Good, man," Tim said, shaking.

The crowd closed around them, pushing
them apart. The red sunset had faded, and
now it was dark purple and dull gold. Alan
remembered the air being cool for summer.
Standing there, he watched his brother take
a few steps backward, then turn to go into
the bar.

Maybe Tim had been right. Maybe Alan
had just wanted to feel superior. Somehow
he had known Tim wouldn't give his blood.
Saving Julia was just an abstraction to him.
He had already thrown her away; why would
he want to save her life? But underneath his
altruistic motive driving to Newport, Alan
had discovered something about himself.

He was capable of hating his own brother.
His own flesh and blood. Speeding across
138, he gripped the steering wheel, hating
Tim's guts. For being a coward who could
turn away from his own suffering child. Alan
felt ashamed to be related to the grown-up

Tim McIntosh. He bore no resemblance whatsoever to the boy Alan fished with off the sandy shores of Cape Cod.

Now, a decade later, Alan felt the same way.

Everything was arranged. Dianne and Julia would fly home, and Lucinda and Amy would drive. Dianne was beside herself. She didn't know which panicked her more, worry about Julia or the thought of her mother and Amy on the road by themselves. Lucinda kissed and hugged her, trying to reassure her.

"Don't you think I'm a good driver?" she asked.

"It's not that," Dianne said. "But I'm worried about emergencies. It's such a long way. With me along, we were two drivers—in case one of us had trouble. What if you get tired? Or if you get lost?"

"I'll be there," Amy said. "I'll talk nonstop and make her drink lots of coffee."

"We'll be fine, love," Lucinda said, holding Dianne's face in her hands. Dianne teared up, staring into Lucinda's eyes. "And so will you."

Amy was gathering Julia's things together, and when she called Dianne to check the bag, Dianne edged away. Alone beside the Winnebago in the airport parking lot with Malachy Condon, Lucinda faced him.

"You're the famous mentor," she said.

"I've been called worse things," he said.

"You did a good job with one of them," she said. "The McIntosh boys."

"Don't remind me," he said. "I'm on the verge of fucking murdering the other one."

Shocked, Lucinda's mouth dropped open.

"I'm sorry," he said, seeing her expression. "This has been an eventful day, and I'm not myself."

They stared at each other. Lucinda wasn't used to checking men out, but she did find Malachy quite attractive. He was big and husky, what Emmett would have called a man's man. His blue eyes were deep set, soulful, and contrite at the same time.

"Don't worry about it."

"I do," he said, shaking his head. "I worry greatly. See, I'm alone ninety-five percent of the time, with no one but dolphins to talk to. Bad habits develop. My own dear wife, Brigid, would've let me have it good for swearing in the presence of a lady." Digging into his breast pocket, he came up with a cassette tape. "Here's a peace offering. For you to listen to on your ride home."

"Thank you," Lucinda said, smiling, taking the tape.

"The other thing is," Malachy said, "I did love those boys. Both of them. In some ways, it was easy to love Tim more. He makes such a mess of things, your heart can't help going out to him."

"Mine can," Lucinda said.

"I tried to talk him into coming to Halifax with me," Malachy said. "But that was just me fightin' a losing battle."

"Today?" Lucinda asked, shocked. "Tim's here? In Nova Scotia?"

"He was," Malachy said.

"What for?" she asked. "Did he ask about Dianne and Julia? What did he say when you asked him to come—"

"Ah, what's the difference?" Malachy asked with both palms turned upward. He sounded like a peacemaker, calm and serene, his voice tinged with regret and, underneath, something much darker. "He can't do what he can't do."

"No, he never could," Lucinda said, her

eyes blurring as she watched Dianne prepare Julia to get her on the plane.

"I wrote him off," Malachy said, his own eyes filling with tears. "God help me, I don't understand such indifference. I told him never to call me again, and I meant it. The selfish bastard. Heartless man."

"Tim McIntosh made his own hell," Lucinda said, patting the big man's hand as they heard the loudspeaker call the flight, watched Dianne hovering anxiously by Julia's stretcher. "Because he doesn't know what this life is about."

The horizon seemed a million miles away, a place Tim would never get to. He steered the *Aphrodite* south-southwest. Occasionally he passed a deserted island, majestic with rocks and pines. Or he would see another lobster boat on its way somewhere, probably going home.

Tim McIntosh felt the weight of failure on his shoulders. He had seen the disappointment, disapproval, hatred in Malachy's eyes when he said he wasn't going to Halifax.

Hatred—from Malachy. Tim had felt it from Alan and Dianne before. But never Malachy.

He shuddered. Burning bridges. Tim had become a first-class expert.

Dianne and Julia were here now, and they needed help. What had Malachy called it—a miracle? In a way, Tim could see that it was. A series of events, coincidences, two people near the same place at the same time. All Tim would have had to do was say yes, follow Malachy up the coast, make everyone happy. All would be forgiven.

Instead, Tim had followed his gut.

Deep inside, he knew Dianne would rather spit poison than look at him. She would be justified, that was for sure. Driving into the wind, Tim's eyes were streaming. The sun made him squint. He grabbed a cap from under his seat, pulled it on with the visor down low. He was crying, and even out there, where there wasn't another human being for miles, Tim didn't want to be seen.

A shot of tequila would help, but Tim wasn't much of a drinking man anymore. He wanted to escape these feelings he was having. He had thought that pulling out of Lunenburg would provide relief, and it had, but not enough. Thoughts of Dianne and their suffering child stuck to him like static. They raced through his mind, telling him what a bastard he was.

He could have stayed.

When Tim was feeling his worst, that's what came to mind. He hadn't had to run in the first place. Twelve years ago, when he and Dianne had gotten the bad news, Tim could have planted his feet beside hers and said they'd go through it together. He could have held her hand, he could have been present at the birth. Instead of leaving her to Alan . . .

Tim blamed his parents. They had screwed life up for him. They'd been so wrapped up in Neil's illness, in chasing their tails to escape it. So many times Tim had stared at the horizon, waiting for his dad to sail into Hyannis harbor from wherever he went to get away. If not for Alan, Tim would have been the loneliest kid in the world. He had missed his father so much.

Tim had never wanted to be that kind of father. A scared loner who'd rather sail the seas than sit at the kitchen table hearing about his wife's bad day. Or good day. Tim should have known he wasn't meant for home life. He had needed Dianne's love so badly; why did she have to get pregnant at all? And why had the baby turned out to be so sick? Tim had had no choice except to leave.

No choice: That's how Tim saw it. Life had left him no choice. It gave him a dead brother, damaged parents, a sick child. Tim was a rogue, and life had handed him tragedy. People found that romantic. He'd show up in portside bars, drink his whiskey, tell whoever would listen about his wife and sick baby. He'd make himself out as a scoundrel, wait for the bar women to say no, he wasn't a bad person, he was just too sensitive for the horrible thing that had happened. Then he'd tell them about Neil, wait for them to put it together.

They'd see too. Of *course* he had done what he did. Life hadn't given him a fucking choice! Losing his brother had hurt too much; he wasn't going to stick around and wait for his baby to die too. No one with half a heart could fail to see that.

No one but Dianne, Alan, and now Malachy. The three people who should care about Tim, love him, feel sorry for what he was going through. But no, not them. Thinking about it, his heart was pounding.

The injustice and unfairness of it all hit him hard.

It made some people feel good to look down on others. That explained a lot of it. Dianne and Alan had been self-righteous for a long time. Malachy though . . . Tim shook his head and wiped tears from his eyes. That hurt him bad, the fact that Malachy had turned against him.

Tim still remembered the look in Alan's eyes the night Tim had refused to give blood. Down in Newport, with all of humanity streaming by, his own brother had looked at him as if he were a piece of shit. Wasn't that what Malachy had called him just a few hours ago? Shit?

Steaming away from Nova Scotia as fast as he could, Tim was traveling fast and far, but he wasn't going back. He wasn't passing anywhere near his family. Tim McIntosh was a loner, and he was going to stay that way. He had been planning to head for Maine, but that wasn't far enough. Maybe New Hampshire, Massachusetts. Maybe he'd skip New England entirely, give up lobstering, try crabbing in the Chesapeake. Or shrimping in the Gulf.

The sun was still bright, and Tim's eyes

were still watering. Cap pulled low, he just held his wheel and steered dead ahead. The sea was empty and endless. At least that was how it looked from the *Aphrodite*'s bridge. Julia would be okay. She'd made it this far, she'd get through this thing and be fine.

Nineteen

Alan met the plane from Nova Scotia. A steady rain was falling, with low gray clouds blanketing all of southeastern New England. He stood on the tarmac by the ambulance, wind blowing his hair and jacket, staring at the sky.

When the airplane came into view, it teetered like a dragonfly. It looked vulnerable and fragile. The wind rocked it from side to side, and Alan's heart was in his throat as he watched the pilot land the small twin-engine at Providence's T. F. Green Airport.

Dianne and Julia were first off the plane. They stood at the top of the stairs, Dianne holding Julia in her arms, shielding her head against the weather. Two stewardesses were trying to urge them back, keep them inside. The EMT crew was ready, taking the stretcher out of the ambulance, but Alan ran up the steps ahead of them.

"You came," Dianne said, looking at him with wide eyes.

"You're here," Alan said, putting his arms around them both.

They formed a small triangle, their heads all touching, and Alan's throat was tight and his chest was constricted and his mind was full of prayers and thanks that they had made it back to him safely, that Julia hadn't died in Nova Scotia, that he was holding them both as close as he could.

"Beeee," Julia said, her voice the barest squeak.

Taking his niece from Dianne, Alan looked into Julia's eyes. A change had occurred. Usually wide and observant, today her eyes were narrow and listless, sticky with sleep. Alan's heart lurched at the difference. The EMTs clambered up, ready with the stretcher, but Alan waved them back. Head down against the rain, cloaking Julia with his jacket, he followed Dianne down the plane stairs to the waiting ambulance.

• • •

Dianne waited while tests were done again. She had sat in Hawthorne Cottage Hospital many times, and she knew many of the nurses. They let her use the nurses' kitchen to make tea and instant soup; they insisted she help herself to chocolate pudding, Jell-O, and saltines. Dianne thought of her mother and Amy on the road, wishing they would get home soon. Reaching into her jeans pocket for a tissue, she pulled out pebbles from the black sand beach.

"How are you doing?" Alan asked, sitting beside her. He wore a white lab coat, his stethoscope around his neck.

"Okay," Dianne said, clutching his hand. "Have you seen Julia?"

"She's having an MRI."

"She had one in Halifax," Dianne said, her voice strained. Julia had been through so many tests: blood tests, urine tests, EEG, EMG, MRI, bone scans, muscle tone tests. MRIs were so confining. She was strapped to a board, expected not to move, and she didn't understand what the technicians were saying, when it would be all over, when she could see her mother.

"I know," Alan said. "But we have to do our own. She'll be finished soon. How are you holding up?"

"Oh, *me*," Dianne said, shaking her head. It hurt her to even think of complaining, with everything her daughter was going through. How could she mention a headache, sore back, pain in her heart, when Julia was fighting so hard? "I'm fine."

Alan put his arm around her. Months before, she might have pulled away. She nestled against his chest, feeling his breath rise and fall and trying to let it calm her, take some of the fear away. She stared down at her lap, where he was holding her hand.

"What's wrong with her?" she whispered.

"We don't know exactly," Alan said.

"We had such a wonderful time," Dianne said, remembering their golden beach days, the magical boat ride, the Ferris wheel, the apple gardens, the sand castles they had all built. "Julia was so happy."

"I got your postcard yesterday," Alan said. "It sounds like it was an amazing trip."

"Was it too much?" Dianne asked, holding his hand tighter. "Did I tire her out? Overstimulate her nervous system? Was the trip too strenuous, all that bumping on long roads?"

"No," Alan said. "Don't do that to yourself."

"The seizure happened so suddenly. There was no warning—"

"There never is, Dianne. It's not uncommon with Rett, several of her conditions. We're narrowing down the problem."

"Just like always," Dianne said, bowing her head. "Just like we've been doing all her life."

Dianne knew there was no cure for Julia. She had neurological disorders, progressive in nature, getting worse as time went on. Growth was slowed, muscle tone reduced, eye contact diminished. Dianne had come to see Julia's hand wringing and waving as forms of expression. She knew that as Julia went downhill, the communication could stop entirely. Dianne had always expected that she would be prepared.

"I'm scared," she said, her voice cracking.

"I know you are," Alan said.

"What's going to happen?"

"We don't know. You're going to keep loving her," he said. "I'm going to keep taking care of her. Other than that, we don't know."

Dianne bit her lip. She nodded. Bells sounded in the hall, and the dinner cart rolled by.

"Thank God you're here," she said in a voice so quiet she didn't think Alan could possibly hear her. "That we had you to come home to."

"Thank God you came home," he whispered back, holding her even more tightly. His body felt solid and strong. Dianne thought of all the times he had comforted her. She had taken it for years, taken his kindness for granted, but now all she felt was overflowing gratitude, and she knew she'd never take him for granted again. She didn't remember ever needing him as much as she did just then.

"How many does that make?" Lucinda asked.

"Let's see," Amy said, squinting at the list. "Prince Edward Island, Nova Scotia—two provinces. Then the actual border between Canada and the United States, that's three. Then Maine, that's four."

They were counting borders, seeing how many they would cross before arriving back home in Hawthorne. Lucinda wanted to keep them occupied, to avoid dwelling on what might be happening to Julia. She could barely stand it herself, and Amy was so nervous, she kept asking how many more miles.

"Is Julia okay?" Amy asked.

"I hope so," Lucinda replied.

"What happened when she started shaking like that?"

"She had a seizure."

"Is that like a fit?" Amy asked.

"Pretty much," Lucinda said.

"I was afraid," Amy said quietly, "when the blood started coming out of her mouth."

"She was biting her tongue," Lucinda said. "She couldn't help it."

"I thought she was dying," Amy said.

"Mmm," Lucinda said, staring at the road.

"Will she, Lucinda? Will Julia die?"

"Someday, honey."

"Someday we all will," Amy said. "Like my dad and Emmett, like Dr. McIntosh's brother Neil. But especially when it's someone young, like Neil or Julia, it doesn't seem right. How can it happen?"

"God decides it's time," Lucinda said. "He decides He needs that person in heaven more than we need them on earth."

"Why does He need Julia?" Amy asked, watching the pine trees go by. "More than He needs me?"

"For one thing," Lucinda said, "it's a mystery. For another, it hasn't happened yet. All we know is that Julia had a seizure and Alan wanted her to come home for tests. She's been through a lot more than this, honey. Julia is amazing."

"I miss her," Amy said, fraying a hole in the knee of her jeans.

"I know. This big old Winnebago seems empty without her and Dianne. But we have to focus on the positive things. We had a great vacation, all together, with wonderful memories to keep our whole lives."

"We have our souvenirs." Amy grinned, thinking about the withered apples they'd gathered from the old orchard, drying in the galley.

"Exactly," Lucinda said. "And we're heading home to people we love. Dianne and Julia . . ."

"My mother," Amy said.

"Alan."

"I call him Dr. McIntosh."

"Mmm," Lucinda said.

"I didn't want vacation to end, but now I can't wait to get home," Amy said.

"Neither can I," Lucinda said.

The highway was easy to drive. There wasn't much traffic for a late summer day. Lucinda had joined an informal caravan of motor homes heading west on the Maine turnpike, driven mainly by old folks like herself. She spied a couple about her age. The man had white hair like Malachy Condon's, and that reminded her of the tape. She had stuck it somewhere . . . Feeling the visor overhead, she found it.

Lucinda plugged the cassette into the tape player. Silence stretched out for a long while, and then the music began.

"Dolphins," Amy said.

Lucinda nodded, driving along.

The beautiful crooning filled the air. The dolphins' songs were ancient and pure, achingly sweet, full of loss and love. Listening, Lucinda thought of her family.

She imagined dolphins swimming together, who had been together since the beginning, who had lost babies and husbands and fathers. Her eyes filled with tears, and as she brushed them away, she glanced over to see Amy doing the same thing. They were heading for home, where they belonged.

• • •

Dolphins were magical. Amy listened to their music and knew they were underwater angels. They swam and frolicked, leaping straight out of the sea with joy. They wore cloaks of silver water that sparkled like diamonds when they hit the light. Dolphins lived in the ocean, but they breathed the air. Had they been people once upon a time?

Amy thought of her father. She had lost him so long ago. For many years she had had a hole in her heart, whenever she thought of how her life might have been if he were with her. Her mother would have stayed happy. There would have been no fights, no misery, no Buddy.

But most of all, Amy would have had her father. She could have grown up as his little girl, being guided and protected through life. He could have helped her to walk, taught her how to ride a bicycle, helped her to do her homework. Russell Brooks had been a good man.

Amy's father was with the dolphins now. She listened to them singing, tried to hear his voice. There was love in the sound. Had her father been a man of love? Had he hated to leave the dock every trip, wishing instead to stay home with his wife and baby? Amy had been that baby. She was his only daughter, his flesh and blood!

Lucinda had spoken of mystery. Amy knew what she meant. Why did life have so many questions and not enough answers? She tried with all her might to block out Amber's hateful words about her father. Amy wanted to trust her own heart, what it was telling her. Could she love her father so much if he was anything less than wonderful?

Amy listened to the dolphins. Love . . .

What was it about love? She was heading home. It was almost time for school to start. What would it be like to go home? She loved her mother so much, but she felt shy about seeing her. Being with Lucinda and Dianne had spoiled her in some ways, for the kind of love that spoke out loud sought the light. She wanted a family that talked to each other. And deep down she was afraid that Buddy would come back.

Buddy had been her mother's boyfriend for a long time. The universe didn't hold many mysteries more confusing than that one. How could a woman love a man like that? As the road slipped by, Amy closed her eyes and tried to let the dolphins teach her all about it, so it would never happen to her.

"Penny for your thoughts," Lucinda said.

"I want to be a dolphin," Amy said.

"Or at least sing like one . . ."

"No," Amy said. "Actually be one. Me and Julia. We could swim free, playing the whole time, go looking for our fathers."

"Oh, honey," Lucinda said.

"They're both at sea," Amy said. "Mine is underneath, hers is in a boat. I love mine so much, Lucinda. I want my mother to remember. . . ."

"Remember what?"

"Being loved by him," Amy said. "When we were all together. When things were good."

"Sometimes remembering the good," Lucinda said, "can be the most painful thing there is."

Amy scrambled out of her seat, retrieved the shriveled apples from the galley, then buckled herself back into place next to Lucinda.

"What good are happy memories," Amy asked, holding the little brown apples, "if they make us so sad we don't want them anymore?"

"When Emmett first died," Lucinda said, "it took me a whole year to be able to look at his picture."

"But you look at it now?" Amy asked.

"All the time," she said.

Amy stared at the apples. They didn't have any pictures of her father up in their house. She had one of her own, tucked into her bureau drawer. The dolphins clicked, their sound friendly and fun. In the background, others cried. She tried to figure out how creatures could be happy and sad at the same time. It seemed to be what Lucinda was telling her, if only she could figure it out.

Twenty

Seizures, by themselves, were not serious, although their underlying causes could be. Julia stabilized enough to go home. She gradually became more alert, her hand waving approaching its usual vigor. Dianne felt overcome with relief. She had been through this before: a bad scare for which Julia had had to be hospitalized, from which Dianne hadn't been sure she would recover.

Alan drove them back to Gull Point. Coming around the bend, Dianne half hoped to find the Winnebago parked in the driveway.

"Mom called from Haverhill, Massachusetts, last night," she said. "She should be here anytime. I can't believe I stuck her with the whole drive home."

"I'm sure Amy's doing a good job as co-pilot," Alan said.

"I should have known it was just a seizure," Dianne said, looking over her shoulder at Julia. "I should have kept my cool, known it was going to pass."

"You know what I wish?" Alan asked, looking across the seat. "I wish you'd know what a good mother you are. The word *should* does you no good here. You made a call, and it was the best one."

Dianne looked down at their hands, fingers laced together. She glanced up at Alan's eyes, and she saw them looking back with warmth and curiosity. She settled back in her seat, smiling at him across her shoulder. Those kisses in the library had stayed with her all through Nova Scotia. The breeze blew through the car, making her skin tingle.

"It's good to be home," she said.

"The marsh is beautiful today," he said, staring out at the golden blanket of reeds. After yesterday's storm, the air was cool and clean. The breeze blew briskly, moving the tall grass as if it were one shimmering sheet of gold.

"That's not what I mean," Dianne said.

"No?"

"I missed you," she said.

Alan smiled as if she had just made him the happiest man in the world. "You have no idea how much I missed you."

"Julia and I never went away like that before," she said. "We had an incredible time. I'll have to tell you all about it, show you the pictures we took, the souvenirs we brought back. We saw the most beautiful beaches in the world, but you know . . ." She smiled, and she had to swallow hard in order to go on.

"What?" he asked gently.

"It felt so good to see you at the airport."

"Didn't you know I'd be there?"

Dianne tilted her head. "Yes. I did. That's the amazing thing. I knew you'd be there— you always are."

"That's what family is for," he said.

"What it's supposed to be," Dianne said, looking from Alan to Julia. She thought of Tim, and she thought of the bad things that had happened under Amy's own roof.

Then it was time to get Julia into the house. They carried her inside, opened the door and windows to air the place out, let the September breeze blow through. Julia was happy to be home. She looked around and patted the air. Dianne sensed her looking for Lucinda, Amy, and the animals.

"They'll be home soon," she said.

"Gaaa," Julia squeaked.

Alan carried Julia upstairs. Dianne walked behind, and she watched how tenderly he cradled the child in his strong arms. He brought her into her room, and he put her down on the changing table. Dianne stepped forward to take over, but Alan was already doing it.

It was such a little thing, watching him change Julia. She kicked her heels against the pad, her hands moving weakly. Alan talked to her the whole time, and she stared at his face. Dianne watched him bend down to kiss her. Reaching up, Julia grabbed his glasses. Julia's gnarled fingers were wrapped around Alan's steel frames; they were momentarily frozen face-to-face.

"Daaa," Julia said.

"I'm glad you're home," Alan said. "You can't believe how much I missed you."

Dianne caught her breath. She reached for his hand, and he took her in his arms.

• • •

Later that night Lucinda, Amy, and the animals were safely back home in Connecticut. The air was as chilly as it had been in Canada, so Dianne lit a fire. Lucinda popped the dolphin tape into the player. They all sat around in non-moose pajamas, updating each other on the last week, reliving their trip. Stella lay on a windowsill, and Orion curled in front of the fire.

"I'm just glad to be in a house without wheels," Lucinda said.

"Yes, I like this campground best of all," Dianne said.

"Dleee," Julia said weakly.

Amy lay beside her on the floor, staring into the fire.

"You're quiet, Miss Brooks," Lucinda said, nudging Amy with her toe.

"Julia sounds different," Amy said.

"She's just recovering from the seizure," Dianne said. "It's normal for her to seem quiet for a week or so."

"Oh," Amy said, still looking worried.

Lucinda didn't want to say anything, but she agreed with Amy. Julia seemed listless, as if some of the life had gone out of her.

Her eyes weren't as bright as before, and her voice seemed to be coming from far away. Julia's regression had always happened in small ways. When she was one, she was able to pick up small toys. But by the time she was two, she had begun to lose her pincer grasp.

Her interest in toys had gone. The hope that her sounds would become words had begun to fade. She was slipping into her own world, and nothing Dianne tried could pull her back. People would urge Dianne to stimulate her more: read to her more often, make her play with building blocks, wrap her finger around Dianne's and get her to pull herself up.

"Don't they think I know?" Dianne would cry. "Don't they think I read the parenting books, that I want to be a good mother?"

"You're a wonderful mother," Lucinda would tell her, but Dianne would cry anyway. It was as if she believed she had failed Julia in some terrible way before birth, cursed her with bad genes, driven away her father.

"Gaaa," Julia said now.

"Hello, sweetheart," Lucinda said. "Do you feel better? Did you have a marvelous vacation?"

"Gaa," Julia breathed.

"When she says 'Ga,' she's saying 'Granny,'" Amy said.

"That's what I've always thought," Lucinda said.

"I wonder how many of our castles are still standing," Amy said. "We built them pretty high up, away from the tide, didn't we?"

"The tide has a way of finding all sand castles," Lucinda said. "It seems to be the tide's mission on earth."

"Maybe not all of them," Dianne said, nuzzling Julia's chest.

Amy had been gazing at Julia, but now she blinked, taking in Dianne and the way she was playing with her child. Lucinda watched Amy watch the mother and daughter, and she wondered what serious thoughts were going through her mind. Their time together had convinced Lucinda that Amy was sensitive, compassionate, and smart, and that she loved using her imagination. Lucinda would try to convince her to enter the library's short-story contest in November.

"Penny for your thoughts," Lucinda said. "All of you."

"Me?" Dianne asked. "I was just thinking I can't wait to get the pictures developed.

That it's good to be home. And that Julia's beautiful."

"Maaa," Julia murmured.

"School starts in a couple of days," Amy said. "That's what I'm thinking. I can go home. I want to and I don't want to, all at the same time."

"That's how I feel about you," Dianne said, squeezing Amy. "I'm excited for you, going home, but I also want you to stay here with us."

"Let's not talk about it tonight," Amy whispered. "Let's just have our homecoming and not think about being apart."

"How about you, Mom?" Dianne asked. "Penny for *your* thoughts."

"I was just thinking," Lucinda said, remembering their long drive, the endless beaches, the shooting stars, the thrill of seeing the *Anne of Green Gables* island home. "That I have the best girls in the world. All three of you."

"Gaaa," Julia said, quietly singing along with the dolphins on the tape.

The next day Amy was to go home. She woke up very early, when it was just getting light. Violet shadows covered the yard and marsh, and the sea beyond was a darkly glistening mirror. Standing in the window of Julia's room, Amy listened to her friend's crackly breathing and wished they could go out and play.

Being away from home had made Amy even more independent than before. She padded downstairs, ate a Pop-Tart, and took Orion out for a walk. With bare feet she ran down the path to the marsh. The old dinghy was there, full of water from all the rainstorms. Bailing it out, she got Orion to jump in.

The Hawthorne marshes smelled like nowhere else. They were full of sea life, warm and muddy, fresh and clean. Amy had learned a lot about confusion on her trip to Canada. The knowledge had sunken in that life could be more than one way at the same time, that a person could feel many emotions and not go crazy.

Rowing across the dark water, she felt grown-up and ready for she-didn't-know-what. Going home, she wasn't sure what she would find. She wanted to get something from the beach, store it up inside herself, make her ready for anything. Pulling on the oars, she wound up the marsh toward the lighthouse.

Beaching the rowboat on the lee shore, she wedged in the anchor as Dianne had done. Orion bounded across the dune, barking at the sun as it rose out of the Atlantic as if it were his own red ball. He whiskered through the beach grass, uncovering fish heads and driftwood. Amy walked along, picking up sea glass, whelk egg cases, and an old wine bottle.

When she got to the lighthouse, she fell to her knees. The sand felt damp on her legs, and she began to dig. Glancing up, she made sure it was the right place. The high tide line was a good twenty feet away. The only reason the sand there was damp and hard was that runoff from the lighthouse had packed it down.

"This one's going to last," she said to Orion.

He barked.

Amy had learned a lot about sand-castle building, watching Dianne and Lucinda. She wanted this one to be as sturdy as a fortress, as lasting as one of the playhouses Dianne made in her studio. It seemed magically symbolic to her: If she could build a sand castle that would survive, Julia would be healthy. Julia would live.

Amy packed the sand extra hard. She made thick walls topped with careful crenellations. She strengthened the foundation with rocks. She fortified the walls with driftwood buttresses. Patting the sand, she thought of building a safe house. A place where no one could ever be hurt.

In a few hours Amy would be going home. The thought made her a little afraid, but why? Her mother loved her; her mother was getting well. Amy's fear was nothing compared to what Julia must be feeling. To have a seizure like that: to bite your tongue and twitch from head to toe without being able to stop. To get on a plane for your first time, go up in the air, zoom through the sky, not knowing if you were going to fall. To have words that no one understood, to have your voice get so weak, people could hardly hear.

The castle was finished.

Orion barked, running in joyous circles. Amy's legs were cramped from kneeling, so she began to run after the dog. All her pent-up energy came out, and she whooped like a puppy, saying things no human being could ever understand. The red sun balanced on the waves, sending rose and lilac ripples into the beach.

The castle was strong. It wasn't beautiful like the ones they had all built on Prince Edward Island. It wasn't delicate and enchanted like some fairy-tale castle high in the mountains, deep in the forest. It wasn't like the castles Amy had seen in movies, the ice-cream-like castle that stood in the middle of Disney World.

It was Julia's castle. It was strong and sturdy and full of hope. Amy had lain awake, worrying that the castles they had made in Canada might have washed away, leaving nothing of them behind. That wouldn't happen here. For extra measure she pulled a postcard and pen out of her jacket pocket and wrote a note. Jamming the card into the bottle Orion had found, Amy walked to the water's edge.

Arm back, she flung the bottle out as far as it would go. The bottle bobbled on the waves, but Amy hadn't stuck a cork in it, so it started to sink. She wanted it to. Staring at the waves, she remembered Dianne teaching her to bodysurf at this very spot. It was the perfect place to build her castle, send her note.

Dear Daddy,
I love you. When I hear the dolphins singing, I wonder if you can hear. I believe you can. Most of all, I want to know you can hear this. Help us, Daddy. Help Mommy be better, help me be good, help Julia get well. She's my friend. If a sand castle can last, so can a girl. I love you. I heard you in the dolphins.
Love, your daughter forever,
Amy Brooks

The bottle sank. The sun rose a little higher, baking the walls of Amy's sand castle even harder. Orion headed back to the dinghy, lay down on the shady side of the dune. Amy knew she was ready to see her mother again, to return home. Pulling on the oars, she rowed across the marsh.

Dianne stood on the bank, watching Amy row across the marsh. She had left Julia inside with Lucinda, wanting a few minutes alone with Amy. She had watched the young girl leave earlier, heard the oars as she slipped away. The water was glass calm. Wisps of mist rose from the surface.

Grabbing the bow, Dianne helped Amy tie up the boat. The dinghy floated with Amy still inside. Dianne gazed down at her. Birds made the only sound. Dianne wanted to say something philosophical and wise, something that would sum up their summer together. But she couldn't speak. She and Amy stared at each other, knowing that this was good-bye.

Dianne climbed into the boat.

Amy sat across from her, her elbows resting on the oars. She sighed. Dianne sighed. They both had tears in their eyes, but they both smiled.

"What a summer," Dianne said.

"I know," Amy nodded, wiping her eyes with the back of her hands.

"And now you're going home."

"Yep."

"Your mother's so happy," Dianne said. "She told me on the phone last night."

"Buddy's gone for good."

"And school's starting. . . ."

"I'm going to do good this year."

"*Well*," Dianne said. "Do *well*." She felt bad, correcting Amy, but she knew if it were her daughter, if it were Julia making the mistake, she'd want to tell her the right way. She glanced over to make sure she hadn't hurt Amy's feelings.

Amy nodded. She looked down at her knees, then up at Dianne.

"Thanks," Amy said.

A school of minnows darted past the boat, speckling the water silver. A blue crab emerged from the mud, waved its claws, resettled in the bottom.

"I mean thanks," Amy said, "for everything. Every single thing. You didn't have to do it all."

"Oh, I wanted to," Dianne said, her chest aching. She thought of everything they had done together, of how much joy she had felt because of Amy. Amy had brought Julia out of herself in ways Dianne had never imagined, she had helped Dianne to see her own daughter as a different kind of girl, a real eleven-year-old girl, not just a sick child.

"You did?"

"Yes," Dianne said. "You've given me more than I've given you."

Amy shook her head. "I don't think so."

"Much more," Dianne said. She looked across the seat at Amy's freckled face. She saw a girl with warmth, humor, and deep intelligence, and she knew Amy would be a wonderful woman.

"When I go," Amy said, her green eyes wide open, "can I come back?"

"Anytime you want," Dianne said.

"I knew you'd say that," Amy said, nodding.

"I don't know if it's possible for one person to have two homes," Dianne said. "But if it is, I want you to feel that this is one of yours."

"I do already," Amy whispered.

Twenty-One

Rummaging through the back of her truck for two quarts of white paint, Dianne found the old birdhouse. She had taken it from Alan's house the day she'd brought him soup, thrown it into the truck bed, and forgotten about it. Now she carried it inside her studio. Propping the birdhouse against her desk, she stirred the paint and put one coat on a little gazebo she had built for a young girl in Noank.

Julia sat in her chair, dozing. Her body curled inward, her knees drawn up, her hands pulled into fists and held close to her heart. Stella rested on Julia's tray, with Julia's forehead pressed into the cat's back. Orion lay with his chin on his paws. Dianne had music on, singing along. While the paint was drying, she decided to look at the birdhouse.

It was a bluebird house. Dianne had made it for Alan twelve years earlier. She remembered taking measurements from a bird book, using a one-inch bore to cut out the hole. The wood had weathered to silver. The nail holes, where it had been attached to the tree, were dark red with rust. The perch had broken off, and the entrance hole had been pecked and widened by bird beaks.

Undoing the hardware that held the roof down, Dianne broke the hook and eye. She looked inside and found a nest filled with three speckled eggs. The nest was coarsely woven of twigs and brown grass, lined with downy feathers and strands of hair. Very carefully Dianne reached in to remove the nest.

"Maaa," Julia said, waking up.

"Look, honey," Dianne said, walking over to show her the nest.

Julia blinked her eyes. Her skin looked as drawn as wax. Her head swayed only slightly, not with the same verve and passion as before. Her hands seemed tired; they clasped and unclasped as if Julia didn't want them to be seen. Stella stretched, slid off the tray, and climbed up into her basket.

"It's a bird's nest, Julia," Dianne said.

"Baaa," Julia squeaked.

"Birds live in here, just like we live in our house." Taking Julia's hand, she ran her fingers over the rough twigs.

"Dleee," Julia said.

Cupping one of Julia's hands, Dianne placed one of the eggs on her palm. The egg was small, no bigger than a large acorn. It was cream-colored, speckled with brown and gold. Julia's fingers closed around it loosely, as if she wanted to make a protective cage.

"A baby bird lives in there," Dianne said.

"Maa . . ."

"A chick," Dianne said, remembering the ride she, Julia, and Amy had taken during the summer. "A feathery, peepy little thing."

Julia tilted her head. She supported the egg, her hand in the air. Dianne gazed at her chick, holding an egg that would never hatch. She wondered how many birds had made their nests in that birdhouse she had built Alan, how many bird families he had watched fly in and out.

"Maa," Julia said, lowering her hand. She was tired. Her head sank down, chin resting against her chest. Gently Dianne removed the egg from her hand. She placed it back in the nest and then moved the nest to her desk. Alan's birdhouse needed a few repairs, and while the paint on her other job was drying, Dianne set about to make them.

Amy and her mother had to get used to each other all over again. Amy got off her school bus the first day and felt the familiar tightness in her stomach as she climbed the steps. Her house looked the same. The siding was peeling off at the corners, the same broken flowerpots lay under the front bushes, the grass was a little too long. But Buddy's car was definitely gone, and that gave her hope.

When she walked inside, she found her mother sitting in the living room, smoking a cigarette. But she smiled at the sight of Amy, leaving her cigarette in the ashtray as she stood up.

"Hi, Mom," Amy said.

"How was your day?" her mother asked.

"Good," Amy said. "I like my English teacher."

"English was my favorite subject."

"We're reading myths," Amy said. For some reason, she felt nervous, as if she were making small talk with a shopkeeper. Her mother had set a box of Twinkies out on the table. Her eyes kept darting to them, as if hoping Amy would just rip into them. But Amy's stomach was turning over too much to feel hungry.

"What's your favorite myth?" her mother asked.

"Well, the one about Orion . . ." Saying the name, Amy got choked up. She had left the dog at Dianne's. Not because she didn't love him, didn't want him with her. But she knew the memory of her house would be too awful, too Buddy-filled, for the puppy to bear. The dog was sensitive as it was, and life in a cage or under the bed was only a few weeks old.

"Tell me about Orion," her mother said.

"He was a Greek hunter," Amy said. "Of great charm and handsomeness, beloved by Artemis. She accidentally killed him. Her sorrow was so horrible, so huge, that she placed him in the sky, along with his dog, Sirius."

"Would you like a Twinkie?" her mother asked.

Amy hesitated. Here she was, in the middle of telling her mother about her favorite myth, which also happened to be her favorite constellation. In science they were studying astronomy, and she had learned that two of the sky's brightest stars, Rigel and Betelgeuse, were in Orion. Amy had never loved school like she did this year, she wanted to talk all about it, and her mother was offering her Twinkies. Dianne and Lucinda would be listening for all they were worth.

"I wanted to tell you about Orion," Amy said quietly.

"I heard you, Amy," her mother said. As she lifted her cigarette, her hand seemed to be trembling. The curtains were open, and light flooded their shabby living room. Amy's mother was wearing clean jeans and a sweatshirt, and there were deep lines of worry and sadness in her face.

"Can you imagine how terrible she felt?" Amy asked, wanting her mother to get it. "Artemis? Killing the person she loved most in the world?"

Her mother nodded. She brought her cigarette to her lips, took a long drag, and blew out a cloud of smoke. Amy's chest filled with rage. She wanted to talk about stars and myths, the love of a woman who had sent her husband to the sky, and all her mother cared about was Twinkies and smoking.

"Mom, it's important," Amy said. "It's tragic, what happened to them, how Artemis felt—"

"Oh, I know how she felt," Tess said.

Amy stopped.

"Killing the person she loved most . . ." her mother said. "I know about that."

"What do you mean?" Amy asked.

Her mother reached out her hand. It was a small hand, and with it hovering in the air, Amy could see that her mother had put her wedding and engagement rings back on. She had stuck them in a drawer during the years with Buddy. Her mother's hand was waiting for Amy to take it, and slowly Amy did.

"What do you mean?" Amy asked.

"There are so many ways of killing," her mother said. "You can kill a person's spirit without even trying. Was I doing that to you? That's what I talk about with my doctor sometimes. I'm so afraid . . . I'm sorry, Amy."

"You didn't hurt me," Amy said. "You hurt only yourself."

"I want to believe that," Tess said. "It's not really true though. What one person does in a family affects everyone else."

"I'm alive," Amy said.

"And wonderful," her mother said. "I'm so glad you like school this year."

"I do," Amy said. "I want to get A's this year. I want to write stories in English. I want to learn every myth." She didn't want her life to be like the myths though. She didn't want her mother to be like Artemis.

"I'm glad you're home with me."

"Me too," Amy said, feeling guilty because it was both the truth and a lie.

"You are?" her mother asked, the worry line between her eyebrows sharp and deep. "You're glad to be here?"

Amy took a deep breath. She thought of her other home, the one with Dianne and Julia, and her throat ached. She was glad to know she could go there anytime she wanted, but she belonged here. This was where she wanted to be.

"Yes. And I'm glad the curtains are open," Amy said.

• • •

One evening in early October, when the
leaves had started to turn yellow and russet,
Dianne asked her mother to look after Julia.
She put on brown velvet pants and a rust
silk shirt and walked out to her truck. A half
moon hung in the sky behind mountains of
purple clouds. The wind blew, and the cloud
mountains were tinged with gold fire.

Driving into Hawthorne, Dianne felt calm.
She took her time, noticing everything.
Because it was chilly, she was wearing a
thick velvet shawl, but she had the truck
windows open. She heard the marsh
grasses rubbing together, the waves cresting on Landsdowne Shoal. The world
seemed sensual and mysterious, and
tonight Dianne felt like part of it.

Since returning from Canada, she had
been completely absorbed in Julia's care.
Recovery from the seizure was slow, but
Dianne was patient. She had trusted she
would know when Julia was well enough to
leave her with Lucinda for an evening, and
tonight was the night.

When she reached the town, her heart
began to beat a little faster. At the same

time, she drove more slowly. She wanted to take her time. She had the sense of doing the absolutely right thing. She had made a wish during the summer, and she had taken her time, letting it come true. Her life was changing tonight, and she wanted to remember every detail: the maples red and yellow in the streetlights, pumpkins on front porches, the sharp chill in the night air.

Alan's house was dark. For a minute she thought he wasn't home. But his Volvo was parked in the side yard. Lights were on in the kitchen, around back. The oak tree where the birdhouse had hung stood in the yard, its branches spreading overhead, the brown leaves rustling in the wind.

Dianne rang the bell. It took a few seconds, but then she heard his footsteps. They came slowly through the house, getting louder. He opened the door wearing chinos and a loose white shirt. With the light at his back, it was hard to see his expression. Dianne registered surprise at first, but then he took her hand and she forgot to pay attention.

"Hi," he said.

"I brought this back to you," she said,

handing him the birdhouse. "It fell out of the tree. You probably didn't notice—"

"I noticed," he said.

Instead of turning on the lights, he led her into the bright kitchen. He had just finished his dinner and had been doing the dishes. Standing by the counter, he looked at the birdhouse. Dianne had rubbed the weathered wood with a cloth, polished it to a soft silver. She had replaced the rusty hinge, attached a new hook and eye. Using a fine birch twig, she had restored the perch. She had sanded the entry hole, smoothed the wood so the birds wouldn't catch their feathers going in.

"I made it for bluebirds," she said.

"I'm not sure I ever saw a bluebird use it," he said.

"There was a nest inside," she said. "With eggs. I checked the bird book. I think they belonged to English sparrows."

"Where's it now?" he asked, lifting up the roof. "The nest?"

"In my studio," she said. "I kept it."

Now her pulse was racing faster. She felt very calm and incredibly excited. The cool air made her skin tingle. The way Alan looked at her told her he was feeling it too.

His hazel eyes were gold-green, expectant. She stepped closer, knowing what she wanted. After all this time she finally knew.

"I wanted to see you tonight," she began.

"I'm glad," he said.

"Are you surprised?"

"I should be," he said after a moment. "But I'm not."

Dianne nodded. He set the birdhouse on the counter, and he put his arms around her. She felt their toes touching. Gently he pushed her hair back from her face. It had grown long during the summer, and it was light blond from all those days in the sun. Brushing every strand back, as if he wanted to see her face, as if more than anything he wanted to look into her eyes, he held her so tight.

"I've waited for you," he whispered. "Since the day I met you."

Dianne tried to breathe. She thought of Tim once again, but this time she pushed him away. Dianne had come to Alan McIntosh after twelve years of fighting him.

"What made you come tonight?" he asked.

"I knew I had to," she said. "Ever since we got back from Canada. On Prince Edward

Island, I thought about you all the time. I thought about the walk we took. . . ."

"Down by the harbor," he said. "To see your house."

"My house." She smiled, thinking that her father would be happy to hear that. "Yes, I thought about that. How I've never shown it to anyone else. How happy I felt to be with you."

"It was a great night," Alan said.

"How we danced," Dianne said. "Surrounded by library books."

Alan waited. Dianne stared into his eyes, knowing that no man had ever looked at her like this before.

"And how we kissed . . ." Dianne whispered.

Alan touched her cheek. He watched her for a few seconds as if he were giving her a last chance to pull back. She wasn't about to, and in fact she stood on her toes to meet him halfway. He wrapped his arms around her and drew her into an embrace that seemed to surround her body with his, and he kissed her.

Somewhere in Alan's house there was a window open, because a breeze blew through the kitchen and made Dianne shiver and moan. She pressed her body closer to Alan's. He was protective and big, towering over her, but Dianne had the sense, deep inside, of wanting to shelter him.

Kissing him, she saw stars and constellations, but from the ends of her toes she felt the fiery desire of wanting to keep this man in safety: to do for Alan McIntosh what he had done for her and Julia all these years.

For every time when Dianne had raged, when she had wept over his brother, when she had pushed Alan away. For every hour he had sat by her side, holding her hand while they waited for Julia to come back from tests or surgery or physical therapy. For every minute he had listened to Julia's heart, rubbed her cramped and twisted muscles, never doubted that she needed hugs and affection as much as any other little child. For all those things Alan McIntosh had done, Dianne stopped kissing him and leaned back in his arms.

She stared at him without looking away, feeling so fierce in her heart that she could barely speak or move. When she opened her mouth, she knew exactly what she was going to say; she just couldn't imagine how it had taken her so long to get there.

"I love you, Alan," she said. She had never said those words to him before, not even as a sister-in-law or a friend.

"I've always loved you, Dianne."

"I don't know why," she whispered, holding his hands tightly, pressed between both of their chests.

"Don't even ask, then," Alan said. "I don't."

"The way I've acted . . ."

"You've acted fine," he said.

"I came over tonight because . . ." Dianne said, her voice breaking.

Alan seemed to hold his breath, waiting for her to go on.

"I wanted to be with you," she said.

Alan nodded. He kissed her forehead, her eyebrows, the tip of her nose. His glasses were crooked, and she reached up to straighten them. As she did, she smoothed his brown, wavy hair behind his ears. She could hear the words she had just said hanging in the air, and she couldn't imagine what to do next.

Alan could.

Lifting her into his arms as easily as he had ever picked up Julia, he carried her down the hallway through his house, through the rooms Dianne remembered from many years ago, and he carried her up the stairs. They went down the dark hallway, into a bedroom at the far end.

His bedroom was spare. A brass bed, an oak writing table, a braided rug, handmade by Dorothea, on the floor. Dianne knew the table had been Malachy's—he had given it to Alan when he'd moved from his house to the tugboat. She already knew Alan's things so well, and she felt moved by their history. When Alan laid her down on the white coverlet, she remembered that it had once covered his grandmother's bed in Nantucket.

Moonlight slanted through the window. It cast lavender shadows around the room. Alan lay beside her, touching her face so tenderly, as if he couldn't believe she was actually there. She could feel his breath on her cheek, and they stared at each other for a long time without smiling or blinking or saying a word.

He brought his mouth to hers, and they kissed. Dianne caught her breath, their lips parting as they held each other tight, grasping as if they could save each other from falling off a cliff. Dianne felt shy at first, feeling him touch the lines of her body. She hadn't been touched in so long.

"It's okay," he said, sensing her unease. "We'll go as slowly and easily as you like."

"It's been . . ." she began. "I've never . . ." She didn't know what to say. It's so easy to forget your body when you're never touched. She was strong, maybe a little too skinny. Would he think she was ugly, unattractive?

"Just know I love you," he said, stroking her back, gazing into her eyes. "Let it start from that."

Dianne nodded. She kissed him gently, her eyes open, willing herself to trust. This was so different from times with Tim—she'd felt crazy, wild, out of control then. Right now she was being guided by love, by her own desires, by the knowledge that Alan would never hurt her.

Alan kissed her neck, the top of her shoulder. Dianne shivered, holding his hand, feeling the sensations all through her body. "Just know I love you . . ." he had said. She thought of those words, and she *felt* them: They unlocked something inside her, and it all came pouring out.

"Alan," she said, reaching for his arms. His

body was strong and hot. She wanted him so badly now, and she didn't even know where to start. Her hands trembled as she felt his muscles, running her fingers down his chest. Twelve years of passion had been stored inside her, and she kissed him hungrily.

They unbuttoned each other's shirts, reaching inside to hold each other close, skin to skin, feeling their hearts beating hard. As Alan slid his hand between the velvet of her trousers and the silk of her panties, Dianne felt so frantic, she couldn't breathe. She trembled, reaching for his zipper.

He helped her out, guiding her hand, slowing her down. She wanted him inside her that second, with no time to wait or explore or take their time, but he trailed her body with kisses, very slowly, making her be patient. Dianne writhed, feeling his hot lips against her skin.

Alan's body was strong and firm, and with his pants off she felt the muscles of his thighs straining against the fabric of his shorts. She felt so conscious of their differences: Her legs were so smooth and his were so hairy, her breasts were so full and his chest was so hard. He kissed her everywhere with tenderness and love, making her arch her back and moan out loud.

"I can't wait," she said.

"Then you don't have to," he whispered.

He cradled her with his arms, rising above her. She reached up to hug him, feeling the heat of his back with her hands, hungrily opening her mouth as he leaned down to kiss her. She guided him inside her, her legs already shaking. Trembling, she tried to lie still, but she couldn't.

"Dianne," he said.

"I can't believe . . ." she said, stars flashing behind her eyes. She grasped his body, feeling their heat as he moved inside her. They belonged together. She had never felt so right in her entire life. She had lived a lifetime for this moment, holding this man, hearing him say her name over and over. She couldn't believe it was finally happening, and neither could Alan.

"Oh, God," she said. "Oh, please . . ."

"Always, Dianne," he said, his mouth hot and wet against the crook of her neck. "We'll always be together."

"Alan," she said, clutching him for all she was worth.

They came together, Dianne sobbing with an emotion she had never known existed. It was joy, sorrow, love, and wonder, nameless and incredible, simple and complicated, all at the same time. Tears were flowing down her neck, into the pillow under her head. Alan was rocking her, telling her he loved her, that he'd never leave her, that this was how it was meant to be.

"I know," Dianne cried.

"At last," Alan said, rocking her, rocking her.

"I'm sorry—" Dianne gulped, "—that I'm crying."

"Oh, don't be, sweetheart," Alan said, cradling her, kissing the tears from her eyes and her cheeks and the base of her neck. It was only then, when she reached up to touch his face, to thank him for his tenderness, that she realized that his face was wet too. That he'd been crying along with her, feeling the same new nameless, extraordinary emotion that had rocked her from the inside out.

An emotion all their own, that they had invented themselves.

"Oh, Alan, I love you," Dianne said. "Love. Love . . ." Because she didn't know what else to call it.

October was a beautiful month. It felt like an extension of summer. The days were warm, sometimes hot. The nights were chilly, never quite cold. On his Wednesdays off, Alan would drive over to Dianne's. They would bundle Julia into a sweater and jeans, and he would row them across the marsh.

Fall was the best time to go to the beach. They had the whole place to themselves. The water was green and clear, and the waves broke gently, as if they were saving all their force for the winter storms that would come later. Alan would run, and then he and Dianne would swim, keeping their eyes on Julia as they dove through the waves.

They touched each other constantly. Once they had started, they could not stop. Alan loved the softness of Dianne's skin, the intensity of her love. She had told him about her new emotion, and he knew what she meant. It was the buildup of all their years together, of wanting each other and not being able to act on it. It was deep, and it filled him with joy, but it wasn't all happy. Because of all the lost time.

Sometimes Alan couldn't believe his life. He would be lying in the sun, Dianne's head on his chest, and he would shudder, realizing that they could die at any moment. He'd have to feel her heart beating against his just to know that they were together, that all this was happening. Why now, why this year? The waves rolled in, the questions kept coming. Alan trained himself not to answer, not to even try.

All he had to do was love her.

"I didn't know you liked the beach so much," Dianne said one day.

"I never did," he said.

"You used to spend your Wednesdays running to the library," she teased.

"Now I run on the beach instead," he said, hugging her. "Wherever you are, love. Wherever you and Julia are."

"Gleee," Julia said. Her head lolled against her chest. It had become harder for her to hold her neck erect. The seizure had taken a great toll, and Alan and all her doctors were mystified as to the reasons. Alan was a scientist, a doctor, but he knew that explanations could not be found for everything. Instead, he pulled Julia onto his lap and rocked her in the sun.

Dianne had been lying on her stomach, gazing up at the lighthouse. The first time he'd felt uncomfortable, coming to the lighthouse beach, remembering that this was where he had come with Rachel. But that was in the past. The wasted past, the years without Dianne, the time he'd spent waiting for her to come to him. He wasn't going to squander any more of it with regrets.

"What do you think it is," Dianne asked, shielding her eyes from the sun, "that lets a sand castle last and last?"

"What sand castle?" Alan asked, holding Julia.

"That one up there," Dianne said, pointing up toward the lighthouse.

Half turning, Alan looked. He saw a square pile of sand, looking more like cinder blocks than the castles Dianne, Amy, Julia, and Lucinda had made on their trip. Dianne had shown him pictures, and those sand castles had been amazing and imaginative.

"It's been there for weeks," Dianne said. "I've been watching it."

"Are you sure it's the same one?"

"Yes," she said. "It's crumbling around the edges, but it's definitely the same. Someone must have made it with mortar. I guess being so close to the lighthouse, it's protected."

"The waves don't get up that high," Alan said.

"Daaa," Julia said, brushing his chest.

"It hasn't rained much," Dianne said. "One good storm, and I think it will go."

"We can always build another one," Alan said.

"I like that one," Dianne said. "I don't know why, but I like that sand castle up there."

"Maaa," Julia said, as if she liked it too.

"Oh, God," Alan said, grasping them both. "Don't ever let this end."

Twenty-Two

* * *

Buddy Slain didn't like the word no. No was his least favorite word in the English language. It filled him with bile, as a matter of fact. It seemed unfair, a great injustice, an impediment to his happiness. When a woman said it to him, the bile became poison.

Driving around town, the word *no* rang in his ears. Buddy's ears rang from amplified rock, the music blasting out of his speakers and the music he played in his band every night. They had a gig down by the water-front, in one of the bars Buddy had been drinking at his whole life. Looking into the audience, it pissed him off, it *hurt* him, to not see Tess in the crowd.

Tess wasn't a beauty. She wasn't rich, she

wasn't brilliant, she wasn't anything overly special, but she was his. Buddy had picked her out of a Saturday night crowd four years before, bought her a drink, taken her out of her misery. Everyone knew Tess Brooks was a widow. She was a homebody with a fatherless girl, a depressed woman with nothing much to live for. Until Buddy.

How quickly she forgot!

Just because the state and some fancy neighbors decided to meddle in their lives, Tess had kicked him out. He had to leave so she could see her kid again. Amy was going to cause her problems, and she'd wish she had Buddy there to help straighten them out. Amy could get herself fat; he could tell from the way her face was plumping up. Tess was too easygoing to ride her about it. You had to watch a kid, especially a girl, to keep her from gaining weight. For the girl's own good.

Getting kicked out of your own house was the ultimate no. It didn't matter to Buddy that Tess owned the property, that she had paid off her mortgage with the settlement she'd received after her husband's death. What seemed important was that she had looked Buddy in the face and said "Leave."

For the time being, he was bunking at Randy Benson's condo. Nice place down by Jetty Beach. If Buddy had the bucks for a place like Randy's, he wouldn't be wasting his time on Tess. On the other hand, she needed him. She was a sad sack with a handful for a daughter. Little bitch had run off with his dog—another serious injustice.

Driving around Hawthorne, Buddy drank a beer and nursed his grudges. First he drove downtown, looking up at the medical building, the place where Saint Alan had his office. Saint Fucking Alan McIntosh, the man who could do no wrong. He didn't know where the jerk lived; high-end doctors like him kept their home numbers unlisted and their addresses private. They loved pulling the strings, doctors: getting people dependent on them, then disappearing into the comfort of total privacy so the little people couldn't find them. Buddy cruised up and down the fancy streets of Hawthorne, hoping to find the good doctor.

Giving up for now, next he headed for Gull Point. Slowly driving down the dead end, he peered at the house, the homestead of the witches who'd stirred this hornet's nest up in the first place. The Robbins ladies.

Mother and daughter and freak of nature. Three holier-than-thou bitches who liked to mess up other families because they were unsexed and unsatisfied. Women like that couldn't be happy unless everyone else around was dry and alone, hating men like they did.

Peeling out, Buddy laid rubber all the way up the road, away from Gull Point.

Last but not least, he drove down his street. His *old* street, he thought, remembering the most bitter no of all: *"Leave."* There was the house. A dump compared to the condo he was staying at now. A royal dump. But Buddy was ready to sacrifice. He'd give up his bachelor luxuries—a fridge full of Molson, premium cable, *Penthouse* in the bathroom—to return to his rightful place, if only she'd ask him nice.

Nice, he thought, driving slowly by. *It would have to be nice.* The curtains were open. He could see in the front windows, and he narrowed his eyes, hoping for a glimpse of Tess. She loved him, whether she wanted to admit it or not. They had had plenty of tender moments, their sex was wild, he knew how to treat her like a queen. Sure, his temper got the better of him sometimes, but that was just his passion coming out.

You couldn't make it in rock and roll being Milquetoast. Tell that to Dr. Saint Alan. Buddy was all about fire and passion. U2, that Irish band, had nothing on Buddy. Buddy was metal, screaming with anguish and heartbreak and dying of love. *Dying* of love. Tell that to Dr. Nine-to-Five. Dr. Suburb, Dr. Perfect.

Driving back the opposite way, Buddy slowed down even more. Okay, there she was. Tess was walking outside into the backyard. It was a sunny day, and she had a basket of laundry to hang on the line. Clothespins in her mouth, she hung the clothes. Amy's shirts, her jeans, her underpants. Tess's nightgown, her bra, her panties. Buddy's laundry should be in there. Buddy's laundry needed washing too.

Parking across the street, he felt angry watching Tess hang up wash that wasn't his. It seemed like another no, another way he was being left out. Beyond the anger, though, was love. That's the thing not many people understood: Buddy was all about love. Buddy would die for this woman, no questions asked. He gunned his engine, just slightly. She didn't hear.

"Love you," he said out loud.

Tess pulled the line, hung another shirt. The sunlight turned her hair auburn.

"Love you," Buddy said again. He kept his voice low. He didn't have to shout. That much he knew. If their connection was half of what he thought it was, he barely had to whisper.

"Hey," he whispered, staring at Tess, his eyes boring into her skull.

Some cars passed by. Buddy slouched down a little. He wouldn't want that CWS bitch catching him there. He checked his watch: two-thirty. Amy would be heading home from school. Her bus wasn't due for twenty minutes, but Buddy didn't want to take unnecessary risks.

"Hey," he said again. "Love you. See you, baby."

Tess brushed her hand across her ear as if chasing away a bee. Probably picking up Buddy's vibe, but didn't know what it was. She was okay. She was A-okay. Not beautiful, not brilliant, not the hottest woman he'd ever had. But to Buddy, Tess was all right. She was his.

October stayed mild, and then one day snow flurries fell. One day the temperature plummeted twenty-five degrees. Amy had gone to school in overalls and a T-shirt, but when she got off the bus at Gull Point, she was freezing, running through the falling flakes to the studio. Throwing open the door, she yelled hello. Orion jumped all over her, licking her face.

"Hey, boy," she said, petting him. "Good dog."

No one but Stella and Orion were there. Amy frowned. Had she made a mistake? Usually she visited Dianne and Julia every Thursday afternoon. She missed coming more often, but she didn't want to act like the old days, give her mother the idea that she preferred this family to her own.

Looking up, she saw Lucinda coming across the yard. She was carrying a big bowl. White flurries danced in the wind, brushing the marsh grass and blowing along the ground.

"Where are Dianne and Julia?" Amy asked. "Is something wrong?"

"They're in the house," Lucinda said. "Julia has a cold."

"Just in time for winter," Amy said, looking out the window.

"I made popcorn," Lucinda said, offering Amy some. "It's a tradition Dianne and I thought of when she was a little girl—we'd make popcorn the first snow of every year."

"Because it's white and fluffy?" Amy asked, munching.

"I guess so," Lucinda said. "Because it's festive."

"Can I see Julia?" Amy asked, looking across the yard.

"Um," Lucinda said. Amy knew the answer was no, and that sent a knife into her heart. She felt awful, and she wasn't sure why: Was Julia really sick? Or did Amy feel bad because she was being banished from Robbins family life?

"How come?" she asked quietly. "Is Dianne mad at me?"

"No," Lucinda said. "Not at all. It's just that Julia's lying down upstairs, and Dianne wants her to rest. She gets so excited when she sees you."

"I'm her best friend," Amy said.

"Yes, you are," Lucinda said. They settled down on the window seat, the bowl of popcorn between them, and Amy relaxed a little. She liked being with Lucinda. Their drive back from Canada had made them close, and Amy imagined this was what it would be like to have a grandmother.

"Tell me about school," Lucinda said. "What did you learn today?"

"I wrote a poem for English class."

"You did? Tell me about it."

"It rhymes," Amy said. She felt a little embarrassed. All the other kids were writing in free verse. Flowing diary-type things about getting shot down in love, hanging out at the beach, sad thoughts of suicide.

"Shakespeare rhymed," Lucinda said. "Keats rhymed. Edna St. Vincent Millay, Elizabeth Bishop."

"Amber made fun of me."

"Well, Amber . . ." Lucinda said as if that said it all.

"It's about the apple gardens," Amy said. "Up on Prince Edward Island."

"Really?" Lucinda asked, sounding excited.

"Yeah." Amy felt in her pocket. The poem was there, folded up. She felt like bringing it out, showing it to Lucinda. But she stopped herself.

"I'd love to see it," Lucinda said.

"It's dumb," Amy said.

"Sometimes writing a poem or a story is easier than letting people see it," Lucinda said. "It takes a huge amount of courage to let someone read your work. It's like letting them look into your heart."

Nodding, Amy felt the paper. It was closed in her fingers. She didn't want to hurt Lucinda's feelings by not showing her the poem, but she was too scared to move her hand. Lucinda was exactly right in what she had said, and Amy wasn't that brave.

"There's something I've been meaning to mention to you," Lucinda said. "It's a contest."

"Huh," Amy said, squirming. She wasn't the winning type. Amber had won the Halloween costume contest when they were in third grade, and David Bagwell had won a prize for hitting the bull's-eye at Ocean Beach. Amy had never won anything.

"It's a writing contest," Lucinda said. "Down at the library. Short stories by anyone who feels like entering. Entries have to be in by Thanksgiving; they can be about anything you want, any subject at all, no more than fifteen pages long—typewritten, double spaced."

"I don't have a typewriter," Amy said. "Or a computer."

"We do," Lucinda said, gesturing toward Dianne's desk.

"I'm not really a writer," Amy said, thinking of writers as rich, brainy people at the heads of their class. "I just wrote this poem. . . ."

"That's what writers do," Lucinda said. "That's all they have to do to become writers: write."

"Huh," Amy said, feeling her poem again.

"Apple gardens," Lucinda said gently.

"Like the ones we went to," Amy said. Looking around Dianne's studio, she gazed up at Stella's shelf. The cat was up there, in her basket. Just below, Amy saw a shelf where Dianne kept wonderful things: a bird's nest with eggs in it, some pebbles from the black sand beach, and the four withered apples.

Amy remembered picking up the apples from the ground. They looked smaller now, dry husks. Their trip to Canada seemed a million years before. Life at home had started off so promising, but lately Amy had come home from school and found her mother napping. She had come here wanting to see Dianne and Julia, and she wasn't going to be allowed.

"See, I haven't seen your poem," Lucinda said. "But I'll bet it's wonderful."

"Maybe you're just saying that," Amy said, tears coming to her eyes. "Because you don't want to hurt my feelings."

"I wouldn't lie about a poem," Lucinda said. "I'm a librarian, telling the truth about poetry is a rule I'll always keep."

"Then why would you think—"

"That your poem is wonderful?" Lucinda asked. "I'll tell you why. It's because you have your eyes wide open, Amy Brooks. You see the world real and true, and you watch its people with kindness. If you wrote a poem about an apple garden, it would be filled with your heart. I know that."

Amy's eyes spilled over.

"And any story you wrote would come from the same place."

"Stories are supposed to be exciting," Amy said. "About orphans and islands and, I don't know, families on the prairie."

"Or about lonely girls and beaten puppies and walks through an apple garden," Lucinda said.

"That sounds like me," Amy said.

"You are certainly worth writing about," Lucinda said.

Lucinda passed Amy the bowl, and the girl took another handful of popcorn. Outside, the snow flurries had stopped. The marsh looked brown and still. Amy wondered when the winter storms would come. She thought of Julia upstairs in the house, and she wondered whether her sand castle was still there.

"Lucinda . . ." Amy said.

"What, dear?"

Amy hesitated. She didn't know how to say she wished she could go see Julia, that she wanted to be part of their family again, as she had been during those days last summer. Why did everything have to change? Her throat ached. The four apples looked so tiny, way up there on the shelf. She had to close her eyes to catch their cidery smell, to bring back that day in the garden.

Reaching into her pocket, her hand closed around her poem again. She handed it to Lucinda, and without trusting herself to say good-bye, Amy ran out the door toward home.

• • •

Julia was wheezing. Her eyes were shut, her lids stuck together with yellow crust. Dianne dabbed them with a damp cotton ball. Alan said Julia probably just had a cold. Even so, Dianne felt nervous. She had known Amy was coming over that day, had been looking forward to seeing her, but she wanted to keep Julia isolated. There were so many germs floating around at school.

"How's your back?" her mother asked.

"What?" Dianne asked. "Oh. It's fine."

"It doesn't look fine," Lucinda said.

Dianne had thrown her back out carrying Julia upstairs. She had felt the strain the last few days, but everything had been fine until she'd felt the pop—something in her lower back letting go. She had to hold herself in a strange twist, favoring the right side.

"It's fine, Mom," Dianne said.

Lucinda settled down in the rocking chair. She had her half-glasses on, and she was reading something—a letter maybe. Dianne turned back to Julia, working amber crystals off her yellow eyelashes with the cotton ball.

"What's that?" Dianne asked without turning around.

"It's a poem," Lucinda said. "By Amy."

"Really?" Dianne asked, smiling. "Will you read it?"

"Mmm," Lucinda said, reading intently.

"Mom?" Dianne asked, feeling Julia's head to see if she had a fever. "Will you read Amy's poem to us?"

"I can't, honey," Lucinda said, rocking. "Amy didn't say I could. I'm sorry, but you'll have to ask her."

Dianne nodded. She felt hurt, a pang in her heart. Amy hadn't been over much in the last few weeks, and she missed her a lot. She understood that Amy had her own mother, her own home, but that girl had added so much to Dianne's existence. She had brought Julia to life. Made her laugh, understood her language, treated her like a best friend. If only Julia didn't have this cold, Amy could be visiting with them now.

"Is it good?" Dianne asked, admiring her mother's respect for Amy's literary privacy.

"It's wonderful," Lucinda said, never taking her eyes off the single sheet of lined paper.

• • •

Alan got to Dianne's house late that night. He had come straight from the hospital, from doing rounds. He came whenever he could, spending every minute he could with her. Turning into her driveway, he noticed an old car parked in the dead-end turnaround. Alan walked out to the street to see who it was, and the car peeled out. Alan stood there watching the taillights, unsettled because he had glimpsed the driver, who looked like Buddy Slain.

Lucinda stood in the kitchen, cleaning up. She smiled when Alan walked in, kissing him on the cheek. This was becoming a pattern. He didn't live there, but he was sleeping with her daughter, and Lucinda seemed to accept it. Even was happy about it.

"I saved you some clam chowder," she said. "I'll heat it right up. Salad and bread, a glass of cider . . ."

"Thanks, Lucinda," he said. "That sounds great. Listen, have you noticed anyone parking on the street lately?"

"No," she said, shaking her head. "But teenagers sometimes do. It's a regular lovers' lane down here some nights. The dead end, and all . . ."

"That's probably it," Alan said, peering out the window again. The old car had had a teenage look to it, with rock band stickers on the windows and the muffler hanging by baling wire. He wished he could remember Buddy's car, but he had never paid much attention. "Is Dianne with Julia?"

"Yes," Lucinda said, her lips tightening. "You'd better go on up."

Alan patted her shoulder. He climbed the stairs. The lights were dim, which meant Julia was asleep. Coming down the hall, he could hear her breath. It sounded loud and rattling, as if she were verging on pneumonia.

Dianne sat stiffly in the rocking chair by Julia's bed. She beamed at the sight of him, watched as Alan listened to Julia's heart and lungs with his stethoscope. But when she tried to stand, to give him a kiss, she cried out.

"What is it?" he asked.

"My back," she said sheepishly.

"What happened?" he asked, touching her spine.

"Oh, I pulled something."

"Carrying Julia upstairs?" Alan asked.

"Yes," she said.

Alan helped her to the twin bed where Amy had slept during the summer. Just sitting down caused her so much pain, her face twisted up. Alan eased her onto her side, then onto her stomach. He put the pillow on the floor so she could lie flat.

"How's her breathing?" Dianne asked, her voice muffled.

"A little rough," Alan said. "I brought some antibiotics for her. Lie still."

"Okay," Dianne said.

He pushed her shirt up. It was a faded blue cotton shirt with long sleeves, very soft and frayed, and as he worked it up to her shoulders and his hands slipped along the sides of her back, her skin felt smooth and warm. He began to knead her shoulders, feel along her spine. She flinched sharply.

"Is that the spot?" he asked.

"It hurts," she said.

Alan lightened his touch. He felt excited by her naked back, by the feel of her body. Leaning down, he kissed the back of her head.

She moaned softly. Reaching around, she took his hand. Guiding it to her lips, she kissed the back of his hand. Gently he eased her arms down at her sides, straightening her spine. She drew in a long breath, letting him do his work. He leaned down to kiss her ear. He rubbed hard in places, soft in others. He worked on each vertebra, counting downward toward her sacrum. She sighed with pleasure. Across the room Julia's breathing was coarse but steady.

"That better?" he whispered into Dianne's ear.

"Much," she whispered back.

Alan nodded. The light was warm and low. He was with his family, the girls he loved. He wanted to seem calm, to help Dianne relax. She hadn't just strained her back; she was carrying around a load of tension. But inside Alan was churned up.

He knew that things were getting to be too much for Dianne. Julia was too big for her to be carrying up and down stairs. They needed a room on the ground floor. Things were changing this fall, and they would continue to change. Dianne sensed what they didn't know for sure; she had begun spending almost all of her time with Julia, in the house, away from her studio and her work.

Julia was taking the turn. Alan couldn't

see what lay ahead, but he felt it coming. He looked across the room. She lay on her side, eyes closed, body drawn into a crescent. She was as much his baby as if she'd been born his daughter instead of his niece. His throat ached with the pain of wanting to be her father, to adopt her before she died.

"Oh, that feels so good," Dianne murmured.

"Good," Alan whispered. "Just enjoy it."

"Mmm . . ." Dianne said. Her eyes were closed, face turned to the wall. Alan rubbed her back, drawing the covers up around her sides, her breasts, thinking she might be feeling cold. He wanted to take her into her bedroom, make love to her. But not tonight. Tears had come to Alan's eyes, and he ducked his face to dry them on his shoulder. But they just came back.

"Thank you," Dianne said.

"For what?" he asked.

"For everything. I'm so happy with you. I never thought I could be so happy."

"Neither did I, sweetheart," he whispered.

"It feels like," Dianne whispered, "we're a family."

"That's all I've ever wanted," Alan said, leaning over to kiss the side of her face.

Twenty-Three

Alan ran before work some mornings, and lately he had found himself going a new way. Instead of circling around Hawthorne Park, behind the library and the arboretum, he had started running along the waterfront. Two days in a row, when he should have been keeping up his pace, he had slowed down just as he reached the big white houses on Water Street.

There it was, the house Dianne had always loved. Running past, Alan noticed the tall windows, the ionic columns, the sunporch, the three chimneys. He saw the wide yard stretching into a meadow, the iron fence, the three outbuildings. From the street it was impossible to guess the layout. The house was large, and he wondered whether there were any bedrooms on the first floor.

Alan wanted to find a new place to live. His house was big and rambling, but it had too many memories. He had lived there his whole time in Hawthorne. Many of Alan's girlfriends had stayed over; Tim had bunked upstairs many nights by himself and, after one late party, with Dianne. He knew she felt uncomfortable every time she came over. The place needed a lot of work; and there were no first floor rooms that would be suitable for a bedroom.

Maybe he was just dreaming. He hadn't asked Dianne how she felt, whether she'd consider living with him. But what if she would? They had gotten closer since she had returned from her trip; it sometimes felt as if their uncomfortable past belonged to two different people. He caught his breath, leaning on the iron fence. The house looked great, in perfect repair. Whoever lived in it kept it up well. The side yard had fruit trees, a vegetable garden, stone walls. Flower beds overflowed with chrysanthemums.

He wasn't sure, but he thought the first floor looked larger in back. As if it jutted out in an L, right behind that boxwood hedge.

They could have their bedrooms back there, his and Dianne's right beside Julia's. So Dianne wouldn't have to carry Julia up the stairs. Buying her this house would mean so much more to Alan than ease and convenience: It would mean making her happy, in as real a way as he could.

Starting up again, he ran toward home. It was getting late, and his first patient was scheduled for nine o'clock. He checked his watch. If he sprinted, he'd have time to shower and change and call his friend Nina Maynard at Hawthorne Realty as soon as he got to the office.

Amy got A's on all her quizzes and tests. She had never made honor roll before, but her teacher told her that if she kept working hard, she'd make it this term. It was going to be a surprise for her mother. Amy felt worried about her mother again, about the way she was still in bed when Amy left for school in the morning, sometimes when Amy came home from school.

"Mom!" Amy called, sitting at the kitchen table.

No answer.

"Mom, want some tea?"

When her mother didn't reply, Amy got up and turned on the stove. The weather had turned cold, and something seemed to be wrong with the furnace. Maybe her mother was staying under the covers just to stay warm. Amy couldn't blame her for that.

Amy found herself making excuses for her mother. *Maybe she's cold,* Amy would think. *Or maybe she was awake during the night, couldn't get back to sleep, needs to catch up on her rest.* Depression was hard for Amy to understand. Her mother's doctor had told her it was anger turned inward. Amy's mother felt so guilty for being angry at her father for dying, she directed that rage at herself instead.

"Why does life have to be so complicated?" Amy wrote. Sitting at the table, she was working on her story. It took place in a small house in a town called Oakville that was an awful lot like Hawthorne. Her main character was a twelve-year-old girl named Catherine who had a mother suffering from depression and a sister who had been born with birth defects. When Amy had especially troubling thoughts, she let Catherine think them. To build her hope for the future, she had Catherine go to the beach, to build beautiful sand castles.

"Hi, honey," Amy's mother said, coming out of her room. She was wearing a pink bathrobe. Her hair was flat on the left side, and her cheek had pillow marks. She yawned and lit a cigarette.

"I'm making tea," Amy said. "Want some?"

"Um, sure," her mother said. She took a seat at the table, and her eyes fell on Amy's story. "What's that?"

"My story."

"What's it about?"

"It's an adventure," Amy said, for some reason feeling self-conscious. It was an adventure, only not about the sea, mountaineering, jungles, or space. It was an adventure about a family, lovables and unlovables, who lost each other for a long time and found each other again.

"Sounds very thrilling," her mother said, but she didn't sound thrilled. Just trying to smile, her lips trembled.

Amy didn't know why that should make her feel so mad, but it did. Why couldn't her mother just smile? Why couldn't she be all-out happy? Amy's own anger scared her a little. She felt so much of it. She kept remembering last summer, when she had shoved Amber and the CWS had practically branded her a violent person. On the other hand, Amy didn't want to turn her fury inward, become depressed as her mother had. It seemed like such a fine balance, so she handed the problem over to Catherine, who was also dealing with oceans of anger.

"Are you depressed today, Mom?" Amy asked.

"Oh, a little," her mother said.

"You seem tired. I get worried when you're in bed a lot."

"Don't be, Amy," her mother said. "I'm doing my best."

"Taking your medicine?"

"Yes," her mother said, trying to smile.

"Would it be okay if I brought Orion to live over here?" Amy asked suddenly. "I miss him, and I think Dianne's too busy to spend much time with him."

"I don't know," her mother said. "He was Buddy's dog. . . ."

"Dickie," Amy said out loud, using Buddy's fictional name from her story before she could help herself.

"Who's Dickie?" her mother asked.

"No one," Amy said. But then, because she felt bad for lying, she said, "He's in my story. He's—"

The kettle began to whistle. Amy's mother stood up, shuffled over to the stove. She took the kettle off the burner, took down two cups, poured the boiling water over the tea bags. Amy had been telling her mother about her story, and she had just walked away. Just as if she hadn't been listening to a word.

"That," Amy began, and it took every ounce of effort she had to say the words, "makes me mad."

"What does?"

"When you just walk away," Amy said. Her eyes filled with hot tears, as if the anger in her chest had boiled the tears before sending them out. Amy was so sick of anger, she could scream.

"I was listening," her mother said. "Finish telling me about Dickie."

"It doesn't matter," Amy said.

"Sure it does," her mother said, settling down with her tea and cigarette, giving Amy the most sincere smile she'd seen in a few days.

Why was it never like this with Lucinda and Dianne? Amy and her mother had been talking for less than five minutes, and Amy was ready to screech like an owl. Everything about her mother made her mad! The fact she'd been sleeping, the fact she was smoking, the way she pronounced "Dickie" with a smile in her voice, as if he was a cute little baby instead of a repulsive middle-aged creep.

"Tell me the rest," her mother said.

Amy took a deep breath. She still felt mad, and she didn't like it. Her mother was trying to be nice. For one second she felt like pointing that anger at herself: *You're a jerk, Amy, for being mad at this nice lady who happens to have given birth to you who's doing the best she can.* But wasn't that turning her anger inward, just asking for depression? She'd have to explore this puzzle with Catherine.

"Mom, where are Dad's pictures?" Amy asked instead.

"Photos of Russ?" Her mother said his name.

"Yes."

"Well, I think most of them are in the attic," her mother said. "It was hard for me to look at them. For so long. You know? Because I missed him so much."

Amy nodded. Catherine's father had drowned, and her mother had missed him so much, she'd stuck all their favorite cassette tapes in the basement. When Dickie had found them, he had moved them out to the garage, closer to the garbage.

"Can I put some up?" Amy asked. "In my room?"

"Sure," her mother said. To Amy's amazement, her mother had ground out her cigarette and pulled down the little trapdoor in the kitchen ceiling. The folding stairs came down, and her mother crawled right up. Amy stood at the base, her heart pounding, and she was still there thirty seconds later when her mother handed her down a brown paper bag.

"Pictures . . ." Amy said. This was amazing. Buddy's prohibition on talking about or displaying pictures of Russell Brooks had been so deep that Amy hadn't even known these existed. There weren't many, only three: her father as a baby, at his high school graduation, and in a suit jacket.

"He's so handsome there," Amy's mother said gently, touching her husband's face. "That's from when he tried to quit fishing and take up selling cars. They made him wear a suit and tie, and he told me he was going to choke to death. This was the picture they had hanging on the wall of the showroom."

"Daddy sold cars?" Amy said, her eyes filling with awestruck tears. Her father had been incredible. A fisherman, a car salesman . . .

"Only for a little while. When I was pregnant with you. I was just so scared to have him go out to sea."

"What kind of cars?" Amy whispered.

"Fords," her mother said.

Amy tried to picture the Ford logo. She needed to find it so she could add the symbol to her collection, her most important memories and significant objects. The Ford logo would be right up there with fishing boats, dolphins, sand castles, and withering apples.

"This picture hung on the wall for everyone to see?" Amy asked. She had never realized that her father was so well known.

"Yes," her mother said, fingers trailing across the frame's dusty glass. "Right down there at Brenton Motors. If only he could have stayed with it . . . if only he hadn't gone back to sea . . ."

"Don't cry, Mama," Amy said, feeling her stomach tighten. Tears flowed down her mother's face, dripping all over the picture frames.

"These old pictures," her mother sobbed, holding them. "They bring it all back. He was a wonderful man, honey. Funny and sweet. Nothing like anyone you've ever known."

"My dad," Amy said, arm around her mother's shoulders.

"Russell Brooks," her mother said. "I was Mrs. Russell Brooks."

"Mama, he didn't drink a lot, did he?" Amy asked, getting up all her nerve. She didn't even like to put such a thought into words, but she had never quite gotten over Amber's vicious lie.

"No, honey," her mother said. "Your father never liked liquor. He didn't want his head all fuzzy way out at sea. He didn't drink much at all."

"I didn't think so," Amy said. She touched her father's picture and thought about her story. Nothing like this had ever happened to Catherine. No way could Amy imagine Catherine's mother wriggling around the crawl space, coming out with her father's pictures, one of which portrayed him as a Ford dealer. In a suit and tie! Amy liked the distinction between her and Catherine; she wondered how many others would emerge before the story contest deadline.

The best part was, Amy's anger was all gone. It wasn't raging outward, it wasn't turned inward. For the time being, it was just *gone*. She had just enjoyed being with her own mother, the same way she loved being with Dianne, Julia, and Lucinda. For the first time in ages, she loved her own family as much as theirs.

Lucinda walked down the road to get the mail. Among the catalogues and bills, she found a check from Tim McIntosh, his monthly payment on the loan she and Emmett had given him, forwarded to her from the library. Staring at his handwriting, she almost didn't notice the car. It was a rusty old thing, parked in the turnaround, tires looking as if they could use some air.

Walking over, Lucinda saw that it was empty. She glanced around. Sometimes bird-watchers came down here. There was always a lot of ornithological activity in the marsh, with herons, plovers, blackbirds, terns, and songbirds—especially during the spring and fall migrations. Artists also favored the spot, setting up their easels in the reeds. But Lucinda didn't see anyone around.

Sticking Tim's check in her pocket, she strolled toward the house. Dianne was inside with Julia. They had been inseparable lately, ever since Julia had caught that cold. Alan would come over every night, examine Julia, set Dianne's mind at ease. Lucinda tried to stay out of their way.

She let herself into Dianne's studio. She didn't know why, but she felt like being alone. Lately, with Alan around so much, with his and Dianne's relationship deepening, Lucinda had begun feeling like a third wheel. Maybe it was time she moved to Florida, joined all the other retirees. Or maybe she should fly back to Nova Scotia, listen to dolphins with Malachy Condon.

Lucinda didn't like getting old, but she accepted it. She had heard sixty-five-year-old women say they felt exactly the same as they had twenty or forty years earlier. That when they looked in the mirror, they expected to see young women. That wasn't true for Lucinda. She had earned every wrinkle, every gray hair. Maybe that's why she liked Malachy: He had seemed unapologetically seventyish, every minute of his age showing. He seemed like someone she could talk to.

Lucinda missed talking. The library had been good for that. True, they had talked in whispers, but she and her young librarians had passed the days with gossip and book talk and deep sharing of their lives. For a while Lucinda had thought that was how it was going to be with her and Dianne: more friends than mother and daughter. But that wasn't turning out to be so. She was Dianne's mother to the core, and that was better than friends any day.

Dianne had Alan, finally! Lucinda had been waiting for years for those two to understand they were supposed to be together. She'd hear them whispering at night, when the house was dark and Julia was asleep. Lucinda would read her books, wondering whether they were planning their lives together. She knew it had to be just a matter of time. Didn't it? What in the world would stop them?

And what would Lucinda do when Dianne

and Julia left? Sighing, she sat down at Dianne's desk. Orion and Stella came over to see if she had any food. Reaching into her pocket, thinking she might have a biscuit left from walking Orion, she came up with Amy's poem. Spreading it on the desk, she read it:

The Apple Gardens

On the island, in the sea,
Northward of the gulf stream's flow,
That is where we came to be,
In the spot where apples grow.

Trees of green and walls of stone
Fill the land that I can see
Anne played here till she was grown
Tell me, what will be for me?

Back at home, my mother cries
My father lives beneath the waves
Tell me, does the one who tries
to love, succeed at being brave?

You see, I'm just an apple girl
And someone came and picked me up
She polished me, just like a pearl
And set me in a loving cup

In apple gardens, let me be
Beneath the stars and wind and sky
The constellations in the tree
I'll love my own life, by and by.

Reading Amy's poem, Lucinda's throat ached. She scratched Orion's head. The cat spied the reflection from her reading glasses, pouncing on the moon of light. Lucinda sighed. She was surrounded by creatures as unloved as she had been. Dianne had pulled Stella from a stone wall, they had all taken Amy and Orion from their dark home until some light could flow in. Lucinda related to Amy's poem so much, her hands were shaking.

Lucinda's early life had been so wretched, and when she'd met Emmett and had Dianne, it was like creating her own heaven. What would happen if Dianne got on with her life? Lucinda had never admired old women who latched on to their grown children instead of getting active, and she felt herself in danger of becoming one.

Or of slipping back into her old state, hurting and afraid. Like Amy, Lucinda had been an apple girl. She knew how it felt to be lying on the ground, waiting to be picked up. Although she was on in years, she felt vulnerable, as if she could fall way back down there if she didn't take care of herself now. She pulled the four withered apples from the shelf and set them on the desk. The dry apples looked like faces.

Little people, little apple girls. Leaning over, Lucinda picked out the one that looked most like her. She had the most wrinkles, but she also looked the wisest. In Dianne's workbench she knew there were fabric remnants left from curtains she'd made for the playhouses. Gingham, pink checks, bright solids.

Lucinda would make dresses, turn the dry apples, the unlovable objects Amy had picked up in the apple garden, into dolls. Maybe she'd shorten a leg of her moose pajamas, sew the dolls some. She and Amy had a lot in common. They both liked tangible reminders of who they were, who they loved.

Twenty-Four

✳ ✳ ✳

"It's really amazing that you called me when you did," Nina Maynard said, shaking Alan's hand. They stood in the circular driveway of the white house, their cars parked by the garage.

"I didn't really expect it to be on the market," he said, noticing the house's gleaming paint, the neatly tended gardens, the discreet security system stickers. "The lights are always on at night. It looks occupied."

"The owners inherited it from her parents," Nina said, checking her clipboard. "They live in Los Angeles, he's in the film business, and they had hoped to use this as their weekend and summer house. They held on for five years, but it just got to be too much.

I think they said they made it back for two summers and six weekends."

"They kept it up though," Alan said, stepping around a yew bush, examining a clapboard for termites or rot.

"No shortage of money," Nina said. "The film business must be nice. Anyway, let me figure out the keys. . . . The owners are very careful, they didn't want us posting signs or advertising it. . . . We always get callers asking about these sea captains' houses, but this one just came on the market."

"Are there bedrooms on the first floor?" Alan asked.

"Let me show you," Nina said, brandishing the key. "Come on inside."

They entered through the front door. The wide plank floors were waxed and gleaming. Bright light poured in tall windows. There was a brass chandelier in the foyer, original sconces on the white walls. There was a double living room, furnished with antiques, with a fireplace at either end. The artwork was abstract, too modern for Alan's taste. French doors led onto a stone terrace, its ivy-covered balustrade curving around the back of the house. The view was of the harbor, with boats dancing on the gray waves.

"It's a real whaling captain's house," Nina said. "Built in 1842 by Captain Elihu Hubbard. Notice the windows? They're original leaded glass, mullioned. . . ."

Alan liked the way the glass held the light before letting it through. It seemed thicker than normal glass, like clear silver, throwing small rainbows on the walls and floor. There were bay windows with window seats, and Nina was leaning over to show him something: letters scratched into the glass.

"It says E-L-H," Nina said. "The legend goes, Elihu's wife scratched it into the glass with the diamond he'd brought her from one of his voyages. I don't know what it means, but—"

"Let's see the rest of the downstairs," Alan said. He didn't want to hear any legends about men going to sea, women pining at home. The fact that this house had been built by a ship's captain was no selling point to him; it reminded Alan too much of Tim. If he could keep the story from Dianne, he would.

"Here's the kitchen," Nina said, "Sub-Zero fridge, Garland stove, tiles brought back

from Italy . . . Look at this great center
island, the Jenn-Air grill—"

"Nice," Alan said, smiling. He couldn't
remember seeing Dianne cook, not even
once, not in all the years he'd known her.
But when Nina pointed out the basement,
leading off the kitchen, and Alan went
downstairs and saw the workshop and tool
bench, the windows and door leading
straight out into the yard, he knew Dianne
would love it.

"You asked about bedrooms," Nina said
when Alan ran back up. "We'll go up to the
second floor in a minute. You'll just adore
the master suite up there, but let me show
you this first. I've been calling it the in-law
wing. . . ." She led him around the kitchen
chimney, down a short corridor.

Stepping into the first bedroom, Alan
knew the house would do.

"It's quite spacious, as you can see," Nina
said. "Beautiful wood floors, a working fireplace, glass doors leading onto this private
terrace . . . a bathroom over here . . ."
Following her through the bathroom, they
entered a study. It was fixed up like a den,
with a desk and bookshelves and glass dis-
play cases filled with awards and photo-

graphs of the owners with people like Lauren Bacall, Gregory Peck, Harrison Ford, and Tom Hanks.

"Everyone loves those photos, a little Hollywood right here in gray old New England," Nina laughed. "Isn't this a great setup? Bedroom-bath-study? A great place to come if you have a fight with your wife . . . or to put your parents when they visit. Are your parents alive?"

"No, they're not," Alan said, picturing where Julia's bed would go, her bureau, the rocking chair. He and Dianne would take the other downstairs room; they could hear Julia crying if she needed them. The bathroom was right there, it was all on the first floor, Dianne wouldn't have to carry Julia upstairs.

"I'm sorry," Nina said. "Well, onward and upward. On the second floor—"

"That's okay," Alan said. Gazing out the window, he wondered whether Dianne would miss the marsh. Harbor views were different: constant action, boats coming and going, the wind whipping up the waves, flags flying at all the boatyards.

"It's not right for you?" Nina asked. "Is there something else I could show you? We have a marvelous listing, just came in, for a stunning contemporary out by the quarries—"

"It's right for me," Alan said. "I'm making an offer."

"An offer?" Nina asked. He could see that she was surprised, but she covered it well. She hadn't told him the price yet, he hadn't seen the upper floors or backyard, but he didn't care.

"Right now," he said. "I want to be in by Christmas."

"By Christmas," she said, smiling slowly as she nodded her head. "Deck the halls!"

They shook hands. Alan had a busy afternoon, and he had to get back to his patients. But as Nina got on her cell phone to call her office and get the paperwork rolling, Alan took one last look around—at Dianne's house.

At *their* house.

That night Dianne dreamed of Tim. She'd been standing on the deck of a boat tossing in the waves. It was a storm, a terrible gale, and the ocean was dark and thick. It seemed more like quicksand than water, trapping everything and everyone that slipped beneath its surface. Dianne felt terror because someone she loved was in there. Although safe in the boat, she was yelling for help.

"Please," she screamed. "Help me, help me!"

Where were they, all the people she loved? Keeping her boat afloat took so much effort and concentration, she was afraid to take her eyes off the wheel. She had to trust that they were in the cabin behind her. "They" was a mysterious collection, and she hoped, but wasn't sure, that it included Julia, Lucinda, Amy, and Alan.

Someone had fallen overboard. A single hand reached out of the sea. Dripping with muck and seaweed, it scared her so much. Would she be able to save the person? Or would the person pull her in? She was crying and sweating, almost ready to sail away. But a calm voice deep inside told her to stay, to have courage and follow her heart. Taking a deep breath, all fears and doubts melted away. She reached overboard, grabbed the nightmare hand, and felt Tim pulling her into the sludge.

Then she woke up.

Julia was crying. Getting out of bed, Dianne felt wide awake and shaken. Julia was wet; her nose was stuffed up. Dianne set about taking care of her, going through the motions she went through every night.

"Maaa!" Julia cried, sobbing as if she had had a nightmare too.

"You're fine, love," Dianne whispered. "We're safe, we're on dry land, we're together."

Julia tossed listlessly, as if she felt uncomfortable but couldn't decide where. Her skin was pale, and Dianne held Julia's hands in her own, warming them up. They were as cold as if she'd been swimming in the sea.

"Is she okay?" came Lucinda's voice from the hall.

"I think so." Dianne nodded, still rubbing Julia's hands. "We had bad dreams and woke each other up."

"Want to tell me yours?"

"It was of Tim," Dianne said, shuddering, facing her mother. "He tried to pull me overboard."

"You were in a boat and he was in the sea?" her mother asked.

"Yes. Should I feel sorry for Tim? Is that the message?"

"Sorry for *Tim*?" her mother asked.
Dianne hugged herself. She was cold too.
As cold as Julia's hands, as chilled as a person who had just come through a storm.
Heat was pouring out of the radiators, but
Dianne couldn't get warm. She closed her
eyes and thought of Alan. She knew he
would save her, would never let her drown.
He would do whatever it took.

But she was still ice cold from her dream.
She knew this was the wreckage from her
past, part of what made up the emotion she
could not name. To love Alan so much, she
had to contend with much regret and sorrow. She started to cry, feeling sorry that
she had dreamed about Tim. Feeling grief
that her life had been shaped by such a
traumatic first love.

Amy was on the school bus. She had finished her story, and she was on her way to
Dianne's to use the computer. Amber rode
the same bus, making life extremely awkward. But Lucinda had given Amy some
helpful advice: Always have a book with
you, and when you feel uncomfortable, get
lost in the story.

Amber and David made fun of Amy. They whispered and pointed, and she heard them cursing her out. Amy cared, but she tried not to show it. She was wearing new school clothes and shoes, a present from Dianne and Lucinda. Dr. McIntosh had bought her fresh notebooks, pencils, and pens.

She had a handful of shells and sea glass, from some of the castles she and Julia had built over the summer, in the zipper pocket of her bookbag. Recently she had discovered Madeleine L'Engle and was halfway through *A Wrinkle in Time*. When Amber and David threw gum wrappers at her, she pretended to read as she thought of the short story contest.

Amy had rewritten the story, ending it with Catherine's mother recovering from her depression, giving everyone hope. In her last scene Dickie was gone for good. She had sent him to California for a new job, but then she ripped up those pages.

Dickie was going to jail for what he had done. He had beaten his puppy, Catherine's mother, and Catherine herself. He was a bad man, and in Amy's story he was going to pay for it. Mona, Catherine's sister with birth defects, was just about to learn to walk.

On the last page, Catherine, Mona, and their mother, whose name was Beth, were kneeling on a beach, building a sand castle. The sand was fine and white: Hawthorne sand. Dolphins were singing in the sea, and you could hear their music. Castles might wash away, but love lasted. The mother had pink cheeks, and her hair fell in golden waves.

Okay, so in the story, Catherine's mother had Dianne's hair.

"Sue me!" Amy laughed. "It's only fiction!"

"Huh?" Amber asked.

"Um, nothing," Amy said, embarrassed.

"Talking to yourself and knocking innocent people down," Amber said, drawing on her own wrist with a ballpoint pen. "Really mature."

"I said I was sorry . . ." Amy said, shrinking.

"Hanging out with the retard has made her retarded," David said, only he pronounced *with* "wit." Amy gave him her steadiest gaze, as if his favorite worm had just died, and she pitied him with all her heart.

Amy couldn't wait to win the contest.

From there it would be easy to imagine her poems and stories getting published in magazines. Amber would open *Seventeen*, and there would be Amy's story about the best friend who became a whore-fink. David would open his stupid heavy-metal magazines, the kind Buddy used to get, and he'd see a picture of Aerosmith thanking Amy for letting them use one of her poems for their newest song lyrics.

Jumping off the bus at Gull Point, Amy didn't look back. She tore straight to the studio, holding her breath until she saw Dianne and Julia inside. She felt so relieved, she could have shouted for joy.

"Hi," Amy called, walking through the door and getting her face licked as Orion went mad with happiness to see her. She went straight to Julia, did a little hand dance with her.

"How was school?" Dianne called from her workbench.

"Good," Amy said. "Got a B on my science quiz. It was a high B, though—eighty-eight."

"You're heading for the honor roll," Dianne said.

"I hope so," Amy beamed.

"Noise," Dianne warned, turning on her saw.

Amy played with Julia for a while, but Julia just seemed tired. She didn't want to move her hands much, and she kept resting her head on her left shoulder. Once again, as she had the last few times she'd seen Julia, Amy felt worried. She glanced at Dianne as if to ask her what was wrong, but Dianne had her eye protection on, was concentrating on cutting a plank with her band saw.

The noise was loud. The stereo was on, and Dianne was singing. Amy pushed Julia's chair over to the desk and pulled her notebook from her knapsack. She glanced at Dianne, looking for an okay. Dianne gave her the thumbs-up, and Amy got ready. They had computers in school. She knew how to use them, but she had never done anything like this before. She had never typed up a story she had written herself. Sitting there, she had a lump in her throat.

She started with the title: "Sand Castles."

"Do you think I'll win?" Amy asked a week later, after the story had been typed, the corrections made, the manuscript ready to be submitted to Mrs. Hunter and Mrs. Macomber at the library.

"It's a great story," Lucinda said.

"But will I *win?*"

"You would," Dianne said, "if I were the judge. You wrote a wonderful story and an excellent poem. I'd give you first place."

"Girls, girls," Lucinda said, pretending to be exasperated. "How often do I have to tell you? It's not whether you win or lose, it's how you see the world!"

"You never say that," Amy said, frowning.

"She does, all the time," Dianne said, rocking Julia on her lap. "She just says it in different ways."

"Like what?" Amy asked.

"Like love each other," Dianne said. "Like forgive the people you don't like."

"Buddy?" Amy asked. "Never."

"Then he'll hold you prisoner forever," Lucinda said.

"Ewww," Amy said, shivering. "Buddy holding me prisoner . . . I'd rather eat bugs. But even so, don't hold your breath on me forgiving him."

"Does your mother like your story?" Dianne asked.

"She hasn't seen it," Amy said quietly.

"Dleee," Julia said.

Dianne reached down to hold her daughter's hand. Lucinda watched her wrap Julia's fingers around her own index finger, try to hold them there. Julia's grip slid away, and Dianne pressed it again. Dianne could be so stubborn, Lucinda thought. Had she realized, talking about forgiveness, that she was still swamped with bad feelings for Tim? That dream . . .

"I still hope I win," Amy said. "Even if I'm not supposed to."

"Gaaa," Julia said.

"You really liked the story, Dianne?"

"I loved it."

"Huh," Amy said. "I'm glad."

Lucinda swallowed. She wondered whether Dianne had noticed that Amy had given the mother Dianne's looks.

"Gleee," Julia squeaked.

"See? Julia thinks I'll win."

"I'll tell you what," Lucinda said, staring at the two young girls, thinking back to when Dianne had been that age. "Win or lose, I'm getting tickets for *The Nutcracker*."

"*The Nutcracker* ballet?" Amy asked. "The one on TV at Christmas every year? That's the one you mean?"

"Mom took me," Dianne said. She looked tired, as if the stress of her life, of just trying to hold her daughter's fingers, were a little too much today. "It was one of my favorite things we ever did."

"And now it's your turn to take Amy," Lucinda said.

Twenty-Five

Julia had another seizure. This time it was the middle of a cold November night, and Dianne heard her kicking the walls like a wild horse banging its stall. Flying into the room, she grabbed Julia and tried to hold her hands, to keep her from punching herself in the face. Holding her child, she could hardly stand the choking, garbled sounds coming from Julia's mouth.

"What is it, Dianne?" Lucinda asked.

"Call 911," Dianne gasped. "Call Alan."

Her mother disappeared. Dianne was alone with Julia. The girl's airway was blocked. She couldn't breathe. Had she swallowed her tongue? Choked on something left in her bed? Julia was turning blue. Panicked, Dianne jumped up. Julia was still seizing. Dianne tried slapping her on the back. Something cracked, as if she had broken a bone. Still, Julia was choking. Dianne tried to turn her upside down. She was frantic, listening for sirens. How long since Lucinda had called? Lifting Julia into her arms, Julia's fists pounding her face and her heels kicking her legs, Dianne tried to carry her downstairs.

Dianne's thoughts were flying: Help was downstairs. Her mother was there, the ambulance was coming. Struggling with Julia, Dianne's back ached. She felt the spasm down low, ignored it. Julia needed air. They could do an emergency tracheotomy. Or they could do nothing. . . . Dianne paused, choking on a sob, leaning against the stairway wall. They could let Julia go, and it would all be over. All her suffering . . .

"No," Dianne said, unable to stand the thought. She kept going, she had to get Julia help, she kept moving down the stairs. "Don't leave me, Julia."

The ambulance was there. Help came all at once. Lucinda had told them Julia was having a seizure, so the EMTs were ready. One shot of diazepam, and the seizure stopped. They cleared her airway: She had bitten her tongue, and she'd been choking on her own blood. Dianne held Julia's hands through it all. She blocked out the furor, concentrated on her daughter's eyes. They were closed, but Dianne knew them by heart. She could see them, enormous and blue, searching her mother's face.

"I love you," Dianne whispered, leaning over Julia as they carried her outside. "I love you, I love you."

Alan met them at the hospital. He made sure Dianne was okay, settled her in the waiting room, then went into the examining room to see Julia. Tubes ran into her arm, nose, and throat. An oxygen mask was over her face.

"She was breathing on her own when they brought her in," the attending physician said. "But she's not now."

Alan nodded. His throat ached as he stared at his niece. Her color was very bad, her lips cyanotic. That purplish discoloration came from a lack of oxygen in the blood, and he checked the flow of oxygen coming from the tanks on the wall. The on-call neurologist wrote orders for an MRI, an

EEG. The cardiologist wrote orders for an EKG. Kissing Julia's forehead, he walked out to see Dianne.

"Tell me," Dianne said, jumping to her feet. She grabbed Alan's hands, stared into his eyes.

"She's going for tests," he said.

"It's worse this time, isn't it?" she asked. "It's much worse. You'd tell me if it was, wouldn't you? Is it? Is it, Alan?"

"I don't know," Alan said. He tried to capture the professional calm that had gotten him through times like this before. He took a deep breath, looked around the familiar ER, reminded himself that he was a doctor. But this was Dianne, and the patient was Julia, and all his training went out the window. His eyes filled with tears. They spilled over as his arms went around Dianne and he began to sob. "I don't know," he said again.

"If anything happens, it's my fault," Dianne cried. "I stopped on the stairs. I wished—it was just a second—but I wished for her to die!"

"Anyone would wish that," Alan said. "For a second. To watch her go through this . . ."

"I didn't mean it," Dianne said.

"I know."

They waited for hours. Alan sat with Dianne in the corner of the bright waiting room, his arm around her shoulders as they watched other people come and go. They watched people with lacerations, sprains, and chest pains. Alan diagnosed each one in his mind. He assessed the damaged, designed the treatment. But right now, when it came to Julia, he was a parent, not a doctor.

"Alan?" Jim Wedstone called, beckoning him over to the desk. Jim was a neurologist of the old school. He preferred to speak doctor to doctor. Jim was the specialist, and Alan was the primary care physician in this case. Jim would tell Alan, and expected Alan to tell Dianne. But that wasn't how Alan wanted it. Taking Dianne's hand, he led her across the ER.

"Jim, this is Dianne Robbins. She's Julia's mother."

"Um, how do you do," Jim said. He seemed displeased or uncomfortable to have to talk to her, but Alan wasn't giving him the choice.

"How's Julia?" Alan asked.

"She's breathing on her own again," Jim said. "Her cardiologist will talk to you, but we feel there's some difficulty in her getting enough oxygen right now. She's not taking it in fast enough to circulate it to her brain, her organs. . . ."

"She's grown," Dianne said, her eyes big as she looked at Alan. "That's it, isn't it?"

"Partly," Alan said. "Maybe."

"I've been afraid all summer," Dianne said, shaking. "Her lungs can't handle . . . is that why she had the seizure?"

"Seizures can happen with these disorders," Jim said, stating one of the many familiar mysteries of Julia's life. Because Jim was a neurologist, seizures were his specialty. He set about explaining synapses and neurotransmitters to Dianne, and the speech sounded so comforting and reasonable; Alan watched her nodding eagerly, her eyes wide, hanging on every word.

It was easier to listen than to think. Julia had grown. What they had feared was happening.

"Come on," Alan said, taking hold of Dianne's arm.

"Just a second," she said, trying to smile, her lips dry. "Dr. Wedstone is just telling me—"

Jim Wedstone could have continued all

day, regaling Julia's mother with theories about seizures in adolescent girls suffering various disorders, but Alan pried her away. He thanked Jim, then grabbed Dianne's coat off her chair. Holding it, he helped her slip her arms into the sleeves, completely aware of the fact that she was miffed at him for the rude way in which he'd behaved to Jim.

"He was just being nice," Dianne said. "Explaining to me, helping me understand about Julia."

"I know," Alan said, buttoning her top button. It was cold outside, with a sharp wind blowing off the harbor. "But let's take a walk."

The harbor was gray and choppy. All Hawthorne's pear trees were bare, their branches tossing in the wind. Dianne tucked her chin inside her coat collar, walking along with Alan. He had been right, encouraging her to come outside. The hospital was stuffy, and she always felt crazy until they let her sit beside Julia again.

Snow flurries swirled down. They hit the pavement, rolling around in white eddies.

Dianne could hardly believe winter was coming. Thanksgiving was next week, and then it would be December, then Christmas.

"When can she come home?" she asked.

"We'll have to see," Alan said. "As soon as she's stable."

"A day," Dianne said. "That's how long it takes her. She's fine, isn't she? That part about not enough oxygen . . . you can fix that, can't you?"

"Let's just walk," Alan said.

Feeling numb, Dianne let him take her arm. They walked briskly along the waterfront, past the boatyards and fishing docks. Most of the fleet was in, their halyards clanking in the wind. Glancing over her shoulder, she wondered how far they were going to walk from the hospital. Julia would be coming to soon, and she wanted to be there.

Rounding the bend, they headed onto Water Street. The wind blew harder here, with no fish shacks or lobster boats to block it. It stung Dianne's cheeks. Huddling closer to Alan, she felt his arm go around her shoulders. She was just about to say they should turn around, go back and see

Julia, when he stopped in front of the house she liked.

"Oh," she said, looking through the gates. Although she didn't have gloves on, she grabbed two of the iron fence posts, holding on with her bare hands.

Alan took her arm. At first she thought he wanted to keep walking, to stay warm, but she pulled away gently, wanting to stop for a minute. She stared at the big white house, the great lawn and scruffy meadow.

"This place," she said.

Alan stood there, hands in his pockets, looking down at her. His face was red, his chin tucked into his collar. She knew he was freezing, but he was letting her have her fantasy. She needed it, to take her away from the reality down the road, what was happening to her daughter, to counteract the terrible thoughts that had gone through Dianne's own mind on the stairs.

"When I was little . . ." she began.

"What did you picture?" he asked. "About this house?"

"Oh, garden parties," she said. Those thoughts were so long ago. "Ladies in white dresses. Little children playing on the grass. Being happy."

"That walk we took last summer," Alan said. "When we stood here . . ."

Dianne nodded. She remembered. They had held hands, walking along in the darkness, in the summer breeze. They had just danced, and kissed. The recollection made her smile. Tilting her head back, she looked into Alan's hazel eyes. They looked so searching and earnest, she would have stood on her toes to kiss him if she weren't in such turmoil.

"I asked you if you thought the people who lived here were happy. You said you didn't know," he said.

"What does it matter?" Dianne asked, feeling despair.

"Come on," he said. Taking her arm again, he began to lead her through the gates.

"Alan," she said, pulling back. She felt shocked that he would even think of trespassing. There were no cars in the driveway, but there was a pumpkin on the front steps.

"They won't mind," he said.

"How do you know?" she asked. "What if there's someone inside? Just because there's no car—"

"I don't think there is," Alan said.

Holding his hand, Dianne reluctantly followed him up the driveway. It was made of finely ground oyster shells that crunched under their feet. The flower beds had been mulched for winter; the yard had been raked. She had never been this close to the house before though, and she couldn't help looking at every wonderful detail.

It was just like the playhouse her father had made her: It had three chimneys, fine white clapboards, black shutters, stately fluted columns, and wide stone steps. As she got closer, she forgot how nervous she felt about walking up someone's driveway. Now she felt excited. There were no curtains at the windows. Maybe she could look inside, just take a peek.

Alan seemed to be looking through his pockets. Letting go of his arm, Dianne inched toward the house. Neat shrubs of boxwood and yew grew almost chin height; she had to crane her neck to see through the window, but when she did, she gasped.

The house was empty.

The white walls were empty, the wide floorboards bare. It upset Dianne to see this wonderful house so vacant: of furniture, paintings, and life. She wanted to see pictures on the walls and books on the shelves. Dianne felt so empty inside herself, so afraid of what was happening to her daughter, she wanted the rest of the world to be full.

"Where are they?" she whispered, her eyes filling with tears. Alan couldn't hear. He was standing by the door as if he expected someone to open it and invite them in. Dianne thought of her daughter, alone in a hospital room just down the road.

Life could be such an empty house. The night before, Dianne had stood in the stairwell of her mother's house and for one dark moment wished her daughter dead. She had no business being here. Whatever tests Julia was having would be done soon. Dianne had to rush back to her, make up for that awful moment.

She turned her head to take one last look. There wasn't a stick of furniture in the room, except one. Dianne hadn't noticed it before: one small chair facing the fireplace at the far end. It had arms and rockers, hand-painted pale pink with tendrils of ivy and blossoms of blue morning glories and red columbine twisting up the wood.

The chair was little. The color pink made Dianne think it must belong to a young girl.

What had caused her parents to leave? Suddenly, she wanted to turn and run. Real people lived here, with their own lives and problems, just like Dianne and Alan and Julia. "Alan, let's go," she begged, tugging on his arm.

"Dianne," he said, holding out his hand.

"We have to leave," she said. "It's wrong to be here. And I have to get back to Julia."

"So do I," he said. "I have to get back to her too. But we have something to do here."

He kissed her. Standing in the cold, in another family's garden, he put his arms around her and gave her the sweetest kiss she could ever imagine. Dianne tried to pull away. Her heart was pounding. Something about that lonely little chair made her care about the family that lived there, made her want to slip away before they came back and caught them interrupting their privacy. Their pumpkin was on the steps, right at her and Alan's feet.

"People live here," she begged.

"I know," he whispered, kissing her face, slipping something into her hand. It felt cold and hard.

"What—" she began, looking down. It was a key.

Alan didn't wait for her to ask more. Taking her hand, he guided the key into the lock. He turned it, and it opened. Dianne stared up at him. She didn't get it. His face was glistening, and the expression in his eyes was fierce.

"Alan," she whispered. "What are you doing?"

"Welcome home," he said, holding his hands out.

She gazed into his eyes, which were full of tears. He put his hands on her shoulders, pushed her gently out the door, then picked her up. Dianne's arms went around his neck, her face pressed against his. She regarded him with a questioning gaze. Tears were running down Dianne's cheeks, and they couldn't stop.

He carried her across the threshold. She was gulping, sobbing, trying to understand what was happening. Her life was falling apart at the hospital, her baby was losing her terrible fight, and Alan was carrying her into the house she'd loved her entire life.

They walked across the empty room, his footsteps echoing, toward the marble fireplace and the little chair. Now that they were closer, Dianne could see that painted across the chair back, across the narrow bar of warm pink wood, was a name:

JULIA

The letters were green stems, and flowers grew off them. The flowers were white, like apple and pear blossoms, and blue, like morning glories. Apples lay at the letters' base as if from wonderful gardens that could produce flowers and fruit at the same time.

"The people have a little girl named Julia," Dianne whispered, stunned.

"They do," Alan said, both arms around Dianne as he lowered her and they stood looking down at the chair.

"Where are they?" she asked.

"They're right here," Alan said.

"Us?" Dianne asked, the word so small and quiet, she could hardly believe she'd said it.

"Us, sweetheart," Alan said.

She looked up into his warm green-gold eyes. His glasses had steamed up, coming in from the cold, and he took them off and tried to stick them in his pocket. His hand seemed to be shaking, so Dianne reached for his glasses and held them in her hand.

"This house . . . ?" Dianne asked, her hands shaking too.

"I bought it for you. For us."

"The chair!" Dianne said, beginning to understand.

"I had it made for Julia," he said.

Dianne wept.

"I want to adopt her," Alan said. "As soon as possible. I want her to be my daughter, Dianne."

"Oh, Alan."

"I want her to be my daughter, and you to be my wife, and I want us to live right here, in this house you've always loved."

"I have," Dianne said. "I've loved it forever."

"I want us to have time together," Alan said. "All of us, as a family. I want us to be here this Christmas, and I want to see Julia sit in her chair by the fire."

"She'll be warm," Dianne said, closing her eyes as she thought of how cold Julia's hands could get. Her daughter had poor circulation, and her fingers and toes were never warm enough. That was why she'd loved the black sand beach, the way that dark sand soaked up the sun. Alan had gotten her a chair by the fire, so Julia could have warmth all year round.

"So, Dianne," Alan said. He took her hand, and she opened her eyes. He looked hesitant, and she reached up to hold him, to let him know he had made her so happy, in some incredible, eternal way, beyond the fears that had gripped her for twelve years, to let him know all those things, but because she couldn't speak, she just held him in her arms.

"Dianne," he said, and now his voice was strong. "Dianne, will you marry me?"

She smiled. Her hand went straight to her mouth, amazed that this was happening. She stared at him, her grin widening. Her eyes twinkled with joyful tears.

"Yes," she said when she could take her hand down and clasp her fingers with his. "Yes, Alan!"

"I love you," Alan said.

"I love you," Dianne said.

The little chair was between them, and it seemed to Dianne to serve as a stand-in for the child herself. If Julia were there, she

would be overjoyed. Dr. McIntosh, her uncle
Alan, the man who had loved her since the
day she was born.

"Julia should be here," Dianne said, staring at the chair. Thinking of how loving, how
thoughtful, a man would have to be to have
such a thing made.

"She will be," Alan said.

"It's time to go back," Dianne said. She
could have stayed there in the house forever, but she had to be with Julia. She'd be
stirring now, not quite waking up, but sensing that her mother wasn't there. They had
to go.

"I know," he said. "Just—"

"I want to tell her," Dianne said, "that
you're going to be her father."

Alan nodded. He seemed about to speak.
He opened his mouth, stopped himself
again. Dianne stared at him, afraid he was
going to say something about Tim. She
didn't know why, it was just a flash of intuition, but she hoped he wouldn't. She
prayed Alan wouldn't say one word about
Tim, bring his brother into this blessed and
amazing house.

He didn't. Holding Dianne's hands, looking into her eyes, he smiled. "Julia knows,"

he said. "She knows I was going to ask
you—"

"Julia . . . knows?"

Alan nodded. "I told her that I bought the
house, that I want to marry you. I asked her,
back in the hospital, when I knew we'd be
walking over . . . I asked her for your hand,
Dianne."

"What did she—" Dianne asked, looking
up at him, "what'd she say?"

"Well, she said yes," Alan said.

Dianne nodded, her eyes bright.

"I told her I want to be her father too," he
said. "But you know, she's heard that before."

"She has?"

"Many times," Alan said. "Many, many
times. Every time you went out of the room
since the day she was born. I've told Julia
that I want to be her father."

"You are," Dianne said, pressing her head
against Alan's chest. "You already are."

He wanted to show her something before
they left to go back to Julia. He led her
straight through the downstairs, through a
solarium where Julia could sit and watch
the boats in the harbor, into the fanciest
kitchen Dianne had ever seen, down a short
hall, into a bedroom.

"It's a suite," Alan said. "With rooms for us and Julia."

"Next to each other . . ." she said, seeing how they connected.

"On the first floor," Alan said, holding her. "So you don't have to carry her up and down stairs."

"Oh, Alan," Dianne said. Her back had been hurting worse than she'd told anyone. That spasm had been so bad this morning . . . she remembered with guilt the thought she'd had about Julia, and knew her own pain had contributed.

"I'll be with you from now on, Dianne," Alan said. "To take care of both of you, you and Julia. I'll make you so happy."

"I already am," Dianne said, looking up into the eyes of the most wonderful man in the world. "You have no idea what you've given me."

"Nothing compared to what you give me," Alan said, kissing her, leading her across the room to the spot where she could imagine putting their bed. He spread his jacket on the hard floor, and they lay down on it. They held each other, eyes wide open, for a long time. Dianne felt their hearts beating together through their clothes. Reaching up, she slid her hand into his shirt, through the space between his buttons.

She thought of the first time they had made love. "Let my love guide you," Alan had told her. He had made it so easy for her. She pressed her hand against his chest, and she found she wanted to do more than that. Very slowly she began undoing his buttons.

"You don't have to—" he said.

"Let my love guide you," she said softly.

Alan closed his eyes. His face was locked in strong emotion, and she watched him pulling himself together. Very gently she caressed his body. She trailed her hand down his muscular chest, his firm stomach. Lowering her head, she kissed his lips.

Dianne had never taken the lead like this. Usually Alan made love to her: She would lie back, feeling the intense sensations, taking all the pleasure he had to give her. That had been all she'd been capable of. Learning to love didn't happen all at once. It took time, and Alan was patient and generous.

Even now he reached up, trying to ease her onto her back. He wanted to take care of *her*, to give her the loving she wanted. But Dianne wanted to do this for *him*.

"There," she said softly, kissing his ear. "Just let me . . ."

"Your back," he said.

"My back's fine," she said.

Very slowly she undressed him. She unbuttoned every button, stopping to kiss each inch of skin. She unzipped his trousers. He squirmed under her light touch, but she pressed his chest, urging him to lie still.

Dianne undressed herself. Winter light streamed in the wide windows, and there was nowhere to hide. She wouldn't have hidden if she could. She wanted to give herself to Alan, every bit. Dianne had been shy her entire life. She had spent more than a decade forgetting she even had a body. But now, as she took off her shirt, her bra, as she saw the expression in Alan's eyes, she knew that he loved *all* of her, and she wanted to give it to him.

"You're beautiful," he whispered.

Too thin, she started to say. *Too bony, too angular, not soft enough.* But she held her tongue. Instead of speaking, she used her mouth to cover his. She kissed him long and slow, their lips parted. She thought of all her insecurities, of how they had no place here and now. Alan had called her beautiful, and the love in his eyes helped her to believe it.

This is our house, she thought, making love to him. *Our home.*

This is our first time making love in our new home.

Alan's arms encircled her as she knelt above him. The light streamed in through the heavy leaded glass, making rainbows on the floor. This man had done so much for her. He had changed her whole life. Dianne saw the world in such a different way because of him, because of how he had touched her.

She touched him now. Guiding him inside her, she felt that by-then-familiar rush of emotion. She wanted this to last forever. She wished she had had these sensations for all the years they had known each other: the tenderness of his gaze, the light brush of his fingers against her cheek, the surge of love within her very being.

"Alan . . ." she whispered.

"I love you, Dianne," he said.

Their eyes met and held. She crouched down, covering his body with her own. Somehow they rolled, so they were lying side by side, still joined together, still moving in a rhythm that reminded her of waves and tides. The harbor was just out their window, the sea just beyond, and she closed her eyes and felt the surge of power. They came in each other's arms, holding each other as the intensity subsided. But lying there, the emotion remained.

Power of love, she thought, grasping Alan for all she was worth. This was the force that built castles, made the sea rise and fall, raised children, called the stars. She had made a life of love for Julia, and now she had Alan too. They had each other.

"Hold me," she said even though he gave no indication of letting go.

"There," he said.

"That's it," she whispered.

"We're together," he said.

"This was my playhouse," she said, cupping his face gently between her two hands.

"I know that," he said. "That's why we're here."

"You've made it my home," she said.

Alan nodded, kissing her.

"We're home," she said, because she could hardly believe it.

Twenty-Six

Thanksgiving was two days away. Dianne and Lucinda stood in the kitchen, each taking care of a different part of the dinner. Dianne always made cranberry sauce, and Lucinda always made the pies. They always polished the silver and washed the crystal goblets. The stuffing had been prepared, so the kitchen smelled like onions and sage. Lucinda had established the rituals long ago.

"I'm so happy, Mom," Dianne said, standing at the sink. She sounded perplexed and amazed, as she had ever since telling Lucinda the news about Alan's proposal several nights earlier.

Lucinda nodded, her hands covered with pie dough. She wasn't surprised at all. Just full of joy for her daughter, bittersweet that it had taken so many years for her to find this happiness.

"I've never done this before," Dianne said. "Lived this way. I don't know what to do."

"Which part don't you know?" Lucinda asked.

"All of it," Dianne said. "I've lived here almost my whole life."

"There was a time you didn't," Lucinda said.

Dianne nodded. She stirred the cranberry sauce, lifted the wooden spoon to her mouth. "When Tim and I lived in the oyster shack," she said. "That seemed so simple. We took some old furniture from your basement, and Alan gave us—" She stopped.

"That was a long time ago," Lucinda said.

"I still . . ." Dianne began. She frowned as if she had something inside, a feeling that had been bothering her all along, and she knew she had to tell someone. "I wish I'd never been married to his brother. I wish Alan and I could just start from scratch. I don't want to have a history."

"I know, honey," Lucinda said. She'd been rolling out the pie crust, but she stopped. She wished she could say something wise and expansive about leaving the past in the past, but she was wishing the same thing.

She thought back to the beginning, when she and Emmett had gone off on their own. They had driven away from the church after their wedding, cans clanking on the back of his truck. They'd moved into the house he built, furnished it themselves, never had to cope with ex-husbands or rival brothers. Their life had been simple. Marriage was hard enough without clutter from two pasts.

"He bought me a house," Dianne said.

"The prettiest house in Hawthorne," Lucinda said.

"It's so big," Dianne said. "When I told him about it, I never expected him to buy it. Never, but he did!"

"I remember how we'd take rides through town, and you'd always want to stop and look at that house," Lucinda said. "You'd ask your father to slow down, and he'd pull right over."

"My playhouse . . ." Dianne said.

Lucinda nodded. She remembered Emmett surprising her that Christmas with the little house he'd made to scale. He had studied the details, getting everything right. She knew how happy he would be to know what Alan had done for their daughter.

"I've built playhouses for the people who are going to be my neighbors down there," Dianne said.

"They'll be lucky to have you as their neighbor," Lucinda said, glancing across the kitchen. She heard the insecurity in Dianne's voice. Lucinda and Emmett were modest people: a librarian and a carpenter. Dianne had spent years supporting herself and Julia by building playhouses for people who lived in mansions. She had rough hands and splinters in her fingers. Delivering her work, she had had to drive up long driveways to houses with pillars, houses that had names.

"Everyone takes their kids to Alan," Dianne said. "They'd expect him to live there."

"With you and Julia."

Dianne nodded, glowing with love and joy.

Lucinda stared at her granddaughter. Julia hardly opened her eyes at all these days. She rocked and slept, trying to work her way tighter into the fetal position, as if she wanted to be a snail. Dianne was so patient. She constantly tried to undo Julia's position, the way the physical therapist had shown her so long ago, so Julia's muscles wouldn't cramp.

"Alan wants to adopt her," Dianne said, following her mother's gaze.

"I know."

"The thing I love the most," Dianne said, "is how much he wants us to be a family."

"He's wanted it for twelve years," Lucinda said.

"Mom," Dianne said, hugging herself as if she were cold.

"What, honey?"

"Do I deserve this?"

"Dianne!"

"For so long," Dianne said, her voice so quiet Lucinda had to lean close to hear, "I'd wonder what I did to bring it on. I'd think it had to be something in me, that I had done, to cause Julia to be born the way she was."

"It wasn't your fault," Lucinda said.

"But I'm her mother," Dianne said. "It must have been something. The food I ate, the food I didn't eat. Mean things I did when I was little . . ."

"You were never mean."

"Sins," Dianne said. "It's funny. I never think about that for other people—look at crippled or blind people, wonder what sins their mothers committed before they were born. But I thought about it for myself."

"You don't anymore?" Lucinda asked, relieved.

"I try not to," Dianne said. "But it's hard. When I see Julia hurting, or having a seizure. When I think about how I'm taking Amy to *The Nutcracker* instead of Julia, because Julia can't go . . . When I think about those things, I have doubts. I think there must be some reason I'm being punished."

"But now," Lucinda said, "you're being rewarded."

"With Alan," Dianne said. As she said his name, her expression changed. Lucinda watched the anxiety go away. She felt the tension leave the room. Dianne was suddenly radiant.

"With love," Lucinda said. Because it was more complicated than Dianne being rewarded with Alan. He was being rewarded with her too. They were kindred spirits, and they had found each other. Against many odds, they were together.

"Can we keep it?" Dianne asked.

Lucinda held her hand. When Dianne was young, she had been full of questions. She had trusted her parents completely, and Lucinda remembered how Dianne would ask her something impossible, like how high was the sky, gazing into Lucinda's eyes with the exact same expression she had right now.

"Sweetheart, Dianne," Lucinda said, "begin telling yourself you deserve love, deserve being happy. Every bit as much as anyone else. And me too. Amy. Julia. We should take every bit of joy that comes our way. Whether it's in a Winnebago or a big white house on the harbor. Or right here."

Dianne hugged herself, looking around the modest house that had been her home her whole life.

"Anywhere at all," Lucinda said.

"My kindred spirit," Dianne said.

"Amy would appreciate that," Lucinda said.

"I'm glad it's Thanksgiving," Dianne said.

Lucinda drew her close. "Be grateful every day," she said. "That's my secret to you. It's what I did with your father, and it's why we were so happy. Because you never know when it might end."

Tomorrow was the day her story had to be submitted. Amy had put her story in the safest place possible: behind her father's picture on the wall of her bedroom. There he was, Russell Brooks, the handsome, trustworthy car dealer, smiling out at her. And behind the picture, just as if it were a wall safe, was Amy's story. She got it down now. She felt nervous, afraid the story wasn't good enough, and she wanted to get another opinion.

"Mom," Amy said, going to her mother's door.

"Shhh, honey," her mother said, lying in bed. "I didn't get any sleep last night. I'm tired."

"Will you read this?" Amy asked.

"Not right now," her mother moaned from under the covers.

"Please, Mom. It's *important*," Amy said, starting to feel angry. It wasn't fair: In the story, Catherine's mother had gotten over her depression, but in real life Amy's mother seemed to be slipping back. Amy felt so worried and panicked, but, at the same time, very mad.

"Later," her mother said, and Amy was pretty sure she heard her starting to cry.

Amy stared with her fists clenched. Lucinda and Dianne were so proud of her, why couldn't her mother be? Her mother's antidepressants were in a bottle on the bathroom shelf. Yesterday Amy had counted them to make sure she was taking them. She stormed into the bathroom and counted them again today: the same number.

"Mom," she said, shaking her mother's shoulder.

"What is it, Amy?"

"Why aren't you taking your medication? Don't you want to get better?"

"I do, Amy."

"But you're not taking your pills!" Amy's voice rose. "I counted, so don't try to tell me you did! Our life is beautiful, we're together, Thanksgiving is here! Why aren't you taking your pills?" She shook her mother hard but with just a fraction of the terrible frustration she felt.

"They make me too sleepy," her mother said, starting to cry. "They make my mouth dry and give me a headache."

"You're not trying!" Amy screamed. "You're not trying at all!"

Her mother just lay there, weeping. Amy stared at her. Why couldn't she be like Dianne? She didn't care that Amy was going to enter a writing contest and, win or lose, go to New York City. Why couldn't her mother take her to *The Nutcracker* instead? Her mother didn't even seem to care that Amy was going to go with someone else. She was too busy lying under the blankets, not taking her medicine.

"We don't even have a turkey," Amy said, her voice shaking. "It's Thanksgiving almost, and we have no poultry at *all*. No turnips, no cranberry sauce. I wrote a story, and you won't even read it."

"I read it," her mother whispered. "When you were at school."

"You did?" Amy asked, getting a funny feeling in her head.

"It made me feel so lousy, that I can't get better as fast as Catherine's mother. She's like me, but so much better. She takes care of her kids, the you-kid and the Julia-kid, better than I ever could. I'm sorry, Amy."

"Mom . . ." Amy began, not knowing what to say.

"Just leave me alone right now," her mother said. "Please? Just let me sleep a little."

Amy backed out of the room, closing the door behind her. She dropped the story on the kitchen table. There was a big glob of peanut butter there, but she didn't even care. Her story had hurt her mother's feelings.

Walking down the street, she found herself heading for the Robbinses' house. Seeing Julia would make her feel better. But when she got closer, she realized she didn't want to see Dianne. Lucinda, maybe, but not Dianne with her pink cheeks and golden hair. Thinking of how her mother must have felt when she'd read Amy's description of the mother, Amy cringed.

Orion saw her coming. He was playing in the yard. Together, he and Amy went down to the marsh. The old dinghy was filled with ice-filmed water. Amy bailed it out. The puppy was growing bigger. He jumped into the boat, wanting to go for a ride. Amy's heart was heavy, but she didn't want to disappoint her friend. Maybe today she'd bring him home with her.

They rowed out the marsh to the beach.

The sky was deep gray, a line of bright gold along the horizon. The marsh looked brown and dead. Amy kept seeing her mother lying in bed, crying because of Amy's story. Maybe that's why she wasn't taking her medication. Amy would throw her story out so her mother would never have to read it again.

Orion bounded over the sand dune. A wintry wind blew off the ocean, shooting Amy's brown hair straight back from her face. Grains of sand blew into her mouth, and she spit them out, climbing the small hill. The dog pranced in excited circles, sniffing everything. He led her toward the lighthouse, and as Amy followed, she almost couldn't bear to look.

The sand castle was gone.

That strong fortress she had built in September, in the lee of the lighthouse, far from the tides and the autumn storms, had washed away. It seemed impossible, but the tide had come up this high: Amy saw bits of seaweed and driftwood, a smashed lobster pot, fish bones, to prove it.

While Orion snorted with joy, smelling the sand and seaweed, Amy fell to her knees. This was the spot. Was it her imagination, or was this a mound of sand? Was it all that remained from the castle she had built? She had had hope in her heart that day. Building that sand castle, Amy had been thinking of Julia.

So much was gone. Amy's mother was back in bed, and Julia . . . Amy covered her eyes. Julia could hardly even talk anymore. Amy's sand castle had failed everyone. Amy began to dig, to push the sand into a thick wall, to build the foundation to start again. But her hands were blocks of ice, and she felt herself shivering in the cold wind. What good would it do anyway?

Orion barked. Amy shivered with a sob. The wind was blowing so hard, no one could hear her, not even the dolphins swimming in the sea. Amy cried and cried. The castle had crumbled, and she didn't have the heart to build it over.

Tess Brooks had gotten out of bed just in time to see her daughter running down the street.

"Amy!" Tess had called out the front door. "Amy!"

But it was too late; Amy had disappeared

around the corner. Sighing, Tess closed the door. A gust of wind had come in, bringing a terrible chill. Tess walked over to the thermostat, stared at it. It was set on sixty-two. Tess couldn't afford to push it up too high; the money from Russ's fund was running out.

Amy was such a good girl. She never complained about the house being cold. She did her homework, more than her share of chores around the house. Her heart was set on being a writer, and she'd put all that effort into her story.

Why had Tess said the things she did? Pushing the hair out of her face, she went into the bathroom, took her pills. She didn't want to be like this: negative and scared. She didn't want to be depressed, hiding under the covers, afraid her own daughter had been better off with the Robbinses.

Picking up a hairbrush, she ran it through her brown hair. One step at a time, her doctor said. He was very nice and kind; he never told her she was wasting their sessions when she cried the entire fifty minutes. She had lost her husband when she was only twenty years old. He had been the only boy she'd ever loved.

Tess had gone to pieces. She had Amy now, and that money from the fishermen's fund, but she felt so alone. She had never had a good job, she had never felt like *enough*. There she was with a bubbly little girl, and Tess hadn't even had the energy to read to her.

Tess had made many mistakes, but she considered that one of her worst: not reading to Amy when she was little. Tess had loved books herself. She had hung around the library when she was young, signing books out as fast as Mrs. Robbins could give them to her. But once Russ died, the world just turned gray. Real life and lives on the page: Tess hadn't cared about any of them.

That's why she had been so happy when Amy had started hanging around with the Robbinses. Mrs. Robbins was such a no-nonsense lady, so upright and concerned about the well-being of young people, Tess had just known she would help Amy. And everyone in town knew Dianne, how she had stuck it out with her deformed baby even after her handsome husband had just sailed away. How could Tess object to Amy spending time with such fine people?

Did it make sense, then, that Tess had seethed with jealousy? That every time she'd heard the words "I'm going to Julia's" or, worse, "I'm going to Dianne's," her stomach had clenched right into a knot? Buddy had been here then, and he had fed those bad feelings, telling her that Amy was starting to prefer strangers to her own home, that pretty soon Amy wouldn't want to be there at all.

Not that Tess could blame her. She sighed, staring at Amy's story on the table. The lower left corner had a little peanut butter on it. The grease was spreading through the paper, turning it clear. Tess wiped it off. She gazed at the title: "Sand Castles." Jealousy was a terrible thing. She wished she hadn't said the things she had. She was glad, sort of, that Amy was going to have the opportunity to see *The Nutcracker*. But why did Amy have to give the mother in the story blond hair?

Twenty-Seven

Amy glanced at the house. If she saw Dianne or Lucinda in the window, she'd go over to say hi. She wanted to see Julia, especially after finding the sand castle gone. In fact, she *wished* they'd look out. She dragged her feet, taking her time.

But it was getting late. She had to get home, make sure her mother was okay. Checking the dinghy one last time to make sure she'd pulled it high enough on the bank of the marsh, and giving Dianne and Lucinda another chance to see her, she walked through the yard.

Orion ran in wild circles. Amy wanted to bring him home, but she knew the best place for him was there, with Stella. Stella had gotten him out from under the bed.

After his life in the cage, only Dianne's little stone-wall cat had been able to tempt him back to life. Orion barked, following her straight out to the road.

"See you, Orion," Amy said, kneeling down to let him nuzzle her face.

Orion licked her ears and eyes. She felt him washing away the tears she had cried on the beach, on the spot where Julia's sand castle had stood. As the dog licked her, Amy felt better. Kisses always did that for her: people's or dogs'. Amy would go home, apologize to her mother, see about getting the peanut butter off her story.

Orion whimpered.

Amy opened her eyes. The puppy was lying on the road, trying to flatten himself into the pavement. He peed: Amy saw the stream trickle from his tail into the gutter. Orion looked terrified, as Amy hadn't seen him look for months. And then she saw the car.

She hadn't noticed it at first. Amy had been so preoccupied with wishing Dianne would see her walking through the yard and invite her in that she had not seen the car. It was parked in the turnaround, its rust-brown color blending with the rushes.

"Hello, Amy," Buddy said, talking through the open window.

"You're not supposed to be here," Amy said.

"I'm not?" Buddy asked.

"No," Amy said.

Orion cried. He just lay on the ground shivering. Go, Amy wanted to tell him. Run like Lassie and bring help! But he was much too frozen. Amy would have to run herself. She'd scream first. Opening her mouth, she didn't even get a sound out.

Buddy opened his car door, took three long strides across the dead end, and slapped Amy across the face. She was so shocked, she touched her cheek instead of hitting back. By then Buddy had Orion by the back of the neck and Amy by the waist, and he threw them into the backseat of his car and slammed the door shut behind them.

"Let me out," Amy screamed.

"Shut up," Buddy said, getting in front.

"You'll be arrested," she said. "You'll go to jail!"

Orion had curled himself up like a snail, cowering on the floor behind Buddy. Amy tried to open the back doors, but the door handles, locks, and window cranks had been taken out. She was trapped!

"Thanksgiving's coming," Buddy said, lighting a cigarette.

Orion looked up at Amy with huge eyes. He reminded her of Julia, of how she could look when she had something she needed to say but couldn't find the words. For Orion's sake, Amy had to make this come out right.

"Please, Buddy," Amy said, trying to keep her voice steady. "Let us out of the car."

"Two days is all," Buddy said. "Two days to Thanksgiving, and poor Buddy has no place to go. No turkey dinner's waiting for me."

"I'm sorry," Amy said.

Buddy was taking his time. With Amy and Orion trapped in back, he didn't seem to be in a hurry about kidnapping them. He smoked for a minute, and then he picked his teeth with a matchstick. If Amy weren't so scared, she'd have remembered to be repulsed. Buddy fiddled with the radio, finding the right station.

"Let us out," Amy said quietly. "I swear, I'll ask Mom if you can come to our house. We'll have pilgrim candles and everything.

Pumpkin pie, that's the kind you like, right?"
she asked, trying to remember from the previous year. She had the feeling that if only
she could forgive him, like Lucinda always
said, if she could just be kind enough to
realize that he felt awful about this, that no
one, not even Buddy, could want to be
alone on Thanksgiving, then Buddy would
feel her goodness and let them go.

"Pumpkin pie?" he asked, his eyes glowing like black coals.

"Yes," she said, her voice trembling. "With
whipped cream."

"Try *mince* pie, you little bitch. It's *mince*
pie I like. Three fucking years under the
same roof, and you don't even remember."
He gunned the engine, still parked in the
dead end.

Now Amy felt the panic shivering down
her spine. The hair on her arms stood up.
She could see Dianne's house, her studio. If
only they would come outside! Just look out
the window! Just then Buddy swore. A car
was coming down the street. Amy craned
her neck. It was Dr. McIntosh!

Amy started screaming, banging on the
windows. Her fists were hard as rocks. If
only she could shatter the glass! Orion tried

to make himself smaller. Buddy slunk down in his seat. Amy saw Dr. McIntosh drive right by, staring full-force at Dianne's house. He was on his way to see her, and he didn't even notice the brown car parked half in the rushes.

"Dr. McIntosh!" Amy screamed. "Help us! Oh, help—"

"He can't hear you," Buddy said, shifting into gear. He laughed.

"Please," Amy said, starting to sob. Buddy was pulling away slowly. Amy's palms were flat against the back window. She had gotten sand under her fingernails from digging on the beach. Orion whimpered. Amy stared up Dianne's driveway: at her house, at the studio.

There, sitting in the window where she always tracked the stars in the sky, was Stella. The little cat saw Buddy's car drive away, watched her friend, the dog Orion, be spirited off, witnessed the whole thing with the helpless despair that only creatures who know love can feel.

Alan had been in such a hurry to see Dianne, he'd run out without his jacket, leaving it at the office. It didn't matter. He rushed from the car to the house. Taking the stairs two at a time, he found Dianne in her bedroom, packing boxes. Crouched by an open drawer, she didn't hear him at first.

"Dianne," he said.

"Oh, you surprised me," she said.

He stared at her. Her hair was messy, tied back with a scarf. She had her work clothes on, old sneakers on her feet. Julia lay on a blanket on the floor, keeping her company.

Alan knelt beside her. His heart was beating fast, as it had been since an hour earlier when he'd left the hospital. Past Thanksgiving weeks he had worked every possible minute. The holiday had meant nothing to him. He had worked normal hours, taking other doctors' on-call schedules. But this year was different. It was only Tuesday, and already he was leaving the office early.

"Don't misunderstand," she said, her skin glowing as she took his hand. "But what are you doing here? I didn't expect you until later tonight."

"I'm taking the rest of the day off," he said.

"You are?"

He nodded. "And I'm getting out early

tomorrow. And the next day is Thanksgiving. I'll be around as much as possible
until you and Amy go to New York."

Dianne glanced at Julia. When she looked
back at Alan, her eyes looked worried, and
she was frowning slightly.

"Is it Julia?" she asked. "Did you get some
test results—"

He shook his head quickly, enveloping her
in his arms. "No," he said. "I just wanted to
be with you. What are you doing?"

"Packing our things, mine and Julia's,"
Dianne said, holding out the summer shirt
she held in her hands. "Getting ready to
move to our house. Why?"

Alan let her go slightly. He thought
about their last long talk. They had discussed Thanksgiving. She had told him
about her mother's words, about how
they had to be grateful every day, to give
thanks for every minute they had together.

"Then I'll help you," he said.

"You closed the office?" she asked, smiling. She held his hand.

"We'd scheduled an early day anyway," he
said. "Usually I take extra on-call duties at
the hospital around Thanksgiving, but this

year I'm asking Joe Bernstein to take mine.
I want us to move in as soon as you get
back from New York," he said, his heart
pounding as he pulled her close again.
"Julia and I will get the place together and
wait for you to come back."

"That's what I had hoped," Dianne said,
kissing him. "That's why I wanted to get
started packing as soon as possible."

"We can start taking boxes over right
away," he said.

"I have about six stacked downstairs,"
she said.

"We're on the same wavelength," he said,
holding her tight.

Amy tried to formulate a plan. Buddy was a
maniac, and Amy had a good mind. He was
like some mad, evil villain, and Amy had
might and good on her side. All Amy's reading, all her hanging around with the Robbinses, had shown her that goodness tri-
umphed over wickedness every day of the
week.

"Been watching your house," Buddy was
saying, cruising along. They were taking
back roads through the Lovecraft Nature

Sanctuary. Nothing but marshland to the right, pine forests to the left.

Orion whimpered. Amy tickled him between the ears. She had to stay calm. She had to maintain alertness. If they passed another car, she'd wave her arms. If only someone would pull up behind them. She could look out the back window, make desperate faces to alert the driver to her plight.

"Watching your house, day and night," Buddy said. "Your mother don't look too good."

"She's fine," Amy said.

"She looks haggard," Buddy said. "That means like a hag."

Orion peed again. Amy could smell the ammonia. Afraid that Buddy would smell it, she pulled off her shoes and then her socks. They were thick Ragg socks, purchased when they made the pit stop at L.L. Bean, and she used them to sop up the puppy's urine.

"Parked outside my own house," Buddy said. "Real nice. But there ain't much action there, her sleeping her life away and all. So I'd drive by other places, see how my enemies are doin'. The good doc, for example."

Dr. McIntosh . . . at the thought of him, Amy's eyes filled with tears. He had been right there; he could have seen her, if only he had looked, if only Amy had been able to attract his attention.

"Dr. Saint," Buddy said. "Or is it Saint Doctor? Whichever. He's a fucking loser. Him and his girlfriend, your foster mother."

"Dianne," Amy whispered.

"That is one sick kid," Buddy said. "Got a good look at her at the grocery the other day. Damn near made me gag the way she smelled. Pretty face though. Worthless arms and so-called legs. All chewed up and spit out. Hey, if arms and legs don't work, are they called something else?"

"Shut up," Amy said. She couldn't bear to hear Buddy say things about Julia. He had no right to put his evil mouth on her, saying wicked things about her friend. Orion nuzzled Amy's bare ankles. His nose was cold, and every panicked breath sent chills up Amy's leg.

"What'd you say to me?" Buddy asked, glaring at Amy in the rearview mirror.

Amy tried to breathe. She had to keep herself calm. This was key. Buddy was the maniac here. Amy had to placate him.

"I'm sorry, Buddy," she said as meekly as she could.

"Thought I heard you say shut up," he said.

She shook her head. The road wound deeper into the sanctuary. Her heart was racing. She tasted something weird, as if her body were even more scared than her mind, as if it were producing some strange chemical of fear. Buddy had cut the door handles out. What did that mean? Amy felt down the crack of her seat, hoping to find a lead pipe. She could cosh him from behind, then she and Orion could climb out the front door and escape.

No lead pipe. She glanced down at the floor. It was covered with empty beer cans and food wrappers. From the looks of things, Buddy liked McDonald's and Dunkin' Donuts. The floor was a junk-food paradise, but Orion was too petrified to explore.

The road had been winding through the woods, and the darker it got, the more afraid Amy became. Hemlocks and white pines grew thick. Flashes of sky were thin and gray. Buddy turned up the music. It sounded like nothing but bass and drums.

To Amy it sounded like blood. The fear-taste grew stronger. She began to whimper like Orion.

Suddenly the road burst out of the forest. They were in the light! There were rock outcroppings on the left, rising to the Hawthorne Hills. On the right was the sea. They had rounded the headland beyond the marsh, and here there was nothing but open water. Staring out, Amy saw waves breaking on rocks: the Landsdowne Shoal.

It was so bright. Hope began to return. Coming into the light was good. If Buddy had been planning something bad, he would have done it in the woods, where no one could see. Where it would take a long time for people to find them.

Here it was still deserted, still the nature sanctuary. No houses around, too cold for people to be hiking. But out at sea there were ships. Amy saw two lobster boats circling their buoys, pulling their pots not far from shore. She waved at them, hoping they would see. Buddy seemed not to notice. He was humming along with the music.

And then he stopped the car.

Amy looked around. The road was wide open. A short distance ahead was a bridge.

She didn't think she had ever seen it before. Her mother had never been one for nature rides, and on their excursions last summer, Dianne had never driven this way. Buddy got out of the car. He had something in his hand, but Amy was too excited to see what it was: He was letting them out!

"Oh," she said, scrambling past him when he opened the door. Orion was right behind her.

"What do you say?" he asked.

"Thank you, Buddy," she said.

She was trembling, but stretching her legs felt good. The wind blew fresh and clean across the wide open road. It would be a long walk home, she and Orion would be tired and cold, but she didn't care. Whatever little lesson Buddy had wanted to teach her, she'd pretend to go along with it.

"Hey, you're welcome," he said.

They were just standing there, facing each other. He had a chipped front tooth and a lightning-bolt tattoo on his neck that she hadn't noticed before.

"We'll walk home," Amy said, trying to smile.

"*You* will," he said.

That's when Amy realized that Orion

hadn't gotten out of the car. He was frozen in terror, trying to burrow underneath the empty food boxes. Amy's stomach lurched. She knew she had to act fast. Orion was as helpless as Julia. If Julia were trapped in Buddy's car, Amy would be just as afraid. Buddy could drive away with him, and Amy would never see him again.

"Here, Orion," she whispered, patting the side of her leg. Her mouth was almost too dry to speak. "Here, boy."

"What'd you call him?" Buddy asked, transferring whatever he had been holding to his other hand.

Amy stared, unable to reply.

"Because I thought I heard you call him something stupid," Buddy said. "His name is Slash."

Amy still stared.

"Slash and I have some unfinished business," Buddy said, shaking out the burlap sack he had been holding. It snapped like a whip, and the dog whimpered.

"Buddy, no," Amy cried, screaming as she realized what he was going to do. She tried pulling his arm, using every bit of her might.

Buddy brushed her aside like dandelion fluff and yanked the dog out of the car. He stuffed Orion in the sack as if he were dirty shirts. The dog had grown since summer; he was sleek and graceful, his dark coat glossy from all the love and good food Dianne fed him, from his days of romping in the sun.

Amy grabbed Buddy's arm, tugging as hard as she could. Orion was in the sack, and the sack was twisted shut in Buddy's hand. Buddy's cowboy boots with their metal studs clicked loudly against the pavement, click-click-click, as he strode rapidly toward the bridge.

Amy was sobbing now, begging. "Don't do it, Buddy," she cried. "Take me. Do something to me. He's just an innocent dog—"

"Shut"—click-click-click—"up."

"Buddy, no," Amy said, holding on to Buddy's shirt. She knew about horrible things men did to young girls. She had asked Marla Arden about some of them back when Marla interviewed Amy to find out what Buddy had done. Amy knew about bad touching and bad talking, and she knew about rape, and that was what she had been expecting when they had driven through the darkest part of the forest.

Weeping now because she had been fear-
ing it so much, that terror had been the
awful unfamiliar taste in her mouth.

The bridge was high.

It was made of ornate green metal, as if it
had been built a long time before by someone who wanted it to look beautiful in this
lovely natural setting. It spanned an inlet,
only about thirty feet wide, of water rushing
to the sea. A brook started it all, up in the
hills, widening as it tumbled over rocks and
moss, entering the wide silver sea at this
spot under this bridge.

"Guard dogs who won't train are worth
shit," Buddy said, looking Amy in the eye.
He drew his foot back as if he were going to
kick Orion in the bag.

"Don't kick him," Amy howled.

"You think you can bargain for this dog?"
Buddy asked.

Amy stared. She heard the lobster boat
buzzing like a mosquito in the distance.
Waving or calling for help wouldn't do any
good. The boat was too far away. This was
between her and Buddy.

"Go ahead," Buddy said. "Bargain."

"Let him go," Amy whispered, watching
Orion move in the bag. She thought of how

dark it must be in there, and she hoped he felt a little safer, the way he felt when he was under the bed.

"Keep talking . . ." Buddy said, touching Amy's hair.

"Please," Amy said, crying.

"Please?" he asked.

Breathing funny, Buddy brought his face close to hers. She felt his slimy fingers on her cheeks, sliding down her neck. He took her hand, pressed it on the front of his jeans.

She squeaked, trying to hold back her sob. She tried to think of Dianne, of her strength, of what she would do. Buddy had been smoking, and he dropped his cigarette on the road. She heard him grind it out with his boot. When she opened her eyes, he was holding the sack higher. Now he had purpose in his narrow gaze, as if he were thinking of Amy now and all he wanted to do was get rid of the dog.

"No," Amy said, seeing him move toward the rail.

"Unfinished business," he said.

And then he dropped the sack.

Amy looked down. The water rushed and swirled. It was dark, brown with weeds and silt from the land. The sack hit the water with a big splash. It floated for a minute. Amy held her breath, tears flowing down her face. She prayed to see Orion's nose, his front paws with their little white tips, emerge from the sack.

The sea carried the sack out the inlet quickly. It moved as it flowed, as if the puppy were fighting to get free. Amy could almost see the dog's legs kicking as the burlap bag tumbled along in the current.

The bag floated for a few seconds more, and then it started sinking.

"No!" Amy screamed.

Orion can swim, Amy thought. If he could just get out. She had seen him swim in Dianne's marsh, on the beach at Prince Edward Island. He was a water dog, a good swimmer! But he was trapped inside the sack, drowning before her very eyes.

"You wanna walk or you wanna ride?" Buddy asked.

Amy bit her lip. She was sobbing blindly, watching the burlap bag sink. She felt his hand on her hair, tugging gently, as if he were just playing. She thought of all the things she'd talked about with Marla Arden, she thought about sinking into the swamp of Buddy's world, and then she thought of Dianne and Julia and life worth living. Amy thought about saving her own life.

Hers and Orion's.

Amy jumped off the bridge.

Twenty-Eight

* ✳ *

Amy swam and drifted. The water was freezing. She gulped, trying to stay afloat. The sea pulled her in, drawing her away from the land. Buddy standing on the bridge looked so far away. He was staring at her, but then he got into his car and drove off. She saw that, the way he just left her for dead.

The current pulled her so Amy hardly had to swim. She was weighted down with her jeans and coat, yanking her under. The waves were small here, but big enough to splash over her head, go up her nose. She tried to yell for Orion, but she couldn't make a sound. She barely had the energy to breathe.

From up above Amy had been able to see

the sack. It had seemed like such an easy thing: to dive in and swim straight to the dog and save them both. She felt the panic of knowing she didn't have time. The burlap bag had sunk, she had seen it, and even now Orion would be choking on seawater. The inlet that had looked so narrow was actually wide, and the sea that was pulling her along was vaster than she had ever imagined.

Daddy, she thought.

He was under the waves, her father. Amy's eyes stung with saltwater and salt tears, and she struggled, feeling for her dog, for Orion. She wanted him to swim up and nudge her; together they would stroke toward shore. Her father was a dolphin; sleek and strong, he could bear them to safety.

The tide was ebbing. It was pulling freshwater from the brooks and streams, ponds and rivers, straight out to the sea. Amy fought against it, knowing the farther out she went, the worse it would be. She cried, struggling against her wet clothes. Waves broke over her head. They were bigger now, because she had drifted so far out.

The waves smashed her down. They

tossed her up and smacked her down. Amy fought them. The harder she resisted, the more it hurt. She could hardly get a breath. The sky was steel gray, and it blended into the waves. Foam filled her nose. She choked, fighting the sea. And then she remembered Dianne.

"Be a seal," Dianne had told her last summer when she had taught her to ride the waves.

Be a seal, Amy thought. She made herself sleek and straight. Not a dolphin, not a black dog. She wasn't thinking straight. *A seal,* she told herself. Free of everything, so slippery, she'd just slide through the crashing waves. Orion and her father were helping her, Dianne was telling her to keep her head down, her arms out straight. Bodysurfing, that's right. So what if it's November, so what if there's no beach?

Amy just thought of the people and dog she loved so much, and she kept her head down just like Dianne had told her, and she made herself sleek like a seal, and she held her breath until she thought her lungs would burst, and that is how Amy Brooks came to ride the waves to safety, straight onto the Landsdowne Shoal.

Only one rock protruded from the sea, and only for one fraction of one hour twice every day. The tide had gone out enough, and it hadn't turned to come back, so that rock was exposed and Amy was able to haul herself up. Sputtering, spitting up seawater, shivering so hard she couldn't control her limbs, Amy climbed onto the jagged brown rock.

A lobster boat was circling a buoy. Amy saw it now. She tried to raise her arm, but when she moved, she lost her grip and began to slide off the rock.

"Help!" she yelled.

The rock was coated with black sea moss as slimy as grease. It was covered with barnacles and mussels, and they sliced Amy's hands with their shells. From up there Amy could see all around. She screamed for help, but she didn't stop scanning the surface for Orion.

"Help!" she called. "Save me!"

There was no one on land. Buddy's car had disappeared. The lobsterman leaned overboard, pulled up one of his pots. His engine was going. Couldn't he hear her? Amy screamed louder. "Daddy!" she heard herself screaming. "Daddy!"

She was just like a baby now. She was sobbing so hard, clinging to a rock that wouldn't hold her, grieving for the puppy she had been unable to save. "Daddy Daddy Daddy Daddy!" rang in her ears.

The boat was going away. She saw it sweep around in a big circle, its wake spreading out behind like a train of white stars. The whitewater churned and foamed, then smoothed into a silver river as bright and wide as the Milky Way. Stars danced before Amy's eyes, through her tears.

"Help!" she screamed one last time, watching the boat leave her behind. "Help me!"

A dog barked.

Trembling, Amy couldn't believe her ears. She clung to her rock, icy water streaming down her body. Straining to listen, she heard it again: a dog's sharp, insistent yelps. *Oh, Orion,* she sobbed. She was dreaming of her puppy.

"Help!" Amy cried. "Help me!"

The boat turned around. Its hull was white with a red cove stripe, and its bow was pointed straight at Amy, coming head-on. She shivered and slipped. The stars were brighter, flashing in her eyes. She spit out more seawater, scrambled to hold on. The barking dog sounded louder. Amy was drowning, going to the sea, Orion was calling her into the deep to be with her father.

"Hang on," a man's voice called. "Just hold tight."

"I can't," Amy cried, her hands sore and bleeding, the waves splashing her feet and legs.

"Here we are," the man said. "Okay, just a second—"

He cut the engine. The boat drifted closer. The man was short and old, with gray whiskers and a yellow slicker over his bright orange overalls. His face was as withered as one of Amy's apples, and his eyes were blue as a summer sky. He was talking non-stop, saying something about having to take care in shoal waters, not wanting to sink his boat before he had the chance to save her.

"Give me your hand," he said, reaching out his arm.

"I can't," Amy said, clinging like a snail to her rock.

"Come on," he said. "That's a girl. What a

brave girl you are, there. Just give me your hand. Come on . . ."

Amy closed her eyes. She didn't want to be such a chicken, but she had the feeling that if she let go, she'd sink under the sea and never come up again.

"Okay, dear," the man said, incredibly patient considering his boat was being dashed against the shoal. "Just let go. Let go of the rock and grab me instead. I'll catch you—"

Amy cried. She thought of Julia having her seizure. Julia's teeth had been chattering just like Amy's, she couldn't stop herself, and there'd been no kind lobsterman to save her. Nothing Dianne did, nothing anyone did . . . if Julia could be so brave, every day, all the time . . . sea gulls were flying overhead, screeching at the bait and lobster in the man's boat, and they sounded to Amy like Julia: "Dleee, dleeee."

If Julia could do it . . .

Grasping the rock with one arm, Amy reached out for the man. His gnarled hand grabbed hold of her wrist.

My daddy was a fisherman, she wept.

But she must not have said it out loud, because the man didn't reply right away. He seemed to be too choked up himself. He pulled a blanket out of a chest and laid it on top of her. Amy was too weak and filled with shock and grief to move. She just lay on the deck and wept.

"There, little one," the man said. "There you go."

"Daddy," Amy cried.

"Got to get us off the shoal now," the man said. "Before we sink."

"My daddy sank," Amy cried.

"Did he? I'm sorry," the man said, giving a little throttle. "But that's not going to happen to us today. Not today, not a lucky day like this."

Lucky, Amy sobbed, shaking her head as she thought of her dog, of how she had failed Orion.

"Not every day I get to pull two young ones out of the cold sea," the man said.

"Two?" Amy asked, confused.

"Two," the man said, reaching down to pull her blanket up a little higher. "You and the pup."

Amy blinked the water out of her eyes. There, standing over her, was Orion. He looked noble and proud, as if he had just swum the English Channel. He was shivering, shaking his coat every ten seconds, but his tongue was red and hanging out in a great happy-dog smile.

"He was swimming out there," the man said, gesturing with his thumb. "Thought he was a seal at first, but it's too early in the year for them to be migrating down this far. Then I thought he was a duck."

"Orion!" Amy cried.

"Just swimming in circles, he was. I pulled him aboard. He was hiding back in the stern, but he must've heard you yelling for help."

"Dogs have the best hearing," Amy said, kissing Orion's ears.

"He saved your life," the man said. "If he hadn't given out that loud bark, I never would have seen you."

"Orion," Amy breathed.

"Ah, he's yours," the man said. "Well, that's fitting. Isn't that fine? A dog saving his young mistress's life like that. Wait'll we tell everyone on the dock about that. Just wait."

"Oh, Orion," Amy said, holding him tight. She'd been thinking it had been the other way around, that she had jumped in to save *his* life. Amy thought of the people who had come to help her on that slippery rock: her father, Dianne, and Julia. Especially Julia. And then the man, the strange and wonderful fisherman who had saved her dog. And Orion, who had barked his head off to save her life.

They passed the red nun and the bell buoy marking the entrance to Hawthorne harbor. The bell tolled deep and true. The three white church spires pierced the pewter-gray sky. There was the brick building where Dr. McIntosh had his office. Flags whipped in the wind. The great white sea captains' houses stretched along the water's edge, and Amy and Orion knew how it felt to return from a dangerous voyage.

Dianne made up the bed in Julia's room. Amy would be staying for a few days. The police had arrested Buddy for kidnapping, and although they didn't believe Tess Brooks was involved, they wanted to make sure. The CWS wasn't taking any chances.

"He's going to jail, right?" Amy asked.

"He's there already," Dianne said.

"Just like in my story," Amy said.

"Where Dickie goes to jail," Dianne said.

Amy nodded. She was sitting on the floor,

holding Julia on her lap. Ever since coming to the house, she had wanted to hold Julia or be close to her; she didn't seem to want to let her out of her sight. Dianne heard Amy kiss Julia's face.

"Gleee," Julia whispered.

"You're my friend," Amy whispered back.

"Gleee," Julia said.

Dianne listened to the children. She loved how Julia's life changed when Amy was around. Julia struggled to be more alert. She unwound from the fetal position. Her voice grew stronger. Her hand began to pat the air. Orion and Stella lay beside them. Stella had been overjoyed to see the dog, and she was draped over his head, licking his ears. No one wanted to be far apart from one another.

"You girls okay in here?" Lucinda asked, poking her head in.

"We're safe and sound," Amy said.

Dianne's throat choked up. Amy's optimism was inspiring. She had just gone through that brutal experience, and she was trying to be cheerful. Dianne knew some of it was an act. Amy jumped at loud sounds. She had seemed subdued when she'd walked through the door with Alan, and he had said that saying good-bye to her mother had been very hard.

"I'm finishing up the stuffing," Lucinda said. "For the turkey. Would anyone like to help?"

"Sure," Amy said, but she didn't let go of Julia.

"The last pie's baking," Lucinda said.

"It smells good," Dianne said.

"What kind?" Amy asked hesitantly.

"Apple, of course," Lucinda said. "For my apple girls."

"No mince," Amy said, shuddering. "As long as we don't have mince . . ."

"I promise," Lucinda said.

"In my story," Amy said, breaking down, "Catherine felt so good when Dickie went to jail. I thought I'd feel better. But I keep seeing his face, the way he looked when he dropped Orion off the bridge. His eyes were blank. He might have just been littering!"

"Don't think about it," Lucinda said. "Don't waste your good mind picturing that horrible man."

"I can't help it," Amy sobbed, rocking Julia.

Dianne walked over to the girls. She crouched down, and put her arms around both of them. She rested her forehead against Amy's.

"Oh, Amy," Dianne whispered.

"Dianne," Amy said, clutching Dianne's sweater.

Dianne understood how a good person's mind could be drawn to the worst in people, the ugliest of human nature. How, with everything gentle in the world, we could fix on the troubled. She had it within herself: All the years she could have been loving Alan, she'd been twisted up with hating Tim.

No summer breeze, calling birds, or shooting stars had been able to chase those feelings away. Dianne had heard Tim's last words, the door slamming, his footsteps walking away, for years and years. Dianne wished Amy could erase her fears, but she feared that Amy would be seeing Buddy's blank stare for the rest of her life.

"Why?" Amy asked. "Dianne, how could a person do what he did?"

"I don't know," Dianne said.

"Maaa," Julia said, her eyelids fluttering.

"I keep trying to figure it out," Amy wept. "How could he be that mad at a little dog?

How could he be that angry but look as if he didn't care?"

Dianne breathed quietly. She just held the girls, rocking them against her body. She wanted to give them the comfort of her warmth, the beat of her heart. Some things in life couldn't be explained or figured out. She had spent years trying to make sense of the senseless. How could any mother understand what had happened to Julia? Why she had been born the way she had. Why her father had left and her mother had stayed.

"He's in jail," Lucinda said. "That's the important thing. Just like in 'Sand Castles': Justice will be served."

"I'm not going to win the contest," Amy said, wiping her eyes. "My story never even got turned in."

"It's not too late," Lucinda said. "I have pull down at the library, you know."

Amy just shook her head, and that pierced Dianne's heart. Amy shuddered as if remembering something so painful she couldn't put it into words.

"Amy?" Lucinda pressed.

"It's a bad story," Amy said. "It hurt my mother's feelings. I don't want to hand it in,

Lucinda. Thank you for helping me, but I just want to forget about it."

"Hmm," Lucinda said. She stood in the doorway. The aroma of apple pie baking drifted up the stairway. Dianne could feel her mother wanting to fix this situation with the story, but she was holding herself back. "Well, if you say so. A bargain's a bargain though. I told you win or lose, you were going to *The Nutcracker*."

"Still?" Amy asked, her eyes a little brighter.

"Of course," Dianne said, thinking of how confident she felt about leaving Julia with Alan. They'd be staying right there, with Lucinda, while he started moving their things into their new house.

"*The Nutcracker*," Amy said, gulping. "Something to look forward to."

"It's so incredible," Lucinda said, "when the ballerinas dance in the falling snow. . . ."

"Just a few days from now," Dianne said.

Alan took them to the train. With both of his hands on the wheel, he concentrated on driving through the snow. Thick snow was falling, making the road slippery. A snowplow went past in the other direction, an orange blur. He found himself wishing Dianne and Amy wouldn't go. The weather was bad, with more snow forecast for later.

But it wasn't the weather. Alan just didn't want Dianne to leave. He wanted to spend the snowstorm with her in their house. They could build a fire and look out at the harbor. They could watch the water turn five hundred shades of gray. They could lie on a blanket on the hard oak floor and stare at the ceiling. He was overcome with love for her, and he didn't want to let her out of his sight.

"So, you come back Sunday," he said instead.

"Sunday night," Dianne said. "On the seven-thirty-two."

"I'll be there," he said.

"My first train ride," Amy said. "My first trip to New York, my first ballet . . ."

"We'll have fun," Dianne said.

"Don't worry about Julia," Alan said.

She looked over at him, and he reached for her hand. Her grip was firm, and he felt their connection. Her gaze was so warm and steady, letting him know she'd never trusted anyone the way she trusted him.

"You're her father," Dianne whispered, giving him the greatest gift he could have. The adoption papers were in the works. His heart was so full, he could almost believe this feeling would never change.

"That's how I feel," he said.

"I've never left her for this long," Dianne said.

"I'll be with her," Alan said. "And so will Lucinda."

"I'm not worried, sweetheart," she said. "As long as she's with you. And I know Mom's happy to have you staying at her house."

Alan nodded. Why did he keep wishing she'd miss her train? He could drive slower. She squeezed his hand. He raised her palm to his face, pressed it against his skin. The windshield wipers swished back and forth. A sand truck drove by.

"Do you think my dress is okay?" Amy asked. "Good enough for the ballet?"

"It's perfect," Dianne said.

"She's bringing those fancy earrings, Dr. McIntosh," Amy said, starting to sound really excited.

"Dorothea's?" Alan asked, glancing over.

"Yes," Dianne said.

"And she's bringing a fancy satin handbag and a gorgeous cashmere cape," Amy said. "She'll look like a movie star."

"Wish I were going," Alan said.

"So do I," Dianne said, smiling over at him. "How about we forget the train?" she asked. "And you can drive us. I'll bet we can get you a ticket for *The Nutcracker*. . . ."

Just having her say that was almost enough, although Alan was tempted by the idea of the city with Dianne. Or anywhere else. But he had made a promise to take care of Julia, and he knew how good it would be for Dianne to get away.

"Girls only," Amy reminded them.

He switched on the radio to hear the weather report. They were calling for more snow, with six to eight inches falling tonight and into tomorrow.

"Maybe we shouldn't go," Dianne said.

"Oh, don't say that!" Amy moaned.

"What do you think?" Dianne asked Alan. He glanced over and saw her cheeks turn pink, and she bit her lower lip and started to smile.

"You don't want to know what I think," he said, thinking of the previous night, how they had made love until after midnight, how they were both so churned up about her leaving that they'd been unable to sleep for hours after that.

"About whether we should go to New York or not," Amy said. "Tell her we should."

"Well," Alan said. They had reached the train station. Snow was falling, and people were standing on the platform, facing east. The train from Boston bound for New York was due in any minute.

"About whether we should go to New York or not," Dianne said, squeezing his hand.

"I'll tell you," Alan said. "We're going to get a snowstorm. If it was a school day, school would probably be canceled."

"Not our New York trip," Amy groaned.

"But in New York," Alan said, "you won't be driving a car. You'll have a nice train ride in, and you'll take a cab to the Plaza hotel. You can find a wonderful restaurant right there, or you can go downstairs and eat at the Edwardian Room."

"And tomorrow we'll see *The Nutcracker*. I can't think of a better way to see that ballet than in a snowstorm."

"It's like magic," Amy said, looking up at the sky.

"Okay. We'll go to New York," Dianne said, gazing steadily at Alan as she held his hand, letting him know how much she loved him, that everything was going to be fine. "And then we'll come home."

"I'll be here," Alan said, "with Julia, when you get back."

The train whistle sounded. The station-master began to make his announcement. Amy scrambled out of the car, lugging her bag, gesturing at Dianne as if she wanted to get on the train before the adults changed their minds.

Dianne reached up to touch Alan's cheek again. He had always loved the depth of her emotion, the way it shimmered in her eyes, in the set of her mouth. But for so long he had believed that intensity of love was reserved for her daughter, for Julia alone. He knew Julia would always come first, but right now Dianne's love was directed at Alan, and he felt it straight in his heart. It contained a promise, and Alan knew Dianne kept her promises. That was who she was.

"Love," she whispered. Just the single word.

"Yes," he said, clasping her hand.

"Julia will be fine?" she asked.

"Better than fine," he said.

"The train," Dianne said, gesturing.

Alan got out of the car. He grabbed Dianne's bag, took Amy's from her. Amy was practically skipping across the snowy parking lot. The crowd was festive. The old-fashioned station was already decorated with Christmas lights, and garlands looped down from the eaves. Alan's throat ached as he pulled Dianne close.

"All aboard!" the conductor yelled.

"That's us!" Amy cried happily.

Alan and Dianne kept hugging. He felt her heart beating right through her coat. It would be so good to lie by the fireplace in their new house, watching the snow fall. He didn't want to let her go.

"Are you sure," she asked, her eyes bright now as she leaned back, "this is a good idea?"

"Like Amy said," he said, kissing her roughly one last time, pushing her up the train as the whistle blew, "it'll be like magic." She waved and he waved until the conductor gently eased her into the car and closed the steel door.

And that was how Alan McIntosh came to put the woman he loved more than anything in the world onto the train that would take her to New York City, into destiny and the path of a yellow cab.

Twenty-Nine

* * *

Dianne lay in the intensive care unit at St. Bernadette's Hospital. Her dreams were vivid and violent: the taxi spinning through the snowstorm, crashing into a crowd of people standing by the Plaza hotel. She saw herself trying to protect Amy, not being able to move fast enough, seeing Amy fly into the air, landing broken on the sidewalk. Dianne lay still, drifting in and out of consciousness, hooked up to tubes and machines, surrounded by doctors. She was so sedated—or maybe just so severely wounded—that she had no idea whether she would live or die.

They had shaved her head. The cut there had been deep enough to warrant stitching and was now covered with bandages. She could see and hear, but she had lost a lot of blood and it took all her energy just to keep breathing.

The best doctors had been called. The top neurosurgeon at St. Bernadette's Hospital was on her case. Dr. Gerard Bellavista was used to bad car crashes, subway accidents, motorcycle collisions. He had tunnel vision, seeing only that section of brain, spine, neurosystem, that required his care. But staring at Dianne Robbins, bruised and bandaged, he could see that she was a lovely woman.

"Where's her family?" he asked the nurse.

"There's a man waiting in the hall," the nurse said.

The doctor nodded and went to find him. A longtime New Yorker, Dr. Bellavista was rarely surprised by humanity. But when he saw the man waiting, he stared. The man was no city dweller. Tall and broad-shouldered, he ducked as if he expected to be shot. His blond hair was mussed-up, his face lined and tan from a life lived outdoors. His brown jacket was made of rough fabric and stained with grease. His blue eyes looked strained and suspicious. His black rubber boots sparkled with fish scales.

"I'm Dr. Bellavista," he said.

"Tim McIntosh," the man said.

"Is she your wife?"

McIntosh cleared his throat. "Was," he said. "She was my wife. Dianne Robbins."

"Then you know who we should call," Dr. Bellavista said.

"Her people are in Connecticut," he said.

"You'd better call them."

"What's her condition?"

"She's had a head injury. That bears careful watching for at least twenty-four hours."

"Can I see her?" Tim asked.

The doctor hesitated. He wanted next of kin there. Dianne Robbins was hanging by a thin thread, and the doctor didn't want to waste any time getting her family down here. On the other hand, this guy was standing right in front of him. He knew the woman better than anyone else around.

"Come back in an hour, when we're done running some more tests. You can see her then for five minutes," the doctor said. "That's all."

Amy was feeling better and better.

She asked every person who came into her room about Dianne.

"She's resting," they said. Or, "She's with the doctor." Or, "Everything is being done, don't worry."

"Don't worry?" Amy cried.

Of course she was worried. Dianne had brought her all the way down to New York City to see *The Nutcracker* as a reward for the story Amy hadn't even turned in. Dianne had sacrificed this time with Julia to be with her, Amy. She had treated Amy like a princess at the Plaza hotel, letting her take a bubble bath in the enormous tub, letting her call room service for an afternoon snack.

"Has anyone called Dr. McIntosh yet?" she asked.

"Who?" the nurse asked.

Amy explained. The man who was here, the one smelling like the ocean and dropping fish scales all over the place, was not the man who should be here. He was Tim McIntosh, the one you couldn't count on for anything, the one who ran off at the first sign of trouble. He had mistaken Amy's identity, thought she was Julia. Never having even *met* his daughter, he had thought for a minute that Amy was she.

Amy had just finished reciting Dr.

McIntosh's number to the nurse, when his brother walked in.

"Um, I just came from intensive care," he said, his face bright red and the skin around his eyes maroon.

"How is she?" Amy cried out.

"She's in rough shape," Tim said. "But they're going to let me see her."

The nurse gave him a mad look, as in don't-you-know-how-to-talk-to-kids? But Amy wanted to know. It was better than lying there in the dark.

"Rough how? Can she walk? Will she come up and see me? Or can I go see her? She's not in a coma, is she?"

"I don't know. I'm not the doctor," Tim said. "Look, I'm sorry I thought you were my kid before. You're the same age, you're with Dianne, I just thought . . ." he trailed off, gruff and confused.

"It's okay," Amy said. She was used to dealing with a bigger jerk than this: Buddy.

"Look, do you know where my brother is? You seem to know him pretty well. I just tried his house, and I got no answer. I think I'd better call—"

Amy glanced at the nurse, who handed

Tim the number Amy had just given her. He walked away without a word to go find a phone. Amy just lay back on her pillows. She felt shocked by what had just happened. That was Julia's father? He seemed so weird and tragic, like an apple person who had been left on the ground. He didn't even have the strength to be gentle to a little kid who'd been hit by a car.

"Good luck," Amy said under her breath. At least Dr. McIntosh would come.

They told her she had a major arm fracture, that she had cut an artery and lost a lot of blood. They had given her new blood, hanging the bright red bags on her IV pole, running it into her body through a tube. The blood had come from other people, ones Amy had never met. It seemed amazing to her, the pinnacle of kindness.

She had strangers' blood coursing through her veins, and it gave her strength and hope. It was like being told she was important, that she mattered as much as anyone. She was just an apple girl, but people cared. She wished Julia were there, lying next to her on the bed. Amy really wished she had Julia to talk to.

• • •

Alan was changing Julia's diaper when the phone rang. He was upstairs at Lucinda's, and he found himself hoping the phone would be for him. So when Lucinda called his name, he quickly finished diapering Julia, lifted her up, and headed for the extension.

Lucinda came bounding upstairs.

"It's your brother," she said. "He wouldn't tell me what he wants, but I thought I should warn you."

"Thanks," Alan said.

Still holding Julia, he picked up the phone.

"Hello, Tim," he said.

"Alan," Tim said.

"I've been trying to get hold of you."

"I heard, up at Malachy's. Listen, Alan. I know we have our differences. You've never been anything but decent to me—better than decent—I'm trying to do the right thing here."

"Slow down," Alan said. He had a lot of anger toward Tim, but just then he could hear the anguish in his brother's voice. He held his brother's daughter, staring into her face. "Take it easy, Tim. What's wrong?"

"They called me, Alan. I was out at sea, and I got the call. I'm telling you, it was a freak they got me at all, but when I heard, I came. I—"

"Came where?" Alan asked.

"To the hospital, in New York City."

"New York?" Alan asked slowly, it dawning on him that Dianne was in New York, that this was one hell of a coincidence.

"St. Bernadette's," Tim said, his voice cracking. "I thought she was my kid. That's the God's honest truth. I walked into her room and thought she was gonna call me Daddy."

"Where's Dianne?" Alan asked, his skin going cold.

"That's why I'm calling you," Tim said. "Here's the thing: She had some old card of mine in her bag. She and the kid, the one I thought was Julia, her name is Amy, got hit by a cab. The hospital called me by mistake. I wanted to do the right thing, I did."

"Hit by a cab?" Alan asked, stunned.

"So I came when they called. I knew I had to call—when Lucinda answered the phone, I damn near died. She's got a voice like ice cubes when it comes to me. Will you break the news to her? What're you doing there anyway?"

"What's Dianne's condition?" Alan asked.

"Bad, I think," Tim said. His voice broke again. "Something about a head injury. They're letting me in to see her in a minute. You're used to this stuff, you see hurt people all the time. The kid's okay, just a broken arm, but Dianne . . ."

But Alan wasn't listening anymore. He had dropped the phone, and he was holding Julia to his chest. She had been sleeping, or at least quiet, but picking up on how upset he was, she began to move. He felt a tremor go through her muscles. She knew, he was sure. This little girl had extra intuition when it came to her mother.

Lucinda was standing in the hallway. She knew something too. Her face was drawn, her eyes expectant. Alan led her into her bedroom, sat her down on the edge of her bed. His face must have shown it all, because suddenly her eyes filled with tears.

"It's Dianne, isn't it?" she asked.

"She's in the hospital," Alan said, staring straight into her eyes and speaking as a doctor, as steady and comforting as he could. "She's been hit by a car. She and Amy."

"No—" Lucinda said.

"I'm going down to New York," Alan said. "Tim says Amy's okay, but Dianne might not be."

"Let me come—"

Alan shook his head. He was trying to stay in control. Still holding Julia, he kissed her head, pressing his lips against her cool forehead for ten long seconds. She was Dianne's flesh and blood. She was the only child of his beloved, and he had held Dianne's hand, wiped the sweat off Dianne's brow, the night Julia had come into this world. He had been present at her birth.

"Stay with Julia," he said, handing the girl into her grandmother's arms. "She needs you."

"Oh, Alan!"

"I'll call you as soon as I know anything," Alan said. He stood up, his car keys in his hand. New York was just two hours down I-95. He was a doctor, trained to stay calm at moments like this. But as he looked into the eyes of Dianne's mother, saw the way Julia was staring up at him, it was a monumental challenge.

• • •

Tim had to wait for over an hour while they took Dianne down for an MRI, then another hour while the plastic surgeons saw her. By the time they allowed him into the ICU, he had been just about to leave. He was sweating like a pig. Hospitals made him nervous. He swore he'd broken out in hives the minute he'd walked through the door. This brought back the days of Neil, when Tim and Alan weren't allowed inside his bedroom at home, when they were told that hospitals were where people went to die. And intensive care units were the worst.

He swallowed his fear. He had gotten the call, and he'd come many miles by land and sea to be there. He had done right this time—now they could forget about Newport and Nova Scotia. Tim had shown up. Did they have any idea what this did to him, walking through a hospital, into an ICU?

He felt like all eyes were on him. He was probably green. The nurse smiled, leading him past a bunch of cubicles. Tim's heart was in his throat. He felt as if he were riding through a hurricane, fighting thirty-foot waves. Dianne was in one of those beds.

Tim was about to see the woman he had once loved.

"Here she is," the nurse whispered.

Tim was speechless.

Dianne lay under white sheets. Her face was cut, black and blue, but she was an angel. She was the girl he had married. The years melted away, and he could see her standing there in her workshop with the playhouse Tim would deliver to Alan. He gazed down at her now, wanting to give her courage. That's what he had come here to do.

But she wasn't moving.

Tim pulled over the single chair. He sat there, pushing his long hair back from his eyes, just staring. Her long blond hair was nowhere to be seen. Her light lashes brushed her bruised cheek. Both hands lay outside the sheet, and something made Tim touch her ring finger, where her wedding band had once been.

Dianne opened her eyes.

Tim's mouth dropped open. He saw the shock on her face. As if she had seen a ghost, or as if she'd been expecting someone else. He thought of the little girl saying "Dr. McIntosh," and he didn't want to go through the same thing again, the humiliation of trauma-induced mistaken identity. So he shook his head and made himself speak.

"Hi, Dianne," he said.

She just stared, her eyes widening.

"I didn't have time to get to a barber," he said. "I know I look like hell."

Her mouth opened and closed, forming words she couldn't speak.

"The hospital called me by mistake," he said. "I was on my way to Florida. You had some old pocketbook with the *Aphrodite*'s name in it. It was a total fluke that they got me. I saw the kid down the hall, and I thought she was Julia. God help me, Dianne. I came here wanting to help. I thought she was my daughter."

Dianne's eyes glistened with tears, and Tim McIntosh let all the years of pent-up emotion flow out. With his head resting on Dianne's pillow, right next to hers, he broke down crying.

She cleared her throat.

Tim let himself cry. He could hear her speaking, tiny words almost impossible to hear. She was probably thanking him, letting him know she understood the pain he was in, how hard this was for him. Finally he raised his head and wiped his face. She was staring across the pillow, straight into his eyes. He'd been right: She was trying to speak.

"What?" he asked, inching closer, touching her bruised cheek with his fingers. "I can't hear you, baby."

"I said get your filthy head off my pillow."

He jerked up, pulling his hand back as if she'd scalded him. Her voice barely croaked. Her lip was cut, and there were stitches over one eye, across her cheekbone, and along her jaw. Was she delirious?

"I came to help," he said, shocked.

She just stared, blinking as if each movement of her eyelids represented great effort.

"It is," she said, "impossibly hard for me to see you."

"I'll leave," he said, sensing trouble and ready to go.

"Knowing that you rejected our daughter. Not just when you walked out on us," she said, her voice weak but rising.

"Hey, Dianne—"

"But in Nova Scotia too."

"Hey, I came to make up," Tim said. He couldn't understand why people talked to him the way they did. Malachy last summer and now Dianne. He was doing his best; he'd always been doing his best. His intentions were good.

"Her name is Julia," Dianne said.

"Hey, lower your voice," Tim said, feeling nervous and looking around. She was squirming around in the bed, trying to get enough of a grip to hoist herself up.

"She's a beautiful, amazing child," Dianne said. "She's so good, she puts up with so much, Tim, and you've never even seen her." The nurse came hurrying over. She tried to ease Dianne back onto the pillows, but Dianne wouldn't lie down. She had gotten strength from deep down, and she had to finish this here and now.

"Look. Hey. You're hurt," Tim said. "You don't know—"

"I *do* know," Dianne said, and her eyes were clear and focused.

"I think about her," Tim said. "I know her name. You act like I don't—"

"You're dirt to me, Tim McIntosh," Dianne said.

"I came all the way—"

She leaned back on her pillow. He could see that she was exhausted, that she had been in a bad accident, but it was those last five words that did it. Tim said them, and he watched her collapse. Her skin was ashen, and she was shaking her head. When she spoke again, her voice was nearly gone.

"You've missed her whole life."

"Sir, it's time for you to leave . . ." the nurse said.

"Dianne, you might not believe this," Tim said, suddenly realizing he was going to walk out the door and probably never see her again. His mouth was dry, and his knees were weak. "But I never meant to hurt you or her. Never. That's the truth."

Dianne was lying on her back. Her eyes were closed and tears were running out of them into her ears and the bandages around her head. Being on his boat was one thing. It was easier to justify his life out at sea. But seeing Dianne like this reminded Tim of everything he had ever thrown away.

"My mother says I should forgive you," she whispered.

"Just understand."

She moved her head—a violent movement. Her eyes were squeezed tight so she wouldn't have to look at him.

"I'll forgive you," she said, her voice full of

tears. "But I can't understand. I don't even want to try. Now leave us alone."

Tim opened his mouth to reply, but the nurse had noticed a change in Dianne's blood pressure. She adjusted the machine, and then she signaled for one of the doctors to come over. Dianne's blood pressure had dropped, and Tim heard them sounding concerned about internal bleeding. The overhead lights were bright, and several nurses came hurrying. Pushed aside, Tim turned away from Dianne. He walked away from the nurses, and he left the ICU.

Thirty

* * *

Alan bumped into Tim coming through the heavy door to the ICU. The two men faced each other, ten feet apart. Alan had expected Tim to be gone by then. He had made the call, summoned Alan, so why was he still there? Alan's body ached. He tensed at the sight of him, wondering what he'd been saying to Dianne, and at the same time he felt old ties of brotherhood.

"The doctor's with her," Tim said, his blue eyes steady. "She's taken some kind of turn."

Alan didn't wait to hear more. He burst through the ICU doors, saw a huddle of activity in a cubicle down at the end. Running through the unit, he was stopped by a nurse and two doctors.

"That's Dianne," he said. "I've got to see her—"

"They're working on her."

"I'm a doctor!" he said, raising his voice.

"Out, please," one of the doctors said, insistent. "You can't help right now. You're going to have to wait outside."

Alan backed away. He felt helpless.

Tim met him in the hallway.

"Did she say anything?" Alan asked. "Did she seem conscious?"

"She was conscious," Tim said.

"How did she look?" Alan asked. His voice broke. He had caught only a glimpse of her from across the ICU. Her face was so pale, covered with bruises.

"She's hurt," Tim said.

"God help me," Alan said, holding his head, pacing in the small hallway. Driving down to New York, he had held it all inside. The fear came pouring out now, flooding out of his body, the pent-up terror of losing Dianne. "Jesus, help me, help us. . . ."

"Alan," Tim said.

Alan's eyes were wild. He couldn't catch his breath. He had witnessed families at the ICU a thousand times, and now he was one of them. Dianne was in there. He shook his head, choked down a sob. His brother stood there, sweaty and filthy with hair that hadn't been combed or cut in a month. He looked just like the little boy Alan had taught to fish, had taught to swim off the sands of Cape Cod.

"I'm leaving," Tim said.

"Tim," Alan said, paralyzed with fear. He realized then he didn't want his brother to walk away.

Tess Brooks hung up the phone. Amy had been hit by a taxicab. She was hurt, lying in a big hospital. She had nearly bled to death! Tess was breathing so hard, she thought she was going to pass out. The house was empty and dark. She walked in circles, tearing at her hair.

After what Buddy had done to Amy! Being dragged into his car, watching him try to drown the dog, nearly drowning herself. And now this! Tess howled out loud. Her daughter had been hit by a car! Oh, what a lousy mother she was. What a crummy, selfish woman.

Tess strode through her small house. In and out of rooms. Her bedroom, the living room, the kitchen, Amy's room. As she did, she saw flashes of the past. Amy's baby shoes, Russell's fishing boat, her wedding dress. Tess had heard of people whose lives flashed before their eyes, but didn't that happen on deathbeds? Why was it happening to her right now?

In Amy's room she stopped before Russell's shrine. Well, that's what it was: Amy had assembled a collection of memorabilia, Tess didn't even know where she'd gotten it all. Russ's portrait smiling out with that honest joy he'd always had. He could have sold a million cars. . . . Hanging from the picture was a fishhook, a cardboard cutout of the Ford logo, a plastic dolphin, and a drawing of a sand castle.

Sand castles were significant to Amy. Tess had never known why until she'd read Amy's story. Tess had gotten all bent out of shape that the mother had looked like Dianne, and because of that Amy had never even turned her story in for the contest. With Tess's life flashing before her eyes, she saw the hard truth: She had dashed her daughter's dream yet again.

"Depression rots, Russ," she said, sitting down in front of his picture. "Why'd you go and leave me?"

No answer.

"I've tried to do it on my own, and look where it's gotten me."

No answer.

"Just look!" she said again, catching sight of herself in the mirror. She had wide, intelligent eyes, a sad expression on her mouth. She tried to smile, but her daughter was in the hospital.

She sighed, staring at Russell's picture again. Photos didn't talk. Drowned husbands didn't return from the deep to console wives who'd screwed up their lives. Or to wait by the phone to hear the latest update on their daughter. Feeling shaky, Tess walked into the kitchen. She opened up the junk drawer, and there it was. Amy's story.

Imagine—her story stuck in the junk drawer.

The corner was glossy with peanut butter grease. Tess tried to blot the oil stain out. No luck, but she could still read the typing. She didn't want to read the words. They still hurt her too much. But Amy had put such effort in, the way she did everything, the way she did life.

The least Tess could do . . . Suddenly she found herself pulling on snow boots. She tugged on an old jacket. The car wouldn't start, she'd need a jump, but there wasn't anyone she wanted to call. Besides, the snow had stopped and the night was clear. Amy was out of danger, and Tess would catch a train to New York in the morning.

She'd walk to the train station, starting now. She rummaged through her junk drawer a little deeper, found her envelope of mad money. That should cover her ticket. Tucking Amy's story in the pocket of her coat, she was glad the train station was so near the library.

The deadline had passed. Amy's story was late being turned in, it was coated with peanut butter, it didn't have a fancy folder. But maybe if Tess called Mrs. Robbins, she could ask that Amy be granted an extension. She could try anyway.

Trying was new for Tess. But she had to start somewhere. Leaving her dark house, she walked out into the cold, starry night.

•   •   •

The night was long. Alan walked the halls. He sat with Amy. He held her until she went to sleep. He read her chart, conferred with her doctor, adjusted the angle of her traction. He telephoned Lucinda. Julia was fine, she told him. She was sitting up with Lucinda, more alert than she had been in weeks. It seemed, Lucinda said, almost as if she knew that Lucinda needed her comfort.

Alan asked Lucinda to put the phone to Julia's ear.

"I love you, Julia," he said.

"Daaaa," she said back.

Alan returned to the hallway outside the ICU. Tim had fallen asleep in one of the chairs. He had been ready to go, but Alan had asked him to stay. Their resentments were deep and ferocious, and they'd stared at each other so long, as if they were squaring off for a fight.

Alan looked down at him now. It felt strange to see his younger brother age. There was gray in his blond hair, deep lines around his mouth and eyes. He slept with his arms crossed across his body, in a position of self-protection and defense.

Sitting down beside him, Alan gazed at the ICU door. Everything worth knowing was happening in that room. His eyes narrowed behind his glasses, staring as hard as he could. He pushed his glasses up, he took them off, he put them back on.

"I used to think they were magic," Tim said gruffly.

Alan glanced over.

His brother was awake, but he didn't look too alert. Arms still crossed, legs extended, he disguised a yawn.

"What were magic?" Alan asked.

"Your glasses. When we were kids and you had to wear them, I used to think you had special powers. They made you smarter, faster, stronger."

"Dorothea used to say I ruined my eyes from reading in the dark. That's about it. The rest was just me being your older brother."

"Yeah, well, I thought you ruled the world."

"I tried," Alan said. "More being the older brother, I guess. Life on a pedestal seemed like a good idea."

"I sure liked knocking you off," Tim said.

"Hmm," Alan said, staring at the ICU door.

"She's not just your sister-in-law anymore, is she?" Tim asked.

"She never was," Alan said, "just that."

"You've gotten involved with her again?"

"I'm going to marry her."

Tim was silent for a long time, but he was definitely awake. He sat up straight, shook his head as if to clear his mind.

"I've loved her all along," Alan said.

"What about my daughter?"

"Julia," Alan said. It felt strange to hear his brother, this other man, call her "my daughter." That was how Alan saw her. Coming from Tim, he knew they were just words, but they tightened up his stomach anyway. "I'm adopting her."

"I could fight that," Tim said, staring at the lighting fixtures. "I wouldn't, but I could."

"I appreciate that you wouldn't," Alan said.

"Eleven years old," Tim said. "Julia's eleven years old."

"She is."

"I was on my way when you got here," Tim said. "On my way back to the boat."

"You said you were leaving," Alan said carefully. He didn't know what had gone on between Tim and Dianne, and he was almost afraid to find out. The old jealousy was strong and deep, and it came back fast. "I appreciate that you stayed."

"Yeah, well," Tim said.

"Well," Alan said.

"You want to have it out with me?" Tim asked. "About what a scumbag I am?"

"Malachy told me about you being in Lunenburg," Alan said sharply.

"Told you and told Dianne, I guess," Tim said. "She hates my guts."

"She said that?"

"She said she forgives me," Tim said, leaving out the rest of what she said.

Alan closed his eyes. His throat ached. Dr. Bellavista was in with Dianne. The ICU door had neither opened nor closed in quite a long time. Alan burned to know what was going on in there. Sitting out here, talking to Tim, felt strange and upsetting, as he thought of everything they had once been to each other back in their Cape Cod youth. He thought about how they both loved the same woman, how Alan was about to legally adopt his brother's child, how Dianne had looked at him with hate in her eyes.

"What's she like?" Tim asked.

"Excuse me?" Alan asked, lost in thought.

"Julia," Tim said, his voice catching. "What's she like?"

Alan took out his wallet. He had her baby picture inside, and he took it out. Handing it to Tim, he watched his brother close his eyes, gather his strength, and look. Alan had sent him Julia's baby picture a month after her birth, but he could tell that Tim had never seen it before.

"Oh, God," Tim said, starting to cry.

"What's wrong with you?" Alan asked. "She's beautiful."

"She's deformed." Tim wept, holding the picture right up to his face.

Alan stared back at the door. Dianne was inside, and it didn't take much for him to spin back in time to the night of Julia's birth at Hawthorne Cottage Hospital. Tim had sailed away, and Dianne was still lost in shock and disbelief. Lucinda was in the waiting room, a team of doctors was on board. Everyone knew the baby had problems, but they didn't yet know the extent.

Dianne lay on the delivery table. Alan was her partner, her birth coach. He was a pediatrician, and he believed he would be ready for anything. Dianne had lain there, going through labor, doing everything she was supposed to to deliver a healthy baby. Breathe, the obstetrician had told her. Push. Breathe. Don't push.

Alan had held her hand. She had the most amazing grip. Clutching his fingers, he wished she might never let go. Her hair flowed down her face, sweat ran from her neck and body. During the early stages she had continually glanced at the delivery room door as if Tim had changed his mind and might come charging in.

The time had come to get the baby out. The doctors gathered around. Sitting by Dianne's head, Alan had held her shoulders. "Way to go, Dianne," he said like someone coaching a baseball team. "You're doing great, you can do it, that's a girl."

She had grabbed his chin. "Tell me," she begged, "that I've done the right thing."

The baby wasn't born yet, they had no way of knowing what her future would be. But Dianne had lost her husband, had signed on for a lifetime of duty for a baby who would never be all right. Alan had no idea, but his answer had come from his heart and soul.

"Yes, Dianne," he had whispered. "You have done the right thing."

"Oh," she had cried. "I hope I have. . . ."

"I promise I'll be there," Alan had said. "For her whole life, for as much as you need me."

"Thank you," Dianne had said, pushing, working, getting her baby born. The room sizzled with anticipation and excitement, every doctor knowing that his or her specialty was about to be put to use. Dianne threw back her head, her skin glistening, hair streaming, the cords of her neck taut as wire. Alan witnessed birth in medical school, but never like this, never when he knew the mother.

"She's coming," the doctor said. "Here we go, another push, Dianne, we have it, let's go, come on. . . ."

The room fell silent.

Dianne was screaming, the joy and relief of having delivered her child, the way every mother sounded when she's just given life, and Alan had expected the room to join in— that collective raising of voices, that choir of those present at a birth. But there was nothing. Every person in the room drew a breath and held it.

"Please," Dianne cried. "Give her to me."

The neonatologist had the baby on the

way to her incubator. Nurses blocked Dianne's view. Dianne was weeping, reaching out, holding her empty arms toward the doctors. No one wanted Dianne to see. The baby was defective. Horribly misshapen, her spine in a sac at the top of her back, her limbs akimbo, her body the mismatching planes of a cubist painting.

Alan rose. Walking across the room, leaving his sister-in-law screaming for him to come back and bring her baby, he gazed for the first time at his niece. He was a pediatrician. He had attended Harvard Medical School, and he had trained at Mass General and Yale. But nothing had ever prepared him for the emotions he felt as he stared into the eyes of that little girl.

"Give her to me," he said.

"She needs—"

Alan was well aware of what she needed. Taking her into his arms, he carried her across the room. Dianne was crying, nodding. She was only in a hospital gown and beautiful. The baby was no bigger than a kitten. Dianne sobbed. As she looked at the baby, her sobs stopped suddenly on one sharp intake of breath.

Alan would never forget what she did next.

With all the pain she must have been feeling from childbirth, from having been abandoned by her husband, and from the anxiety of bearing a damaged child, she put all of those feelings aside. She looked at her baby. And she nodded. She was trembling, it would be hard and there would be setbacks, but she was ready to try.

"Give her to me," she said, her voice shaking.

Alan placed the baby in Dianne's arms.

"Sweet baby," Dianne whispered. "Little girl . . . I love you. I love you. I love you. And I'll never leave you. Never."

Now, sitting outside the ICU, Alan watched his brother Tim cry as he stared at that baby's picture. Alan waited while Tim pulled himself together. For a few seconds Alan considered telling his brother the account of his daughter's birth, but he held himself back. That story belonged to him and Dianne.

"Dianne kept her at home?" Tim asked.

"Yes," Alan said.

"She never sent her away?"

"Never once."

Tim nodded, wiping his eyes. Just then the ICU door opened. Both brothers rose to their feet. Dr. Bellavista stepped out. His expression was serious, but Alan could see in his eyes that he had good news. He looked from one McIntosh to the other.

"She's improving," he said. "Her vital signs are better, and she's responding, coming to. She wants to know if Alan's here."

"That's me," Alan said.

"Go on," Tim said.

Alan hesitated. He wanted to say the one right thing. Waiting these last few hours with his brother had brought him back to a time when they had been close. It couldn't last, they were too different, and there was too much water under the bridge. But he remembered when they had been close.

"Do you think she meant it?" Tim asked.

"Meant what?"

"That she forgives me?"

"If she said it, she meant it," Alan said. He knew that much about Dianne, and it was something that never wavered.

"I hope she does," Tim said. His eyes widened and filled with tears. Alan knew Tim was about to walk away and he'd never see his brother again. "I never should have been with her. She belonged with you all along."

"Then there never would have been Julia," Alan said, which was the closest he could get to his own brand of forgiveness.

"Make her happy," Tim said into his brother's shoulder, giving Alan a last hug. "Do what I never could."

"I will," Alan said.

They shook hands, and Tim McIntosh walked down the clean hospital corridor, leaving a glittery trail of fish scales behind him. Alan was inside the ICU before Tim even made it to the elevator.

Thirty-One

* ✳ *

JULIA'S STORY

Well, they don't think I know, but I know. And they don't think I understand, but I do. They speak in poetry and songs, and I love their words and I love to sing. When my mother is near me, her voice wears a smile, no matter what, no matter what is going wrong in her day. My mother loves me, and she shelters me with her happiness.

My body is my body. It is different, heavy, and cumbersome. My arms and my legs don't work, so they get in the way. I see other people moving with ease, and I want to fight through my skin, break free so I can run down the beach, through the grass, into the wind, like everyone else.

I was born into the world with two people there. My mother and my uncle. For a long time I thought he was my father, but as my hearing developed and I began to understand words, I realized that my real father had gone away, that the reason my mother cried all the time was that he had left us. What does it matter? I wanted to know. We have this other father, this wonderful father, this father who loves us like the sun.

To me, the sun was warm and always there, and it shined on the garden and made Granny's flowers grow, and my father Alan shined on me and Mama and made us happy and safe. He is always there.

He brought me Amy. To have a friend has made me happier than I ever thought I would be. I see the way people look when I go by because I am different. My body is broken and ugly, but I want to tell them: That's not me! Inside I'm beautiful and light and free! But they frown and turn away. They would rather pretend I don't exist. It hurts my feelings, and I cry inside.

But never Amy. She gazes at me with curiosity and love. She makes me laugh, the faces she makes and the jokes she tells. When Mama turns her back, Amy and I do our hand dances and our signal. I stick out my tongue, and Amy touches her ear. When she pushes my chair she goes fast, to let me know how it feels to have legs that work. This is how kids run, she told me, so I would know.

And now I know!

My granny is holding me now. She is crying, tears spilling on my head. Something has happened to my mother and Amy, and they are in the hospital. I shiver, because the hospital is a scary place. Everything there is too bright. There are no beautiful shadows, no silver shade, no delicious night with my mother coming in to see that I am all right.

But the hospital is good. It is where they take care of people like me. I find it hard to imagine my mother and Amy like me, helpless and needing other people to lift and feed them and move them. But at the hospital I have seen people, normal people like them, come in and go out.

"Gaaa," I say, saying her name, wanting my granny to know I love her.

"Oh, darling," Granny sobs, holding me.

"Your mother was in a terrible accident. Alan went down to see her and Amy. He'll call us soon."

Granny is so worried. All will be well, I want to tell her. I try to move my hands, to pat her face, but I feel so tired. My body is fading away. I am happy about that, because when my body is gone, I will be free. I will be able to run and laugh and swim through the sky. I can feel the day coming. Not now, but soon.

There are things to do first. I know, although I don't know how it is possible. Maybe because God gave me a body that doesn't work, he gave me the vision to know more than others. I don't ask, because what would be the point? I lie in my bed or sit in my chair, waiting for everything to happen. And nothing I do or wish can make it happen any faster. But somehow I know. . . .

There will be a wedding. That day is coming soon. My father, Uncle Alan, has bought my mother a ring. He showed it to me yesterday when he took me to see our new house. It is big and beautiful, and he told me it is made of love. He showed me my room, where I will be able to watch the boats in the harbor, the fishing boats and the sailboats moving across the water with the freedom of spirits.

He showed me Mama's ring.

"It's a diamond," he said, opening the soft velvet case. "It's the symbol of eternity, Julia, because it's as old as forever. It's the hardest material in the world, and I'm going to prove that to you before we leave."

"Gleee," I said, which is my word for wonderful!

"Look," he said, holding Mama's diamond to the light, letting rainbows dance all over the ceiling, walls, and floors. Oh, if only Stella were here, I thought. My kitty would be chasing those rainbows like crazy, and Amy and I would laugh our heads off.

"I'm going to propose to her, honey," my daddy said. "I'm going to adopt you and marry your mother, and we're going to be a happy family."

"Daaaa," I said. That means "Daddy," because I have never thought of him in any other way, and I believe that we are a happy family already.

"Right here," he said, carrying me over

to the bay window in our new living room. "This is where our Christmas tree will be. Can you picture it? We'll decorate it all together, you, me, your mother, Amy, and Lucinda. We'll string up white lights, thousands of them, so bright the boats in the harbor will think we're a lighthouse."

"Dleee," I said, because I liked that idea.

"And I'm going to marry your mother right here," he said. "Right in front of the Christmas tree. If she thinks I'm waiting till the new year, she's got another think coming."

"Daaa," I said. I listened carefully to this part, because it was about time. Time is the thing for me. I'm eleven years old, which for me is a long time. My heart is so tired. It has to work so hard. This terrible body takes a lot of work, and I am wearing out. But certain things must be done. It is part of my job, and my gift.

"Right here, Julia," Daddy said. "You and Amy will be the bridesmaids. You'll both carry flowers, the most beautiful bouquets you've ever seen."

"Gaaa," I said to remind him that Granny would know what kind to get. Granny loves flowers. She has all kinds in her garden in summer: roses, peonies, bluebells, lilies of the valley.

"You'll wear white dresses with silver sashes," Daddy said. "Because your mother once told me she dreamed of garden parties here, with ladies wearing white dresses."

"Baaa," I said because I love brides. Mama will be the bride, and Amy and I will be bridesmaids. In books and on TV, brides are like fairy princesses. Mama will be the prettiest of all, smiling with joy.

"Lucinda will give your mother away," Daddy said.

Right now Granny is holding me. She has stopped crying, and she carries me downstairs. She sighs every few minutes. Outside the window, snow has stopped falling. The clouds are clearing, and the stars are coming out. Granny sighs again, and she holds me tighter.

"Gaaa," I say. That makes her happy. She snuggles me, kissing my head. I love her kisses and her hugs. She is full of love, the person who has seen my mama through all her worst times. She talks to me like Daddy, she tells me stories of the past, she has shown me the apple dolls she made for our Christmas presents, from the ruined fruit Amy found that day in the apple garden.

Everyone tells me their secrets. I am lucky, because the secrets are full of love. They show the ways my family wants to help each other, bring meaning to the hard times we all have known. Granny's apple dolls mean that the unlovable can be loved, and Daddy told me a story that he didn't want anyone else to hear.

He told it to me at our house, the place I will go to live for my last days. It was in the living room, by the bay window, where our Christmas tree will stand. There is a pane of glass there, ancient blue-leaded glass, wavy and flecked with bubbles of trapped air. There are scratchings on the pane, and Daddy stared at them with anger in his eyes.

"I wanted to break this window, Julia," he told me. "When I first saw it. The Realtor told me the letters meant something romantic about the original owners. Some sea captain and his wife. Well, you know how I feel about sea captains—"

I waved the air.

"I wanted to break the glass, get rid of it before your mother saw it. The last thing I want is to remind her of Tim."

"Daaa," I said, wanting him to know it didn't matter, Mama didn't love Tim, Alan was the only father I could ever want, he didn't have to worry.

"But I got to thinking," he said. "Maybe I was looking at it the wrong way. The letters read E-L-H. E-L-H. The owner was Elihu Hubbard, so I thought maybe his middle initial was L. But I checked the original deed, and it was S. Then I checked at the library, found a history of Hawthorne that had this house in it, and I saw that his wife's name was Letitia."

I waved, because I loved hearing him tell me this story.

"E-L-H is their monogram," he said. "Elihu Letitia Hubbard. What they became when they married each other. She scratched it into the glass with the diamond he brought her back from his voyage. So that is what I'm going to do too." He brought out the velvet case, removed Mama's ring.

"Maaa," I said because I wished Mama were there to see this.

"Scratch our monogram right next to theirs."

Diamonds were the hardest material on earth. He had told me already. Born of fire deep in the earth, they lasted forever and cut glass without breaking. I watched my daddy take that ring and use Mama's diamond to carve their monogram into the thick blue glass: A-D-M.

"Alan Dianne McIntosh," he said. And then he did something I couldn't believe, the very thing that made me so happy he was my father: He added a J. "For Julia," he said, kissing my head.

Granny sighs again. She holds me at the kitchen table. The lights are out, and her heart is racing through her sweater, waiting for the phone to ring. I breathe as quietly as I can, not wanting to disturb her. Granny will be upset until my mother comes home. I know, because that is how Granny is.

That's the thing: People are who they are. Twelve years of silence have taught me that above all. I watch and I listen. I cannot change the flow of events. If I could, I would tell Granny that Mama will come home again. I have this shimmering sense, this sure sight that lets me know. I am connected with my mother right now. My eyes are closed, and I am touching her face.

My mother is hurt, and she lies just about as close to death as I am. It is near, tugging at our blood. But the thing Granny and Alan don't know, and neither does Mama or Amy, I am moving toward it and Mama is moving away from it. I yearn to leave this body, this cage. I will love them no less when my body is gone. My spirit wants to break free. But my mother has many things left to do, and she must stay alive.

Stella meows. She knows too.

My kitty jumps up on the window ledge. Orion pads across the kitchen floor, cries for Granny to give him some attention. She pets his head, saying, "There boy, there, boy." That is enough for him, and he circles once and lies down on the floor. But Stella waits.

She keeps her vigil. Her turquoise eyes blink, gazing into mine. I blink back. Our eyes speak to each other, as we have learned to do over the years. She is telling me she knows how I feel, that I want my mother to come home. She misses my mother and Amy too, and she will call to the stars tonight, trying to bring them home.

Granny sees.

"Stella," she says, her voice barely a breath. "Are you watching Orion in the sky?"

I wave my hands, telling Stella to call the stars.

"Oh, kitty," Granny said, "you think you live in that constellation, don't you?"

Stella says nothing. With regal elegance she turns her back on us. She gazes toward heaven, her body tense with longing. She implores her friend, the hunter in the sky, to make my mother well again.

"Gaaa," I say.

"Sweetheart," Granny whispers, kissing my head.

I wave my hands, wanting to comfort my grandmother.

Granny is so smart. She knows stories and plays. She knows poems by heart, and watching my cat, Stella, she thinks of one and recites it now.

She says out loud:

"Evening Star,
Hesperos,
you bring all good things.

You bring home all the bright dawn
    disperses,
bring home the sheep,
bring home the goat, bring the child
    home to its mother."

"Bring my daughter home!" my grand-mother implores the evening star in the velvet sky.

"Gaaa," I say to let her know that all will be well.

I close my eyes and think of the four apple dolls. They each wear a different dress, made from Mama's curtain fabrics. But it's their faces I love. Their faces are made from the wrinkled, withered apples Amy picked up in the apple gardens.

Granny has hidden the dolls.

They will be a surprise for us on Christmas morning. Me, Mama, Amy, and Granny herself. As Amy once said, those apples are us: funny looking, fallen from the tree, not good enough for pie.

My granny's crying now, and I want to tell her:

All will be well.

We are all, all of us, approaching the end of our time on this earth. We all have gifts to bestow, but not one of us is finished yet. We are girls of spirit, angels in broken bodies, apple dolls come to life. We've seen sand castles built, and we've seen sand castles wash away.

Mama has more left to do here, and she's not leaving yet.

I need her too much.

About the Author

Luanne Rice is the author of *Secrets of Paris, Stone Heart, Angels All Over Town, Home Fires, Crazy in Love, Blue Moon,* and *Cloud Nine.* Originally from Connecticut, she now lives in New York City with her husband.